A Mary MacIntosh Novel

POISONED BY PROXY

Maureen Anne Meehan

www.maureenannemeehan.com
info@maureenannemeehan.com

Table of Contents

Chapter 1

"Please wake up, mommy! It's me–Levi. I promise I'll be a good boy!"

Why won't she get up off the cabin floor? I've been calling her name forever, but she's still not answering me. I'm getting scared because it's dark and cold in here. Where are we again? I think I should go and get help, but I don't know what I'm supposed to do. If I leave, maybe she will get mad when she wakes up and finds out that I left her all alone out here in the woods–wherever we are.

Am I on the right path to get back to the main road? I can't remember which path we took after mom wrecked the car. I hope I can find my way to the road, because I'm pretty sure we need help. But what if it's a bad guy that stops? I'm so tired. I've been walking for so long. Why does my head feel so fuzzy? Oh yeah, I bumped it when mom ran our car into the ditch. I feel dizzy. Mom's water tasted icky. What was in there?

I think maybe I should go back to the cabin because mom is going to get mad at me for leaving. She gets mad a lot these days. Wait–are those headlights?

* * *

Judge Binnard fastened his black robe, and in doing so he immediately commanded the attention of every lawyer seated in his courtroom.

"In the matter of Cassie S. Counsel, state your appearances for the record."

"Your Honor, Macy Green of the Public Defender's Office, appearing on behalf of the mother. Your Honor, before we begin I have to get on the record that this case is nothing more than a horrible tragedy. Car accidents happen every day, and my client was merely a passenger in a car driven by her father. The only thing that could possibly make this accident different from any of the many others is the fact that my client's infant died. My client is grieving this loss now, and should be allowed to focus on the pending funeral—not the justice system. She is distraught beyond words—"

"Save it for the trial, Ms. Green," Judge Binnard interrupted. "Today's only the detention hearing, and as you know has an extremely low burden of proof. You should know better." It was obvious to the judge that Macy was trying to put on a show for her client, and Judge Binnard disliked such theatrics in his courtroom. He'd worked juvenile cases for the past twenty years in the quaint Wyoming town of Sheridan, and had become well aware of the unique emotional environment involved in these sorts of child abuse cases. He was not about to let anyone in his court try to misuse that emotion in an attempt to bypass the relevant rules of law.

"Your Honor, please let me—"

"Ms. Green, we haven't even made it through introductions. Don't push me today." The judge knew that courtroom control was always important in these cases, but even more so today; he was not willing to risk losing any control over the attorneys when it came time to call the pending Levi L. case.

"With all due respect, Your Honor, my client desperately needs you to understand that—"

"Understand what? That she was traveling with an infant on her lap in the front passenger seat of a car? That she wasn't wearing a seatbelt? That she failed to secure any of her three other children with seatbelts either, before her drunk father T-boned a pickup truck? Or did she want me to understand that she's had four previous DUI's, which now puts her in a dead heat with her father, who was just issued his fourth?" Judge Binnard looked disapprovingly at Ms. Green before he continued, "Are you actually suggestion that despite all that, your client's three surviving children should be returned to her under the theory that they are not in substantial danger of physical or emotional harm while in her care?" Judge Binnard didn't have to think long or hard to come up with the answer to that question.

"But, Your Honor, I feel obligated to address the issue of detention of these three children on the record," Macy Green whined.

"Ms. Green, I suggest you exert your energy on ensuring that your client obtains the alcohol treatment she obviously needs. I know your client was also drunk that night, and I also know that her license has been revoked for too many DUI convictions. Perhaps her reasoning was impaired by the alcohol, but the fact remains that she made an irresponsible choice that ended the life of a newborn. She's lucky that her other three children were not more seriously injured. These facts alone make the detention of your client's other children a foregone conclusion."

Judge Binnard was normally extremely gracious to the parents on his docket, and he was well known amongst local attorneys to bend over backwards to provide parents every possible opportunity to reunify with their children. Cases such as Cassie's, however, provoked an entirely different reaction in him.

"But Your Honor," Macy Green began before she noticed the angry expression on the judge's face. Although she'd only been working the juvenile calendar for a few months, she'd learned enough to realize when to cut her losses. She longed for the day when she'd complete the mandatory juvenile court rotation and return to the land of murderers, rapists, and thieves. Juvenile cases were simply too draining. "I apologize, Your Honor," she said as she wisely took her seat next to her client.

"Ms. Green, you've certainly heard my lecture before. We need a license to drive, marry, and vote. If we choose a particular career path, we're obligated to pursue proper schooling, degrees and certifications. The most important field in life, and the one that ties all of these possibilities together, is being a parent—a good parent. Regrettably, there's absolutely no training or other prerequisites involved with beginning the biological process of swapping DNA.

Judge Binnard's voice turned slightly softer, and he looked pointedly at the public defender in front of him. "I know you're new to my court, Ms.

Green, but you've been here long enough to know my position when it comes to parental responsibility. Parents need to take their responsibilities more seriously, especially when the unfortunate has occurred and one or more of their children have already been removed from their home. If a parent in my courtroom doesn't exert every single effort into fulfilling their duties as a parent, they have no hope of regaining custody in their case. Sadly, baby Cassie is never going to be able to return home. Mrs. Sheldon's three surviving children will not go home either, until she proves to me that she is capable of fulfilling her parental obligations. Next case."

Mary MacIntosh sat in awe as she watched the proceedings unfold. She took copious notes because in her fifteen years as an attorney, she'd not once handled a juvenile matter. She knew that whatever information she could glean from these initial cases on the docket would help her when Levi's case was called. Her big, brown eyes shot wide open as she listened to Judge Binnard rule on the Cassie S. matter in such a swift and assertive manner. She began to doubt her decision to accept representation of her newest and youngest client, ten-year-old Levi.

When Mary MacIntosh told her law partner about her desire to expand their criminal and civil defense firm, Harry's response was immediate. "Let me guess, Mac," he said in his predictably sarcastic fashion, "your body clock is ticking and you think that hanging around abused or neglected kids will fill that void until that selfish boyfriend of yours finally commits to having a family with you." Mac defended her choices to Harry by rationalizing how important it was to provide community service. Harry didn't buy it for a minute.

Mac had worked for Harry her entire legal career and was accustomed to his fatherly disposition. Harry partnered the Jackson Hole office, while Mac managed the Sheridan office, making their long-distance legal partnership a respectfully healthy one. After winning a large verdict in an environmental case, Harry gave Mac complete freedom to choose the types of cases she wished to champion, but that didn't restrain Harry from offering his advice. Mac, a forty-year-old single, attractive woman with long auburn hair and warm, brown eyes, valued her distinguished boss, as Harry held great respect from all members of the legal community.

As Mac listened to the juvenile court calendar, she considered Harry's comments regarding her motive for defending Levi. Maybe Harry was right. She had no experience in this area of the law, and Levi's case appeared to be complicated and high profile. She had studied as much about this area of law as she possibly could in preparation for today, but was still having trouble understanding how the county attorney could prosecute these types of cases while balancing two distinctly different and competing interests: prosecuting parents for their criminally neglectful or abusive parenting, while also promoting reunification of the family unit.

"In the matter of Theresa D.," the county attorney called out the next case without skipping a beat. Karl Swensen had served as Sheridan's county attorney for nearly twenty years and had practiced before Judge Binnard most of his career. They had a respectful rapport despite the fact that they shared very little in common. Karl was a right-winged Republican, with a strong belief in the death penalty, strict judicial sentencing, tough love parenting, and stream-lined budgeting. He was tall and lean, with sharp features, contrasted with Judge Binnard's stout frame and round face.

"Judge, I will submit on detention in this case," Macy Green stated, though not quite as firmly as she had in the Cassie S. case. "But as to visitation, however, I'd request–"

"Forget it, counsel. Your client was charged with impregnating his fourteen-year-old daughter. No visitation. We'll set statutory trial dates. Next case."

"In the matter of Sara Q.," Judge Binnard called without missing a beat.

"Your Honor, detention is not an issue in this case. The minor is sixteen and refuses to live with her father," Karl Swensen said. "Sara ran away after her father caught her on MySpace and decided to beat her up for it. Sara wants to stay at the shelter and doesn't want any form of visitation until her dad has completed anger management counseling. The People request statutory dates."

And so the calendar continued. Mac sat and listened, taking notes as to the procedure of Judge Binnard's court. She wore her form-fitting navy suit with a cream blouse, pearl earrings and necklace from her grandmother's estate, and navy heels. As she sat in the back of the courtroom, her thoughts slowly drifted to her current love life and whether she'd ever satisfy her maternal instincts. When Judge Binnard called the Landers case, Mac was caught off guard and jumped in her seat.

"In the matter of Levi L.," Judge Binnard announced. The courtroom clerk motioned to the judge and the two of them began to whisper. The clerk picked up the phone and spoke softly into it while cupping the receiver. A minute later, the door to the judge's chambers cracked open and a small boy with blond, curly hair and emerald eyes slowly approached the clerk. An extremely large woman escorted the little boy to the left side of the courtroom and showed him a shelf of toys. Judge Binnard was quiet as he watched the boy sheepishly select a *Hardy Boys* book.

"Good afternoon, Mrs. Kelly," Judge Binnard said to the rotund woman, before turning his attention to the little boy. "And you must be Levi."

The little boy looked up and nodded.

"Have you ever been in a courtroom before?"

Levi shook his head.

"No? Well, let me introduce myself. I'm Judge Binnard, and this is my courtroom. I'm very pleased to meet you, and I want you to know that you're in a very safe place right now. You can tell us anything you want here. If you'd feel more comfortable talking to me up here, then you can sit next to me behind the bench. Or you could chat with my clerk, Joanne, who has seventeen grandchildren of her own." Joanne gave Levi a little grandmotherly smile and wave. "I've already appointed you your very own attorney, Mary MacIntosh, and she's here today to be something we call a 'guardian ad litem,' but that's a rather big and awkward word, isn't it? We chatted already, and she told me that you could just call her Mac, okay? Ms. MacIntosh, will you please step forward?"

Mac walked up the center aisle of the courtroom and pushed open the countertop-high gallery door with her knee. She walked up to Levi and kneeled down before him while extending her hand. Levi looked at Mac's hand held in front on him briefly before quickly turning his attention to Mrs. Kelly and then back up towards the judge.

"It's okay, Levi," Judge Binnard prodded. "Ms. MacIntosh is here to help. You can shake her hand."

Levi tentatively reached his small hand out toward Mac and gently shook her hand. As Mac made this initial contact, she couldn't ignore the dirt under his fingernails and the deep scrape on his thumb. Mac looked into his eyes and offered a warm smile. His sallow skin flushed as he garnered a half- grin, and then, suddenly, his look changed. The half-grin turned into a scowl and Levi jerked his hand away. Mac tried not to react to this behavior and instead began asking him questions about the things he liked, such as sports or cars or playing with other kids. Levi did not answer her questions. As they faced off in an awkward silence, Mac noticed how frail Levi looked in his tan pants cinched tightly at the waist.

"How old are you?" Mac asked. "Let me guess. Twelve?" She knew that he had just turned ten but was hoping to earn brownie points for guessing too high.

"I-I-I'm ten," Levi stammered.

"Wow, you're really mature for a ten-year-old," Mac countered. "I see you've chosen a *Hardy Boys* book," she said, turning the book in her direction. "That's pretty tough reading for a boy your age. You must be really smart." Levi began to smile a little bit at this comment, perhaps a bit broader than before. "When I was a little girl, I read every *Nancy Drew* book I could find. My brother read *Hardy Boys*. We used to argue over who was the better detective. Maybe you can tell me about the book after you've read it." Levi looked to the side, afraid to commit. Mac offered him the book back and he grabbed it. She let go, and gently patted him on the shoulder.

Mac stood and looked at the judge, unsure about the next courtroom procedure. Judge Binnard made some legal findings on the record as the court reporter pressed the keys of her stenographer machine.

"Ms. MacIntosh, you'll need to schedule a time to meet with Levi at the foster mother's house. You can follow Mrs. Kelly into my chambers to make those arrangements. The meeting can be now, if that works with everyone's schedule. I will make all appropriate rulings, and Macy Green will call you with future court dates. I will ensure monitored visitation and a no-discussion order, so that no one may discuss the matter with Levi unless you are present." The judge's voice softened somewhat as he continued. "Thank you for agreeing to take this case. It's going to be a complicated one, I think."

With that, Mrs. Kelly took Levi by the hand and motioned for Mac to follow them through the judge's private entrance. After Levi was out of earshot, Judge Binnard finished the hearing.

"Bailiff, you can escort the parents into the courtroom now." The bailiff's voice boomed out into the hallway, requesting that the Landers parents join the hearing.

Evelyn Landers walked in alone. It was immediately apparent that she was not typical of the mothers in Judge Binnard's juvenile cases. Her five- foot-one-inch frame was sheathed in a beautiful St. John knit black pantsuit, while her medium-length, dark hair was stylishly layered and tucked behind her ears. Her makeup was lightly applied, with a sheer lipstick in a neutral shade. She gracefully sat down in the front row next to a gentleman.

"Ms. Green, since Mary MacIntosh is representing Levi, I assume that you will be representing the other three Landers children?" Judge Binnard asked.

"Yes, Your Honor. I accept appointment as counsel for Austen Landers, age sixteen, Ben Landers, age fourteen, and Lauren Landers, age twelve. If a conflict arises, I will advise the court immediately."

"Thank you. I assume that Dr. and Mrs. Landers have each hired private counsel?"

"Yes, Your Honor," a voice said from the front row of the courtroom. A tall, red-haired man stood and straightened his gray tie. "Harold Neiman on behalf of Dr. and Mrs. Landers."

"Mr. Neiman, I'm afraid that you are not going to be able to represent both parents in this case, as Dr. Landers and Mrs. Landers most likely have divergent interests in this matter. Have you spoken with your clients about this possibility?"

"Yes, Your Honor. If a conflict arises, I will represent Mrs. Landers only. Dr. Landers has agreed to retain his own counsel at that point in time."

Evelyn Landers shifted in her seat looking nervous, unsure as to whether she should remain seated or stand up beside her lawyer.

"That time is now," Judge Binnard said. "I assume that you've had an opportunity and a desire to read the social worker's report in this case? Mrs. Landers is being accused, among other things, of deliberately poisoning her son with perphenazine. Now, our justice system presumes her innocence, of course. But the court must assume that Dr. Landers has an opinion on this subject that may not favor his wife."

"Your Honor, you are assuming–," Harold Neiman started.

"Please approach the counsel table when addressing the court," Judge Binnard brusquely interjected.

Harold Neiman walked forward and stood next to Macy Green. "I've read the jurisdiction report and there is nothing in there that even hints that these allegations are true or that Dr. Landers has any interest other than those of his family."

"Mr. Neiman, it is readily apparent to me that the parents have conflicting interests. You may represent Mrs. Evelyn Landers. Dr. Luke Landers will have to hire his own lawyer. I assume he can afford one, correct?"

The county attorney smirked at the suggestion. Dr. Landers was the top-paid OB/GYN in Sheridan County, and perhaps in all of Wyoming.

"He can afford his own lawyer, Your Honor, but Luke and Evelyn Landers are a united front. They support one another one hundred and fifty percent and are absolutely positive that the petition will ultimately be dismissed with Mrs. Landers being exonerated on all charges against her. Dr. Landers fully supports her position and has signed a waiver of conflict–"

"Mr. Neiman, you are an experienced lawyer, right?"

Harold Neiman looked quizzically at the judge.

"I know that you are. It was a rhetorical question. I knew your dad, and if you are anything like him, you could run circles around half the attorneys in this town. But there is one thing I can assure you. Mothers and fathers often disagree on childrearing–even when they are happily married and live a united front. When one parent is accused of a crime against one of their children, there is a substantial probability that this united front may fraction. If and when it does, I don't want you crawling into court begging to be relieved as counsel. Therefore, I'm telling you now that you must make a choice as to whom you wish to represent."

"Fine. I will represent Mrs. Landers," Harold huffed in response. " I'll call John Trainor and let him know that he will be representing Dr. Landers. We talked about the possibility before the hearing."

"Very well," Judge Binnard said. "Speaking of which, where is Dr. Landers?" The judge looked around the courtroom in an exaggerated fashion before focusing his attention squarely at Evelyn.

Evelyn stood and slowly approached Harold Neiman, nervously glancing at the judge and her lawyer, wondering whether she should answer.

"He-he's delivering a baby. It was an emergency C-section. He couldn't be here."

"He has medical partners, doesn't he?" Judge Binnard asked.

Evelyn looked surprised by the question. "Well, yes."

"And his medical partners are qualified to perform C-sections, correct?"

"Of course," Evelyn stiffly replied to the judge's challenge. Her jaw clenched and she crossed her arms over her chest.

"Then the next time we have a hearing and I order Levi's parents to attend, please communicate to the good doctor that I mean both parents. Surely, his son's well-being is more important than the almighty dollar."

"Your Honor," Evelyn started, "I don't like what you are–"

"What my client means, Your Honor," Harold Neiman interrupted, "is that Dr. Landers will be at the next hearing. Thank you."

"This case may prove to be logistically difficult, counsel. We are going to have to be mindful of the fact that children are going to be asked to testify about both their parents and siblings. Levi will not be allowed in any hearings involving this detailed sort of testimony or when either of his parents are present, though, because that will clearly be too stressful for him. Dr. Landers will need to be apprised of this." Judge Binnard firmly stacked a file of papers on his desk and closed his manila folder. His clerk quickly whispered something to him, reminding him that he needed to set further hearing dates and make findings regarding visitation.

"Oh yes," the judge continued. "With respect to visitation orders, the court orders that Levi remain in foster care pending disposition and that Mrs. Landers be allowed monitored visitation three times per week for two hours a visit. Dr. Landers' visitation will be addressed at the next hearing when his lawyer is present. Mrs. Landers is ordered not to discuss the facts of the case with Levi when visiting. Our next hearing will be next Tuesday in order to further address visitation and discovery. We are adjourned for lunch."

"But Your Honor," Harold Neiman said, "Mrs. Landers is an extremely involved mother who needs more than just a routine visitation schedule. She's a stay-at-home mom who has been Levi's sole caretaker his whole life. She's in the PTA and is also on the Chamber of Commerce, the Women's Charity League, active in her church and serves–"

"Save it for the trial, counsel. She could be Mother Theresa, Mr. Neiman, but if she has done what the petition alleges, then she is going to face losing her parental rights. This hearing is adjourned."

Evelyn turned to Harold Neiman and whispered in his ear while gesticulating with her right hand and shaking her head.

"Your Honor, Mrs. Landers is not happy that she is being forced to see her son in the presence of a monitor, and is upset that her husband is disallowed visitation for a week. She feels that he has constitutional rights to see his son and that you are depriving him of those rights."

Judge Binnard took a slow, deep breath through his nose–so loud in fact that the microphone on his desk made a piercing, windy sound. Harold knew he was in for a tongue-lashing, and his shoulders hunched toward his ears as he awaited the verbal assault.

"Mrs. Landers is upset? Well, so am I. I'm irked that her husband didn't bother showing up. I'm irked that I went out of my way to hold this hearing over the lunch hour so that she could be afforded privacy. I'm irked that my staff is missing out on *their* constitutional right to eat their lunch in peace and quiet. You can tell your client to voice her ire to her husband outside of my courtroom and after this hearing is over."

With that, Judge Binnard removed his reading glasses and stood. He quickly whispered something to his clerk, unsnapped his robe, and then exited the courtroom.

Evelyn Landers turned to her attorney and said, "You told me that I'd get my son back today and that the state had no case against me. What kind of attorney are you?"

After pointedly collecting the papers in front of him into his briefcase and closing it, Harold Neiman turned to his client with a somber expression and said, "The only attorney in town who is willing to defend you."

Chapter 2

"I've been workin' in the foster care system as a foster parent through Social Services for twenty-three years, and in all that time I ain't never seen a case like this. I feel so sorry for this little guy," Mrs. Kelly whispered into Mac's ear as they walked through the back hall of the courthouse. Levi trailed slowly behind, looking out each window they passed as they made their way towards the exit sign. "Staircase is on the left. We can take it down and the exit is near the parking lot. Where'd you park? You can follow me to my house and meet with Levi while I make his lunch."

"I walked. My office is just down Main Street," Mac answered. "If it is not too much trouble, would you mind giving me your address so that I could meet up with you in just a few minutes? I really need to check in with my secretary first so that I can make sure there isn't anything pressing waiting for me at the office. I didn't expect this hearing to take so long."

"These hearings always take a long time," Mrs. Kelly tersely responded. "You just have to get used to it. When I started workin' in foster care, I had to sit in the danged courthouse half the day. I complained about it loud, too, 'cuz I had kids to tend to and I wasn't gettin' paid extra to be sittin' around all day at court. Plus, I had to get a sitter just to show up at court. Nowadays, they at least pay me to come to court so I can afford gettin' a sitter."

Mrs. Kelly reached into her oversized handbag and retrieved a pen and a crumpled up Wal-Mart receipt. She wrote her address and telephone number on the receipt and then immediately handed it to Mac. "Want me to make you some lunch?" she politely asked.

"Oh, no thank you. I brought my own. I'll grab it from my office and eat with Levi at your house."

"Suit yourself," Mrs. Kelly responded, and then added almost as an after-thought, "I make a mean Sloppy Joe."

"I bet you do. I'll take you up on that offer another day," Mac said with a little laugh as she knelt down next to Levi and began to look directly into his eyes. "I'm going to come and have lunch with you," Mac said gently to the frail boy in front of her. "Maybe we could talk a little, and then you can show me around Mrs. Kelly's house?"

"Don't care," Levi mumbled in response. He looked agitated, yet Mac couldn't shake the feeling that he was much more afraid than he was angry. Mac reached out for his shoulder, hoping that a gentle pat on the back would assure him that she was a friend. Instead, Levi recoiled as he pulled back and stared down at the ground and began to knock his tennis shoes together at the toe.

Mrs. Kelly rolled her eyes. "This kid is a piece of work," she mumbled under her breath and then grabbed Levi by the hand as she began to cross the street with him towards the parking lot.

Mac watched as Levi proceeded to walk away from her. His tiny frame was in direct contrast with Mrs. Kelly's ample one. Levi turned briefly and nervously glanced back towards Mac. She quickly waved to him, but he turned his body back in the direction of Mrs. Kelly, without waving back.

* * *

As Mac headed towards her office, she walked directly in front of the courthouse, which architecturally was an amalgamation of old and new. Built in 1905 and placed on the National Registry of Historic Places, Sheridan's courthouse sat majestically on top of a hill, and had the look of a capitol building, complete with a dome top. In the summer, the grassy slope resembled a velvet carpet leading up to the courthouse steps, with fifteen-foot tall pine trees intermixed with cottonwoods whose limbs were heavy with brilliant foliage.

The old section of the courthouse had an underground tunnel which previously connected the county jail to the sheriff's residence. The jail had long since been relocated, the sheriff no longer lived amongst inmates, and the former sheriff's home was now the juvenile court annex, carrying with it the flavor of a colorful history. The new wing to the courthouse was added a few decades back, and provided the government with the space it needed for additional offices. This extra space was necessary for the government of a growing western town, but the new wing was fashioned in a manner that successfully balanced the historical elegance of the original structure.

As she crossed Main Street on this bright day in late September, Mac admired the old dome brightly shining in the mid-day sun. Fall was on its way, and the leaves on the beautiful trees surrounding the courthouse were beginning to show ebbs of color. Autumn was peaceful in Wyoming with bright, crisp days. But sometimes, without much warning, a warm Chinook breeze turned into a violent pre-winter snowstorm which dusted the grandiose peaks of the Big Horn Mountains with a light layer of snow. Mac smiled to herself as she thought that this uncertainty of the weather made the season interesting.

As Mac continued to walk south along Main Street, her thoughts returned to the Landers family. Mac had not met the other Landers children, but had read about them frequently in the local newspaper. As a sports enthusiast, she regularly consumed the pages of *The Sheridan Press*, and the Landers children were often the focus of local sports coverage. She felt as though she already knew them based on all of the reports she'd read in Levi's court file, as well as the local press. Mac began to recall some of the stories she had read about each of the kids.

Austen was a tall, charismatic young man. She knew that he was a senior in high school and that he played varsity football for the Sheridan Broncs. He had been the starting quarterback since his sophomore year and college scouts had been watching him since early this season. Austen was also the forward on the school's varsity basketball team, and the third baseman for their baseball team. He had dark hair and dark blue eyes just like his mother, balanced with his father's height. Intuitively, Mac knew that Austen was considered popular.

Ben Landers was a sophomore in high school and a member of both the varsity wrestling and football teams. Whereas Austen was tall and dark with blue eyes, Ben was short and brawny with dark eyes. Mac pictured a burly, serious young man with an undercurrent of anger and energy furrowing deep inside. Based on court reports, Mac knew that Ben had a reputation for being surly and not being afraid of getting into a fight. Mac immediately recalled an episode following a football game during his freshman year that firmly backed up his reputation.

Lauren Landers was in eighth grade and was a feminine version of Austen. At five-feet-nine, she stood quite tall for a twelve-year-old girl. Lauren was a tad lighter in color than Austen, having both light brown hair and eyes. She was also an avid sports enthusiast, playing basketball, volleyball, softball, tennis, and golf, all while maintaining an active membership with her local swim team. Mac pictured her as a typical 'tween- ager–rarely caught without her MP3 player plugged in her ears. Mac smiled to herself as she imagined that Lauren's iPhone and music likely had the added benefit of tuning out her overbearing mother from time to time.

Levi was much more petite and fair skinned than his siblings. Unlike his siblings, Levi had blond and curly hair accompanied by a set of piercing green eyes. Similarly, Levi did not have the height that his siblings clearly inherited from their father, but he certainly had his father's haunting good looks, though without an athletic frame it came across as a somewhat hollow and fragile appearance.

Mac reflected on Levi's appearance in court that morning. She didn't see any overt signs of abuse or illness, though his voluminous medical records suggested otherwise. Levi appeared afraid and guarded, but what child wouldn't under the circumstances? Mac decided to get to know Levi on a more personal basis before diving into the medical records which would undoubtedly provide Mac with the other side of the story.

* * *

"I am so glad you're here," a breathless Mrs. Kelly said to Mac as she flung open the front door of her foster home. Mac was alarmed at Mrs. Kelly's flushed face and by the manner in which she was panting. "We just had quite an episode."

"An episode? What do you mean?" She had only been away from Mrs. Kelly for forty-five minutes, as she made sure to be brief while checking in with her law office staff after court.

"It's Levi. He's had another outbreak."

"I'm not sure what you're talking about, Mrs. Kelly. Is Levi hurt? What happened?"

Mrs. Kelly squinted her eyes at Mac. "How much did the judge tell you about Levi's conduct disorder?"

"I didn't have any conversations with the judge about this case," Mac explained to Mrs. Kelly. "The public defender's office called me requesting my assistance on a case. I only recently accepted, and I don't even have a complete file on Levi to review. Please tell me what's going on."

"Them doctors—they call it a conduct disorder. They don't say what it is. I've been around the block enough times to at least call it like I see it. I ain't no doctor, but I've raised enough kids to know that Levi is a bully. But bullies don't just get themselves born. Somethin' happens to 'em to make 'em inta bullies. My money's on one of them elder brothers, I tell you. I bet they knock him around and without no way to defend against them bigger brothers, he picks on younger kids or throws a tantrum when he gets any chance. And that's exactly what happened when we got home from court. He darned near went crazy, throwing stuff 'round the baby's room. That boy done fished out a dirty diaper and wiped the baby's stinky crap all over the walls. I've had my share of delinquent foster kids, so don't think I can't handle it—but he keeps this up and he is out the door. I'm too old for this, and I'm not willing to deal with it for much more. I've had kids steal my car, steal money outta my purse, set fires in the woods, blow up frogs with firecrackers—you name it, I've dealt with it. But I am not gonna be wipin' no shit off no walls. You hear me?"

Mrs. Kelly took a deep breath and without another word, she motioned with her head for Mac to follow her into the house and towards the room where Levi was sitting.

The house was an old Victorian, but it had long ago lost its glamour. The rooms were small, and a musty smell permeated throughout. The furniture inside the house was sparse and tattered. Paint was peeling from the walls. The living room had one old couch with a small television in the corner sitting on top of cinder blocks. TV trays were lined up in front of the couch with what appeared to be the remains of breakfast on each plate.

Mac followed Mrs. Kelly to a closed door near the back of the house. Mrs. Kelly knocked twice before turning the door knob. She pushed on the door, but it only gave way an inch. "Oh, what has this kid done now?" she shouted to no one in particular before using her weight up against the door. When the door responded to Mrs. Kelly's attempts by only moving another inch or so, Mrs. Kelly tersely shouted out for Mac to give her a hand.

Mac helped push on the door, which only began to open after the sound of furniture moving escaped from within. "Damn kid put the crib in front of the door," Mrs. Kelly unnecessarily explained to Mac.

With her narrow frame, Mac was able to squeeze herself through the partially opened door, and when she entered the room, she immediately saw Levi crouched in a corner with his head between his knees and both arms crisscrossed over his head. Mrs. Kelly, who was far too wide to enter, was unable to follow Mac into Levi's room.

"Levi, I'm Mac. Remember me? I met you at the courthouse a bit ago. I am here to help you."

Levi did not flinch.

"Can you tell me why you are so upset?"

Again, Levi did not move. Mac could see his chest heaving, probably because he was either crying or out of breath from his tantrum—or both. His blond curly hair was matted to his head and was wet with sweat. Mac looked around the room. Mrs. Kelly was right. It appeared that Levi had taken diapers out of the Diaper Genie and smeared feces on the walls. The baby's crib had been moved behind the door, as was evidenced by the scratches on the hardwood floor. The linens had been tossed around. Toys were broken. Heads had been ripped off teddy bears and the stuffing spewed out. Levi's hands were filthy, and he smelled.

Mac took a seat next to Levi on the floor and sat there in silence for a few moments just listening to him breathe. She sensed that he was calming down after a few minutes.

"When I was little, my dad died," Mac started. Levi did not move. "I was so angry that he left me. I didn't understand what happened or why, and I just wanted my daddy back and for things to go back to the way they were before he died." Levi's head picked up a bit. "I even got so mad one time that I cut the hair off my favorite doll. My mom scolded me, but that didn't stop me. A few days later, I broke the wheels off my brother's G.I. Joe Army truck. Now, that didn't go over too well, as you can imagine. My brother was hysterical and my mom got really mad." Levi pulled his head up just a bit higher. Mac could see his watery green eyes. She kept on telling him the story.

"I was so mad at my mom because I thought that she made my dad die. All she did after he died was curl up on her bed and stare off into space. It made me hate her. One day when she was curled up in a ball, I marched into her bathroom and broke off all of her Avon lipsticks. Later when my mom found my mess, she went berserk."

Mac scooted a little closer to Levi. He didn't move away from her, so she kept on talking.

"After that, my mom made me go stay with my grandma. I don't remember how long I stayed at my grandma's, but I tell you, it was boring there. There were no toys. No cartoons. Nothing at all to do. It was winter in Colorado, so it was too cold to go outside. I just sat there. It seemed like forever. I wanted to break something at my grandma's house so I could go back to my mom's. I remember walking around their house, which smelled like a giant mothball, looking for something to break. I remember finding the perfect thing: a coo-coo clock in the back bedroom. Every hour the little blue bird came out of the top window of the clock that was shaped like an A-frame house. I waited and waited until it was ten o'clock in the morning and when that silly little bird came out for her seventh 'coo,' I pinched her with my fingers and pulled real hard. The clock came off the wall and broke into a million pieces." Levi's head raised up another inch. Tear tracks had made their way down his cheeks, and droplets dripped from his chin onto his pants. He wiped his runny nose with the back of his hand.

"My grandma came running in that room so fast. It was the fastest I'd ever seen her move. I could tell by the look on her face that she was really mad. I expected her to spank me and yell at me and send me home, but she didn't." Mac paused, baiting Levi. She looked at him for a long time, hoping that he would ask her what happened next. He stared into Mac's deep brown eyes, silently begging her to go on, but Mac wanted him to speak. She hoped that she could invite a connection between them. She waited another minute, and then another.

"W-w-what did she do?" he finally asked, his voice quivering.

Mac smiled and slowly inched forward towards Levi. "She held me in her arms so tight that I could barely breathe."

"Was she hurting you?"

"No, Levi. She was loving me. She gave me the longest teddy bear hug you can imagine. And then she helped me pick up all the pieces to the clock and together, we glued them back together. The clock never worked again, but she kept it on her wall anyway. Every time I went to her house from that point on, I looked at that clock and felt so bad that I had broken it."

Levi nodded. Tears continued to drip down his cheeks. Mac reached into her purse and retrieved a tissue. She thought about offering the tissue to Levi, but realized that she had an opportunity to connect, so she seized it. She reached over and blotted his tears while continuing to talk.

"This all happened when I was about five. When I was seventeen and packing my suitcases for college, do you know what she did?"

Levi shook his head, not knowing. "What?"

"She hid the clock in one of my bags. When I later got to college and unpacked, I found the clock. Inside, there was a letter from my grandma telling me that sometimes we can't fix what is broken. The clock was unique—my father had given it to her after he returned from a business trip to Europe. It wasn't replaceable, and it was something very special to her. Just like my father. And me. She told me that she loved me no matter what I did."

Levi looked away. The tears had returned.

"Mrs. Kelly is upset because you messed up this room. Why don't you and I clean it up together? She has a right to be upset, just like you do, Levi. You have a right to be sad right now. It's okay. I understand. We need to learn something from this. What do you think we should learn?"

Levi did not answer. Mac reached out to touch his face, but he pulled back.

"We don't have the right to break other people's stuff just because we get upset. I had to learn that lesson too, Levi. I could not understand why God took my dad away. I was so angry. I wanted–"

"How did he die?" Levi asked, looking back toward Mac with large, hungry eyes.

"A car accident. It was snowing. He and my mom had an argument, and he left the house to calm down–and while he was gone he had a terrible accident."

"Were you mad at your mom for making him die?"

Mac was surprised by his question. She drew in a deep breath and tried to think of an answer that would be appropriate, but she found herself at a loss for words.

"Well, Levi, my mom didn't make my dad die. It was just an accident."

Levi shook his head at Mac, insistent as he responded. "No it wasn't. My dad says there are no such things as accidents."

Chapter 3

"I know you're upset, Evelyn, but these allegations are serious. We have to discuss them today," attorney Harold Neiman said.

Court had apparently left Evelyn Landers quite shaken, evidenced by the mascara running down her otherwise flawless cheeks. As she walked with her attorney towards her champagne-colored Range Rover, she said, "I will look at my schedule and see if there is a good time this week for a meeting."

"You're not planning on coming with me to my office right now?" Harold asked. "This is extremely important, and we can't just wait until a time later this week. These aren't matters easily discussed outside of my office, and I certainly won't discuss the facts with you on the street. There are eyes and ears around, if you know what I mean. I'm surprised that the *Sheridan Press* isn't following us to your car."

Evelyn Landers's demeanor stiffened as she approached her car. She turned towards her attorney and brusquely dismissed his suggestion to work on her case. "I have a million things to do today. I didn't expect for this nightmare to happen. You may not realize this, but it's currently my busiest season for philanthropic work, and I'm committed to more projects than I care to count. I can't just drop everything because an overly zealous prosecutor has decided to drum up an unsubstantiated case against high- profile citizens in the midst of election season. Believe me, anyone with a little savvy in this town knows exactly what Karl Swensen is doing. Unfortunately for my family, we're going to have to endure these ridiculous allegations until our name can be cleared–which is your job, Harold. I trust you will be getting this matter properly dismissed."

"Evelyn, accusations of child abuse do not just get *dismissed* without an investigation. Social Services is going to continue snooping around and digging into your family's background. I'll object, of course, but you have to understand that they have a right to investigate this case. *If* they don't find enough evidence to support pursuing this case–the key word being *if*–then they'll dismiss the case on their own. But I've done this for long enough to know that cases like this don't get filed without there being some evidence out there to support it. This is serious stuff. Your philanthropic commitments are commendable, but they're going to have to play second chair to your current family predicament until the case gets adjudicated."

Evelyn unlocked her car and sat on the posh, tan leather seat. She put her keys in the ignition and started the car, leaving the door ajar, thus causing the safety system to beep repeatedly. While Harold was pleading with her about adjusting her priorities, she applied her peppermint frost Estée Lauder lipstick. While confirming that it was properly applied in the overhead lighted mirror, she said, "Thank you for your concern, Harold, but I am perfectly capable of managing my own priorities and don't need the lecture. I've raised four kids, three of whom excel both academically and athletically. I've managed to perform my duties as the '*doctor's wife*,' remain an active and avid volunteer, all the while managing to tend to my last child–who is *quite* a handful. But, since you seem to know what's best for me at the moment, I will follow you to your office for a chat. But don't expect me to stay long, as my day is quite booked."

* * *

"That's exactly what I don't get, Evelyn," Harold Neiman said to her once they were settled behind closed doors in his corner office of Neiman and Wiley. "I know you are an incredible mom and a dutiful wife, and that you constantly go out of your way to keep giving yourself to charitable causes. But right now, when your family needs you the most, you seem almost put off by the demands placed on you by the judge. From what you've described, Levi has been a challenge since birth. You–"

"A *challenge*?" Evelyn nearly shrieked in response. "A challenge is kicking a fifty yard field goal. A challenge is running a sub-five minute mile. I know all about challenges, Harold. Describing Levi as a challenge is an injustice to the word." Evelyn uncrossed her legs and re-crossed them again, shifting her weight in the high-backed, maroon leather wing chair. "You have no idea what I've been through. Not only has this little guy been throwing tantrums since he broke my ribs during my seventh month of pregnancy, but he's constantly testing my ability to trust my own motherly instincts when it comes to childhood illnesses. My other kids got sick, and I was able to deal with it without any problem because they got normal kid illnesses: the flu, chicken pox, ear infections, pneumonia, you name it. But nothing Levi has had could be considered normal by any stretch of the imagination. In fact, he's probably had everything but the normal stuff, and it's taken every ounce of my strength to see to it that his ever-changing needs continue to be met. You can't even imagine how much of my time tending to Levi has taken away from the other kids. Do you know how many sporting and other special events I've missed? And after all these years of me bending over backwards to make sure that Levi gets loved and cared for in *every* way, I'm being accused of purposefully making him sick! I can't even begin to tell you how unnerved I am over this. It's like a cold slap in my face, after everything I've done for that child."

"I agree with you, Evelyn. It is offensive," Harold replied, trying to slowly lessen the degree of tension that had been bubbling between them. "And you certainly do not fit the profile of a Munchausen by Proxy mother. In fact, you have demonstrated–"

"Have you researched this disorder?" Evelyn hissed. Without giving her lawyer a chance to respond, she venomously continued, "I have. I looked it up in Luke's medical book and on the Internet, and I'm horrified that anyone would even consider applying that disorder to me. It's vile and disgusting. What parent in their right mind would purposefully induce an illness in his or her child to gain attention or sympathy? And who would think that I could be that type of parent? *That* does not describe me in the slightest. I have made sure that Levi's medical needs have been met, but that's by responding to the medical condition–not creating it. I don't consider the attention that I receive in the process to be anything remotely like a benefit–it's a burden. A burden I willingly and lovingly assume, as it is being done for my son whom I love. I apologize if I'm coming across strong to you right now, but I want to make sure that there is no confusion between us when it comes to my treatment of Levi: I have never sought medical treatment on his behalf simply because I was bored or needed attention."

After catching her breath, Evelyn stood up from her chair, walked over to the wet bar and began pouring herself a glass of water.

"There's Scotch if you need something stronger," Harold offered. "It's been a trying day."

Evelyn turned to Harold, and began to speak to him once again—but this time, in a more subdued tone. "I have too much to do today, Harold; otherwise, I'd definitely take you up on your offer of a good, stiff drink. I still need to drop off baked goods at the church, pick up Lauren from volleyball before taking her to swim practice, get Ben to his private wrestling coach, drop off Austen's waiver form so he can run for Homecoming King, and make dinner for the kids," Evelyn paused for a moment, clearly getting worked up for the tasks ahead of her. "To top it all off, tonight there is a benefit dinner for Luke's new wing at the hospital. I'm sure my family's dilemma will be gossiped about non-stop. I've seen the whispers, the nods, the looks—I'm not an idiot, Harold, and it hurts. It kills me to think for one second that there are people who might actually believe that I'd do something as despicable as poison my own son!"

Evelyn sighed. "That drink is sounding better and better. If only I didn't have to drive." With that, Evelyn began to pack up her bags to leave Harold's office.

* * *

"You forgot to pack my conditioner, Mom," Lauren Landers whined while rummaging through her swim bag on the way to the YMCA.

"I'm so sorry, Lauren," Evelyn said, releasing a sigh, "I've had a straining day."

Lauren rolled her eyes. "You always say that, Mom. You have your usual headache, too?"

"As a matter of fact, I–," Evelyn started before stopping herself. She was exhausted, and didn't need to justify anything to her twelve-year-old daughter. Evelyn found herself apologizing to Lauren a little too much lately, because it seemed that she was never able to do everything "just right" in Lauren's eyes. Wasn't it just yesterday when she had reached out to hold her mommy's hand? Didn't she beg Evelyn to play Barbies with her and to have tea parties? Now, it seemed that Evelyn's only involvement in Lauren's life was making sure that she owned the hippest clothes, ensuring she had a fully charged cell phone, and providing her with a constant supply of Bumble conditioner. *Where did my darling little girl go?*

Evelyn looked in her rear-view mirror and focused on the young woman in the back seat–the sweaty, muscular young woman wearing a volleyball uniform. Didn't she realize that her mom had spent all day in court fighting to get her little brother back? Was she that self-absorbed that she didn't even realize that today was the day they were supposed to get Levi back from foster care?

"Levi has to stay at Mrs. Kelly's house." Evelyn watched Lauren's reaction in the rearview mirror as she slowly uttered those words.

Lauren lifted her head up for the first time since she jumped into the Range Rover and returned her mother's obvious stares in the rearview mirror. Lauren's face softened a bit. "I thought Dad said that the judge would have to give him back today."

"That's what we thought, honey, but the judge decided that Levi should stay in the foster home for a little while longer. They aren't finished evaluating the case, but I am sure that it won't be long until–"

"Is the judge going to give Levi to another family?" Lauren interrupted. "Jessalyn Jones, this girl in my geometry class, said that they can make kids live in new families forever if they want to."

Evelyn turned left on Dow Street and accelerated toward the YMCA. She had suddenly become anxious to drop off Lauren, as the conversation had begun to make her head pound. Evelyn carefully calculated her response. "They are not getting Levi a new family, Lauren. And who exactly is this Jessalyn Jones girl to be educating you on the foster care system?" Evelyn spit the words out like cotton balls, thick and stringy.

"She's a girl in my geometry class," Lauren calmly replied. A few minutes went by before Lauren started up on the topic again. "Ben said that the judge has no case against you. He said that if you were gonna poison one of your kids, it would be him instead of Levi. Ben said that–"

"What?" Evelyn gasped. "That's not an appropriate thing for Ben to say, Lauren. You know that I would never harm any of you." Evelyn's foot began to press harder on the accelerator, and she found the car skidding to a stop in front of the Y. "Have a good practice, Lauren," Evelyn conclusively stated. "Borrow conditioner from Amy."

After Lauren hopped out of the car, Evelyn sped off. As Evelyn scooted away from her inquisitive daughter, she glimpsed at the mothers around her who were cautiously escorting their young children into the YMCA. *What happened to the days when I was one of those moms? Was it that long ago that I had to wheel Levi in a stroller across this parking lot, while escorting Austen, Ben and Lauren to swimming lessons?* A thought unexpectedly popped into her head: *what if Ben was thinking that I'd poison him back then?*

Ben was the second-eldest Landers child–and possibly the brightest, but cloaked with entitlement and aggressiveness. He was fourteen now, just weeks shy of his fifteenth birthday, and a sophomore in high school. Despite his honor roll status and varsity wrestling prestige, Ben had a chip on his shoulder the size of Mt. St. Helens. He relentlessly picked on Levi, and frequently engaged him in "friendly" wrestling matches. Evelyn sighed as she thought about those wrestling matches, which were more similar to a gladiator battle than a brotherly tussle. Ben was three times Levi's size and five times his weight. Levi didn't stand a snowball's chance in hell during the matches, though he never turned down an opportunity to interact with his older brother–even if it meant he'd be tossed around like a rag-doll.

Evelyn considered the fact that Ben and Lauren were discussing the probability of her poisoning her children. Did they really think that she was capable of poisoning one of them? What kind of a monster did they think she was? They had no problems entrusting her with cooking for them, cleaning for them, running them around town to every event imaginable, heading up their fundraisers, and planning their family's lavish vacations, but they didn't trust that she would never poison any of them?

Evelyn raced up Fifth Street toward the high school, completely unaware of her speed. She wanted to turn in Austen's Homecoming King release form and then hightail it back to the sanctum of her home. What she needed now, more than anything, was to close herself off from the world. In a way, it was nice not having Levi home. She missed him, for sure, but she sure didn't miss his endless demands. He was always sick. He had constant doctor appointments and lab tests. When Levi wasn't at the doctor's office or in a hospital emergency room, he was in the principal's office for fighting at school. It wasn't uncommon that one of his classmate's mothers would call under the guise of conversation, only to reveal the true nature of the call—that Levi had said or did something to her son or daughter that was offensive. Evelyn was tired of making excuses for Levi, tired of apologizing for him, and tired of trying to figure out what was wrong with him.

Evelyn was so deep in thought that she didn't immediately notice the flashing red lights in her rear-view mirror. When the siren finally drew Evelyn out of her reverie, she immediately pulled the car over to the shoulder of the road and anxiously awaited the officer's approach.

"In a hurry?" the officer asked. Evelyn didn't recognize him. He must have been new to the force.

"I'm sorry," Evelyn managed to reply. "I've had a lot of things on my mind, and I obviously didn't realize how fast I was going. I've had a difficult day and—"

"All my days are difficult, too, ma'am. That doesn't excuse me from the speed limit, though, does it?" the officer callously replied, before asking Evelyn for her driver's license and registration. Evelyn was definitely flustered at this point and watched as he took her documents back to his squad car. From her side mirror she saw him begin speaking into his two-way. The conversation seemed to last forever; Evelyn expected that the officer was radioing her information in to dispatch, but couldn't imagine why it was taking so long. Ten minutes later, the officer, appearing both angry and disgusted, finally returned to Evelyn.

"Here you go, ma'am." The officer abruptly handed Evelyn her driver's license and registration.

"Sir, I haven't had a ticket in over twenty years—I'm an extremely safe driver. I apologize for losing sight of my speed, but you have no idea how awful my day has been. As it is, I'm going to be late picking up my son from wrestling practice. Would it be possible to just issue me a warning instead of—"

The officer interrupted Evelyn's pleas and handed her a piece of paper. "The date on the ticket tells you when you need to appear in court. You're probably familiar with that."

Evelyn looked incredulously at the officer. "What's that supposed to mean?" she asked, not sure exactly why he would take that sort of an attitude with her. She certainly was not about to take flack from some rookie cop.

"It means exactly that. Good day, Mrs. Landers," the officer somberly replied. Without so much as a blink of his eye, he began walking back to his squad car. Evelyn could only presume from the snide remark that the dispatcher was filling him in on the details of the juvenile charges pending against her.

As she shifted her car back into gear, she made a mental note to herself to complain about the officer's disposition.

* * *

"Why didn't you get him back, Mom? Dad said that—"

"Your father wasn't in court today, Ben, I was. Alone. Delivering babies is apparently more important to him than bringing his son home." Evelyn winced as the bitter words escaped her lips. She knew that her statement was unfair and that she was speaking out of frustration. "I'm sorry," she quickly added, "I didn't mean that. I'm just upset."

Ben slipped off his seatbelt and reached into his wrestling gear bag, which was sitting on the back seat. He pulled out a baseball cap and put it on his wet head. He'd just finished wrestling practice and wanted to be dropped off at the YMCA to lift weights with the football team. Normally, Evelyn would have objected and insisted that he come home with her so that he could do homework and she could make dinner, but she didn't have the energy. She nodded and put the car in drive, careful to obey the speed limit on her way back down the hill.

"When does he get to come home?"

"Do you miss him?" Evelyn asked, in a hopeful tone.

Ben rarely missed an opportunity to pick on Levi. Evelyn suspected that if Ben missed his little brother, it was only because he didn't have anyone to tease. Ben didn't dare pick on Austen. Austen was two years older and the quarterback of the football team. Ben lived in Austen's shadow. And Lauren could hold her own. She was two years younger than Ben, but she was very athletic and confident, and if she couldn't out-run Ben, she certainly could outwit him.

That left Ben with ten-year-old, defenseless Levi. Levi was either whiny and sick or angry and throwing tantrums. He provided constant fodder for Ben. Levi never figured out that if he didn't react to Ben's taunting, Ben would eventually get bored and leave Levi alone. Instead, Levi played right into Ben's trap–crying to Evelyn the minute Ben looked at him sideways, or worse–running full bore at Ben with his little fists hammering wildly. Ben would clobber Levi to the ground with one quick swipe. Levi would holler out in frustration or pain, and Evelyn would come to the rescue, scolding Ben and babying Levi. It was a never-ending cycle that drove both Levi and Evelyn crazy.

"Yeah, I miss the little squirt. It's too quiet at home without him bawling about something."

Evelyn shot Ben a scowl before letting out a large sigh. It wasn't worth the confrontation to remind Ben that his little brother was alone and scared, trapped in a stranger's house. Evelyn wasn't sure that Ben really even cared about anyone other than himself. She had thought about making him see a psychiatrist, but Luke vehemently objected to her suggestion.

"Well, I miss him very much," Evelyn said. "I'm sure that Austen and Lauren miss him, too."

When Ben didn't respond, she changed the subject, inquiring about school and homework and Homecoming events.

After she dropped Ben at the YMCA, Evelyn drove home to throw something together for dinner and to change into a nice cocktail dress. She was not in the mood to socialize tonight, but at least the benefit dinner at the country club gave her an excuse to dress up and take her mind off her baby.

It was so painful to think of another woman getting Levi ready for bed, reading him a story, helping him under the covers, and tucking him in. She wondered whether he missed her goodnight kisses. She worried if he would come down with a fever in the night and his foster mother would not know of it. Evelyn religiously checked on Levi during the night. What if he had another seizure? What if he vomited while asleep on his back and choked? What if–Evelyn's mind started racing through the heinous possibilities, all of which haunted her. She wanted her baby back. Soon.

She feared that Judge Binnard had no intention of ever giving Levi back to her. She wondered how much the judge knew about her past, but she was too afraid to ask her attorney. She didn't trust Harold–she couldn't trust him. He might be loose-lipped like a lot of other people in this small town. She had no one to talk to, and she needed to talk to someone now more than ever. She needed a friend, someone with whom she'd feel comfortable confiding. Evelyn realized now that there was no one in her life that she could trust in that way other than her housekeeper, Ginny. She ran through all of her friends, but realized that none of them were more than ladies to golf and play bridge with and to meet for lunch and talk about the kids. She had ladies in her sorority group and her book club and ladies from church–but none of them were the type of friend that she could trust with her personal feelings.

And she certainly could not trust her husband.

Chapter 4

Mac felt unsettled from her conversation with Levi, and pondered why he thought that there were no such things as accidents. He spoke with such an earnest conviction that Mac had little doubts that he held those thoughts deep in his heart. What did Levi think when he fell down and scraped his knees? Or when he inadvertently ran into someone on the playground at school? Did he think that these situations were intentional or calculated?

Mac fully intended to continue this conversation with Levi–to explore his psyche and to find out the depth of his feelings–but she knew that it was too soon to get much of a response out of him. She needed to build trust and gain his confidence before she could ask such a provocative line of questions. She was impressed with his willingness to help clean up the mess he'd made at Mrs. Kelly's house and when Mac had said her good-byes to Levi, she had promised to come back and visit him soon. Levi's tentative wave back to Mac left her with hope that perhaps this conversation wouldn't be too far off, and that she might actually be able to build a relationship with this little boy.

She drove back to her office and entered the two-story brownstone on Main Street through its rear stairwell. Her secretary, Megan, was busy on the phone when Mac entered. Megan waved at Mac and handed her a thick stack of messages. Megan flipped up the microphone to her phone headset as she said, "A large box of documents arrived from the doctor's office on the Landers case. I put them on the couch in your office. And you received phone calls from both Mrs. Lander's lawyer and Social Services. And your boyfriend called too."

Mac walked into her corner office that overlooked Main Street, and saw her yellow tabby cat, Ted, on the windowsill monitoring the hustle and bustle of small-town life. Mac walked over to the window and gave Ted a scratch behind the ears. Ted began to purr and nudged her hand with his head, beckoning more attention. Mac knew that if she didn't comply and give Ted a good petting, he would undoubtedly jump up onto her desk and rest himself on the papers she needed to read, so she rubbed and scratched his cheeks to appease him.

Mac logged onto her e-mail and sighed as she saw how quickly her inbox filled with e-mails lately, and longed for the days of solely snail-mail communication. She first opened the message from her boyfriend, Dr. Jeffrey Plattenburg. Jeffrey worked for the FBI as a profiler and was trained as a specialist in tracking serial killers. Mac had met him while he was on assignment in Wyoming hunting down a killer. Jeffrey was an avid runner, like Mac, and they shared many interests. Since Mac desperately wanted a husband and a family, she hoped that their relationship of nearly six months would work. Jeffrey had previously been married to a doctor in Washington D.C. Though he had no children from his former marriage, he was noncommittal on whether he actually wanted to have any children. Well . . . strike that. Jeffrey had actually made his desires not to have any children quite clear, but Mac was convinced that she could change his mind. She just needed a little time to accomplish that. Jeffrey was a very regimented and precise man, and Mac wondered whether he was even suited for the chaos that children can bring into a home. Mac paused for a bit as she reflected on that thought. Mac sighed—why does everything have to be so complex? Why can't life ever provide you with an easy answer, or a clear-cut choice? While she truly liked Jeffrey, she was not interested in wasting time in a relationship. Jeffrey might not even be worth her taking the time to contemplate, as they didn't see each other often and were presently a geographically undesirable couple.

Mac logged off her email and lifted a stack of documents out of the cardboard box containing Levi's records and began to review the first entry on the chart of his medical history. It described Levi's birth in strictly statistical terms, and included a succinct description of how the event had transpired. Mac now knew Levi's official birth date as June 10, 1997 and that he had been a breach baby that resulted in an emergency Caesarian. His birth was otherwise uneventful, and that he had emerged a healthy, robust baby scoring a nine on the APGAR scale. Though Levi was born slightly jaundiced, after being treated with additional light in the hospital, he was released to his family as a thriving and healthy baby boy.

The first sign of any potential healthy issues presented themselves approximately one month later when Evelyn took him for his regular check- up, complaining during the visit of his lackluster eating habits. According to the records, all three of her older children breastfed heartily and had no problem latching on and getting plenty of nutrients. Levi, on the other hand, struggled to latch on, and suckled for only a few minutes before losing interest. Evelyn described to the doctor that Levi fussed with her a lot and constantly pulled his knees to his chest. He was not gaining weight, so Dr. Kerr, the pediatrician, recommended supplementing with formula.

Apparently, Evelyn took offense at the suggestion to begin formula feeding Levi, and the doctor at this visit thought it important enough to document in Levi's charts. "Mother is upset with recommendation. Feels that it is her fault that Levi not getting enough to eat." The chart associated with this notation showed that Levi's weight at the time was only five pounds and ended with the emphatic note that Evelyn nevertheless continued a steadfast refusal to supplementing Levi's diet.

After the one month check-up, Mac saw that Levi's medical history showed frequent visits It appeared to Mac that Evelyn called or "dropped in" the office every few days, and that these unscheduled visits were the result of Evelyn's continuing complaints over Levi's weight. Levi's pediatric medical chart reflected these visits and his overall status in the following way:

7/20/97: Baby–6 weeks: Mother believes that baby suffers from "failure to thrive" syndrome and wants baby seen by a specialist. Baby weighs 6 pounds and has not gained significant weight since hospital discharge.

Told mother breast milk might not be nutrient-rich enough as baby is fourth child in seven years. Mother dissatisfied with formula option and convinced lack of weight gain has nothing to do with breastfeeding.

Referred her to lactation specialist to have breast milk analyzed. Mother declined while again requesting "failure to thrive" specialist. Gave referral to Dr. Abrams in Denver, Colorado.

7/25/97: No lab results/reports from Dr. Abrams. Mother continues to complain about "failure to thrive."

7/29/97: Mother reports taking Levi to ER night prior due to vomiting and dehydration. Discharged after overnight IV. Baby appears listless. No fever. Able to cry tears. Repeated recommendation for a supplement.

8/7/97: Baby–8 weeks: Well check. Immunizations: DTaP; MMR. Mother highly questioning efficacy of giving immunizations to a "failure to thrive baby." Baby seen by Dr. Abrams in Denver. Lab tests completed. Results faxed. No diagnosis for failure to thrive. Reviewed Dr. Abrams's finding with mother. Mother continues with complaints of "failure to thrive" and questions efficacy of immunizing baby. Repeat recommendation to supplement breast milk. Mother again refused. Weight:

6.2 lbs. Length: 23 inches. Slow growth. Infant asleep during visit. Mother asked for additional referral. Gave her referral to Dr. Leslie Myers in Billings, MT.

8/20/97: Baby–10 weeks. Weight: 5.8 lbs. Length: 24 inches. Weight loss. Mother discussed possible colic. Baby cries all the time and pulls knees to chest. Diarrhea daily. Reflux issues. Elimination 10-12/day.

Suggest Mylecon drops to settle stomach and lactose-free formula supp. Recommend supplementing with formula. Mother refused to supp breastfeeding.

Mac read through every entry in Levi's charts and noted that they occurred with much similarity to the ones posted leading up to his ten-week visit. Weekly entries showed very moderate weight gain. Levi had been seen by a doctor almost daily for the first three months of his life. Mac wondered about how Evelyn could manage three other children with this sort of schedule and began to consider how Evelyn was able to tend to her family during those days. Did she have a nanny to assist her with the other kids? Austen would have been in the first grade by then, and Evelyn would have had to get her eldest child to his first day of school during this time frame. Ben further would have undoubtedly required some sort of preschool program. Mac recalled that Luke had started his private medical practice around that time, meaning that he wouldn't have been able to help Evelyn much with the kid shuffle.

Mac noted the time, remembering that she had an appointment with Dr. Kerr. She had scheduled a meeting with Levi's pediatrician almost immediately upon receiving his case. She put a sticky-note in Levi's medical file to remind herself where she had stopped reviewing the notes, and began to grab all the items she would need for the appointment. She put on her long, tan wool jacket and affixed her faux-Burberry scarf before she exited down the back stairs of her office. Two streets later, Mac had arrived at Dr. Kerr's office–a Victorian home painted eggshell blue with pink trim.

* * *

Dr. Kerr had a successful practice, evident by the number of kids of all ages packed into his waiting room. Adolescents jammed out to the music pumping through their iPods and iPhones. Grade school boys energetically thumped their thumbs on the keyboards attached to their GameBoy or Ninetendo DS. The toddlers were focusing their energies upon the toy box that was permanently affixed within the waiting room, and Mac saw them alternately digging in the treasure trove of toys provided by the office or with the toys undoubtedly supplied by their mom's diaper bags. Moms easily engage one another in conversation while awaiting their child's appointment.

Mac tip-toed around the frenzy surrounding her as she made her way to the receptionist, a pleasant middle-aged woman with frosted, short hair and sincere, kind eyes. After a quick introduction, the receptionist picked up the phone and dialed the doctor on his intercom line. As she presumably conversed with the doctor, the receptionist began nodding into the receiver, apparently sympathetic to what the doctor was telling her. She then gracefully yet gently put the phone down and returned her attention to Mac.

"Dr. Kerr is terribly sorry, but he's not going to be able to meet with you today as scheduled. We've had an unexpected number of same-day appointments due to an early flu onset. Dr. Kerr has been tending to one emergency after the other, and this pushed all of his appointments back a bit. He apologizes with all sincerity, but he is going to have to reschedule your conference with him today."

Mac was slightly annoyed. If Dr. Kerr's day had proceeded as was just described, then having someone call her to reschedule their appointment would have been a no-brainer. Mac recognized the futility in pointing any of this out to the receptionist, and proceeded to pick a new time to meet with Dr. Kerr.

Just as she was preparing to turn and walk out the door, an internal office door opened and a buxom blond popped her head out. "Ms. MacIntosh?" she called.

Mac turned around abruptly, surprised to hear her name being called by the woman. "Yes," Mac answered.

"I'm Dr. Kerr's head nurse, Janie Johansen. I have access to all Dr. Kerr's patients' files, and know nearly as much as Dr. Kerr on the individual patients. Would you be interested in coming back and meeting with me, since you're already here?"

As Mac listened to Janie Johansen's introduction, she couldn't avoid the fact that the head nurse was extremely attractive. Nurse Janie, as her nametag stated, was nothing shy of stunning. Mac had seen her around town from time to time, though didn't know the woman or her occupation before today. When Mac had seen her in the past, it was usually walking up or down Main Street with shopping bags on her arms. Though she applied her make- up lightly, she always appeared well dressed and coiffed to perfection. She had long, curly blond hair that was frequently tied back into a ponytail, and huge electrifying green eyes. She looked to be around thirty-five or so, and Mac had never noticed a ring on her wedding finger.

"I'm not sure," Mac replied. "I really need to speak with Dr. Kerr about some of his impressions, and I'm not sure this would have been noted on his files. It's okay, though, I've already rescheduled my appointment for tomorrow."

"You're already here, and I might be able to answer some of your preliminary questions. Why don't you come back to the office and chat with me? At worst, it might save you some time during your meeting with Dr. Kerr tomorrow." Nurse Janie offered Mac an encouraging and dazzling smile as she continued, "I've cared for Levi since his first visit to our office, and I really think that I can offer you some assistance." This last comment came out with a smile, but it was stated more firmly and seemed much more like a command than a question. Janie began hurriedly motioning to Mac to follow her back into the inner office.

Mac was a bit taken aback by the nurse's comments, and was surprised that Dr. Kerr's nurse knew why she was there. Never mind, Mac thought to herself, Sheridan is a small town, and small towns have few secrets.

Mac followed her back towards Dr. Kerr's personal office. As Mac followed Janie's lead, she noted that the nurse walked heavy with purpose, her narrow hips swinging slightly yet pointedly with each quick step, as she entered the doorway marked, "Dr. Kerr." His office was both sparsely and plainly furnished, with a wooden oak desk and a wingback maroon leather chair. In contrast, the walls were heavily cluttered with framed certificates and awards. His bookshelves were also littered with medical journals. Mac watched Janie straighten a pile of papers on Dr. Kerr's desk as she offered Mac a place to sit on the short, black fabric couch.

Nurse Janie gave Mac a knowing smile, and opened with a comment that Mac considered ripe for interpretation. "I've worked for Dr. Kerr for a long time, so I'm intimately familiar with the families that he sees."

"How long have your worked for Dr. Kerr?" Mac asked.

"Eleven years. Got the itch," Janie said, with a smirk. Mac didn't get the joke at first, and after a few seconds of awkward silence passed, Janie followed up on her failed joke. "Get it? Eleven year itch?"

"Oh, I get it," Mac said, as she began to rub her temples. "I'm sorry, Janie, but I'm feeling a bit slow today. It's been one of those days," Mac paused briefly before continuing. She pulled a water bottle out of her attaché case, unscrewed the cap, and proceeded to take a long gulp of water. "So you've known the Landers family for some time?"

"You could say that. I've known them eleven years, and Ben was the first patient I ever had. He was about three then, and absolutely adorable. A lot sweeter than he is now." Janie added the last comment almost as an afterthought, but immediately continued. "He came in for a pre-school check- up. Lauren came in for that visit too. She was a sweetie-pie and just learning to walk, I think. Austen was with them for his Kindergarten shots. Mrs. Landers was pregnant with Levi, and definitely appeared to have her hands full, as I remember."

When Janie paused a moment, Mac prompted her to continue. "So, it sounds like you know the whole Landers family, including Evelyn, pretty well?"

"Mrs. Landers? You could say that." Mac noticed an unmistakable change in Janie's tone with this answer–almost defiant. Mac wanted to make sure that her read of Janie's response was accurate, and so it definitely required some sort of follow-up.

"Do you think that Evelyn Landers is a good mom?" Mac gently prodded, hoping that this question would prompt the nurse to continue with her unspoken thoughts on the Lander's family mother.

The nurse noticeably paused a moment before responding. "She's dedicated to her kids, if that's what you mean." Janie crossed her arms firmly over her chest, revealing her large cleavage.

Returning to the matter at hand, Mac realized that she might have to be a bit more pointed in her questioning. "I don't really have a definition of a good mom in mind," Mac said. "Can you explain what you mean?"

"Well, like I said," Janie started, leaning in toward Mac, "she is very dedicated to the kids. She's involved in everything, and I do mean *everything* they do. Those kids are way over-booked in the extracurricular department. And Evelyn is involved in every one of those activities, which sure would give her control over the kids' day-to-day lives. She also keeps a finger on every social event in this town by volunteering on practically every committee there is. She's something, to say the least."

"Do you like her?" Mac prodded.

Janie paused a brief moment before answering. "I don't have anything against her, but we're most definitely not friends, either. I guess that I basically don't have a strong opinion on her, one way or the other."

Mac decided to continue with the interview in a different angle entirely. "Have you heard about what's going on with Levi and the court?" Mac watched the nurse closely, intent on seeing her visual reaction to the question. Janie lifted her eyebrows and sucked in a deep breath.

"Of course I know. Everyone in town knows. It's awfully scary. I'm glad that someone is finally doing something about it, too. That poor kid has undergone every test under the sun and has seen more doctors than most residents do in medical school. She's nuts when it comes to poor little Levi."

Mac was glad that she had asked Janie a follow-up question as she did, because the response she received clearly indicated that the nurse's previous statement that she had no opinion of Evelyn was a bit off the mark. Without any additional prodding by Mac, the nurse continued with a lengthy response.

"She was a pretty normal mom with the older three kids–maybe a little neurotic–but nothing too dramatic," Janie continued. "But when it comes to that little guy, she's got something crazy going on. I don't know what it is, but she's obsessive when it comes to Levi. I've heard people around town whisper that it may be some sort of manifestation of the 'empty nest' thing. I've heard other people say that she acts out with Levi the way she does because deep down she wishes she were a doctor like her husband. By getting so involved with Levi's medical conditions, she gets to be seriously involved in the medical community, in a roundabout way. I really don't know the answer." Janie paused momentarily before adding a final comment. "All I know is that I am happy to hear that Levi is now out of her grasp and safely in foster care."

Mac was startled to hear the nurse's last comment. It was shocking to Mac to think that Levi needed to be saved from his mom–a woman who by all accounts appeared to be a dedicated and involved mother. "How do you know that he's in foster care?"

"This is a small town, Ms. MacIntosh. How long have you lived here?"

"A few years."

"Well, it shouldn't take you much longer to realize that *everyone* knows *everything* about *everyone* in this town. I guarantee that there are people talking right now about the fact that you and I are meeting about Levi. Trust me on that. The minute someone sees something going on, they get on the phone and tell someone else. The gossip chain is made of platinum here." Janie took a breath and leaned back in the couch. She uncrossed her arms and relaxed her position.

Mac returned the nurse's cool smile and continued the interview in a way that she hoped made it appear that she was entirely nonplussed by the nurse's last remarks. "Are you the only nurse in this office?" Mac asked.

Mac considered herself successful at pulling the smugness out of the nurse, as Janie's face clouded before finally responding to the question. "Yes . . . and no. Up until last year I was the only nurse, but then Dr. Kerr hired an assistant. A Physician's Assistant. Though it sounds more technical, the P.A. isn't really any different than a nurse. So while I am by title still the only nurse on file within the office, there truly are two of us now. However, I work full time, and the P.A. works part time."

"Have you been involved in Levi's pediatric care since he was born?"

Janie snapped back. "What do you mean by that?"

Mac, trying to assure the clearly perturbed nurse, back-pedaled a bit on the question. "I'm sorry, Janie, if that came across in a negative way. Let me rephrase the question, because I meant no disrespect. What I was simply wondering was whether you were present as the nurse for all of Levi's medical visits to this office?"

Janie relaxed and responded, "Oh, yes. Yes. Like I told you, I've been working here for a long time, and I've been here for all the scheduled and unscheduled check-ups for the Landers kids." The nurse began to smile a tight and seemingly forced smile back at Mac, before apparently pondering the implications of Mac's question. "Why?"

"I don't mean anything in particular by asking any set of questions—these are just basic questions to give me a broader picture on Levi's family history. Following up on that, though, have you noticed Mrs. Landers' behavior change in any way over the years?"

"Change? In what way?" Janie responded. For a moment, Mac was afraid that she had offended the nurse again and caused her to close up entirely. Fortunately, Janie continued after a brief pause. "I mean, everyone changes. Her kids are older and therefore a bit easier to manage. She was a bit more frazzled when they were little, though not remarkably so. Then Levi came along, and he was exceedingly sick, which ended up making her even more frazzled."

Mac noted that Janie appeared to be justifying Evelyn's previously described unacceptable behavior as towards Levi. Mac wanted her to be the angry and accusatory nurse that responded with fervor as she had previously. Mac paused for a moment, deciding on an open-ended question to help re- direct Janie back to a heated description of Evelyn. "Would you characterize her as a stable mom?"

"I'm not a psychiatrist, Ms. MacIntosh. I'm only a nurse. I give kids shots and eye exams and measure how much they've grown. I don't do psychoanalysis on the parents."

"I'm not suggesting that you do. As you know, I represent Levi. I'm trying to find out whether it's safe for him to return home to his mother's care. Social Services seems to think that Evelyn Landers *intentionally or recklessly* harmed Levi, and so it's my job to determine whether these allegations are true. If I do ultimately consider them to be valid allegations, then I must in turn decide what the best course would be for Levi and, possibly, the rest of the Landers children."

Mac paused, looking for the nurse's reaction before summarizing. "If I find that the allegations are false, then it it's my duty to ensure that Levi is returned. I scheduled an appointment with Dr. Kerr to get his professional opinion on these matters, and at my meeting with him, I fully intend to ask these questions. Since you graciously volunteered to meet with me, I'm now asking you for your professional opinion on the same." Mac hoped that by adding reference to the nurse's professional opinion she would completely assuage any of Janie's potentially hurt feelings, as the nurse's desire for professional recognition came across loud and clear.

Before Janie had an opportunity to respond to Mac, a soft but insistent knock was heard coming from Dr. Kerr's door. Without hesitation, Janie got up from the couch and opened the door. The receptionist poked her head in and said to the nurse, "Dr. Kerr is requesting you in Room Four." When Janie began to somberly nod in response, Mac realized that their brief meeting must be over.

Mac stood up, assuming she needed to leave. Janie responded to her earlier question in a loud tone, "If you are trying to get my professional opinion on whether Evelyn is purposefully making Levi sick, then my answer is . . . probably. I can think of no other medical explanation for what's happened to that sweet little guy. Knowing Evelyn, she enjoys being in the spotlight at all times. That's true whether the attention is coming from the PTA, the church, or the Doctors' and Dentists' Ball." Janie then looked pointedly at Mac as she stated, "Evelyn always has the newest clothes, and I've never seen her repeat a dress or outfit twice. That kind of tells you something about a person, especially a mother of four, don't you think?"

Mac was confused. "I thought you said she was a good mother."

"No, Ms. MacIntosh. You asked me whether I thought she was a good mom, and I remember my response specifically. I said she's dedicated to her kids, a comment which is clearly and intentionally subject to interpretation."

Janie immediately turned and walked away.

The receptionist raised her eyebrows at Mac and whispered, "She's way too opinionated, if you ask me. And she pays too much attention to that kid."

Mac had still been focused on Janie's parting comments, and it took a few seconds for the receptionist's words to process. Mac turned to the receptionist and asked, "I'm sorry, what did you say?"

The receptionist's eyes began to nervously look around, before she responded to Mac. "You did *not* hear this from me. Janie has seniority around here and she lets all of us know it; if she found out I told you this, she'd make sure I got fired." The receptionist's eyes were wide open and her dislike of the head nurse was apparent. "She bosses all of us around like it's her office."

"Did you say that Janie pays too much attention to Levi?"

The receptionist leaned closer to Mac and said, "I've only worked here for five years, so I don't know everything, but every time that kid comes in here, which is often, Janie drops everything and whisks him back to Room Two. There can be ten kids waiting for their turn to see the doctor and it doesn't matter. She puts him ahead of all the rest and sees him first."

"Is that because he has such a long health history?" Mac asked.

"I don't know," the receptionist said with an inflated tone. "She seems *obsessed* with that entire family–she doesn't just do it for Levi. When the other Landers kids come in for their health check-ups for sports and what-not, Janie drops whatever she's doing and makes sure she's the nurse that handles them. Even the routine stuff that other employees could handle. It's weird."

"Is she a personal friend of the family?"

"I don't think she's a friend, though I've heard that she used to baby-sit for the family when the kids were younger."

"I see," Mac said as she followed the receptionist out of Dr. Kerr's office and back down the hallway toward her work station. Mac found the receptionist's comments unnerving, though, without mistake, insightful. Mac decided to try for as much information as she could and threw in one last question. "You've worked here long enough to observe Levi's visits. What do *you* think about Evelyn Landers?"

The receptionist glanced sideways at Mac, and her eyes narrowed. Her face clearly gave away that there were many more thoughts that she wished to share, but she appeared to catch herself. "I–I don't really know anything," she stammered in response. The previously forceful receptionist was now replaced by a meek woman who was suddenly unsure of herself. "I need to get back to my post. Phone's ringing."

As the receptionist walked towards the front desk and put her headset back on. She waved goodbye to Mac while simultaneously cupping the microphone on her headset and silently mouthed, "She's crazy," while making little circles with her index finger around her right ear.

Chapter 5

Mac logged onto her computer and did research when she returned to her office and opened up a medical website and plugged in the term, "Munchausen by Proxy." She was surprised not at the medical definition, but at how far reaching the condition could be. The syndrome impacts a caregiver, usually the mother, who then feigns or induces an illness in another person, usually her child, to gain attention and empathy as the "worried" or "devoted" parent. The caregiver seeks comfort from medical personnel and is often on a misguided mission to feel special which is temporarily satisfied each time doctors, family, or friends perceive her as the heroic caretaker of a tragically ill child. Some caretakers crave a pertinacious relationship with doctors in which they simultaneously engage and defeat the treating physician through carefully-crafted deceptions.

Most caretakers diagnosed with Munchausen by Proxy have serious personality disorders that make them behave in this odd and destructive manner. They were often abused as children themselves, and tend to abuse their own children, particularly when the caretaker is experiencing high stress in her life. Any time a health care professional suspects a case of Munchausen by Proxy, they are required by law to report it.

Mac continued her on-line research and easily found many legal websites dedicated to the prosecution and defense of Munchausen cases. One site warned that every parent who seriously advocates for his or her ill child becomes a potential target of investigation. The defense attorney who crafted that particular article explained that mothers in Munchausen investigations get emotionally raped, publicly slandered, criminally charged and, in the most egregious cases, jailed. A large majority of mothers who are falsely accused end up divorced, or worse, commit suicide. The defense lawyer cautioned that in many of the Munchausen cases, the child is used like a "carrot," causing the mother to falsely "confess" and agree to counseling and other services to enable a quicker reunification with her child.

Mac pondered both ends of the spectrum of possibilities. It was possible that Evelyn Landers was a devoted, doting mother, falsely accused of Munchausen by Proxy. She seemed to be the type of woman who would do anything for her children. On the other hand, it was possible that she forcibly made Levi sick to get attention. Mac made notes on her yellow legal pad. *Why would Mrs. Landers need attention from medical personnel? What was her personal history? Luke is a doctor -- did her husband ignore her? Was her marriage healthy? Does she have a history of child abuse? Domestic violence? Criminal record?*

Mac made a few more notations and then asked her paralegal, Pamela, to research background information on both Evelyn and Luke Landers. Mac left Pamela busy digging into the Landers family past, and began to return to the courthouse to observe a juvenile court trial. From her research into juvenile law, the entire legal procedure seemed different to Mac. For example, she discovered that there are no jury trials in these types of cases, and that cases proceeding to trial were heard solely by the presiding judge, who was the ultimate truth-finder. The social worker's and police reports were allowed into evidence despite the hearsay contained in them, as the goal of protecting the child's welfare appeared to outweigh the standard evidentiary rule of exclusion. Also, there appeared to be no spousal privilege like there is in adult civil and criminal cases, and parents are often times forced to testify against one another. Because a juvenile case bended all the legal rules that Mac relied upon up to this point in her career, she decided that it would be a huge benefit to witness a juvenile trial and see how the different legal rules were applied.

It didn't take long for Mac to make it to the courthouse, and she was happy to see that Judge Binnard's court was in the midst of a trial. Even better than simply witnessing a juvi trial would be witnessing one in front of the judge her case was scheduled in front of. As Mac found her way into the courtroom, Judge Binnard's clerk was swearing in a witness. The woman was young, probably around eighteen, and was tearful and shaking. Mac whispered to the bailiff, who was seated near the gallery. "What's this case about?"

"Punk kid got in a fight with his grandma because she wouldn't let him watch TV. Set the garage of grandma's house on fire after backing her car out. He took the car and picked up his girlfriend. They did a bunch of meth and when he was tweaking, he threw the girlfriend out of the car and took off. Unfortunately for the girlfriend, her jacket got caught in the passenger door on the way out. The little punk didn't stop for his own girlfriend, and he dragged her about five hundred feet before the jacket finally tore free from her body. That's the girlfriend about to take the stand."

Mac nodded at the bailiff and pondered the story. She looked around the courtroom and saw an elderly woman sitting in the gallery. The punk kid was seated next to public defender Macy Green. The kid looked like Opie from *The Andy Griffith Show*, with short, strawberry blond hair and freckles. There was no way anyone would even consider this little kid to be capable of the rage that had just been described to Mac. The girlfriend was cute, with short, dark hair and big blue eyes, and in Mac's mind did not look like a druggie.

Mac turned back to the bailiff and asked, "Where's the kid's mom?"

"Jail. Drugs. Kid was a meth baby fifteen years ago. We had his detention hearing back then. Grandma adopted him because mom lost her parental rights. Now, we have him back here. Funny how that works."

Mac shook her head in amazement, simultaneously paying closer attention to the young woman on the stand. Mac listened to the teenage girl testify about doing drugs and the injuries she sustained as a result of being dragged by the car. She'd undergone four surgeries and would never be able to walk again without a limp. The part of her scalp where her hair was ripped out at the root would likely not grow hair again due to scar tissue. She needed more skin grafting on her leg, but would have to wait until the current graft healed.

Upon cross-examination, the young lady admitted that she suffered no cognitive impairment that she was aware of, and even if she did, she couldn't be sure whether the methamphetamines had anything to do with any brain damage she might have sustained.

Despite repeated and urgent hearsay objections made by Macy Green, the witness was able to testify that her former boyfriend admitted to setting the garage on fire and stealing grandma's car.

After the young lady's testimony was concluded and both sides had their respective opportunities at cross-examination and re-direct, a police officer took the stand. Mac wasn't sure what role the officer taking the stand playing in the incident, but figured it out as his testimony was ultimately elicited. After his testimony, Mac saw the punk's grandmother take the stand in her grandson's defense. Mac was amazed at Karl Swensen swift yet totally effective line of questioning which immediately drew into question the grandmother's testimony. Finally, Mac saw the juvenile himself take the stand. It wasn't entirely shocking to Mac when she heard him ultimately blame all of the actions on the girlfriend, claiming that it was her idea to take the car and start the fire.

The witness testimony was much quicker than Mac was used to, as was the judge's ruling. Mac's prior cases had long closing statements after which the judge read complicated jury instructions. She was then used to a jury deliberating for hours, or days, and a decision rendered some time after. However, in the punk's case, after brief closing statements, Judge Binnard immediately entered his findings that the petition was true beyond a reasonable doubt and sentenced the boy to Juvenile Hall for thirty-six months.

After the hearing, Mac was able to hear a few plea bargains in several completely unrelated juvenile cases. Again, Mac marveled at the swiftness of justice in the juvenile system. One case that she heard in particular burned in her mind, and she wished that she hadn't heard its fact pattern. In that case, a thirteen-year-old boy was babysitting his six-year-old cousin. When the young cousin was playing video games, the older cousin asked him if he wanted a lollipop. The little boy said "yes." A few minutes later, while the little guy was engrossed in his Nintendo, the older cousin said, "here's your lollipop." When the little boy reached for the candy, he saw that the older cousin was standing next to him with his pants down, penis erect. The older cousin was being sentenced to a sexual predator rehabilitation camp in Montana, and part of his plea bargain included being labeled as a "sexual offender" for the rest of his life.

Mac reflected on the boy's sentence, amazed at how this one act had affected his entire life to come. He would have to register in any county he lived. His life was forever changed by that one single act. It was a terrible act, and Mac didn't discount it, but she felt somewhat sorry for the teenager. Most crimes committed as a juvenile did not carry over into adulthood, unless the crimes were serious felonies, like murder, rape and armed robbery. Sexual offenses, however, did carry over if the juvenile admitted the offense and agreed to the term of sexual offender as part of probation. Despite rehabilitation at the youth camp, he would carry the heavy burden of being a registered sex offender and he was practically guaranteed that future neighbors would whisper and demand he move from their neighborhoods. As a teenager, he could not possibly understand the implications of this plea bargain; yet, Macy Green seemed unmoved by the implications of such a bargain. She put the agreement on the record, watched as the boy was escorted away by the sheriff, and without so much as the blink of an eye, proceeded to call her next case.

The next case in court that day involved a kid who brought a hunting knife to school to impress his buddies. Unfortunately for that kid, his school had a "zero tolerance" policy with respect to weapons on school grounds.

Mac listened raptly to the rest of the calendar. When Judge Binnard finally called recess for the day, Mac was too energized by the long docket to immediately return to her office. She decided to approach the prosecutor and see what else she could learn that day.

"Long day?" Mac asked of Karl Swensen, the County Attorney who had just handled the multitude of cases that she had watched.

"Not really," Karl said comfortably, as if he had been conversing with Mac at the end of a long docket for years. "Pretty easy, really. Juvenile delinquency days don't get to me much, because it's really not much more than kids doing stupid things. In fact," Karl said while looking from side to side, "a lot of the things they get charged with are the same things we did as kids. The laws are just a little different than when we roamed the streets with eggs and toilet paper and shaving cream." Karl smiled at his last statement, and began sorting through the paperwork from the long day as he continued chatting with Mac. "The more serious offenses, like the ones you saw today, are a *little* tougher, but not much. The cases that seem to get under my skin, though, are the dependencies. I hate that part of the job. When pregnant moms do meth–that pisses me off, but I get to go after those women with a vengeance. I hate husbands who beat their wives, especially when they do it in front of the kids, but I get to lock those bastards up. But what can I do after watching poor little kids cry when the bastard dad is being taken into custody? What's even worse is that usually, after all the crap he puts the family through, those kids still love the guy."

Mac completely understood what Karl was saying, and wondered where the Landers case fit into that scheme. "What about a case like Levi's? How do you feel about that?"

Karl Swensen stopped putting his paperwork away for the time being and pushed his round frameless glasses up the bridge of his nose. After a few seconds of silence, Karl shrugged his shoulders slightly while saying, "If I put my prosecution hat on and don't think of anything other than the evidence as it appears in the reports, then I can honestly tell you that Levi's case is one of the most egregious cases I've seen."

Mac felt a chill go down her spine. If someone as experienced as Karl could say that about the abuse in Levi's case, just what other evidence is there for her to familiarize herself with? Pushing that alarming thought from her mind for the time being, she continued gleaning as much information as she could from the prosecution. "What would your answer have been if you considered it without your prosecution hat on? Looking at the case only from the perspective of the players in the case, without regard to any of the reports involved?"

Karl Swensen slowly shook his head. "You've seen Evelyn Landers. She's the epitome of the perfect mom: beautiful, rich, and dedicated to her husband and kids. She's raised three other healthy and incredibly athletic kids, something that doesn't just happen in a vacuum. She obviously knows how to mother children. She's involved in the community and doesn't appear to need to draw attention to herself–she gets plenty of attention from her role as mother and philanthropist."

"Does that change, though, if she feels unfulfilled?" Mac asked. "My mom was a bit that way. She was very involved in raising me, my brother and my step-siblings, and involved in the community, but she was unfulfilled. She went back to work as an interior designer, which seemed to make her very happy. She liked taking business trips and being away from home sometimes. I didn't like it, but as an adult, I understand."

"She didn't poison your baby bottle with feces, did she?" Karl immediately pounced.

"Well, of course not."

"Well, that's the part that makes me scratch my balding head."

Mac let out a small laugh. Karl often poked fun at himself–which was an endearing trait. "Have you spoken with Harold Neiman about the case?"

"He called earlier, interested in working out some type of a deal. Unfortunately, I'm not in a position to do that yet. Neither Levi nor Evelyn have had their psych evals yet, and without them I'm unable to even consider a plea. Plus, no one has had the chance to interview Luke Landers. His involvement in this will be important, and must be included in any potential negotiations."

"Meaning?"

"Well, meaning, did he know about it? Did he facilitate it? Did he participate in it?"

"If that's a serious question, then why wasn't he charged?" Mac asked, earnestly. "He is a doctor. He should have known that something was wrong and done something about it."

"I don't have any evidence as to Luke yet. While the case has been charged as to Evelyn, it remains under an active investigation. The evidence that the investigation has produced so far only leads to Evelyn, so that's the only parent we can charge–at this point."

"I know that you can't tell me much, but can you tell me how you came to suspect that something was wrong?"

"You'll soon become familiar with the term 'mandatory reporters'," Karl directed at Mac with somewhat of a smirk. "Physicians fit into that group, as they are required to report any cases in which they suspect abuse. Munchausen by Proxy has only recently been recognized by the American Medical Association and the American Psychiatric Association as a real disorder, so when a doctor suspects it in one of their cases, it usually ends up being a pretty serious case. The only problem is that when a doctor diagnoses Munchausen instead of identifying any potential physical abuse, they tend to put themselves at risk of being investigated by their ethics board. That's why the cases that ultimately do get reported are the ones that leave little doubt in one's imagination." Karl paused during his response to Mac's question, making sure that she was following his logic up to this point.

"In Munchausen cases, you generally are presented with medical records that are oftentimes contradictory, especially considering how many doctors were involved and the variety of previous illnesses diagnosed. Further complicating matters is the fact that non-medically trained individuals, like prosecutors, for example, often have a difficult time determining what is or isn't ethical so far as diagnosis and treatment of illnesses. All I can do in these types of cases is rely on experts, and in a case like this that takes place in such a small town, you can imagine my difficulties finding an expert. Levi has been seen by almost every doctor here, and as you know, those doctors can't be used as experts. That means that I have to go to neighboring communities or even cities to find experts." Karl sighed, apparently considering the enormity of the task. After visibly shaking the thought from his mind, Karl asked, "Have you gone through his records yet?"

Mac, who had been standing in her black high heels for a half hour while talking to Karl, decided to answer the question while more comfortably seated at the prosecution table. She subconsciously began straightening her gray skirt as she responded, "I started to, but then I had to go to a meeting with Dr. Kerr."

"You already met with Dr. Kerr?" Karl asked with undisguised astonishment.

"Well, not quite. I said I had a meeting with Dr. Kerr, not that the meeting actually took place." Mac gave out a sarcastic laugh as she continued. "Dr. Kerr was a no show, claiming an unexpected inundation of sick kids."

"I'm not surprised. It usually takes my wife weeks to book an appointment with him for our kids' check-ups."

"I did speak with his nurse though," Mac offered.

"Janie? What did she have to say, if you don't mind me asking?"

"She was actually a bit odd, to be completely honest. She seemed very eager to speak to me at first, but then it seemed like she couldn't wait to get away from me."

"She's a friend of my wife's sister. They are both single. I think she's a little flighty," Karl said. "Did she tell you anything of interest?"

Mac was not the type of lawyer who tried to hide the ball from other lawyers involved in a case. She liked cordial relationships and firmly believed that cases went better when all parties cooperated. The problem in this case was that it was too soon for Mac to know where she stood in representing Levi's interests with respect to Karl's obvious legal position. If it turned out that Evelyn was innocent, then it would be in Levi's best interest to reunify with his mother. In that situation, Karl is an opposing party because Mac's legal arguments would be aligned with Macy Green's, the public defender. On the other hand, if Evelyn were to be found guilty, then Karl would become an ally, as Mac's legal arguments would be aligned with his position against Evelyn's continued caring for Levi.

Mac chose to answer carefully. "Janie Johansen appears to be very interested in the Landers family."

"So I've heard," Karl dryly responded. "In fact, I've heard that she's interested in some more than others."

Chapter 6

Evelyn walked into the lobby of the Sheridan Country Club and checked her floor-length mink coat with the attendant. The weather really didn't call for the warmth of a mink, but she wanted to make a grand entrance into the club. She knew that people would be watching her every move. Though part of Evelyn secretly enjoyed this attention, deep down she knew that it was going to be unpleasant as she would surely be analyzed and dissected as if she were an amoeba under a microscope. Evelyn needed a drink. She dabbed her lips with a little extra gloss and then headed through the dining room toward the bar.

As Evelyn hunted down a strong shot of liquor, she marveled at the sights around her–or rather, the lack of sights around her. She couldn't believe how generic the country club was, after all of these years and after all of the chances for it to bring itself into the current millennium. Worse, it was in dire need of a simple remodel. Evelyn began to dream about the other, swankier club in Sheridan, and wished that this were even minimally on par. It was obvious which club didn't get any influx of money from the methane gas industry. Without that money for minimal updates, it was unlikely to attract the only real other source of revenue for similar business out here from the increasing number of Hollywood-types who enjoyed a reprieve from the spotlight. The reclusive and private nature of this small, Wyoming town, coupled with its sheer beauty and the fact that Wyoming did not have a state income tax, made the area highly desirable. In the past decade, several new country clubs and golf communities had been built, but the old country club still had its appeal.

There was something familiar and inviting about the old country club that made Evelyn feel the need to keep on returning. The clubhouse was constructed in wood, painted white, and had the look of a large, plain home. The shake roof was dilapidated and was in need of replacement. The bar was similarly unremarkable, however, it served its purpose–and its purpose for Evelyn tonight was a dry gin martini, straight up, with an olive. She sucked half the drink down in one swallow, and held her head tilted back even after the long swig was over, savoring every last second of feeling the warmth trickle down her throat.

She took another swallow and then set her glass back on the bar for a refill. While waiting for the bartender to take notice of her empty glass, she reapplied her lipstick and tugged at her black long skirt. She'd gained a few pounds over the last few months and was self-conscious of the gentle tightness around her waist. She grimaced, knowing full well that Luke would take inventory of her figure as soon as he walked through the door. Before proposing to her twenty years ago, Luke made sure to point out that no wife of his was going to be fat and homely. Rather, Luke's wife was to be thin, refined, graceful, and elegant. During all of her pregnancies, he monitored her weight gain closely to ensure that she didn't pack on any unnecessary weight. Not only did he keep a firm thumb over her caloric intake, but he kept daily tabs on her exercise routine.

Evelyn sighed just thinking about her husband's control over her body. She'd grown so tired of his relentless obsession with ensuring his wife's polished appearance that she had let herself go a teeny bit in silent protest. She didn't have the gumption to challenge her husband on the issue, so packing on a few extra pounds was her only real way of rebelling against his criticism. Feeling how snugly the dress fit over her middle section made Evelyn start to ponder whether she had rebelled against Luke just a little too much. She self-consciously rubbed the small roll of skin that gently pushed against the waistline of her dress. Luke called it her muffin top and suggested an additional personal trainer to help with this new problem spot.

Luke had yet to arrive at the club, but by this point in their relationship his tardiness no longer seemed to register with Evelyn. Luke used to explain to her that the obstetrics business didn't allow for timely dinners with the family, but he no longer bothered with any sort of explanations as to his whereabouts. He rarely made it to a ball game on time, nor could he volunteer to coach any of the kids' teams because he was frequently paged to see a patient in crisis or deliver a baby. It wasn't that Evelyn minded his schedule–she expected it. But it would have been nice if he would call and give her an update. He used to call. He used to try. But something changed years ago. Evelyn couldn't remember exactly when she noticed the change, but it happened gradually, over time.

At first, he rushed in the door, apologetic for being late for dinner. But as time passed, dinner with the family wasn't that alluring. Four noisy kids at the table, spilling milk, arguing over whose turn it was to set or clear the table. And Levi. Levi was often sick by dinnertime, and the whole family had to cater to his needs.

It seemed like the larger the Landers family became, the more frequently Luke had to deliver babies in the late afternoon. Evelyn wondered whether this was intentional. Not that a doctor can plan when a woman is going to go into labor, but did he deliberately schedule inductions later in the day to guarantee a miss at the family table? She wasn't sure. She didn't dare ask.

It seemed like Luke's presence was needed more frequently at medical conferences too. When they were first married, he seldom went to a conference without her. The conferences were generally in nice places, like Hawaii or Aspen–and they made an expense-paid vacation out of it. But as Levi continued to get sick, Evelyn didn't feel like she could leave him with a sitter. Luke continued to go–perhaps on a more habitual basis. Was there a correlation? Evelyn didn't know the answer to that question, but did know that this second martini was really hitting the spot.

Evelyn lifted her mind from her negative thoughts regarding her family, as it was making her feel depressed to think about Luke and the lack of respect and support he showed her. She wanted to go and socialize with other people, but she didn't dare turn to see who else was present at the evening fundraiser as she was quite sure that every person attending was staring at her–whispering about what had happened in court that day. She could only imagine the gossip chain. She could practically hear the women in the room huddled together, exchanging theories of how she poisoned her youngest child. It made Evelyn's stomach tighten. It had crossed her mind several times that afternoon to just stay home, and she nearly did, but after deep contemplation decided that might make matters worse. If she were to withdraw from her normal charitable events, people might start to think that she was guilty and reticent to be seen in public. As difficult as it would be, she decided that she would have to continue conducting her business as usual—attending all events with her head held high, and a stiff drink in hand. With that thought, Evelyn tossed back another needed gulp and began to think of her husband again.

While Evelyn drummed her fingers on the bar pondering Luke's whereabouts, she tried to calm her frayed nerves by reflecting upon his earlier phone call. She hadn't expected him to follow up with her after the hearing, but he had called during the day to see how it went. That was a nice surprise, Evelyn thought. When she told him what the judge said about him needing to hire his own attorney, he groaned about the cost of attorneys and the ridiculousness of it all. Luke kept nagging at her about the case and about the difficulties it presented to their family. Couldn't their lawyer just get the case dismissed? Couldn't they just agree to share the one attorney? Couldn't they just hurry it all up?

While Evelyn was pleased that Luke had called, she did recognize that he hadn't asked her how Levi was or how he looked. He didn't ask how long before he could see him again, or even how long it would be before their next court hearing. The main concern that Luke drove home during this phone conversation was regarding the expense and inconvenience of the case. Of course, this made Evelyn very upset, but she knew enough by this point in their marriage that it was best for her to keep these thoughts to herself. If she criticized him for his lack of concern, he would get angry and remind her that it was "her actions" that got them into this mess.

As she stood in the bar waiting for Luke and thinking about their predicament, the whispering around her was no longer at the levels that she could try to ignore. More people were arriving for the event and she felt the intensity of the growing number of cold stares. Not one single person had even bothered to approach her, in solidarity or in opposition. By this point, Evelyn would have been grateful for an uninviting guest to approach her.

She continued standing alone with her back to everyone in the room, looking out the window and focused intently on the sun setting behind the majestic Big Horn Mountains. Rays of sunlight illuminated Cloud Peak like the long fingers of a parent stretched out toward a child. The rays were bright red but were gradually fading to pink before retreating to a light yellow and then disappearing entirely. It reminded Evelyn of the hot flush of fear through her body when the Social Services worker accused her of making her baby sick.

When the social worker had first approached her at Dr. Kerr's office, she assumed that there was a mistake. As the social worker continued to clarify the issues and there was no doubt that she was the correct party in their investigation, anger swelled in her heart. The anger only grew as she continued to listen to the social worker detail the specifics of the case against her, but ultimately shifted to the pink light of panic and then to the yellow hue of fear. She feared first for her baby, then for his siblings, then herself–and lastly for Luke. Reflecting, she realized that she didn't fear for Luke's emotional state but did fear an angry reaction from him.

It never occurred to her that Luke would defend her or support her. She assumed, from the minute the Social Services workers introduced themselves and explained the purpose of their visit, that Luke would accuse her of wrongdoing. During the whirlwind of the few days following Levi's removal from their home, she hadn't contemplated the fact that Luke was being fairly supportive. He hadn't blamed her or accused her or shamed her. Instead, he quickly made a telephone call to his lawyer and found out who could best represent them. *Them*–not her or him, but them. His support came as such a surprise to her that she was unsure how to react to it.

Evelyn was considering why she feared her husband when she felt a cold hand on the small of her back which sent shivers up her spine. She turned. It was Luke. His face was flushed, as if he'd jogged to the country club from the hospital. He ordered a glass of red wine, pinot noir to be exact, and gave Evelyn a light peck of the cheek.

"Sorry I'm late. Induced Kathleen Kesselman. She is now the proud mother of twins. Luckily, she couldn't deliver vaginally so we took them C. I need all the Cs I can get if I'm going to be paying two lawyers."

Without waiting for a response from Evelyn, Luke grabbed his glass of wine and turned toward the dining room. Before Evelyn uttered a single word–not even a hello–Luke left her to join a group of men standing near the large fireplace.

Ah, Evelyn thought to herself, *the old Luke is back.*

Luke did not seem overtly upset about the fact that Levi would have to stay in foster care. He was, however, very unnerved that they would have to pay for two lawyers to represent them. Not because money was an issue for them–it wasn't, as Luke was making plenty of it. Luke just believed that Evelyn was perpetually reckless with her spending–and found herself honored for her donations, both in time and money. She also was competitive with other families and made sure that her children had the best of the best when it came to clothing, gadgets and toys. To top all of it off, their home was the product of a high-end designer. Luke often complained about her spending habits, but he backed down when she threatened to go back to work if what they needed was more money. The last think Luke wanted was to be strapped with more responsibility with the kids, and Evelyn knew it.

Before she followed Luke away from the bar, Evelyn ordered herself another martini. If she was going to face Luke, she might as well be prepared, she thought. After Evelyn had been standing by Luke for several minutes without any sort of acknowledgement, she decided to give up. She set her glass down on the mantle of the fireplace and made her way to the door without saying good-bye.

* * *

Wednesday morning came early for Mac. She got up at five-thirty and headed out from her two-bedroom apartment for her usual five-mile run. She showered, dressed in a black A-line dress with a leopard belt and matching leopard boots, and then headed to the kitchen for a quick breakfast. She poured herself a strong cup of coffee before heading to the office.

As Mac walked into her office that morning, Pamela was waiting for her with wild-eyed excitement. "I did some background checks on the Landers family. You're going to find this *very* interesting," Pamela said as she set down the bottom half of her bagel and handed Mac a manila file full of papers.

"Summarize it for me," Mac said, handing the file back to Pamela.

Pamela followed Mac back to her corner office and plopped herself down on the leather couch. She pulled an inch-thick stack of papers out of the file and thumbed to the page that had the yellow sticky note attached to it. "Evelyn met Luke while in medical school."

"Okay," Mac said.

Pamela looked disappointed with Mac's lack of reaction to this statement. "Did you hear me? She met him while *enrolled* in medical school. Evelyn went to medical school! She met Luke during her junior year at UC San Diego School of Medicine. Luke was a sophomore. She dropped out to support him."

Mac turned towards Pamela, as the words started to register. "You're kidding me."

"No, I'm not. Not only that, but she was a straight-A student in undergrad at Stanford. Biology major. And she was also getting A's in medical school, before she dropped out, that is. Luke, on the other hand, got a baseball scholarship to Arizona State and finished after five years with a three point three grade point average. How he got into med school is a mystery. And he didn't get great grades in med school either."

"That is interesting," Mac reflected out loud. "The way he's treated, you would have though Luke came from that kind of an educational background, not Evelyn. I guess it's possible that after she dropped out and got a job to support him and now that he's reaping all the rewards from it all, she's starting to resent the hell out of him for being the big-shot doctor," Mac said.

"You may not be far from the truth. I found an archived article in the San Diego Tribune that profiles him winning some beach volleyball tournament during the time frame when he was in med school."

"Were you able to figure out where Evelyn was working during Luke's time at medical school?"

"Of course!" Pamela enthusiastically responded. She really liked it when Mac peppered her with questions that she was prepared to answer. "She worked at the hospital as a research assistant for an undergrad professor."

The intercom buzzed in Mac's office. Mac pushed the button. Megan explained that a hysterical Mrs. Kelly was on the line and needed to speak to her immediately about Levi. It was an emergency, according to Mrs. Kelly, and she needed Mac to hurry over to help.

Pamela stood and handed Mac the contents of the file. "There's a lot more in there. Wait until you read about how Evelyn's twin sister died."

* * *

Mac raced to Mrs. Kelly's house, and was immediately greeted by an out-of-breath Mrs. Kelly when she answered the door. She wore a floor-length nightgown and her hair was clipped back off her face with bobby pins. The dark circles under her eyes appeared to be a combination of mascara and a lack of sleep. She invited Mac in.

The TV trays from the previous day were still lined up in front of the television in the living room. Dried, crusted food speckled the plates and the house still smelled of a combination of rotten food and dirty diapers.

"Where's Levi? Is he okay?" Mac asked as she began to look around the house, searching for the crisis that prompted to emergency visit.

"He ran away, Mac, he ran away! In all my years . . . oh dear, he ran away!" Mrs. Kelly shouted at her, in between puffs of breath. "I called the police. They're on their way. Oh Mac, what am I going to do? Levi ran away! He got so upset this morning, you just wouldn't believe it."

"Worse than yesterday when he wiped a dirty diaper on the wall?" Mac asked.

"Much worse. I don't think I've ever seen a little guy so . . . so *angry*. He had this demonic look in his eyes—like he was capable of killin' someone. My kids ate their breakfast in the biggest of hurries and ran to the bus stop without me even so much as hollerin' at 'em. That never happens."

Mac felt the need to get Mrs. Kelly back on track, as she had a feeling that this conversation could easily get steered away from Levi. "Mrs. Kelly, slow down. Take a breath." After a few seconds passed and Mac watched the woman follow her orders, she asked Mrs. Kelly, "What was he upset about?"

"I can't say for sure. My eldest foster said that one of the girls teased him for the diaper incident. No big deal, right?" Mrs. Kelly asked rhetorically.

"Wrong."

"His face turned bright red, like his whole head was going to explode and then he started to shake. He didn't make a sound. He didn't scream. He didn't go after any of 'em. He just ran to the kitchen, got a paring knife, and jabbed it into his own thigh! My fosters freaked out. He stabbed himself–just like that." Mrs. Kelly demonstrated holding a knife and pretended to jam it into her rotund thigh. "That's when I called the police. I thought he would go after us."

"What happened next?" Mac asked.

"He dropped the knife on the floor, like he was in shock or something. He didn't make even a whimper of pain. He stared at everyone with this look of the devil himself, and then he bolted out the back screen door. He was wearing only his t-shirt and skivvies." Mrs. Kelly paused as she reflected upon Levi's dress when he ran away. "Well, I can't imagine he'll go far dressed only in his skivvies. His leg was bleedin' pretty bad."

"Did you call paramedics?" Mac asked in a panic as the facts slowly started to sink in. When Mrs. Kelly shook her head "no" to indicate that 9-1-1 hadn't been called, Mac went into overdrive. As Mrs. Kelly began to justify why she hadn't thought of calling for an ambulance, Mac interrupted her shouting, "We need to find him! It is cold out this morning–it can't be more than forty degrees. Plus, he's bleeding and desperately needs medical attention! Which way did he go?" Mac shouted, moving quickly toward the back door.

"He went that way," Mrs. Kelly said, pointing to the creek that ran perpendicular to her house. "He went down by the crick."

Mac ran out the screen door and down the back sidewalk. She could see droplets of fresh, crimson blood on the cement. She unzipped her leopard print high-heeled boots and tore them off her feet.

"Call for an ambulance," Mac yelled before disappearing over the banks of Goose Creek.

Chapter 7

Big Goose Creek was a narrow waterway that traversed through Sheridan. Its banks lined the border of Kendrick Park and narrowed to an overflow near the General Crook Monument. At that point, it joined Little Goose Creek and together, the Big Goose and the Little Goose became simply Goose Creek.

Mac followed Levi's muddy footprints from the back yard of Mrs. Kelly's house. Mud squished between her toes and she winced each time she stepped on a sharp rock or a rough tree root. Mac realized that the trail of Levi's footprints was leading her through Kendrick Park, but then, suddenly, his footprints vanished. Mac surveyed the area to ensure that she wasn't mistaken, but there was no doubt that at the edge of the park, Levi's footprints stopped. Mac could only interpret the sudden cessation of tracks to mean one of two things: he crossed the creek, or he was hiding. Considering his age and size, Mac decided that the former was less likely than the latter.

Mac calculated her options, recognizing that she had precious little time to work with. The temperature was dropping quickly—the first winter storm was on its way. Mac was only wearing a long-sleeved black dress. She had no coat on and felt the chill in her bones. She could see her breath forming puffs of steam and she knew that Levi must be freezing. She needed to find him quickly.

She retraced her steps to where she'd last seen his footprints, which brought her to the edge of the creek. She looked up and down the river bank on her side, but could not see any movement. She then looked across the creek and down river a few hundred yards, and to her amazement, under the cement planks of an old, washed-out bridge, sat a little boy, curled up in a ball, wearing a filthy shirt.

Mac wanted to call for help, but realized that she would have to physically run to a local house in order to get that help, as she did not have her cell phone on her. She was afraid that if she went to the nearest house to call for help that she would lose sight of Levi by the time they returned. No, Mac thought to herself, this is the time for her to act. There was no time to play with, and this was going to be her only chance to catch Levi.

She hiked her long, black dress up to her thighs and proceeded to take a tentative step into the cold, swift creek. The water was moving rapidly, but it was nothing that Mac couldn't handle. She silently thanked her stars that the creek wasn't moving as swiftly as it would were it Spring. She sighed as her toe touched the water, realizing how messy and cold her rescue attempt would be. Mac sucked in her breath and began the journey across the creek, moving carefully and quickly. She knew that she could make it across as long as she watched her step; the rocks at the bottom of the creek were slippery with tendrils of moss. Mac lost her step more than once, but didn't lose momentum. Each time she felt her balance shifting, she simply braced herself for a fall with her right hand.

As Mac was making the journey across the creek, she realized that Levi had seen her. Mac wasn't hiding from him, but didn't necessarily expect for him to be drawn from his emotionally vacant state to notice her approaching. As frequently as she could while traversing the creek, Mac looked directly at Levi to make sure that she did not lose sight of him, should he decide to run. Throughout her slow journey, Levi remained seated underneath the washed-out bridge, just watching. Once Levi caught sight of her, it appeared that he didn't take his eyes off her. Mac hoped that this meant that he was appreciative in his own way of the expected contact. She anticipated that he would run if he saw her, but he didn't. He just sat, crouched down in a fetal position, and watched her cross the creek.

As Mac took her last step in the creek and slowly lifted her legs out of the cold water and back onto dry land, she realized the impact the journey had on her small frame. She was soaking wet and her drenched dress weighed about five pounds. Her feet were bleeding in a few spots and her calves were freezing cold. She stepped into the sludge, feeling her feet sink into the thick muck. Her steps were heavy and deliberate. Mac was afraid that Levi's apparent comfort with her pending approach would change once she exited the creek and began to move in his direction, but the fear was without merit. As she approached, Levi simply lowered his head onto his curled up knees and placed his arms over the back of his neck.

Mac made a mental note to analyze Levi's physical reaction just then—pushing himself further and deeper into the fetal position must have some psychological significance. She didn't have the time to contemplate Levi's response any further, and she continued her approach slowly towards the young boy. She could not see any part of Levi's face—it was completely hidden from her view, protected by the web of his arms. She could, however, see a deep gash in his right thigh, and realized that Mrs. Kelly's story was accurate. Damn, Mac thought to herself. There was not as much blood as Mac thought there might be, based on the blood trail that she followed from Mrs. Kelly's home, but Mac thought that the cold water from the creek crossing probably washed away the blood that had been dripping down his leg. The cold water might actually have been a blessing as it probably slowed the bleeding by shrinking the capillaries and blood vessels around the wound.

As Mac got within arms reach of Levi she finally began to verbalize her presence. "Levi? Are you okay?" Mac asked. Levi did not respond. "Levi, I know you are upset. I understand. It's okay to be upset." Mac inched her way closer to Levi and sat down at his side. Her black dress, which was previously just about seventy-five percent wet and twenty-five percent muddy, was now entirely covered in mud. She considered the dress one hundred percent a loss as she nudged herself closer to Levi, and though it a worthy sacrifice if she were able to get him some help. She noticed that he had large goose pimples on his skin and that his legs were shaking. She wished that she had a coat or blanket to put on him, but she had nothing but the drenched and muddy dress on her own back—and that simply wouldn't be of any help.

As Levi remained silent, Mac decided to continue speaking softly to the little boy. "We need to get you warmed up, buddy." And then, even more softly, "Will you let me take you back to Mrs. Kelly's house? We could get you some hot cocoa and–"

"No!" Levi shouted, his head still in his hands. Mac was startled by the suddenness of his reaction and the strength of his voice. Before she could say anything, though, Levi shouted, "I'm never going back there!"

Mac contemplated an appropriate response to Levi's outburst. "Are you upset because one of the girls teased you?" Levi did not answer. "That wasn't nice of her. I'm sure she's very sorry for being so rude to you. If we talk with the other kids and explain that you don't like to be teased, will you let me take you back?" Mac could see that Levi was shaking even harder now—a combination of the air getting colder and the possibility that he was crying. Although she could not see his face, she reached over and put her hand on his arm. Levi flinched before pulling away. "Levi, I'm not going to hurt you or tease you or do anything that's gonna make you sick. I'm here to help—"

"No one is making me sick. That's a lie!" Levi said, as he raised his head up from his hands. Mac could see that he was crying, and his lower lip trembled as he spoke. He looked older than yesterday in court—yet somehow more vulnerable. "I'm sick because God makes me sick. My mom is nice to me. She loves me. She is the *only* person who loves me."

"Levi, there are a lot of people who love you. Your dad and your brothers and—"

"My brother *hates* me."

"Austen?"

"Ben. Ben hates me. He thinks I'm stupid and weak and a crybaby."

Mac decided that it wasn't a good idea to respond to Levi's comments about Ben, but better to perhaps point out all of the other people that loved the little boy. She could spend more time discussing his thoughts about Ben later, as she responded a simple, "Your dad loves you."

"No," Levi said, and Mac noted that his crying had temporarily stopped. Levi looked Mac dead in the eyes when he continued, saying, "My dad loves his job and he loves my brothers and sister because they're good in sports. He thinks I am a crybaby too. Just like Ben."

Mac was at a loss, but realized that she was getting some serious headway into the young boy's frame of mind. "Does your dad call you names, Levi?

Has he ever called you a crybaby?" Mac slowly scooted herself even closer towards Levi, so that by now their hips were side-to-side nearly touching. She put her arm around the fragile little boy, and pulled him as close to her as he would let her. She took the end of her black dress and applied pressure to his wound while waiting for him to answer, but he remained quiet. "Does your dad tease you?"

Mac looked into Levi's emerald-green eyes. The reflection of the water flowed through his eyes, like the waves of the ocean. She pushed a few strands of his curly blond hair away from his eyes, and then began to gently apply more pressure to his wound. Levi winced at her pressing onto his cut leg, but he didn't recoil. Mac took this as a sign that Levi knew he was safe with her; at least she hoped he realized that she was safe and would not betray or hurt him.

"Ben teases me. So do the kids at Mrs. Kelly's house." Levi pulled away from Mac's embrace and scooted down the river bank toward the water. He dug a rock from the mud and threw it into the creek. "I am *never* going back there. *Never.*"

"I understand how you must feel. I'll talk to the social worker and see if we can find you another place to stay."

"The social worker is the one who took me away from my mom. She'll make me go back. She doesn't care about me."

"I understand you're angry, but you must know that your social worker is doing her job. You know that she's trying to make sure that you don't get hurt, just like her job requires her to do. She's working hard on your case to protect you from any possible harm, and whether you are really in danger is something that we can only find out with time. She has to be careful, Levi, to make sure that while you are out of your mom's care that you don't get injured. Your social worker loves children, and she just wants to make sure you're in a healthy environment. She's not trying to hurt you or your mom or–"

"Yes, she is!" Levi interrupted. "She took me away from my mom because she wants to hurt us. I know for a fact because my dad said so." Levi finished his statement to Mac with somewhat of a smirk on his face, apparently getting some satisfaction in citing authority to Mac in her retort to her.

"Your dad told you that?" Mac asked, totally bewildered at the suggestion that Luke Landers had actually made such a comment.

Levi did not answer, so Mac asked him again. Still, Levi remained silent.

Mac decided that Levi had shut down, and if she had any hopes of continuing their conversation, she would have to take an entirely different approach with him. "Do you trust me, Levi?"

No response.

"Look at me," Mac said. Just as Mac was getting ready to move herself directly in front of Levi's field of vision, he turned his head toward Mac. "You *can* trust me. I know it's hard to know which people you can trust, especially when bad things have been happening. I don't know all the answers yet, but one thing I can promise you is that you can trust me. I'm here to help you, Levi."

After a momentary pause in which Mac secretly was hoping that Levi was contemplating what she just said to him, Levi looked at her and said somberly, "They pay you dollars, don't they?"

Mac shook her head, somewhat taken aback. "What do you mean?"

"The judge–you're getting paid in dollars. You're not here with me because you want to," Levi said while looking coldly into Mac's eyes. "That's what my dad said."

Mac was horrified to hear Levi's statements. Of course she was getting paid, but how does one explain to a kid of Levi's age how the system works, and that she took his case only because she really did want to help? Mac was more worried, though, by the comments Levi kept making regarding his father. What was the doctor telling his son? Why would he fill his head with such negativity? Or perhaps Levi just overhead his father making some comments on the case and he misinterpreted them? Whatever the reason, she realized that this was a serious problem.

"When did you talk with your dad, Levi?" Mac made sure that she asked this question as softly and sweetly as she could because she knew that she risked losing Levi entirely if he felt she was accusing his father of something bad.

"Last night. He said that the judge pays you to stick up for me."

Mac thought about this, and realized that if what Levi was saying were true then the conversation with his dad would have had to have occurred outside the visitation orders set by Judge Binnard the day prior. Mac wondered if Luke went to Mrs. Kelly's house, or whether he was able to contact Levi over the phone while he was in foster care. There was no doubt that what Levi was saying was extremely serious, but before she considered all of the corollary issues involved, she realized that she needed to take advantage of the situation at hand. Levi had opened up to her by commenting on some inner family dynamics, and if she didn't respond appropriately, she would lose the opportunity to make a serious connection with him. She thought of the best choice of words, knowing that she had to be utterly honest with him.

"You're sort of right, Levi," Mac started off. "I'm getting paid to help on your case, but I don't *have* to work on your case. The judge can't make me sit here right now and talk with you, all wet and dirty like I am. My job is to review cases, like yours, and make a decision on whether I want to be involved. When the judge asked me to work for you, I could have said 'no.' Regardless of payment in dollars." Mac smiled, as she used Levi's own word choice to explain her salary. "I'm not afraid to say 'no' to the judge and turn down a case, Levi. I've done it before. But when I read your file, I knew I wanted to meet you. The papers I read told me that you're a good, nice, smart, young man—one that I very much wanted to meet."

Mac described the process as simply and honestly as she could, fudging a teeny bit only on the lack of any hesitancy she might have felt when accepting the case. There was no need to share her initial doubts with Levi because that would only muddy the waters and be too complicated to explain.

Mac seemed to have gotten through to Levi, perhaps just a tiny bit. He cocked his head to the side, and after a moment of obvious reflection, responded, "My dad said that lawyers are greedy."

"That's interesting," Mac said. "There are some greedy lawyers out there, so your dad's right, Levi. But we're not *all* greedy." She reflected on what she just said and realized that she should probably take her response a bit further to drive home the point. "There are greedy people all around us, Levi, and greedy people can work in a bunch of different jobs–not just as lawyers. I'm sure there are tons of greedy mechanics and doctors and plumbers. You know that there are good people in life, and then there are a few bad people. That's the truth regardless of their job choices. And, sometimes a good person can make a mistake. In fact, we all make mistakes. We all do things we wish we didn't do."

Mac was pleased at her response, which had come out of nowhere. While answering his question, she was able to subtly make a point that might apply to Levi outside of their discussion. She let Levi think about her response for a minute, and noted that he remained seated, holding his knees close to his chest. Mac's attention was drawn to Levi's pink, goose-pimpled skin and blue lips. While their conversation was a dramatic turn in their relationship, she realized that there was no way that it could continue from their soggy perch.

Mac lowered her head to eye-level with Levi and said, "We need to get warm, honey. It's too cold to stay out here. Where can we go where you will feel safe?"

"Y-y-your house," he stammered, probably fearing her rejection.

Mac lifted her head back up and calculated her best response. She was aware that he was putting her to a test, challenging her to prove he should trust her. In his ten-year-old way, he wanted to see if she was who she claimed she was. Mac had no doubt that she would get scolded for taking Levi to her home, but she also knew that she had no hopes with this child if she did anything short of the same. She internally sighed, as she realized she would have to just let the social worker–and judge–object to this, *after* the fact. Mac's job as a guardian ad litem was to be there for the little guy, and there was no other way for her to do that with him. She was going to have to take him back home with her.

After what Mac hoped was only the briefest of moments, she responded, "Alright. I'll take you to my house. We have a slight problem though. The emergency people like the police and ambulance are looking for you. Mrs. Kelly called them when you had the knife, before she called me. Guess where my car is? Mrs. Kelly's house." Mac looked Levi directly in his eyes, hoping that the significance of their current situation would sink in. "Because of all that, we can't go back to my house right away. Plus, we need to get your leg fixed, and it looks like you're gonna need stitches. We're gonna have to go to the hospital first, or possibly call a doctor."

"No!" Levi shouted, and Mac feared that she'd lost whatever ground she might have gained with him. "I hate the hospital and I hate doctors."

"Then you shouldn't stick sharp objects into your skin, Levi. If you're gonna hurt yourself, you're gonna be going to the places you hate. I took your case, Levi, and that means that I have to get you medical care. I *have* to get you stitched up. Maybe next time you'll think about that before you stick a knife in your leg."

Levi paused, and Mac hoped he understood their situation. He was shivering uncontrollably by now as he said, "C-c-can we call Nurse Janie? Could she fix up my leg?"

Mac was surprised as this was the last thing she'd expected Levi's response to be. "You like Nurse Janie?"

"Yeah, she's nice." Levi smiled as he apparently thought of the nurse. He looked up to Mac when he said, "And she's pretty." Levi then blushed, and looked away. Mac smiled to herself at the young boy's body language.

"Yes, she is nice–and pretty. I'm not sure if she's allowed to give stitches though. I'm pretty sure that only doctors can do that. What about seeing Nurse Janie, but having Dr. Kerr fix your leg?"

"No! My dad says that he's the one who got us into this mess."

"Honey, I'm not sure if that's true, but if it is–it is only because Dr. Kerr thought you needed to be helped. If he didn't like you or your mom, then he wouldn't have cared who got hurt."

"My dad says Dr. Kerr is jealous."

"Jealous? Did your dad say what Dr. Kerr was jealous of?"

"N-n-no. I guess not."

"Do you know what jealous means, Levi?" She couldn't place her finger on it, but she sensed that there was potentially significant information to be had. Why would Luke suggest Dr. Kerr was jealous of him?

"Yes. It means you want what someone else has."

"You're very smart, Levi," Mac said as she helped him to his feet. She pulled him by the hand up the bank of the creek. He followed her over a large, white fence and into a corral. Mac was glad that Levi didn't resist her, and didn't object outright.

"Where are we going?"

"I have a friend who is a veterinarian. He works in that building," Mac said, pointing to a brown structure in front of them. I'm gonna see if he can help us fix your leg."

"My dad says that veterinarians are doctors who are too chicken to work on people."

Mac chuckled at Levi's comment. That boy really looked up to his dad, she thought. At least this comment wasn't one that she found herself having to defend. "Oh really? Your dad sure has a lot of interesting opinions. I can't wait to meet him."

"I know you'll love him," Levi earnestly replied. "He's so smart. Much smarter than my mom."

Mac reeled at that comment. She turned to the little boy, wondering where that comment came from. "Why do you say that?"

Levi shrugged his shoulders as he got up with Mac's help. "'Cuz dad says so."

Chapter 8

"You what?" Senior Social Worker Linda Sterling shouted into the phone. She was in charge of placing Levi in foster care with Mrs. Kelly and was not pleased with Mac's news. Mac had delayed calling her, knowing her response wouldn't be supportive.

"I said I have Levi with me and, he is safe," Mac calmly repeated. "I had his leg stitched and I am going to–"

"No, no, no! You're his lawyer, Ms. MacIntosh, not his pediatrician. You're not allowed to get medical attention for Levi without express written authorization by one of his parents or legal guardians, and you definitely know that you don't have the right to aid and abet in his absconding. You've just rewarded him for his behavior! What Levi did was criminal, and depending on the mood of the juvenile prosecutor, he could end up getting charged with brandishing a weapon or making terrorist threats at his foster family."

"This is a crucial time for this little boy, Linda," Mac replied. "We can't just sit around and watch him self-destruct, not if we truly have his best interests at heart. We have to make sure that he is in a safe environment. Don't get me wrong, I think Mrs. Kelly is a wonderful person, but Levi is in a very fragile state right now. We have to make sure that his foster family appreciates and responds to his delicate psyche. Levi needs to be in a very controlled, safe environment where he is not teased or triggered. As a social worker, I'm sure you agree."

"I'm sorry, I didn't realize that you were also a child psychologist," the social worker snidely remarked.

Mac let that remark slide. She was aware that Linda and Mrs. Kelly were long-time friends and that no matter how she tried to spin it, both ladies would think that Mac was trying to undermine them. Mac realized that she would have to make the best of an imperfect situation, which meant more involvement in this case than she truly desired to spend. She'd gotten to know Levi a little bit by this point, and felt that she owed it to him on a personal level. *Damn*, she thought to herself, realizing that she'd been sucked into the emotional roller coaster of the case.

At least the wound is not infected, Mac thought. Their impromptu visit with her veterinary friend worked out fairly well, considering the circumstances, and Levi's thigh was sutured closed. After the veterinarian put three stitches in Levi's right thigh and gave him a painful tetanus shot, Mac called Pam at her office and asked her to take them to Mac's apartment. She wanted to get him into a nice, warm bed and let him sleep. The vet allowed them to borrow a few blankets and told Mac to take Levi directly to his pediatrician or to the emergency room. Mac sheepishly agreed, knowing that her intentions were otherwise. If she took him to another doctor, Levi would lose faith in her. She needed to protect him now—more than ever—so that she could find out the truth. She prayed that her delaying the follow up medical care would end up being a wise choice. Mac was starting to realize that life with children involved prompt decision-making without much time to reflect on the situation at hand. Not everything regarding childcare was as black and white as Mac had imagined it would be.

As Mac requested, Pam brought Levi's medical files with her, along with the investigation into the Landers family. Mac needed to stay by Levi's side, but figured that she could work while he slept. She really couldn't afford to waste any time, considering how many questions there were that needed to be answered.

It wasn't long after she tucked Levi into her bed that the little boy fell asleep. Mac had held off on placing the call to Linda Sterling until she was absolutely certain that Levi was completely out for the night. If she called earlier, the social worker would have insisted that Levi be taken to the hospital—which in any other circumstance, Mac might have agreed. Being involved in this unusual scenario gave her a different perspective, however, and she knew deep down that what Levi needed more than anything else was a little time away from the system.

Mac fixed herself a cup of tea and tried to relax on her couch as she reflected on the craziness of her day, but she could not ease the knots that were angrily forming on her shoulders. All Mac could do to protect Levi, for now, was to provide him shelter from the outdoors and a brief respite from doctors and hospitals and social workers and foster care. She wanted to further procrastinate placing the call to the social worker, but knew that any additional delay might jeopardize her relationship with Linda Sterling. Therefore, Mac picked up the phone and dialed her number.

"Ms. MacIntosh, I think you've gotten yourself too close to the situation to adequately represent Levi's best interests. I am going to ask the district attorney to make an ex parte motion to have a new attorney appointed for Levi, and I'm going to ask that it get filed by tomorrow."

"Please don't do that, Linda. That would be a terrible mistake. The one thing Levi is lacking is stability, and someone to trust. In the short time I've had with him I've worked very hard to start building a bond between us, and I really feel that I'm getting somewhere. If I were to leave now, what kind of message would that send to him? Really, Linda? Don't you think that it's your job to make sure that Levi has someone–"

"You've had this case for less than forty-eight hours, Ms. MacIntosh. Two days. I don't know what makes you think that you've been able to build anything between you and Levi in the course of just a few hours. I'm happy that you feel a connection to him and that you're taking an interest in the case, but this isn't my first case, and I've learned that in order to professionally handle a caseload of this nature, you have to make sure to maintain a professional distance. Decisions can't be made with emotions. They need to be made with objectiveness and clarity. You're dealing with more than just a case, after all, but with people's lives. Children's lives. I take my job very seriously, and my job is to process this case with a plan of reunification while maintaining Levi's best interests at the forefront. That's what juvenile law is all about–reunification consistent with the best interests of the child. If a professional involved in such a case gets too attached, they may lose sight of reunification–and as a state agency, the constitution mandates that we not lose sight of that goal. Do you understand?" Mac was smart enough to know that she was just put in her place, and wished that Levi weren't asleep in the next room so she could appropriately respond to the social worker's condescending reproach. Maybe she was lucky that Levi was snoozing, as Mac had no choice but to respond in a calm and quiet voice. She took a deep breath and a sip of warm tea before responding to the social worker's allegations.

"I understand very well," Mac said in a hushed tone. "But what *you* don't understand is that I am trained to be objective. Even when I feel a personal connection, I am able to sufficiently distance myself and maintain my professionalism. I'm an attorney, and that is what I do." As Mac continued, she tried desperately to keep the sarcasm out of her voice. "No amount of training, in social work or otherwise, can provide a black and white outline on how we're supposed to tackle our jobs of providing for the best interests of a child. Every person is different, as is every situation. When I was with Levi, I didn't have a guidebook to follow. I had to listen to my gut instinct and I hope that if you were in my shoes, Linda, you would have responded similarly–because it was the only response that was entirely in Levi's best interests. And as he's peacefully sleeping in the next room, I'm busying myself reviewing his extensive medical files so I can get a better understanding of his history. I presume Social Services felt the facts in this case supported Levi's removal from Evelyn and Luke's care, so I want to make sure I get familiar with those very facts which ultimately brought Levi to me forty-eight hours ago." Mac paused briefly to catch her breath before finally concluding her desperate plea. "Please give me a chance to continue representing Levi, because I know that's the only decision that's truly in his best interests."

Mac was greeted by silence on the other end, making her wonder if her call got dropped and she made the heartfelt plea to a dead line. Finally, Mac heard Linda clear her throat. "Your home has not been approved by our agency. I'm afraid Levi won't be able to stay with you, Ms. MacIntosh."

Mac shook her head in disbelief. While Linda's response appeared to concede Mac's continued involvement in the case, the suggestion that Mac was unqualified as a temporary placement of Levi was insulting. "I'm sorry, Ms. Sterling, but did you just say that the extensive background check that I endured to take the bar examination in this state and appear in front of a juvenile judge in Levi's case is somehow insufficient to ease your concerns over a simple overnight visit? Did you really mean to imply that my home might not be suitable? I'm a single woman without a criminal record or any roommates. I don't do drugs and I don't have any crazy ex-boyfriends. I work extremely hard at keeping my home clean, and my only vice in life is running. These are the very things about me that were scrutinized when I underwent a thorough criminal background check prior to my admission to the bar, and I highly doubt that there was anything left out that would have completed the picture for me to get approval by your agency."

"Ms. MacIntosh, our agency has a protocol to follow. We have to approve all placement facilities in order to get state and federal funding. We must—"

"I don't want funding," Mac said.

"Whether you do or don't, we still have to formally and officially approve your home before Levi is able to stay with you."

"Fine," Mac responded in obvious defeat. "I'll do whatever you want, jump through whatever hurdles you make me, but for God's sake please don't take him from me tonight after all he's been through today."

Linda Sterling let out a loud sigh. "Like I told you, it's against policy."

"Please," Mac urged. "Please . . ."

"Fine. But the *only* reason I am agreeing is that I don't have any other places to even consider placing Levi at this hour of the night. And Mrs. Kelly refuses to have him back because her kids are terrified of him, and I'm left with very limited options. So, until I can find another foster family who doesn't mind having a child who wipes feces on the walls and tries to stab the other residents of the home with a butcher knife, my only choice appears to be letting him stay with you—his court-appointed attorney who has never raised a child and has no idea what she is in for."

"I appreciate your vote of confidence," Mac said dryly.

"This isn't a game, Ms. MacIntosh. This child has physical and emotional problems that you are not trained to deal with. I hope you know what you are getting yourself into."

* * *

Seconds after ending her call with Linda Sterling, Mac dialed her paralegal's home phone number and spoke softly into the receiver so as not to wake Levi, who continued to sleep soundly. "Thanks for everything you did for me today," Mac said to Pamela.

Pam had picked them up from the vet's, took them to Mac's house, gathered the Landers files and brought them to Mac, went grocery shopping and delivered kid-friendly food, got a ride from Megan to Mrs. Kelly's and picked up Mac's car, and delivered her car to her apartment–all in under two hours–all without being asked.

"I have your back," Pam said.

"I read the obituary for Evelyn's twin sister that you copied for me," Mac said.

"Wasn't that strange? I don't think I've ever heard of anyone dying from *saffron* poisoning."

"Me neither. The article said that Evelyn's family was in the clothing manufacturing business in California and that the saffron was used to make yellow dye for the clothes. I didn't realize that saffron was used in anything but cooking."

"Me either. Now that I think about it, I use saffron when I cook Mexican food. Guess I should be more careful."

"Lots of recipes call for it," Mac agreed. "My mom is a gourmet cook, and she uses saffron all the time. There must be a part of the plant that's poisonous, like rhubarb or mistletoe."

"Yeah, but on Christmas Day? How twisted is that, to die from a cooking spice on such a celebrated day? I mean, she was only twenty-four-years-old. I wonder if Evelyn was there when it happened."

"Meaning?" Mac asked.

"Well, it would be interesting to know what kind of effect that would have had on her, watching her twin die right in front of her. Or, whether she had anything to do with it."

"Pam, that's a pretty big leap."

"Why? She's being charged with poisoning her son. Her sister died of a mysterious poisoning," Pam retorted. To further tighten her point, she added, "I bet that when her twin died, Evelyn was left with an exclusive right of their inheritance. I can bridge the gap."

"Good thing you don't prosecute crimes," Mac chuckled in response. "You need more of a connection than that to consider filing criminal charges."

"Sure, it's circumstantial—I'll give you that. But circumstantial evidence gets people locked up every day."

"No, I didn't mean that you didn't have a valid point, Pam, I just mean that there has to be a stronger connection of the dots in order to jump to that legal conclusion." Mac then gently added, "But that doesn't make it any less interesting."

"Well, I guess I just assigned myself my next task, then," Pam said.

"What do you mean?"

"I'm gonna find that connection for you," Pam said firmly, before hanging up the phone.

Mac crossed over to the kitchen counter to place the cordless phone back into its charger, and when she turned around she saw that Levi was standing two feet away.

"Huuuuuuu," Mac gasped, stepping back and sucking in her breath. Levi appearing out of nowhere nearly caused her to have heart failure. "My God, Levi. You startled me! I didn't hear you get up."

Levi stood, staring at Mac in a trance-like state. He did not utter a sound nor did he move. His eyes were rimmed in a hue of red and he squinted at her with a look of pure hatred. He was wearing a pair of sweatpants that were two sizes too small—borrowed from Pam's daughter, and one of Mac's t-shirts.

"Levi? Are you okay? Do you remember where you are?"

He remained silent, but started rocking back and forth on the balls of his feet.

Mac stared at Levi, unsure what to think. Was he angry? Was he even awake? Was Mac finally witnessing the beginnings of one of the tantrums she'd heard about? "Are you thirsty? Can I get you some water? Or milk? Maybe you are hungry. You didn't eat much today."

Levi lowered his chin, but he made sure to keep his eyes firmly fixated on Mac. His stare bore a hole through her, like he was trying to pierce her with hate. Mac didn't know what to do. She was ashamed to admit that she actually felt fear run through her veins, and her mind went back to the social worker's warnings to her over the phone. This was just a little boy, Mac tried to assure herself. All he needed was comfort and love. Still, the look on Levi's face reminded her of a scene in *The Omen*. Mac took a small step back into her kitchen and reached behind her to flip on the light.

Suddenly, Levi charged at her. He had only been a few feet away, yet as soon as Mac turned on the light he was lunging towards her in what Mac thought was an attempt at tackling her. She stepped right to avoid contact, which ultimately sent Levi vaulting toward the countertop. He smashed his head into the cupboard causing the boy to tumble down to the floor with a bounce. Mac was mortified by the cracking sound his head made when it made contact with the counter, and couldn't help but feeling horribly guilty. She knelt beside him and rolled him over onto his back. A goose-egg-sized lump had already started to form atop Levi's head.

"I'm so sorry, Levi. I thought you were trying to hurt me."

Tears ran down the outer edges of his eyes and formed two distinctive streams connecting into the tributaries of his hairline. "I-I-I was scared. I woke up and didn't know where I was. I was just going to give you a bear hug, just like I used to give my mom before bed." The tears were no longer streams, but now rivers. Mac's tears started flowing too.

"Oh, baby. I am so very sorry. When you didn't respond to my questions, I thought that something was wrong. I am so sorry for dodging your hug. If I'd known that you were coming in for a bear hug, I would have never moved an inch. Let me grab some ice."

Mac gently set his head on the kitchen floor and reached over to open the freezer. She grabbed a few cubes of ice from the tray and wrapped them in a baggie. She placed the baggie in a napkin and placed it on his head. Levi winced when the ice touched the bump. She held it there for a moment and then persuaded him to walk with her into the living room.

"Between the gash on your leg and the lump on your head, you look like you've been in a war." Mac smiled halfheartedly at her weak attempt at humor, and hoped that Levi would, too. "You're a pretty tough kid, you know that?"

"I have to be," Levi responded, cracking something that could be described as a smile. "Otherwise Ben would have kicked the crap out of me by now."

Mac gasped in response to Levi's crude language. He was too young to be speaking in such a way, though she didn't truly fault him considering the point they were at in their conversation. Still, she felt obligated to ask him, "Is that how you talk at home?"

Levi gave her a sideways glance before responding. "No. Well, not in front of mom. She'd make me write sentences for saying the 'c-r' word."

"Who have you said that in front of?"

"Ben. Only because that's how he talks to me." Levi looked up at her, almost questioning her reaction before quietly saying, "I hate him."

"You don't hate your brother, do you? Really?" Levi nodded. He looked like he was serious. Mac knew that they would have to come back to the topic of Ben at a later date, and that she might be able to get a much better insight into the family dynamics by focusing on the second Landers child, but she decided not to press her luck for the time being. "Do you love Austen?" Levi shrugged, somewhat noncommittally in response. "What about Lauren?"

"Lauren is nice. She takes care of me when I am sick and plays in my room to keep me company. She gets me medicine sometimes because she says that she likes it when I am happy. I wish she didn't fight with my mom so much."

"Why do they fight?"

"I don't know. Sometimes they fight about how she dresses, or how often she's on her cell phone. Her staying too long in the bathroom. Stuff like that."

"Girl stuff?" Mac thought back to the things she argued about with her mother when she was a teenage girl. She remembered having arguments over monopolizing the bathroom and over tying up the only phone line.

"No, I guess I mean boy stuff. My mom thinks that Lauren dresses like a boy and does sports like a boy and only has friends that are boys. It makes my mom mad. My mom thinks that she should dress in lacy crap and talk to her girlfriends on her cell phone and be a cheerleader. They fight about it all the time." Levi tried to throw in the "crap" word nonchalantly, but Mac caught him looking at her out of the corner of his eye for a reaction when he uttered it.

"Hmm."

"My dad and mom fight about it too," Levi continued. "My dad thinks that Lauren is just fine how she is. He is glad that she likes sports and thinks that Lauren is better off staying away from mean girls who make her feel left out."

"What do you think?" Mac asked.

"I think that my dad is right," Levi said earnestly without a second's hesitation. "Lauren is the nicest person in my family. And the smartest. She's even a better athlete than Austen—and she's way better than Ben." Levi smiled for a second, thinking of how his sister outshone his mean older sibling. The smile was short lived, though, and a seriousness came about Levi's expression as he finished the thought. "Ben thinks he is the best at everything. The only thing he's really good at is being mean."

"Sounds like you don't like Ben much."

"I hate Ben. He makes me eat gross stuff."

"What do you mean by that?" Mac asked. By now, she'd fluffed a few pillows behind Levi's neck and had him reclined on her living room couch. She was sitting crossed-legged on the floor next to the couch as she was talking with him.

"One time he wrapped dog poop in a Tootsie-Roll wrapper and made me eat it. I threw up."

"That's gross." Mac gasped, as she thought of actually having to eat such a concoction. As she pictured that, she started to think about what else Ben might have forced down Levi's throat—and the consequences of it. She was nervous about what Levi's answer would be, but knew she had to ask the question. "What else has he made you eat?"

"Dog food. Cat food. Fish food. Rat poison."

"*Rat poison?*"

"Yeah, but at least he got in bad trouble for that one. He made up a club, acted like it was all cool to be a member. All it really was just an excuse for him to do mean stuff to the members of his club. Once he put a dead snake on Jimmy's garbage can lid. He thought it was so funny when Jimmy's mom emptied their trash, 'cuz he could hear her screaming bloody murder. Ben made Jimmy tell his mom that he had put the snake there, so that Jimmy could get in Ben's stupid club."

Mac couldn't help it, but her eyes were wide open. There was much more to Ben's role in the Landers family than she would have guessed, and she knew that there could be more beneath the surface. If Ben really were so sinister . . . ? Mac couldn't finish the thought, so she just prompted for Levi to continue. "Go on. Tell me about the rat poison."

Levi didn't hear Mac, or was too caught up in his reverie to answer her pointed question. "One time Ben made Tommy's little brother Justin lie down on the ground under their motor home and drink the gas that was dripping down out of it. Justin got sick and had to have his stomach pumped. Ben made Tommy say that it was his fault, so that Tommy wouldn't lose his membership in Ben's club."

"What else? Tell me about the rat poison."

"Once he took rat poison from our garage and fed it to Justin's rabbits. The rabbits died. Ben tried to make Justin take the blame for it, but Justin wouldn't. He told Ben that he didn't want to be in his stupid club and he was going to tell his mom that Ben was the one who fed poison to the rats. Ben didn't want to take the blame, so he forced me to eat the rat poison.

When I was going to the hospital to get my stomach pumped, Ben told Justin's mom that *I* was the one who did it."

Oh my God, Mac thought to herself. "Why didn't Justin tell his mom what really happened? That's serious!" Mac tried to keep a calmness about her, but she couldn't. Rat poison!

"Ben told Justin that if he told anyone, Ben would make him eat rat poison, too. He said that he would put the poison in his school lunch and when he didn't expect it, he would die in his sleep from rat poison. Justin knew Ben enough to know that he wasn't bluffing, so Jerry didn't tell."

"Have you told your mom about any of this?"

"No," Levi said. He took the ice off his forehead and handed it to Mac. The bump had gone down considerably, but a deep purple bruise was already forming.

"Why not? Why haven't you told on Ben? He is a bully."

"He'll beat the crap out of me if I do."

Chapter 9

"Luke Landers is the non-offending parent and should retain custody of his son," John Trainor said to Mac over the phone.

Mr. Trainor was Luke's lawyer, who obviously didn't have the common sense to avoid making the phone call at six thirty in the morning. Mac had let Levi sleep in her bed, which meant that she was delegated to the couch; Mac barely slept enough as it was, so this call was definitely not appreciated on many different levels. Normally, she got up at five and went out for an early morning run, but with Levi there, she couldn't go. Probably just as well, Mac thought.

"The case is under investigation, Mr. Trainor," Mac said. "Dr. Landers has not been adjudicated as anything as of yet, namely 'non- offending.' It may be that the investigation substantiates his lack of involvement, but he's not getting Levi until the Social Services Agency and the court make that determination."

"There is no reason that Levi should be living in foster care, or worse," John spat into the phone, "living with his *lawyer*, during this process. The little guy needs his family."

"I agree with you, Mr. Trainor, wholeheartedly. I can't make that happen, though, until the investigation proves that would be in Levi's best interests. And that means we're going to need to get to the bottom of who is making him sick."

John ignored Mac, and continued his unappreciated tirade. "My client is absolutely furious that you didn't return him last night. I had to make him promise not to call you. You have no legal right to have him in your care. I have half a mind to call the State Bar and report you–"

Mac sighed as she listened to John go on, and hoped that this phone call didn't signify how her day would proceed. What a crappy way to start the day, Mac thought, and then smirked at her use of the word "crap." Finally, Mac interrupted John's litany to put him back in his place, somewhat. "I got temporary permission from the social worker, Mr. Trainor. That means Levi is appropriately placed with me, so there would be nothing for you to report." Mac almost left her comment at that, but then decided to add in a more emotional note. "Believe me, it is not what I expected to happen when I volunteered for this assignment. What happened with this little boy yesterday was absolutely crazy and–"

"You made it worse by absconding with him. You basically told Levi that running away is okay, because you get what you want when you do. You then took him secretly to get fixed by an animal doctor, no less, and then secreted him back to your own private home. How do you think that looks, Ms. MacIntosh? It doesn't take a genius to realize that my client does not feel that you are fit to be his son's temporary guardian, let alone his lawyer."

"With all due respect to your client," Mac said as she took a long gulp from her steaming espresso, which she had managed to brew while listening to John rant and rave, "Levi has some serious trust issues. Without breaching the attorney-client privilege, I'll just say that Levi fears certain members of his family. Returning him to such an unstable environment is not going to assist in his therapeutic needs. This little boy–"

"Therapeutic needs? Good Lord, Ms. MacIntosh! You sound like one of those psychodrama lawyers. Are you in therapy? If you're not, you should consider it," John snorted. "It sounds to me like you've gotten yourself in way over your head, and you're now *personally* involved." John emphasized the word "personally," spitting it out as if it were distasteful for him to simply utter it.

"Personally involved?" Mac practically shouted back at the defense attorney. "You say that like it's a crime, and not the best way to represent a young child as their guardian ad litem. That's my job, John. Levi is suffering–from what, I don't know, but I do know that it's my job to protect him."

"Oh. I see," John said with heavy sarcasm, "I get it now. Your time clock is tick-ticking away and you see this little boy as an antidote to your unfilled desire to be a mom. Well, this isn't the time or place–"

Mac dropped the phone loudly on the counter, but not to sever their connection. The last thing she needed was a lecture on her biological clock, and hanging up on John seemed too polite a response. She decided to let him continue to rant through the phone to no one in particular, and hoped that he heard the loud "plunk" as the phone hit the counter. She went to check on Levi before returning to the phone, and when she did return, the line was dead.

* * *

"What in the hell was wrong with you last night?" Luke asked Evelyn through the master bathroom door. "Storming out of the country club like a scorned lover? I'd have thought you'd want less attention directed towards you, not more. You do realize that you were the talk of the party after you left."

"No doubt you did nothing to dissuade that."

"What's that supposed to mean?"

"Just what I said–you didn't defend me. You never do," Evelyn said.

"These days it seems I have to hire lawyers to do that for me, Evelyn. I can't defend you alone anymore."

Luke stayed at the party far too late, and he was paying the price for that right now. He needed to grab a shower and get to the office, but Evelyn wouldn't open the bathroom door. She'd already shuffled the kids off to school by the time Luke arose. She knew that he needed to use the bathroom and appeared to enjoy the momentary power she held over him as she listened to his pleas for her to hurry. He stood in his boxer shorts with disheveled hair and dark circles under his eyes, knocking every thirty seconds. After several minutes passed without any signs of movement on the other end, Luke gave up and went to use Austen's shower.

When he finished showering, he wrapped himself in a white fluffy cotton towel and headed back to the master. His closet was attached to the master bathroom, which was closed off from the master bedroom by French doors. Those were the very doors that Evelyn had locked him out of previously, and they still remained closed and locked. Luke was furious, and he began pounding on the doors again. He pounded hard.

"I need to get dressed, Ev. I have patients waiting."

"Scorned lover, huh?" Evelyn huffed through closed doors. "Did you really think that's what I looked like when I left the party last night?"

"Huh?" Luke had no idea what Evelyn was getting at, but at least she was responding. Perhaps now he'd actually be able to get dressed sometime soon.

"You said that I stormed out of there like some scorned lover."

Luke sighed out of frustration. "Whatever, Ev, just let me in so I can get dressed."

"Well, maybe you're right. Maybe I am a scorned lover. Did you ever think of that?"

"Listen, Ev, I simply don't have time to play these sort of games. I have got to get to work and you need to let me in so that I can get dressed. Someone needs to pay for this house and the cars and the sports and the vacations," Luke grumbled, then added almost as an afterthought, "and don't forget your wardrobe."

"What about *her* wardrobe? Who pays for that? Don't you need to rush off to work so that you can also pay for her townhouse and her car and her wardrobe?"

"Evelyn, let me in. I have no idea what you are talking about. Have you taken too many pills again?" "*Again*? Since when have I taken too many pills? You're just trying to change the subject, as usual. You like to twist things around so that it is deflected from you."

"Right, Evelyn. You're always right. Now can you unlock the doors? Or better yet, throw my tan slacks and my blue dress shirt out and then I'll be on my way. You can sit in the bathroom all day for all I care."

"I'm not getting anything for you. Why don't you ask *her* to help you out this morning? I'm sure that you keep a spare set of clothes at *her* place. Go there, you bastard."

"I have no idea what you're talking about," Luke said, his frustration growing by the second.

There was a considerable pause in the conversation. Luke thought that he heard Evelyn sniffle. As angry and frustrated as he was, Luke realized how much Evelyn apparently needed him. His busy workload meant that he wasn't there for her as much as she obviously needed, and right now she needed him to listen to her and be there for her. Luke sighed as he realized he was going to have to walk away and hope for the storm to pass; Evelyn seemed to be having another one of her episodes, and those were only cured by time.

Luke wrapped the towel extra tightly around his waist, and began to exit the bedroom as he proceeded towards the laundry room. After Luke headed down the two flights of stairs leading to their basement, he found their maid Ginny diligently doing their laundry. Luke flipped through the stack of freshly ironed clothes that were folded on the pantry shelves, searching for a pair of clean pants. When he found a suitable pair, he began to search through the rack of pressed shirts that Ginny had hung up on their laundry rack. When he found a shirt that moderately matched the pants in his hands, he began to head back to his eldest son's bathroom. This is one of the benefits of having teenagers, Luke chuckled lightly to himself. What would he have done this morning without Austen's shaving supplies and deodorant? Luke wondered. After tidying up with Austen's grooming accessories, he finished getting dressed and headed to the office.

* * *

Evelyn was in frenzy, and she didn't know what to do to calm herself down. Normally, she would be one her way to Levi's classroom, as she volunteered as a teacher's assistant every Thursday morning. After all, this was expected of her, as all the stay-at-home moms volunteered in the elementary school classrooms. Evelyn knew that the fourteen-thousand-dollar-a-year tuition they paid should have been enough to cover teachers' assistants without her contributing her Thursday mornings, but she did it to put on the airs Luke expected of her.

When Levi was in first grade, Evelyn realized he tended to act out when she was physically present in his classroom. At first, he would just act silly and play the role of class clown, but as the school year went along, his acting out escalated to the point of physical outbursts. Evelyn commented on her observations to the first grade teacher and suggested that perhaps it would be better for everyone if she not continue her work in Levi's classroom. Of course, Ev's comment was met with derision from the school administration–suggesting that Evelyn simply didn't want to be involved with Levi's behavioral issues at school. Despite her better judgment, Evelyn continued to help out on Thursdays–just not this Thursday.

Paradox has its way of finding a person at just the right moment and as Evelyn thought back on her suggestion three years prior not to volunteer in the classroom, she realized that the administration's allegations were partly true. She didn't look forward to the dull time she spent as a classroom volunteer. She found photocopying worksheets tedious and boring. After raising four kids, she didn't enjoy teaching kids to read or memorize math facts. She would have rather been fundraising for a noble cause or lunching with friends. Evelyn couldn't help but realize, in this moment, the irony she was living because the type of dullness that the school volunteer routine offered was exactly what she needed now to keep her mind off her present legal and marital problems.

But going to Levi's class wasn't even an option at this point, as she was ordered by the judge to not work in Levi's class. The judge considered this an inappropriate "unmonitored visit," despite the fact that Levi was surrounded by other third graders, their teacher and other volunteer parents. So, here Evelyn was, sitting on her master bathroom floor, in tears, wishing for the first time that she could help the teacher make photocopies.

Evelyn heard a light knock on the door, and lost herself for a moment in the thought that it was Luke returning to apologize. Evelyn wasn't surprised that it wasn't Luke, though, but their maid. "Mrs. Landers? Mrs. Landers, are you okay? I was going to put away some laundry. May I come in?"

Ginny had been part of the Landers family for nearly ten years. Once Evelyn was kept out of the house so frequently tending to Levi's medical problems and doctor visits, she no longer had the time to keep up with the demands of housekeeping. Luke was a bit slower to come to that conclusion, though he ultimately did after finding himself without clean underwear one too many times.

"Mrs. Landers?"

"I'm fine, Ginny. Just give me a minute, please."

"Yes indeed, ma'am," Ginny was quick to reply. "I'm sorry if I intruded, I just ... Do you want me to make you another pot of coffee?"

"Thank you, Ginny. I could really use some fresh coffee. Would you start making that for me in about an hour, though? I think I'm going to get myself outside first and enjoy some fresh air and exercise."

"Um ... why don't you try your treadmill?" Ginny nervously responded. "I could put on some nice, soothing music for you instead. Don't you think that would be nice?" Ginny tentatively asked.

"No, Ginny. I want to go outside and get some fresh air." Evelyn was surprised at Ginny's interference with her plans. That was unlike her.

"I think you'd enjoy the treadmill better, Mrs. Landers. I could put the cable to the digital scenery channel and you'll feel really calm and relaxed that way–like you were outdoors," Ginny continued. Her approach to get Evelyn to stay inside was both curious and infuriating at the same time.

"What is going on and why don't you want me going outside?"

Ginny momentarily paused before responding. It would be insubordinate of her not to answer directly. "Ma'am, there are people out there with cameras. They've been there for an hour or so. Doctor almost ran them over on his way out."

"Do you mean reporters?" Evelyn asked, as she began to slowly exit the bathroom. "People from the newspaper?" "I-I-I don't know, ma'am. That could be."

"Well then, call the police. If there are people on my property without my permission, then they are trespassers. Report them immediately. I won't stand for anyone invading my privacy, and I refuse to become a prisoner in my own home."

"Yes, ma'am." Ginny hung her head as she dutifully turned around, prepared to make the call. She hesitated for a moment before turned around and asking timidly, "Mrs. Landers, what exactly should I say? I've never called the police before."

"Never mind, Ginny," Evelyn said in an exasperated tone. "I will handle it."

By now, Evelyn was outside of the bathroom, pacing in the master bedroom. Ginny didn't wait a second before entering the bathroom, grasping tightly to the basket of clean laundry. She clearly hoped that Evelyn wouldn't change her mind.

As Ginny set the basket down, she glanced at Evelyn, who had stopped pacing and was curled up on the bedroom floor with her knees pulled to her chest. Evelyn's hands were up against her face, trying to cover the obvious tears that were flowing. Ginny hesitated before taking action, but ultimately abandoned the clean laundry and sat down on the floor immediately next to Evelyn.

"Mrs. Landers, it is okay to cry."

Evelyn pulled her head up from her knees and looked at Ginny's concerned face. Ginny was plain-faced and plump. She wore black stretch tights and a large, white T-shirt that used to belong to Dr. Landers. Her long, dark hair was pulled back into a ponytail and she looked older than her forty- seven years. Evelyn turned toward Ginny and allowed Ginny to pull her in close. She was surprised to find herself feeling safe and warm around Ginny, enough to start crying in front of her. Ginny rocked lightly back and forth, comforting her. The phone rang several times, but Ginny did not move from her post and Evelyn was grateful for that, too. Eventually, Evelyn stopped crying and when she did, she popped up to her feet and started scurrying around, as if nothing had happened.

"Ginny, I am planning on having Chateaubriand for dinner with that Waldorf salad with chopped truffles. You will need to go to the market and pick up a few things. I will leave you a list. And the kids' gym bags are in the garage with their workout clothes. They need to be washed and re-packed for tonight's practices." Ginny popped back into action, recognizing that their momentary connection was over.

"I already took care of the gym bags, ma'am. I will go to the market."

Evelyn nodded, while tying her tennis shoes. "I am going to walk on the treadmill for an hour or so. I'll leave the list in the kitchen." Evelyn started down the staircase and then she turned, holding on the ornate wrought-iron banister and said, "Thanks, Ginny. You are a good friend."

* * *

Evelyn felt that the women in town were jealous of her because she "had it all"–the big, beautiful house, four children, a handsome husband who made plenty of money as a doctor, nice cars, expensive furniture and clothing, and nice vacations. Because of that, Evelyn was confident that there were many women in town celebrating her downfall, and taking pleasure in her suffering.

Evelyn hadn't always played her cards right when it came to friendships. She had a nervous habit of talking–constantly. Any mom will admit that their best source of conversation is their own children, and Evelyn was never at a loss for material, given that her kids were the star quarterback or the star wrestler, or the star swimmer. Evelyn never missed an opportunity to talk about what accomplishments Austen or Ben or Lauren had achieved. As if this weren't annoying enough, Evelyn's slim frame was usually dressed in a new outfit, her nails were perfectly manicured, her hair recently colored and styled, and her make-up freshly applied.

Evelyn could not even imagine the dislike she had incurred during those momentary conversations amongst people who weren't truly her friends, but just putting on a front and pretending to listen to her boast. In fact, she was so self-centered that she never seemed to take notice of the body language of the women to whom she was addressing. They would be at a ladies' luncheon and Evelyn would talk about herself or her family non-stop. At the end of the luncheon, she would dash out–claiming that she had to take Levi to the doctor or something along those lines, and the women lagging behind at the luncheon would start talking–behind Evelyn's back. They called her "Little Miss Perfect" to point out to one another how far from perfect she actually was. Most of them knew about Levi's problems long before Social Services ever did. In fact, it was one of those moms who called Social Services, after finally getting fed up with Evelyn's incessant stories detailing the dutiful trips to Levi's medical appointments.

The single call isn't what made Social Services investigate, however–it was the accumulation of calls that ultimately forced their hand.

What Evelyn didn't realize is that the gossip amongst her so-called friends wasn't entirely focused on her obsession with Levi's medical issues: often times, the ladies gossiped about Luke.

Chapter 10

Dr. Luke Landers was a very busy man. Had there been the type of medical testing there is today back when he was a child, he probably would have been labeled ADHD instead of merely hyperactive. He was easily bored and couldn't sit still for a minute. His OB/GYN practice shared in his energy, as it, too, was constantly on the go, twenty-four/seven. It wasn't that Luke was the most skilled practitioner in town—but what he lacked in skills, Luke made up for in a variety of other ways.

Luke made every woman feel loved and beautiful—whether he was delivering a baby or chaperoning a high school dance. The first thing he did when he entered an exam room was ask the woman how she was feeling and if she had any concerns she'd like to share with him. He would sit in his chair and wheel himself up next to the woman's face, look directly into her eyes and smile. He was disarming and charming at the same time. He listened to any complaint, no matter how small, and made copious notes in charts; after all, it's an ego boost to have a physician remember minute details that were randomly shared during their last visit. Luke knew how to work a woman, and work her well indeed.

Women loved him because he actually listened. His fan club did not end with his female patients, as he knew the names of every parent that his kids came in contact with. Remembering names wasn't a gift he was born with, but since he considered this an important skill he modified a pneumonic device into a game that worked for him. Whenever introduced to someone new, he'd make up a rhyme that involved the person's name and something unique that he would associate with them. "Julie Harn made juice in a baseball barn with Connor Harn." The rhymes themselves weren't particularly clever, but incorporated all of the elements he needed to remember facts with names. The next time he ran into Julie, he'd make sure to address her by name when asking how Connor was doing in baseball. Luke silently chuckled, knowing that Julie would eat it up.

While it seemed obvious that women would love him, men actually seemed to admire Luke, too. He was a scratch golfer and was happy to join a foursome even at the last minute, and was never afraid to share helpful tips to anyone he was playing with, in a completely non-threatening way. Though Luke wasn't able to schedule any activity due to the nature of his practice (women went into labor when they darned well felt like it, regardless of his calendar) he made sure to spend any of his free time at the country club in hopes of squeezing in a quick round of golf. Fortunately, the old-fashioned Sheridan Country Club had only nine holes, so a round of golf could actually be played quickly.

Luke was a natural athlete and helped coach Austen's teams when Austen was young. During these early years of parenting, he went out of his way to offer encouragement to all on the team and made sure to point out the positives in each of the children—Luke knew that it was the little things like this that made a difference.

The Landers family owned a boat, and they weren't afraid to share it with their friends. It was routine for the Landers kids to be accompanied by any of a variety of their young friends waterskiing during the summer at the local lake. Luke patiently circled the novice water skier and offered encouragement and advice until the kid was able to get up and ski around the lake. For some kids, it was the highlight of their summer. He was an avid snow skier and snowboarder as well, and allowed his kids to invite friends to join them on their family ski vacations. Luke had taught probably twenty kids to ski or board.

Luke's patience with kids, and the human race in general, was in direct contrast with his apparent ADHD behavior. While he normally felt driven to keep himself constantly moving and on the go, when it came to helping a child get back up on their skis, he felt uncommonly patient. He might express frustration through some small gestures, like sighing out loud each time the kid fell, but as long as the kid wasn't a "quitter," Luke had no problems with being patient. This did not hold true in cases where the child gave up or refused to try–Luke was simply not able to put up with that sort of behavior.

Enter Levi Landers.

Levi quit the second he couldn't accomplish something, which frequently occurred on his first attempt. Levi cried with the slightest of injury. Levi had troubles holding a baseball correctly. Levi refused to get into the water at the lake. Levi hated skiing. Luke was frustrated just thinking about Levi's failures, regardless of the events leading up to them. Levi shouldn't take the things Ben says to heart, anyways, Luke reasoned. After Ben mentioned that rattlesnakes were in the water during one of their waterskiing trips, Levi refused to go in–no matter how many times Luke pointed out that only one person had been bitten in the past twenty years. When Ben called Levi "pukeface" on one of their trips, Levi began to detest their ski trips. Never mind the fact that Levi got carsick on the ride up the windy mountain and vomited all over the place. Luke chuckled, remembering Ben's quick wit with the nickname choice. That boy is smart as a whip, he thought. Evelyn tried to butt in once Luke starting calling Levi puke-face, he remembered dryly.

Why does she always have to do that, he thought? Doesn't she know that's the only way to teach Levi to grow a backbone? Plus he hates being put into a situation where he has to put her in her place in front of the kids. Of course, this makes Levi cry even harder, because he's so damned emotional. As if her overzealous defense of Levi didn't already reinforce the kid's wimpy behaviors, she had to go and force his hand.

But that was Evelyn–always forcing something on someone. Luke didn't have to force himself onto others–he was charming and witty and well-liked by all. Or so he thought. But not everyone liked Dr. Luke Landers, especially not Dr. Kerr. As the oldest pediatrician in town, Dr. Kerr was already practicing in Sheridan when Dr. Landers arrived. When Dr. Landers applied for privileges at Sheridan County Hospital, Dr. Kerr was the only board member who voted against him. Dr. Kerr was not impressed with Dr. Landers' credentials, and during the interview he felt that Dr. Landers's answers were disingenuous. While unable to articulate his specific reasoning, Dr. Kerr felt that the young doctor was flippant and uncharacteristically informal while being interviewed. Of course, Dr. Kerr was outnumbered and Luke was promptly awarded hospital privileges. The rest of the board was excited to have a new, young, energetic OB/GYN on staff.

Still, Dr. Kerr distrusted Luke from the minute they met. His dislike grew when Levi was diagnosed with "failure to thrive." Back when Levi was about four months old, Dr. Kerr was making his hospital rounds when he bumped into Luke, also on hospital rounds. Luke arrogantly asked how Dr. Kerr's life was "shaking." When Dr. Kerr tried to redirect the conversation to Levi's medical diagnosis and proposed treatment plan, Luke remarked that Levi was simply a finicky eater and that he'd grow out of it. In Dr. Kerr's opinion, Luke showed absolutely no concern and did not take the diagnosis seriously. In fact, Dr. Kerr recalled Luke saying something about Levi becoming a linebacker for the Bronc's one day.

Dr. Kerr was also bothered by the fact that his nurse babysat for the Landers family. He knew it wasn't any of his business how his nurse spent her evenings or weekends, but Dr. Kerr found it odd nonetheless. Plus, there were a few times that he spotted Janie driving Dr. Landers' Mercedes, which appeared above and beyond her job as a babysitter. When questioned about it, Janie *claimed* that her Subaru wasn't big enough for all the Landers kids. That answer simply didn't hold water, when you considered that the Landers family owned a family car that would have been far better suited for the kids than the Mercedes.

Dr. Kerr knew that he was overly critical of the Landers situation. He didn't think he was jealous of Dr. Landers. Dr. Kerr had a sweet wife and two nice kids–grown now and off living their own lives. He couldn't put a finger on why the hairs on his neck rose every time he had dealings with Luke Landers–but it happened, over and over again.

* * *

Mac hadn't been to an elementary school since she had attended one herself–circa nineteen seventy-something. She parked her car in the drop-off zone and proceeded to the passenger's side to retrieve Luke and walk him into his classroom. No sooner than she'd done this, Mac felt as though she'd been plunged into a war-zone. The crossing guard began running in Mac's direction while yelling at her, "You can't park there! It's a drop-off zone." The principal blew her whistle and yelled something similar, and several moms in their SUVs were honking repeatedly for her to move her car.

Mac motioned for Levi to stay put while she pulled forward and parked in what she prayed was a parking zone. Mac took Levi by the hand and carried his backpack for him. Levi still walked with a limp, and since his stitches wouldn't get removed for four more days, he wouldn't be allowed out during recess. Mac introduced herself to Levi's teacher, Ms. Kendrick, who was a pudgy, cute, youngish woman with long curly hair and square teeth. Ms. Kendrick's face lit up when she saw Levi and warmly welcomed him back. It was Thursday, and he hadn't been at school all week. She told him how the class had missed him and that he would need to stay in at recess to catch up on some of his fourth-grade work.

Mac told Ms. Kendrick about the leg injury and about the foster care problem. The teacher seemed to understand, and Mac considered that perhaps she'd already been informed of these issues. She did not express an opinion, however, but simply offered solutions to Levi's special needs.

"I know Levi pretty well, Ms. MacIntosh," Ms. Kendrick said. "I was also his second grade teacher. I moved up this year to fourth. I have a pretty clear history of his physical and mental health issues."

"I'm sure you know way more than I do," Mac said. "If there's anything you think I should know, please feel free to speak with me." Mac handed her a business card and wrote her cell phone number on the back. "I have to warn you that I might not be very sharing in return. I have to be careful and make sure I don't accidentally waive potentially privileged information, because if I do you'll find yourself getting grilled about that conversation on the stand during a trial. So, if I just listen and don't talk much, don't be offended. I'm just trying to do what's best for Levi."

"I think it is best for Levi to carry on with the routine of life, so I'm very glad to see that you brought him to school. He likes school. He likes the certainty of the daily routine, though that doesn't include recess, which can be chaotic. Levi is happy to stay inside, so today works out just fine that way. In second grade, he used to beg me to stay in, but I forced him outside because I thought that it was imperative for his social growth to experience playground life. Half of what we need to know as far as social skills and negotiation tactics we learn on the elementary school playground. Then we ship them off to high school and they somehow forget it all. Anyway, I'm digressing. My point is that Levi'll be safe here with me during the day. Will you be picking him up?"

"Yes. There is a chance that he'll be placed in a new foster home, but for now, I'm the designated responsible adult."

"I hope they leave him with you," Ms. Kendrick said in a whisper. "Most of the fosters in town just do it for money and don't really care about the kids. But you didn't hear that from me."

"Of course not," Mac said. "The Social Services Agency, in particular, Linda Sterling, might drop by to see how Levi's doing. Otherwise, I'm supposed to remind you that his parents are not allowed unmonitored visits with him while he's at school—at least not for the time being."

"I understand. I'll call SSA if there is a problem, and I'll call you also. I know the drill. Been there, done that."

"I'm sure you do."

"Thursdays are normally the day when Mrs. Landers volunteers in my classroom, so I'll make sure that she doesn't do that today."

"Oh. I wasn't aware of that."

"Her absence won't be noticeable. She hates being here. It is written all over her face."

During the conversation between Mac and Mrs. Kendrick, Levi had been sitting at his desk drawing on a piece of homework paper. Before Mac left, she went over and kneeled beside him. The desk and chair seemed so small to her, and Levi looked bigger sitting in it. He was wearing a pair of new blue jeans and a long-sleeved rugby shirt, thanks to Pamela; Mac's paralegal had gone to the Landers house and retrieved some of the boy's clothing from Ginny. His curly blond hair was clean and neatly combed back off his face, revealing his almond-shaped green eyes.

"Are you okay with me leaving?" Mac asked. "Ms. Kendrick said that she'd take extra good care of you today and that you get to stay inside at recess. You okay with that?"

"She doesn't need to take extra care of me. I can take care of myself."

"Enough with the tough-guy thing, Levi," Mac said. She put her hand on his shoulder and looked him in the eye. He turned his face in the other direction, suddenly taking great interest in the cursive writing cards up on the blackboard. "I know you're ten and I know you're fairly self-sufficient, but people who can take care of themselves don't stab themselves in the leg with kitchen knives. I'm your friend and I care very much about you. I'm doing my best to take care of you. We all need to be taken care of from time to time and it would make it a whole lot easier if you would be nicer to the people who are trying to help you."

Mac patted him on the shoulder again and started to walk toward the door.

"I'll be fine," Levi said.

Mac turned and smiled at him. "I know you're going to be fine. I believe in you." Levi gave her a half-smile back, which to Mac, was like receiving a dozen long-stemmed roses. She walked out of his classroom feeling like a competent parent must feel and it was quite rewarding.

As Mac approached her car she heard a familiar voice call her name. She turned. The face didn't register.

"I'm John Trainor," the man said, holding out his right hand. "Dr. Landers's lawyer."

"Oh. Nice to meet you."

"I see you're taking on the mommy role, walking Levi into class. I have to say that I'm greatly disturbed by the notion that my client can't take his son to school, but you can."

Mac sized up the man standing before her. He was not tall, maybe five-foot-eight, with thinning blond hair, soft brown eyes with strangely long eyelashes that pointed down. He was well dressed, in a black and brown pin- striped suit.

"Did Dr. Landers take Levi to school on a regular basis, Mr. Trainor?" Mac asked.

"That's irrelevant."

"Is it? From what I gather, Dr. Landers has never, or I should say, almost never taken Levi to school. I read the intake sheet from the SSA and Dr. Landers admitted as much." Mac turned her attention away from Luke's attorney, and began to walk towards her own car.

John Trainor tensed his lips and showed his ability to think quickly on his feet. "Dr. Landers supports a wife, four kids and a full-time nanny. He also raises a good deal of money for charitable causes in this town, so his time is quite valuable. Let's not forget that he is at the beck and call of women going into labor, so he does not have a set schedule. That's why his stay-at-home mom has historically taken Levi to school. Since Mrs. Landers is suddenly prohibited from bringing her son to school, which is a travesty in and of itself, then Dr. Landers should be afforded the opportunity." Mr. Trainor had a pained look on his face, and spittle was flying out the edges of his mouth as he continued speaking. "When did our country decide to make up ridiculous laws regarding parents? What kind of country have we become when good parents like the Landers get their kid snatched away and told that they can't even visit him, when if you look around the country, there are thousands of abandoned kids–or kids whose parents are on drugs–or I could go on and on–I mean, what kind of laws are we making? And how in the hell does the SSA have so much power over parents and their kids?"

"Mr. Trainor, I–"

"John. You can call me John."

Mac buttoned her navy suit jacket and folded her arms over her chest. The air was cooling, and Mac could smell that rain was on its way. Without missing a beat, John continued on, his decent human face becoming pinched up and not so decent looking.

"I don't see how the Agency can vest you, or anyone else, with authority to parent the Landers's child. Part of me thinks that you're doing this because you don't have kids of your own and you're lonely. There. I said it. I know that I'm outspoken and I sometimes speak out of turn, but I have to tell you–"

"John, you already shared that opinion with me on the phone, right before I hung up on you." Mac was seriously annoyed by this man, and hoped that her encounters with him would remain minimal throughout her involvement in this case. Unfortunately, she didn't think she stood much of a chance of that happening.

"Then give him back to his parents, for God's sake."

Mac turned away, and hoped that John could read her body language. She was late for a client meeting, and based on her last contact with him she knew there was little chance of this conversation improving. "I can't do that, John. It's not my decision to make, and you know that. Oh wait, I'm sorry, did you know that? See, the way it works, John, is there's a judge in our case, and he's the one who actually makes these types of decisions, not me." Mac was pleased that she took the time to look Luke's attorney up on the state bar website after tucking Levi into bed, because she found out that John had been a transactional real estate attorney for the three years that he'd been practicing law.

Mac hoped that her derisive tone might have shut John up, but he had a dagger for her in response.

"Maybe you should start watching your back, Ms. MacIntosh. Dr. Landers knows where you live."

"Is that a threat, *John*?"

Chapter 11

"Perphenazine is a highly potent neuroleptic agent used for the treatment of psychotic patients, particularly those with schizophrenia, but also for patients presenting with manic phases of bipolar disorder."

After Mac's client meeting, she opened the box of documents on her office couch and began to read Levi's medical history. She received a portion of the documents on Tuesday, and began processing as many documents as possible in reverse chronology. Initially she had intended to begin her review starting with Levi's birth, but given the voluminous nature of the documents she decided that might not be the most appropriate use of her time. Mac kept looking for any indicia of what the final straw was for Social Services while reviewing the multiple medical documents. Surely they had been suspicious before they took action; what ultimately pushed Linda Sterling towards filing a petition?

Mac almost immediately had her answer, and that was Perphenazine. When Levi's blood test showed a presence of this drug, the Agency finally was forced to step into the picture. It wasn't actually the fact that Levi had the antipsychotic medication in his bloodstream that caused concern, because the boy had been prescribed Risperdal about six months earlier when he was diagnosed with "Oppositional Defiant Disorder and Childhood Antisocial Behavior Disorder." What caused Social Services to take a look at Levi's condition was the fact that Evelyn Landers had been issued a prescription for Perphenazine the spring prior–before Levi had been diagnosed with anything.

* * *

Evelyn flipped on her treadmill and hopped on the track, increasing the speed until she found herself at a fast jog. As Evelyn was jogging she began to wonder on the life she'd given up by dropping out of medical school. Would she have been happy? Would she have still married and had kids? If Evelyn would have married in that case, she was confident that she wouldn't have chosen to do so with Luke. If she had chosen her career before Luke's, she was pretty sure she would have been in an entirely different situation than she was now. Evelyn began to daydream about the man she would have married in that scenario and how nice and humble he would be. Evelyn clearly pictured her smart family and smart kids, who would have lacked in athletics but made up for it with love and respect.

Evelyn increased the speed of her jog, as she realized how much she envied the life she'd given up. Jogging helped her forget, and that's what she needed more than anything else at the moment. Soon, Evelyn wasn't able to distinguish between the good sweat she'd worked up and the salty tears that were flowing.

Since Levi's court hearing, Evelyn had plenty of "friends" calling, but none of the calls seemed to be made out of genuine support or concern. Evelyn knew the motivation for these calls was simply to get new material to gossip about. For some reason, Evelyn found herself not able to shake one call in particular from her head, though upon reflection there wasn't really anything unique or noteworthy about it. The call was from an acquaintance of hers that she knew only from their work together on a local Animal Shelter Board, which is possibly the reason she found it so unusual.

"Oh, Evelyn," Clara Evans had breathlessly said, "I had no idea that you were bipolar–you hide it so well. Rest assured that I feel the same way about you regardless. My brother is bipolar and he's normal eighty percent of the time. When he has an episode, we all know how to deal with it–assuming that he's properly taking his prescribed medications. Feel free to utilize me the next time you have an episode, because I have valuable experience dealing with it."

Evelyn certainly was taken aback from the woman's boldness for she didn't really know the woman all that well. She considered herself an emotionally stable woman, excluding a mild bout of depression she'd had following her last pregnancy. The "baby blues" were well known these days, and women were no longer embarrassed to share the fact that they had succumbed to the condition. Evelyn was surprised when she got the baby blues following Levi's birth, but only because she hadn't had it during any of her other pregnancies. She suspected that the stress in her relationship with Luke made her more susceptible, as she was confident that she wouldn't have developed the temporary depression based on either factor alone. Luke suggested she give Paxil a try.

After years of taking it, Evelyn thought of Paxil as more of a vitamin, given that it just helped her adjust to the new bite life seemed to take following Levi's birth. Paxil worked slowly and imperceptibly, easing her anxiety, and she noticed the cloud of depression lifting from off of her shoulders. Ultimately, Evelyn forgot how awful she'd truly felt before Paxil, and decided after a few years on the drug that she no longer needed the stuff. It wasn't until then that Evelyn was able to actually witness how well the drug had been working, because unlike when she started, the effects of eliminating the drug from her system produced an immediate response—the anxiety immediately came rushing back. Therefore, she continued taking the drug on a regular basis, and today was no exception. She'd already taken one to help her get out of bed, and another about an hour later. She wanted to take a third, but knew she was unable to as she'd already taken two and it wasn't quite noon yet. Dammit, she thought, realizing how unusually low she felt.

Her mood certainly hadn't been helped by the most recent phone call she'd received from another of her "friends." For some reason, one of Levi's classmate's mothers felt an urgent need to share with Evelyn that Levi had been dropped off by Ms. MacIntosh this morning. The thought of her son holding onto that woman's hand as they entered the building, looking at her with his young and innocent eyes as they walked in to meet the teacher, ripped Ev's heart right out of her chest.

Evelyn's chest was tight with memories of her children, and how her life with Luke changed once they came along. When she and Luke were first married, she had no qualms accompanying him on his many business trips, and actually enjoyed the opportunity to get out of the house and spend quality time with her husband. That all changed once the kids came along. They'd only taken one vacation since the first three kids were born, and it was a five- day trip to Acapulco that she'd totally despised. Being away from Austen, Ben and Lauren ended up causing her more stress than she could have anticipated, and she realized that the stress from her busiest day as a stay-at- home mom paled in comparison to the stress she suffered from worrying about their safety when she was away. Since then, she's not had a private vacation with Luke.

Luke continued taking his trips out of state, and Evelyn realized that their marriage suffered as a result. Luke's business trips frequently took him to a romantic vacation destination, and Luke used to request Evelyn's attendance by his side. After Evelyn declined more than a few times, Luke no longer bothered with an invitation. While Luke would attend his luxurious business trips, Evelyn was left at home with their four kids—one of whom required extremely high maintenance. Evelyn had become to hate Luke's return from his business trips, because he was always glowing. Evelyn found it grating, because she was undoubtedly harried from frequent carpool runs or Levi's frequent medical visits.

There had come a time when Evelyn decided a trip with Luke would help her marriage more than her absence from home would hurt the kids. Levi was about five years old at the time, and he'd just gone for several months without any medical issues. Evelyn was excited over Levi's progress, which made her start to feel warmer and fuzzier than she had in a while. When Luke had a business trip during that time frame, Evelyn was ecstatic. She wanted to go with Luke, and work on their relationship. Evelyn thought Luke would be happy to hear his wife consider attending with him, as it'd been many years. She was devastated when Luke ended up talking her out of going, insistent in his desire that she remain at home. Luke claimed that he would have personally loved her to accompany him, but that he was worried that leaving Levi home all alone would be too risky, should he experience an emergency. Evelyn couldn't believe it, and immediately began to suspect that Luke was having an affair. There was simply no explanation that made any sense to Evelyn, given Luke's otherwise lackluster view on Levi's medical needs.

Evelyn was disappointed when Luke's recommendation proved correct and an emergency requiring her presence did occur, though it didn't involve Levi. While Luke was on that particular trip, Ben was seriously injured at school. Evelyn was called to the school to take Ben to the emergency room, and several x-rays were taken of his spleen. On their ride home from the hospital, Evelyn called Luke in the Bahamas to update him on Ben's condition. Evelyn was fully prepared to give Luke praise for what ended up being a good decision on his part, but was not expecting for a woman to answer his hotel room phone. Evelyn was so shocked to hear another woman's voice answer the call, that she was left speechless and ultimately hung up without having said a word.

Because this all happened in the days before caller I.D., Evelyn assumed Luke was none the wiser as to her call. Nevertheless, Evelyn made sure to fill Luke in on that call as soon as he came home. Luke denied an affair, and adamantly denied having any women in his room throughout the entire trip. At the end of the confrontation, Evelyn ended up on the defensive as Luke accused her of being both jealous and paranoid.

When Luke's next medical convention came around six months later, Evelyn had the foresight to book herself on the same flight to Mazatlan as Luke. Evelyn was sly about her plans, and did not let Luke know that she would be with him until the last minute. As soon as Luke found out that Evelyn would actually be accompanying him, he found some bogus excuse to cancel the trip. After Luke cancelled that trip, Evelyn briefly considered the "d" word. Ultimately, Evelyn decided not to follow through with a divorce, because she couldn't imagine another woman being involved in raising her kids. In Evelyn's mind, staying in an unhappy and difficult marriage was the better choice when considering the consequences. Over time, Evelyn's viewpoint varied on the subject, especially when her suspicions grew. Evelyn was certain that Luke was having an affair and finally consulted with a family law attorney to consider all of her options.

Evelyn wasn't pleased with what the attorney explained to her, as custody, support and visitation were far more complicated than she could have imagined. Evelyn left the attorney's office in tears and, of course, needed an extra dose of Paxil that day.

Paxil was such a blessing, Evelyn thought. The friendly little pill proved to be such a help in so many different parts of her life, and Evelyn had learned to depend on it. For instance, her tiny-little-friend was always there for her when Levi began suffering through another one of his outbursts. Paxil never let her down.

Evelyn remembered the first incident with Levi following the cancelled trip, and sighed with pain as she envisioned it. In the middle of that winter's holiday performance by the kindergartners, Levi got angry at a little girl for standing too close to him and clapping too loudly in his ears. Levi pushed the girl down from the bleachers, forcing her into three other children on the way down. Since then, Levi's aggressive behavior seemed to increase, and each time the behaviors escalated. It was around that time that Luke offered Evelyn a doubling of her dose of Paxil, and she hungrily accepted.

Evelyn sighed as she reflected on the fact that society continued to treat women differently from men. So long as a man was successful, he could pretty much get by with anything. He could have affairs or be a crummy father who never attended any of his kids' events, but society would overlook it due to his success in the business world. Many rationalized that the behavior was simply a result of hard work, and the man's nose being pressed too firmly to the grindstone. Affairs were accepted as the obvious consequence to this, considering the wife too busy with the kids when the man's needs ultimately arose.

Women were never granted the same latitude, even successful, working women. In fact, it seems that when women put their career first in life, they immediately become designated a neglectful mother. *"Why does so- and-so even have children? The nanny raises them and they are brats. What's the point?"* Evelyn heard this type of conversation many times while attending bible study or volunteering with the Women's League. Women were judged on an entirely different playing field. If a woman had an affair because her husband beat her or treated her with disdain, the woman was forever labeled the "Hester Prynne."

Affairs in general were treated so differently when considering the sex of the offending party, Evelyn thought. A man who cheated on his wife was still treated the same among men within the community. Guys would approach the adulterer male and talk sports and kids and business as if nothing was going on. They would not discuss affairs or gossip or cheating. It was just business as usual.

And this was the case with Luke. Luke could show up at any event and the men would congregate around him to talk shop or baseball or whatever they shared in common. There was no judgment or ridicule. Boys will be boys.

This type of attitude made Evelyn crazy. If she were to cheat on Luke, Evelyn knew damned well that the women in town would ridicule her for splitting up the family. Evelyn sighed, as life simply was unwilling to cut her a break.

Evelyn would have thought that her selfless behavior of putting Luke through medical school would have earned her some respect from her husband and the community. All she really wanted was to have a happy, healthy, normal family–didn't sacrificing her career on so many different levels at least get her that? She easily could have allowed nannies to raise her four children as she returned to finish her medical career, and then proceed to work long hours in the field, if that were what she wanted. But that's not what she wanted. Or was it? Upon reflection, maybe deep down she was quite jealous of her husband's successful medical practice.

* * *

Mac had no idea what the protocol was for picking up kids from elementary school, but she was pretty sure that she would end up violating whatever it was, given her morning experience dropping Levi off. She knew she needed to pick up Levi by three twenty, do a bit of homework, give him a snack, and then rush him to his soccer practice at the YMCA by four. Mac decided to follow the lead of the mothers ahead of her as she entered the pick-up zone, and spotted Levi sitting on the grass in front of the school. Levi's head was in his hands, and he seemed oblivious to the honks that were coming from Mac's car. Mac pulled forward to get out of the pick-up zone, knowing full well that had she parked where she was, she'd quickly get devoured by the arriving mothers behind her, and she knew she needed to go to Levi.

"How's my star soccer player? Ready to go to practice?" Levi did not look up.

"How was your day? Do you have homework?"

Still no response.

Mac finally grabbed Levi's backpack and tried pulled him up by the hand. He tried to pull back but she didn't release her grip.

"My day sucked," Levi said.

"So did mine." Mac responded, fully aware that Levi was testing her patience by using an obviously prohibited word. At least it was better than "crap," Mac thought. "I feel like I didn't accomplish anything today, and so overall my day sucked, too. I know that if I get up and exercise when I feel this way that I'll usually start to feel better. Why don't we go to the Y so you can kick a soccer ball really hard, and I can see if I can scrounge up a pick-up game of basketball? Then, we've got a shot of walking out of there in better moods. Shall we?"

Levi was not used to being the center of attention for his dour mood. He got plenty of attention when he was sick and he got more attention than he wanted from his evil brother Ben, but he was not used to someone understanding what it was like to have a crappy day and to offer a solution that might work. Mac drove them both to the YMCA, and made sure to pay close attention to Levi when he played in the soccer game. Mac cheered for Levi, and threw out comments indicating that she was paying attention to his game. When practice was over, she had him do his homework while she played in an intramural basketball game.

Mac was a good shot. Levi liked that about her. And she wasn't a sissy about taking an elbow or throwing one from time to time. Every now and then she made eye contact with Levi and mouthed "watch this" as she maneuvered around the poiont guard and made a lay-up. Levi caught himself smiling. So did Mac.

By the time the two of them finally arrived at Mac's apartment, they were starving. Mac loved to cook, but was unsure as to what a ten-year-old would eat. She made something simple–pasta with a marinara sauce, French bread, a salad, and milk. Mac decided that her dinner choice was appropriate, given that Levi ate everything on his plate.

After homework and a shower, Mac offered to read Levi a bedtime novel. Mac suggested that she read to him the book called *Hatchet.*

"I'm a big kid. Grown-ups don't read to big kids. They read to babies."

"That's not true, Levi" Mac responded. "Sometimes adults like to be read to because it can be so calming and enjoyable. A lot of adults buy books on tape just so they can hear the soothing voice of someone reading to them. Let me at least try and give that to you. I'll start off reading the book, and if you get sick of me reading to you, you can finish the book by reading it yourself or reading it back to me. What do you say?" Levi grumbled, but agreed.

The story started with a boy named Brian whose parents had recently divorced. Brian was flying alone with only a pilot in a single-engine plane from New York into the Northeastern wilderness to visit his father, who had moved there after the divorce. The pilot had a heart attack in the middle of the flight, and the plane crashed into a mountain lake. Brian survived the crash, but he was young–not much older than Levi–and he would have to survive a winter in the wilderness alone if he'd hoped to be rescued. All he had with him was a hatchet, which had been a gift from his mother.

Levi ended up loving the story, and begged Mac to read more. He kept listening intently until well over an hour past his bed time. Finally, Levi fell asleep during the part when a moose was attacking Brian. She tucked him in, gave him a kiss on the forehead, and settled herself on the couch.

Mac booted into her email and checked messages. She was glad to see that she had a few messages waiting for her from her boyfriend, Jeffery. She read them and then responded, filling him in on what had transpired with Levi. After logging out, she flipped the overhead lamp off and closed her eyes.

* * *

In the middle of the night, Mac felt a soft tap on her shoulder, which caused her to awaken with a start. Mac was greeted to the image of Levi standing over her, with tears running down his pale cheeks. Mac flipped on the floor lamp and motioned for him to sit next to her on the couch. She wrapped her blanket around his shoulders and asked him what was wrong.

"He came to visit me again in my sleep," Levi said.

"Who came to visit you?" Mac asked, pulling Levi close to her and wiping the tears from his face.

"The Baseball Man."

"Who is the Baseball Man?"

"He comes and talks to me when I sleep."

"You have a dream about a Baseball Man sometimes?" Mac asked. Levi nodded. "What does he talk with you about? Baseball?"

Levi sniffled as he nodded. "He shows me baseball cards."

"Oh. Do you like baseball cards?"

"Yeah. I collect them. I have a shoebox full of them in my room at home. It's under my bed. I hide it so Ben can't steal my favorite ones."

"What cards are your favorites?"

"Willie Mays. I have the 1979 Cooperstown Collection card. He was the National League Rookie of the Year in 1951 and the MVP in 1954 an 1965."

"Wow. You know a lot about baseball."

"Yeah. My favorite team is the Giants. I have a Willie McCovey and lots of Barry Bonds." Levi answered with a bit more energy, apparently getting distracted from the source of their current conversation.

"Are they some of your favorites too?" Mac asked, still waking up. She glanced at the clock in the kitchen: it read two-forty-three.

"Yeah. I have Lou Gehrig and Mickey Mantle and Babe Ruth and Hank Aaron too."

"Maybe you can show them to me sometime," Mac said. "But how about we both try and go back to sleep for the time being? It's still the middle of the night and you have school in the morning."

Mac watched the moon set in Levi's eyes. She knew immediately that she'd made a mistake. This was the first time that Levi wanted to talk with her—really share with her—and she was shutting him down because of the time. Mac internally kicked herself, and hoped that she'd be able to smooth over her dimwittedness. Perhaps she'd be able to revive their conversation.

Mac smiled and stood up. "Do you want to go by your house tomorrow after school and get your baseball cards? We could look through them together over the weekend. I would enjoy learning more about your favorite teams."

Levi didn't respond, and Mac feared that she'd shut him up for good with her selfish desire to sleep. Mac didn't give up, though she felt that the end result had already been determined.

"My favorite team when I was a little girl was the Cincinnati Reds. Back then, Colorado didn't have a professional baseball team. Once we got the Rockies, they quickly replaced the Reds as my favorite team. Have you ever been to a professional baseball game?"

Levi didn't speak or acknowledge her. She'd lost him. She gently took him by the hand and walked him back to her bedroom. After tucking him back into bed she gave their conversation one last attempt. "Levi, who is the Baseball Man?"

Levi shifted his eyes to the right and left, as if he were looking for an actual person within their room. Mac tried to follow the young boy's gaze, but as she'd expected she didn't see anything out of the ordinary within her room.

"Do you see him when you're awake?"

"No." Levi softly responded, as if he were debating whether to answer Mac at all.

"You only see him when you sleep?" Mac gently followed up, in the hopes that she'd be able to revive the teeny spark that had just been offered her by the young boy.

"Uh-huh."

"Does he do anything other than show you baseball cards?"

"Yeah. Sometimes he teaches me things."

"About baseball?"

"He shows me how to run the bases and stuff."

"I bet you're a good player. I want to come and watch you play when the season starts back up. Would that be okay with you?" Levi shook his head, a slight smile reappearing. "Maybe we should get your glove and a few balls from your house tomorrow, too. We could go to a park after school and play catch. I have to warn you though that my throwing arm isn't what it used to be. You might have to give me some pointers."

"It's okay. Some girls can't throw balls." Levi chuckled with the comment, before adding, "Don't worry, I won't tease you. I'll teach you."

Mac smiled and then leaned over to ruffle Levi's hair. "Go back to sleep and dream about baseball. I'll wake you up for breakfast, okay?"

"Okay."

Mac clicked the light off as she left Levi alone in her room. She lay awake on the couch for the next hour wondering about the Baseball Man, who he was, and what he subconsciously signified to the young boy. Levi had a forensic psychological evaluation before the detention hearing, but she hadn't read anything about a Baseball Man in the report. She wondered whether the psychologist addressed the dream issue in his report, or whether Levi even shared it during the evaluation. She made a mental note to review the results of the evaluation a bit more closely after she dropped Levi at school.

When Mac finally resigned herself to follow up with Levi about the topic, she began to finally feel sleep to return to her. Just as she'd started to slowly drift off, she was again awaken with a start. This time, however, it wasn't from a simple hand on her shoulder.

Chapter 12

Austen Landers walked down the hall with a confident gait and his head held high, reveling in his recent nomination for Homecoming King. Austen smiled as he recalled passing his high school's marquis just moments before, casually perusing the postings when he spotted his official nomination. He smiled broadly, thinking how great his life was–and he was only four weeks into his senior year! He was starting quarterback, scouts were eyeing him for college, he had more friends than he knew what to do with, and his girlfriend was one of the most desired girls in their school. Austen grinned mischievously as he thought of the only thing possibly better than his recent nomination, and that was the secret his girlfriend had recently shared with him: she was ready to have sex. He practically laughed out loud with glee. No one denies Homecoming King on Homecoming night!

Life simply couldn't be any better for Austen, that is, if you ignored the fact that his little brother was in a foster home and his parents fought like crazy.

Austen sat in his physics class and watched his teacher write a complex formula on the blackboard. He began copying the formula down, but his mind had become focused on thoughts of Levi. Austen's baby brother was truly a mystery to him. Let there be no misunderstanding, Levi loved the little guy, but he just couldn't understand what was wrong with him. For that matter, he couldn't figure out what there was about Levi that caused their parents to fight over him so much.

Austen's mind lifted from the momentarily bleak thoughts, and he began thinking of how fun it was to be around Levi when he wasn't sick. Austen loved to throw the baseball as high as he could in the air and watch

Levi focus in on it and catch it. The smile on Levi's face when he caught the ball was so darned endearing that Austen couldn't help feeling a little twinge in his heart.

Levi was a bright little kid, too, Austen thought with pride. The little guy had a rolodex memory when it came to baseball trivia, and Austen loved to stat-quiz him on his favorite players. Levi was so good, in fact, that sometimes Austen felt that his detailed questions weren't even challenging to his baby brother. He remembered when he asked Levi what he thought was a tough question, what year Mickey Mantel was inducted into the Baseball Hall of Fame. Levi didn't pause for one second before he accurately responded, "1974," immediately followed by a smile and a request for another stat-quiz question. It was quite obvious to anyone observing the two interact in this little game that Levi adored his oldest brother and loved every second shared with him.

That was definitely not the case with Ben, though, Austen thought dryly. At least Ben was smart enough to know not to pick on Levi when Austen was around. Austen would not tolerate bullying in the Landers house, regardless of whom it involved. Whenever Austen saw his siblings bickering, he'd go out of his way to put a stop to it. Even though his patriarchal influence amongst the kids was well known, it had little influence on Ben. Austen let out a slow sigh as he thought of how hard Ben could be on Levi, regardless of Austen's presence. There were countless times requiring Austen's intervention in defense of Levi, but that didn't seem to deter his bully of a younger brother.

"Mr. Landers, care to share your answer to the equation with the rest of the class?"

Austen snapped out of his reverie and back to his physics class. Unfortunately, by this point everyone in Austen's class had their eyes intently focused on him. "I'm sorry, Mr. Donohue. I was thinking about something else."

"I assumed you were finished, since you weren't writing anymore."

"No, sir, I'm not. I'm sorry, sir."

Austen put himself to work on his assignment, and tried to force the thoughts of his inner family dynamics to the back of his mind. While Austen diligently began to attack the physics assignment in front of him, though, he couldn't entirely ease the nagging worries in the back of his mind. After all, his youngest brother was being brought to school by a complete stranger lately, and that was not easily forgotten. Austen tried to qualm his uneasiness by thinking of Levi's likely return. He realized that there was only one week left before Homecoming , and that there was a good chance that Levi would be home by then. Austen thought of how nice that would be, celebrating two homecomings at once. That would be perfect. No, Austen grinned, topping off the two homecomings with his girlfriend's acquiescence would be perfect.

* * *

Mac rushed to her bedroom while rubbing sleepily at her eyes. As soon as Mac entered the room and saw him standing on her bed, it was clear that her quick response was warranted. Levi's eyes were wide open and he had a frightened expression on his face, but he was standing at attention focusing all of his energy directly on Mac's closet door. She cautiously approached him, gently calling out his name. Levi's eyes didn't move and his body didn't flinch, as he remained completely fixated on the closet in front of him.

"What's wrong, Levi? What are you looking at?" Mac asked.

After what felt like an eternity to Mac, Levi finally responded in a slow and monotonous voice. "He's back," Levi said.

Mac continued to wipe at her eyes as she slowly began to approach Levi. "I'm sorry, honey, who do you mean is back? Do you mean the Baseball Man?"

"Uh-huh."

Mac looked at Levi and followed his stare. "Is he in the closet?" Mac asked him, as she began to follow his gaze towards the closed closet door. When Mac got no response from him, she decided to slowly begin approaching the closet. After passing her queen-sized bed and then her medium sized dresser, Mac found herself hesitating in front of her closet. Mac brushed her uneasiness aside, realizing that Levi's fear was irrational and reassuring herself that no one was insider her bedroom closet. When she looked up at Levi, she saw that he hadn't moved an inch and his eyes remained fixed.

"Should I open the door to make sure that there's no one in here? Would that be okay with you?"

Levi finally took his gaze from Mac's closet. "He's gone now," Levi responded while shaking his head no.

"Are you sure? I can check to see."

"No! He's gone! I told you he's gone. He is, he is, he is, he is." Levi had gone from zero to sixty in under five seconds, as he was now jumping up and down on the bed and yelling at Mac in what can only be described as a fury. What do I do now? Mac thought to herself. Is this what the Social Worker meant when warning her about biting off more than she could chew? After a brief pause, Mac decided to get onto the bed with Levi, and hold onto him tightly. As Mac put her arms around the little guy, she grabbed onto him and tried to restrict what she assumed was a tantrum. He kept jumping, but Mac didn't let go. Levi eventually began to jerk back from her in a way that she assumed was him awakening from the trance-like state. After a minute, he jerked back from her and he seemed surprised to see her standing on the bed with him. He stopped jumping.

Mac loosened her grip on him and looked into his eyes. "Are you okay, Levi? Did you have another bad dream?" Levi looked quizzically at her, as if he didn't understand.

"I'm so tired," Levi whined, as if he had suddenly been awakened from a slumber by Mac herself. "Why can't you just let me sleep in peace?"

Mac crawled off the bed as silently as she could, and watched Levi slip back underneath her comforter and close his eyes. Within a minute, his breathing became deep and rhythmic, and there was little doubt that he had fallen fast asleep. Mac was curious at Levi's reaction, and his ability to resume sleeping as though nothing had happened. Mac couldn't help but think of how bizarre this kid was, so sweet and adorable in one minute, and practically possessed in the next.

A stream of thoughts rushed into Mac's mind, and she was nearly overwhelmed by their sudden approach. Why am I representing Levi? Am I the best person suited for this case? Am I even capable of handling this case? Do all juvenile cases require this much energy and personal attention? What do I do next? Mac shook her head firmly back and forth, trying to shake the worry from her mind. It was too late for her to worry about these types of questions now, as she had found herself firmly in the midst of Levi's family battle.

After easing her mind somewhat from her worries, Mac quietly walked over to her closet and slowly pulled the door open. The closet was its usual mess, which made Mac think about the task of cleaning it up that undoubtedly faced her. She pushed the thought of tidying it up to the back of her mind, and summarily glanced over each item in her closet. Too many sweaters and jeans on the shelves? Check. Row upon row of business clothes tightly lined up on the hanging rod? Check. Mac sighed as she closed the junky closet, which was exactly as cluttered as she'd left it. Other than the fact that her closet was too small, Mac didn't find anything wrong with the image that greeted her from inside her closet. Certainly, the Baseball Man was not lurking about in there.

Mac closed the closet door as she began to ease herself out of her bedroom. Just as Mac thought that she had successfully exited without stirring Levi, she began to hear some sounds coming from the lump tucked into her bed sheets. Mac turned, disappointed to see that she had awoken him.

"Harm. Kill. You."

"Levi? Was that you? Did I wake you?"

"Harm. Kill. You."

Mac couldn't be certain, but was pretty confident that he said "Harm Kill You." She walked closer to the bed and reached out for Levi's hand. "Levi, wake up." Levi jerked her hand away and repeated the ominous phrase several times, before Mac was successful in awakening him. When

Levi looked confused and startled at her standing in front of him, Mac felt a gentle explanation was in order.

"You were talking in your sleep again, honey. Were you having another bad dream?"

Levi shook his head 'no.'

"I thought I heard you say 'Harm Kill You.' Is that possible? Do you remember that? Do you think you were dreaming that someone was trying to hurt you?" Mac asked.

Levi looked at Mac with a furrowed brow, and Mac thought that he might drift off to sleep again. Eventually, Levi returned Mac's gaze and appeared to be more cognizant of his surroundings. "The Baseball Man," Levi said slowly. "The Baseball Man came back and wanted me to meet Harmon Killebrew." Levi turned his body towards Mac as his voice became more firm and his words came out more quickly. "I remember Harmon was on first base and I had to go to him there, but I couldn't get there in time. The Baseball Man was angry because I was too slow."

"Who is Harmon Killebrew?" Mac asked.

Levi let out a huge sigh. "Duh - only the most famous first baseman for the Twins. He was a home run leader with Reggie Jackson and Frank Howard in 1969." The thought of who Harmon Killebrew was seemed to have lifted Levi out of his gloomy dream, as he seemed to perk up a tiny bit while he was explaining this to Mac.

"Oh. I didn't know that." Mac responded, pleased to see Levi react a bit more calmly. "See, we need to get your baseball cards so that you can teach this sort of stuff to me."

"He left me a card on first base before he left."

"Harmon Killebrew left you one of his baseball cards in your dream?" Mac asked.

"Yeah, but not the one with his stats on it, the one with his picture in his light blue Twins uniform. He's swinging his bat, but there's no stats on the back."

"I see. Well, dreams can be like that," Mac said, as she pulled the covers back up to his chin. "I'm glad you're okay and just having vivid dreams. Get back to sleep. I'll be out in the living room if you need me."

"Wait," Levi called as Mac had turned her back towards him. "I didn't get to tell you what was on the back of the card!" Levi called.

Mac turned around, curious.

"Harmon's card had a message for you on the back."

"For me? What do you mean?" Mac asked, feeling a strange tingling down the back of her neck.

"There was a note written to you on the back. It told you to go check on my mommy. She's sick."

"Oh. That's a strange message for a first baseman to put on his baseball card." Mac was relieved to hear the message for her in Levi's dream was as benign as it was, considering the awful possibilities that ran through her mind in the moments since Levi mentioned it to her in the first place.

"Will you call my mom?" Levi asked, his attention fully turned to Mac and the worry in his voice came through loud and clear. "Please? I want to make sure that she's not sick."

"Okay, honey. We'll call her first thing in the morning."

"Now, we have to call her now!" Levi whined loudly.

It's very late, honey. I promise we'll call in the morning, but it's too late to call anyone right now."

"Please call. *Pleeaassee*. I'm scared she's sick. I know she's sick." Levi needled her further.

"No, Levi, I told you it's too late." Mac stood firmly as she told Levi again how late it was.

"I know she's sick! I know it! She needs me to call."

Mac saw the nervousness in the young boy increase, and thought she could calm him somewhat by referring to logic.

"How could you possibly know your mom is sick? She was fine when I saw her last, and that was just a few hours ago."

"The messages on the cards are always right."

Mac snapped to attention, immediately forgetting about logic and reason.

"What do you mean that the messages on the cards are always right? Have you had these dreams before?"

* * *

Luke Landers was not a happy man. It was the second night in a row that his wife had locked him out of his master bedroom, and this time it came after a mere suggestion that she take a double dose of her medicine Friday morning. Evelyn went berserk, claiming that he was trying to make her sick like he'd done to Levi.

"How dare you suggest that I've made Levi sick," Luke yelled through the bedroom door. It was three-thirty in the morning and the fight ensued. "You're the one who constantly hauls that poor kid to the doctor. Half the time I don't have a clue why you even think he's sick. I'm half inclined to think that maybe the social services agency is on to something. Maybe it is you that's made that kid sick."

As Evelyn opened the door and was about to unload on Luke for making such a rude, cruel statement, the phone rang. Both Evelyn and Luke turned towards the phone at the same time, and it felt as though time had temporarily stopped. Luke didn't hesitate, though, as he was used to middle- of-the-night phone calls, given his line of work. Normally, the hospital paged him, but there were occasions when his pager didn't sound and a follow up phone call was required.

"Dr. Landers, I'm so sorry to bother you so late. This is Mary MacIntosh."

"Is Levi sick?" Luke immediately asked, causing Evelyn's eyes to widen in fear.

"N-n-no, *he's* not sick, but he is convinced that his mom is. Would you mind putting Mrs. Landers on the phone so that Levi can hear for himself that she's okay? I don't think he'll be able to go back to sleep until he knows she's alright."

The worry that Mac thought she'd heard in Luke's voice just moments before were gone, and a loud sigh reverberated through the phone lines.

"You don't need to have children of your own to be able to recognize when you're getting manipulated by one." Luke continued. "Levi is just manipulating you so he can stay up late. He does it all the time."

"Dr. Landers, I know you know him better than I do," Mac said, "and I know that kids sometimes stall bedtime, but Levi was asleep before this all happened. Levi awoke from a bad dream and he really needs to hear his mom's voice. That's all. I'm fairly certain that once he hears that she's fine, he'll go back to sleep. He's overly tired from a stressful week; please just let him speak with her for a moment."

There was a long pause on Luke's end of the line.

"Dr. Landers?"

"I'll have to call you back," he said and then he hung up.

Levi was standing next to Mac when she placed the call. When Dr. Landers hung up on Mac without Levi hearing on his own that Evelyn was alright, Mac was burdened with figuring out an appropriate explanation to give the overly worried boy.

"She's going to call you right back," Mac promised, hoping that Levi's parents wouldn't make her into a liar.

"She's sick, isn't she? My dad told you that she was sick and couldn't talk right now and he'd call back."

"No," Mac said, beginning to question herself whether this had happened before. "Your dad was in the middle of something and said he'd call right back."

"He's in the middle of a fight with my mom. And she's sick. And he won't call back."

"Don't speak about your parents like that, Levi." "But I know that's what's happening," Levi urged.

Mac was almost afraid to ask, but she was unable to hold the question back. "What makes you think you know for a fact, Levi" Mac asked.

"Because Harmon Killebrew told me."

The only thing that freaked Mac out more than Levi's comment was when it was proven true. Levi was right. Luke didn't call back.

* * *

Luke had solid reasoning for his failure to return her urgent call. Luke intentionally lied to Evelyn, telling her that he was mistaken when he mentioned Levi's name earlier. Luke told her it was just a wrong number, and that he had wrongly jumped to the worried conclusion that it was Levi calling. He was shocked that Evelyn believed him, because his explanation didn't make much sense given his reaction and subsequent explanation to Mac over the phone. Regardless, he was relieved that she was easily convinced that it was a wrong number. Luke was afraid if she knew it was Levi on the other end that it would make her crazier and she would once again blame him for the fact that her baby was somewhere else—not home in his own bed where she could comfort him.

* * *

Weekends in Sheridan were usually working weekends for Mac, unless Jeffrey was in town visiting her. Sometimes they met in other cities if his FBI work brought him elsewhere, but it mainly was in Mac's hometown. If she didn't spend her weekend with Jeffrey, her normal routine was to sleep in until seven or so, go out for a nice, long, leisurely run, and then go to the office for a few hours of quiet catch-up. On Saturdays, the phone didn't ring and her staff didn't interrupt, and Mac could get through a stack of paperwork in a few hours.

It was still too early on Saturday morning, however, and Mac was being awoken this time by a poke to her arm. She had fallen asleep on her bed at some point while awaiting Evelyn's call, but she could not recollect how late she had stayed up waiting with Levi. Regardless, Mac was reminded of the situation at hand by Levi throwing one hell of a fit in the middle of her living room. Mac had to physically restrain him by pulling him into a bear hug to prevent him from breaking the framed photographs that lined the shelves of her armoire. Once she'd settled him down, she sat next to him on the edge of the bed and distracted him with stories from her childhood. During the course of these stories, she curled up on top of the bedspread, and eventually drifted off.

All too quickly, Mac was again awoken with a start, but this time it was from poking on her left arm. While Mac had expected that Levi fell back to sleep along with her, she came to realize that he'd been up watching cartoons for hours. He hadn't slept at all.

"I'm hungry," Levi said. "I get doughnuts on Saturday."

"You do?" Mac said, calculating how strong she would have to brew her coffee in order to survive the morning. "Well, then, let's let Miss Mac make herself some strong coffee and I'll take you on a doughnut run. How's that sound?"

"Okay. Can my mom come?"

"Oh. Well, that's an idea," Mac started, "but I would need to check with the social worker. I'll call and see if we can get some doughnuts and take them to a park or something and meet your mom there."

"My mom doesn't like doughnuts."

"Maybe we can bring her a croissant or a muffin."

"My mom doesn't eat that stuff. Let's just see if she can come."

Mac looked at Levi's blond tussled hair and sleepy green eyes. He could use a few doughnuts. He was still wearing his pajamas and Mac could see his collarbone through the fabric. She grabbed some sweatpants and a sweatshirt and dressed in the bathroom. She set out clothes for Levi and when he was in the bathroom, she brewed her coffee and made a few calls.

Chapter 13

"The kid is still with you?" Jeffrey Plattenburg asked in a tone that was clearly not sympathetic. "You can't keep a ten-year-old kid in a one-bedroom apartment forever. When is he going back to his family?"

"Like I told you the other day, he can't go back to his family until his dependency trial is concluded, and right now there simply aren't any foster families in town that will take him." Mac defensively added, "He's . . . well, he's a challenging child."

"You don't know how to handle kids, let alone challenging ones. Why is he with *you*?"

Mac was offended by Jeffrey's suggestion that she couldn't handle the situation. "I'm doing my best. We're doing okay, actually."

"How does this affect next weekend? Are you still coming to DC?"

"Oh. I forgot," Mac said, and kicked herself as soon as she said it; this was an event that shouldn't have been easily forgotten. She was supposed to fly on a red-eye next Thursday to attend a gala thrown by the FBI in his honor for his solving a serial killer case. "I'm not sure I can make it now."

"Because of the kid?" Jeffrey incredulously asked, again not even trying to mask his annoyance.

Jeffrey had made it very clear at the beginning of their relationship that he didn't want children. He was married before, and his wife left him in large part due to his lack of any ambitions to become a parent. Since leaving him, his ex had remarried and had two children. Jeffrey didn't feel slighted by this, but considered himself lucky that the kids weren't his.

Mac, on the other hand, wanted children very much. Even though Levi was an unusually difficult kid, she was very happy to have him staying with her. In fact, his presence had quite an impact on her. Mac had long been toying with the idea of upgrading her home, and Levi had unknowingly provided her with the additional push she needed to make such a move. Mac began to think of the particular house she'd had her eye on—the quaint Victorian on Coffeen Avenue with two stories and three bedrooms. It would be nice to provide Levi with not only his own room but also a playroom, Mac thought. Mac decided that it was probably wise for her to start to seriously consider contacting the rental agent to see if it was still available.

Mac returned her attention to Jeffrey, and thought of a careful and calculated response to his question. "Only partly because of Levi, but mainly because I'm really behind at the office. This case has taken a lot of my time, and my workload has really piled up. Pamela and Megan are about ready to form a mutiny if I don't get full day in soon to put a dent in it. You know how it goes. When you have a big case, you put the rest of the world on hold."

After a brief pause, Jeffrey asked her a question that caught her off guard. "Have you given any more thought to taking the Virginia Bar Exam? Or have you forgotten about that too?"

"Look, Jeff, I understand that you're not happy with my choice, but right now Levi really needs me."

Mac could hear Jeffrey sigh.

"There's another guy who needs you, but I guess he's not quite as important."

"That's not true, and you know it. Just give me some time, okay? Things will settle down, I promise. Think about how you felt last month when your case was coming to a head and you couldn't meet me in Denver. I was supportive because I knew how important it was for you to solve that case. Can't you afford me the same courtesy?"

"This event isn't a courtesy, Mac. This is a major career milestone for me, and attending such important events is what people do when they love and support each other."

Mac wanted to respond in more detail to ensure that they didn't leave the matter unresolved, but she heard a loud crash coming from the bathroom. "I gotta go," she quickly said to Jeffrey before hanging up and rushing towards the sound.

* * *

Luke Landers delivered a baby in the early hours of Saturday morning. He'd become quite used to being paged by the hospital in the middle of the night, but he couldn't seem to catch the hang of being disrupted from an intense love-making session. Janie, on the other hand, had become quite used to the interruptions, and simply encouraged him to come back later to resume their "sleepover." Luke sighed, just thinking of how easy Janie made it for him to want to come back.

Evelyn, on the other hand, had a gift for making it hellish on him. As Luke pulled up to the driveway, he honked his horn to announce his presence. Luke had called just a few minutes earlier, hoping to get Ben ready for his arrival without his having to actually enter the house. Luke had to take Ben to a wrestling tournament, because there was no one else available. Austen was to drive himself to football practice, and Evelyn was to take Lauren to her swim meet. But when Ben exited the home a few minutes later, Austen and Lauren followed close behind him.

"What's going on?" Luke asked.

"Don't ask," Austen said. "I'm taking Lauren to the swim meet on the way to football."

Luke noticed Lauren's eyes were swollen from tears. "What's going on? Is everything alright?"

"You know the drill," Lauren sniffed. "She totally wigged out."

"I'll take her," Luke said to Austen. "You're late." Luke took a moment to exchange schedules with his eldest son, and collected all of the required sporting gear into the back of his car. As Luke began to back out of the driveway, he noticed in his rearview mirror that Evelyn had come out of the house and was standing in the middle of the garage with her arms tightly crossed over her chest, and was still wearing her bathrobe. When Luke noted the black streak of tears cascading down her cheeks, he promptly hit the garage door button and gunned the accelerator.

129

* * *

Linda Sterling scheduled the supervised visit with Evelyn at ten o'clock in the morning in Kendrick Park. Given the unusual circumstances involved in Levi's case, Linda decided that her presence was required throughout this visit. After Levi stabbed himself in the leg, Linda had no other choice but to place him in the unlicensed care of his attorney. She knew she needed to cover all her bases in this major case, and her attending the first supervised visit following all this was a smart choice. Plus, Linda needed to document how Mac interacted with the boy in her care, and ensure that she provided adequate supervision.

Mac and Levi arrived early with doughnuts, coffee and a container of fresh fruit. Mac set the items on a picnic table and followed Levi to the jungle gym. She hadn't been able to run that morning, so she figured that chasing Levi around the park would constitute as her daily exercise. She was reminded how physical a park could be, as she'd long forgotten how difficult it was to scale the monkey bars. They played hide and seek, tag, and raced each other from one end of the park to the other. By the time Evelyn showed up, Mac and Levi were side-by-side on the swings as they tried to blow off some of the sweat they'd worked up.

Evelyn had transformed from the woman in the garage a few hours earlier. She had showered and was wearing a watermelon-colored sweater set and creased jeans. Her face was sallow, and Mac noticed that she was thinner than a week earlier at the detention hearing.

As soon as Levi saw his mom, his eyes lit up with excitement and he jumped off the swing to greet her. Evelyn opened her arms wide and appeared overjoyed to accept his loving embrace. She held him tightly for a few moments, clearly not wanting to let him go. When she finally did release him, Evelyn gently grasped Levi's hand so they could walk towards Mac and Linda Sterling together.

"He's so complicated," Linda whispered to Mac. "His psych eval came back, and the results were very interesting. He's intelligent and insightful, but he has a terrible anger management problem."

"If someone was deliberately making me sick and I spent half my time in a doctor's office, I'd be mad too," Mac said.

"Did he tell you that?"

"No," Mac said, and then quickly added "though he did say that he was sick of being sick. And that he worried his mom was now going to be sick, too." Mac considered throwing in the part about the Baseball Man, but something inside her told her to hold off on that. Mac didn't know how significant this detail might be, and decided to protect Levi's confidence for the time being.

"How much do you know about his illnesses?" Linda asked.

"Not enough. I haven't had time to review the rest of his medical records. In fact, I haven't been to my office much in the last few days."

Evelyn and Levi were now within earshot, so Linda couldn't finish what she was saying to Mac. "I suggest you read on. He's had some very peculiar diagnoses."

Mac nodded to Linda, making a mental note to drop by the office and grab the box of Levi's medical records. She figured that she could read them after Levi went to sleep that night, before realizing that sleep was something she'd gotten little of herself lately. She'd slept very little since Wednesday, and was basically surviving on coffee and sugar.

When Evelyn approached the picnic table, she held Levi's close to her, as if she was protecting him from the enemy. Mac stood and held out her right hand. "I'm Mary MacIntosh. I didn't really get a chance to meet you in court the other day. It's a pleasure to meet you."

Evelyn shook Mac's hand and then took a step back.

"Mac is doing a good job of taking care of Levi, Mrs. Landers. I hope you know that—"

"The thing is, Linda, Levi doesn't need someone else to take care of him. I've been doing a great job of loving and caring for my son for a long time, and it's offensive to me that anyone thinks otherwise. The idea that my son needs an attorney appointed by the state to visit with me, in a supervised setting no less, is beyond offensive. I'm a good mom—"

"Levi," Linda said, "why don't you go and play on the equipment for a few minutes while we ladies have a little visit. Would that be okay?"

Levi quietly backed away from the group of ladies and made his way toward the play equipment. He looked back to see what was going on a few times, aware of the fact that he was the subject of the conversation and controversy.

"Mrs. Landers," Linda continued, "the judge was very clear about you not speaking about the case in front of Levi. Please don't do that again. It's hard enough on him to be in this situation. Hearing your words only makes him more uncomfortable and confused. This isn't easy for him."

"It's not easy for *him*?!" Evelyn shrieked. "Do you think this is easy for *me*? Or my family? This is hell on earth. He's part of a functioning family, and his absence is traumatic for all of us. Don't lecture me on what I can and can't speak about in front of my son. I'm his mother and I can make that decision myself."

"Not so long as this case remains active, because the judge specifically ordered you not to speak about this case in front of Levi. If you continue to disregard his order, you could be providing a basis to have your parental rights terminated. I'm sure you've spoken with your attorney about this– and if you haven't, I certainly suggest you do. We're focused on Levi first and foremost. You should be too."

Evelyn glared at Linda, obviously not getting the picture. "Don't lecture me. You don't know me or my son. I'm a damn good mother. I've raised four intelligent, responsible children in a world where half the kids I know are complete losers. I've a proven track record. I don't need a court or an agency judging me. This is ridiculous. I've done nothing but try to keep my son healthy, which has been grueling hard on my marriage, my friendships, and my other kids. I've put Levi first every step of the way, and to have you second guess me is rude and offensive."

"I'm sorry you feel that way, but that is my job and this is my case. As I said before, so long as this case is open I'm going to continue to monitor what you say and do around Levi, and document my observations in his file. Perhaps that would motivate you to behave more properly around him."

Mac stood on the sideline of the conversation and watched it like she would a tennis match. She didn't dare speak.

As if Evelyn could read her mind, she promptly changed the subject and turned all of her attention towards Mac. In a much quieter and more appropriate tone, she said, "How's he doing?"

"Levi?" Mac asked, tentative to join in on the conversation for fear of having Evelyn snap at her again. "He's doing okay. He doesn't sleep well, and he's finicky about eating sometimes, but we're adjusting. He seems to like school and his teacher." Mac paused for a moment, contemplating whether to mention anything about the problems she'd observed. Mac decided that it would probably be better to bring it out in the open, since it was going to be brought to Evelyn's attention sooner or later. Might as well get her reaction and input sooner, and apply it to Levi while he was still staying with her. "I am a little concerned about the fact that he hurts himself or breaks things without much provocation. Is that normal for him, or is he acting out because of what is going on?"

"I think he's acting out. He's been ripped from his home and his family and he's confused," Evelyn said. "I would do the same thing."

"Isn't it true, Mrs. Landers, that he's had a history of acting out?" Linda interjected. "His self-mutilation started when he was seven, according to the medical records."

"Self-mutilation?" Evelyn stated in a defensive tone. "Where do you get such terms? I wasn't aware that you were a psychologist."

"Actually, I am both a sociologist and a social worker. I read his entire medical history and it doesn't take a degree in psychology to understand a psych eval. It was written in fairly plain English."

"As far as I'm concerned, most psychologists need a psychologist. They look for things to exaggerate in order to justify the diagnosis."

"Levi stabbed himself in the leg this week, Evelyn. And before that? He took an eraser from school and rubbed in on his hands until they bled. Should I go on? Let's see, he burned his arms with match tips, he swallowed an entire bottle of Ibuprofin, he has a documented history of head banging and self-hitting. I could recite a number of other incidents if need be. I'd say it's pretty clear that he's trying to harm himself."

"I'd harm myself too if someone snatched me from my mother and made me live with *her*."

Mac was surprised to see Evelyn throw a cheap shot at her like she just did, throwing her into the match with Linda. Mac shot Evelyn a disdainful look as she responded. "I don't deserve your disrespect. I'm doing you a favor by taking care of your son."

"Don't bullshit me; I know you're in this for the money."

"*Money?* Are you kidding me?" Mac sputtered in surprise. "I don't make squat here, Evelyn. Not only is the court paying me a pittance to cover this case, but it's taking me away from working on higher paying private cases."

"Then why?" Evelyn asked.

Chapter 14

"Ladies, as you may be aware, we have a court hearing on Tuesday regarding jurisdictional issues. Until that time, Levi will continue staying with Mac, assuming she's still willing to take care of him." Linda turned her head towards Mac with that last statement, and saw Mac shift her head up and down in a sort of non-committed nod of approval. "Is there anything Levi could benefit from his own home that might make him more comfortable at your place, and make things easier for you pending this hearing?"

Mac thought about it for a bit. "He has mentioned his baseball glove and set of baseball cards a few times to me during conversations. He likes to talk about baseball a lot."

"Can we get those things from you?" Linda asked, now turning her attention towards Evelyn.

"Fine." Evelyn snorted. "If you want to come and get them, I'll put them out on the front porch."

"And if he has any other favorite toys, it would be good to have some. I don't have anything like that in my place."

"It figures," Evelyn snapped.

Trying to play referee, Linda slightly positioned herself in between the two women. "Why don't you pick out a few things you think Levi might like, Mrs. Landers," Linda interjected. "That would be very helpful to your son, and I'll make sure to note of it in the case plan. Include anything you think he might like, but please make sure to include some additional clothes. For the time being, why don't you spend a little time with Levi, while you have the chance. Mac and I can sit here and talk business for a bit."

Evelyn didn't like that Linda was dismissing her from the conversation. She marched away in a huff.

While it was obvious that Evelyn was out of earshot, Linda and Mac finally began to speak. "I'm thinking about renting a house."

"Mac, Levi living with you is only a temporary arrangement. As soon as we're able to find a suitable foster placement for him, we're going to have to move him. I don't want you to go to the trouble of moving in the event we locate an alternate placement, because he will be removed if we do."

"I know, Linda, but really—I've been contemplating a move for a long time. I think the situation with Levi is a sign to finally take the big step, whether he's able to stay with me in the new place or otherwise. Having Levi with me has been the motivation that I needed."

"Suit yourself, but be prepared for the judge questioning the conflict of interest issues that his placement with you represents. Even if we can't find any other placement for Levi, the judge might order us to figure something out to get him out of your home. You've gotta admit that it's a bit hard to stay unbiased about what's in Levi's best interests if you've already fallen in love with the little guy and want to keep him in your home." Linda leaned over and gently patted Mac on the back as she said this, hoping not to offend the God-send that had offered a place for her most troubled case. "Try not to get emotionally involved, Mac. Levi is a difficult child and he's going to test your loyalty and love. Each time he tests you will get harder, and it might even put you into the difficult situation of finding out more information about yourself than you cared to learn."

"What exactly do you mean by that?"

"Each time you have an incident with a child in your care, you learn something about yourself in how you reacted to the situation and how it made you feel inside. It's very difficult for me to explain, but you'll eventually see what I'm talking about with Levi. Having a child in your care will change your life." Linda thought perhaps she had gone too far in this heart to heart. "I'm here for you if you want to talk. I'm also here for you if you decide that parenting Levi is too much for you. Don't try to be a hero. If it's not working out, it will be in everyone's best interest if you're honest."

"Of course I'll be honest, Linda."

"Mac, may I ask you a personal question?" Mac nodded. "How serious is the relationship you're in?"

"I don't know, serious enough. We've spoken about the future. Why? Does that impact Levi's ability to stay with me some way?"

"Not really," Linda responded. "I'm just curious if your future might involve children?"

Mac looked over at Levi swinging and smiling, thinking deeply about the question before her. Mac finally returned her attention back to Linda, who was peering deeply into Mac's eyes searching for an answer. She thought about the question for a few more seconds before she finally responded.

"It does for me."

* * *

Mac parked her car in front of the Landers's two-story light yellow house, and asked Levi to stay put while she ran to gather the items Evelyn had hopefully set out for Levi. Mac was relieved when she arrived on the wraparound porch to see two large duffle bags awaiting her, as she feared there would be nothing left for her to pick up. How would she explain that to Levi? Fortunately, that's a question she wouldn't have to bother with, as the bag contained fresh clothes, a baseball card album, a baseball glove, and a Nintendo-DS handheld game. Mac grabbed the two bags with relief and began to run back to her car. Before Mac was off the porch, though, the front door to the Landers house opened loudly.

Mac turned nervously, afraid of what she would find waiting for her on the other end of the front door. She found Evelyn staring at her. Mac stood frozen for a moment, unsure of her best response. Mac briefly made a hand gesture to Evelyn in a way that she hoped indicated she would be right back, and then ran quickly to the waiting car to drop off the duffle bags and check in with Levi.

"Thanks for the bags." Mac breathlessly said to Evelyn upon her return to the front porch. "Levi was very happy to hear that he'd be getting his baseball stuff and video games."

"He can play that Nintendo for hours. Don't let him." Evelyn sniffed, apparently grateful for the distraction. "It over-stimulates him and usually creates behavioral issues after long. I usually only let him play for a half hour at a time–and no more than an hour a day. That's probably too long, but it seems to occupy him while we wait for doctor appointments or other commitments. Levi does not have a long attention span, unless he's playing that thing."

"I won't abuse it. Thanks for the information. Anything else I should know?"

"Watch his diet carefully. Bland foods are best. He has gastro-intestinal problems."

"I've noticed that, but he seems pretty good today. Yesterday wasn't bad either."

"Good. He also likes stories. He likes you to make up stories to tell him–or for you to read to him. It calms his nerves."

"I've found that. I'm reading *Hatchet* to him now, and he likes the story a lot."

Evelyn wasn't too emotionally overcome to give Mac a look over from head to toe. "I'm impressed," Evelyn finally said. "I thought you didn't know much about kids."

Mac wasn't sure whether to be offended or pleased by the comment, so she decided to ignore the negative implications and keep the conversation moving towards closure. "I'm not entirely oblivious when it comes to children, though I don't have any of my own yet."

"I hope you do someday. It will give you some perspective on how this entire case has emotionally drained my family. I know you're just doing your job, but I want you to think about it from my perspective. I'm raising four good kids, one of which has health issues, which is not that uncommon, and one day, the police and the Social Services Agency show up and take my baby from me." Evelyn's voice began to quiver slightly. "I've done nothing but care for my kids for sixteen years, and now this. Can you imagine how this makes me feel? My kids are my life. I have devoted myself to them. I am in utter shock that an agency that is supposed to be looking out for children's well-being could even consider me a bad mother. I can certainly understand when a child is taken away from abuse or domestic violence or drug addiction. None of those things happen in Levi's world. He gets sick and I take him to the doctor like any good parent would. I–"

"I'm sorry, Evelyn," Mac interrupted. "I really would love to talk with you about this, but I can't. I hate saying that, because it makes me feel so rude–especially when you're sharing personal thoughts with me. Because I'm representing Levi, however, and you have your own attorney, the ethical rules prevent me from having any substantive conversations with you about this case. I have to be very careful what I say, though, because I can get in trouble and I don't want to lose my license."

Evelyn sniffed somewhat, as she lifted her chin up a bit defiantly. "I wish lawyers could just be normal people. You always have your lawyer hat on. The world would be a better place if you had your human hat on. If you thought like a compassionate person first instead of an advocate, the courts wouldn't be clogged up with ridiculous cases."

"That might be true, Evelyn, but you must understand the logic that prevents me from speaking with you about this case without your attorney present. How would it look if you shared with me a fact that ended up having legal significance in the case? No matter how honestly you were in sharing it with me, my legal obligations to Levi mean that I'd have to use that information in his case–despite however heartfelt our conversation was. Without your lawyer present, you'd have no idea about that–and I'm not the one to educate you on that. We may be on the same side on some issues, but we're still opposing parties and by us chatting we could be creating many legal and ethical problems. The ethical rule preventing us from speaking is not only applied to lawyers, but doctors, too. I know Luke doesn't speak with you about any of his patients' medical histories or disclosures."

Evelyn nodded in frustration and turned to head back into the house.

"Evelyn," Mac said, reaching out for her arm. "I want you to know that I'm trying to take very good care of your son. If you want to see him, call me. I would be happy to meet you again at a park or somewhere else.

I know he needs you and misses you. I think Linda would be okay with me monitoring additional visits between you two."

"The idea that I have to have a monitor to see my son makes my stomach turn," Evelyn grimaced. She then turned herself back towards Mac, and softened her voice somewhat. "That being said—thank you for the offer. I *would* like to see him again tomorrow if it's not too much trouble. My other kids have some sporting events. Maybe you could meet us at one with Levi?"

"I would be happy to do that." Mac responded. "Here's my card. I wrote my cell phone down on it, which is the best way to reach me at any given moment. Call me anytime," Mac said, as she handed Evelyn her business card. Evelyn accepted the card and studied it for a minute.

"You have your own firm. That must take a lot of work."

"It does. Luckily, I have a good staff to help me."

"How are you going to juggle work and Levi? He requires constant supervision. I sleep with one eye open, worrying that he's going to get sick in the middle of the night. Do you know his history? Do you know how many times I've had to rush him to the hospital in the middle of the night? Do you know what to look for?"

Mac fumbled for a response.

"I thought so. You don't know."

"I'm planning on going to my office now and picking up the rest of his medical records and reading them after he goes to sleep tonight."

"I hope he doesn't have an episode while you're deep in thought reading. He's at risk being away from me. I'm the only one who knows what to look for."

"Perhaps you can tell me. It would expedite things—and it would be in Levi's best interest for you to tell me. So long as you limit yourself to instructions I need while caring for Levi, I don't see that there would be any problems with it. I'll call your attorney as soon as I get home to update him on our conversation."

"I don't give a damn what my attorney thinks. This is my son. This is about what's best for him. I can't sleep knowing he's not under my roof and under my care. I'm the *only* person in his life who truly loves and cares for him. His father doesn't. He's demonstrated over and over again that he puts his own needs before his kids–especially Levi. He's been flaunting his–," Evelyn paused mid-sentence and shook her head in disgust. "You can't possibly understand what we've been through–"

"Then go ahead. Tell me about Levi's health history."

Evelyn took a big breath and closed her eyes for a long blink. "If we're going to be candid, I need to know that I can trust you."

"Well," Mac started, carefully choosing her words, "As I said earlier, I represent your son and you have your own attorney. I can't promise you that my allegiances are with you first and foremost because legally my allegiances are with your son. With that, though, I can tell you that I won't share your comments with anyone unless absolutely necessary. And I do need to tell your attorney about our general conversation."

"Allegiance? That sounds ridiculously cold. This is his *life* we're talking about."

"I realize that, Evelyn. I don't take this matter lightly. I just don't want to make you promises that I can't keep. With respect to his medical history, I can assure you that if the information is in his medical chart, then what you might tell me probably won't affect matters greatly, but if you confide in me with respect to your problems as a mother, then I'm torn. You have to understand that. As much as I want to be your shoulder to lean on, there are some things that I am legally prohibited from doing. If you don't tell me stuff that can't be found somewhere in his charts, though, then I think we should be just fine."

Evelyn paused, obviously contemplating her words given Mac's comments. "He has long health history–and it will take some time. It's complicated."

Mac looked to Levi sitting in her car. "I can't leave Levi in the car for a long time," Mac said. "What do you suggest?"

"You can come in and he can play in his room–his natural and comfortable surroundings–and we can talk."

"I'm afraid that might confuse him, and leaving would prove difficult. We need a plan B."

Evelyn thought for a moment. "Why don't we go to his school? It's the weekend and no one is there on the playground. He can play, or sit at the picnic table there and play his Nintendo. We can talk."

Mac thought Evelyn's suggestion over for a second, realizing that it might actually work. "Sounds good. Do you think you could grab a few snacks for him and a juice box? I had my secretary get some of that for me, but it's back at the office. I don't have any snacks with me."

"Sure," Evelyn said with a smile, pleased with the unexpected meeting with Mac and additional time with Levi. "I'll be right out. I'll follow you in my car."

Mac waited in her car with Levi happily playing his Nintendo. Just a moment later Mac saw the garage door opening, and Evelyn's Range Rover backing out. Mac started the engine back up to her Equinox, and followed Evelyn's car to the elementary school. When their cars settled into adjoining parking spaces, both Evelyn and Mac got out of their cars. As Mac was opening the passenger door on her car to get Levi out, Evelyn sidled up next to her and addressed Levi, making sure that her instructions came before any Mac might provide. She told Levi that he could bring his games out with him to the swing set, and that both Mac and Evelyn were going to sit and watch him.

Levi didn't wait to hear if Mac gave her approval, as he immediately jumped out of the car and raced towards the swings. He sat, twisting and twirling on a swing as he played his hand-held games. Mac and Evelyn sat at the picnic table.

"How much do you know from his records?" Evelyn asked Mac, after they had both got themselves situated on the picnic table's benches.

"I left off when he was a baby–suffering mostly from a 'failure to thrive' diagnosis."

"Oh, wow, that's a really long time ago. I'll try to give you the abridged version from that point. He's had about one hundred diagnoses since then. I'm not sure I can even remember all of them." Evelyn looked up into the sky, as if for inspiration and took a deep breath.

"I think the next diagnosis was Reactive Attachment Disorder which is a condition found in children who do not form a healthy emotional attachment. They diagnosed him with that around age two. You can imagine how that made me feel," Evelyn said, looking directly at Mac. "I strongly disagreed with that diagnosis, because I was with him twenty-four-seven and constantly ensured that he was soothed, comforted and cared for. Looking back, I can admit that Levi was detached to some degree. He certainly was unresponsive, or at least resistant, to any form of comforting. I still disagree with the diagnosis, but he did display several common characteristics of the disorder."

Evelyn paused and turned her attention towards Luke on the swings. "How you doing, honey?" she yelled towards him. Levi grunted in response, too intent in the video game to offer any more human of a response. Evelyn smiled and sighed before continuing.

"Levi was a disaster in playgroups and in nursery school. He didn't make friends easily and other children didn't like playing with him. I can understand why, because Levi's always been either antisocial or acting out in a physical way. Regardless of how many times he was redirected, Levi loved to hit and bite–not a great way to make a friend. This was a result of his explosive anger, which in turn led to him having problems sleeping. Anyway, I could give more examples, but the point is that the doctors eventually backed off this diagnosis, but cautioned that he might suffer from depression as a teenager due to the possible diagnosis. And the doctors insisted that we, as a family, ensure his safety and reinforce healthy familial relationships. Of course, having Social Services take him away is the worst possible thing if this diagnosis was true."

"From what I hear, Ben isn't very nice to him. If he has Reactive Attachment Disorder, having an older brother pick on you wouldn't help much."

"Did Levi tell you about Ben?"

"Yes," Mac admitted, keeping mindful of her precarious position as Levi's attorney. She didn't want to say too much. "What was the next diagnosis?"

Evelyn uncrossed her legs and shifted in Mac's direction. "Well, we had a number of minor issues come up. He had a series of elimination disorders during his post-potty training days. He was diagnosed with encropresis and enuresis. He wet the bed constantly and sometimes pooped in his underwear at school. He hated going to unfamiliar bathrooms, such as a public restroom, which was a nightmare because we spent most of our weekends at a ball field or gymnasium for whatever sport the older kids were engaged in. But, looking back, I realize that it really wasn't a big deal. I was upset over it then and I wish I hadn't made such a fuss. I insisted that he be medically and psychologically treated. I think he felt like he was being punished and he felt so guilty each time he had an accident. It was really terrible for both of us."

"Is he cured now? I've noticed that he waits until the last possible second to tell me that he needs to use the potty. He's sometimes in panic mode when we get him to a restroom."

"I think that could be the fall-out of over-reacting to the problem at the time. He does put off elimination and his diet is often very low in fiber, by his choice."

"I'll concentrate on the fiber," Mac offered. Evelyn smirked and then continued.

"The next diagnosis was a doozy. A specialist in Denver thought Levi had Pervasive Development Disorder, which in my humble opinion was a way of saying that he didn't know what was wrong with him. This particular doctor was well known in the field of autism and when he had a hunch that something was wrong with an intelligent kid, he apparently used this broad diagnosis to cover things like Asperger's syndrome."

"I've heard of that. Didn't Bill Gates have that diagnosis?"

"I'm not sure, but it's possible. It's like autism, but kids with

Asperger's usually have high intelligence quotas and above average language and cognition. Levi wasn't given this particular specific diagnosis.

In fact, it ended with PDDNOS–meaning pervasive development disorder not otherwise specified."

"That sounds pretty broad."

"I'd say. It was frustrating, because kids with this diagnosis tend to have problems with communication and play, but are too social to be considered autistic. Levi certainly fit this criterion by age five, but I still felt that diagnosis was wrong. He was not social and he was smart, but he was sick–physically sick–most of the time. I felt like the doctors were so focused on his behavioral issues that they were overlooking the fact that Levi was in the lower five percent in height and weight and that he had diarrhea and vomiting almost weekly."

Mac looked at Levi twisting happily in the swing, his thumbs moving rapidly on his Nintendo. He was frail and thin, highly focused, determined, overly angry at times. The diagnoses that Evelyn described seemed plausible, given her own observations. Mac had noticed the repetitive body movements when his attention wasn't focused on something like a game, and could see how a doctor could make that diagnoses.

"How did these diagnoses come into play? I mean, would you go to the pediatrician with complaints, and he would refer you to these specialists?"

"Sometimes. Other times, Dr. Kerr or his staff would notice problems. His teachers also made comments. It wasn't just me complaining that something was wrong with him all the time. Other people noticed things too."

"What about Luke? As a doctor, did he notice problems with his son?"

"Luke didn't have time to notice, if I may be so frank with you. Let's just say that by that time, he was preoccupied."

"With?"

"Work. Sports. Other things."

Mac wasn't sure whether she wanted to pursue that line of conversation, and thought that Evelyn's evasiveness was based on their conversation earlier. Mac wanted to know more, but knew that would head the conversation into dangerous territory, and therefore decided to continue focusing her questions directly on Levi. "What was the next diagnosis?"

"The flu."

"The flu? That's pretty normal isn't it for a kid to have the flu?"

"One would think so. My other kids had it from time to time. But when Levi got it, it was a whole different animal. He got the flu at five, but it wouldn't seem to go away. He threw up every single day for a month. *Every single day*. And he had diarrhea. As a result, he was hospitalized for dehydration, of course. When he was in the hospital, I was so worried that I insisted that tests be run. I thought he had mono and I wanted a blood test done. So, Dr. Kerr ordered a blood test and they noticed his white blood cell count was incredibly high. Janie and I did research on the Internet and based on his lab results and his symptoms, we were sure that he had cancer. I had him flown to Denver and further tests were performed. And that is when we started down the yellow brick road of cancer diagnoses."

"Plural? You mean to say that he was diagnosed with more than one cancer?"

Evelyn shook her head yes. "The first was called the 'Two-Hit Leukemia.' It's basically flu-induced leukemia which they call acute lymphoblastic leukemia. I was right when I thought that he had mono or something. There is a virus called HTLV-1 which directly causes a kind of leukemia. Burkett's lymphoma can be triggered by reactivation of latent Epstein-Barr virus infection. So, Levi had a sort of mono and then the flu and this somehow triggered cancerous growth in his blood. He was given chemotherapy for two months and by the time he was five, the symptoms were in remission. I'm quite sure that I saved his life on that one." Evelyn snorted, noting the irony. "The doctors had no idea what they were doing."

As Evelyn continued to detail Levi's medical history, Mac paid close attention to the manner in which she spoke. Evelyn had a very authoritative tone, as though she knew more than the doctors. From what Mac had researched on Munchausen mothers, this was apparently a common trait–they often diagnosed illnesses before medical staff had all the tests and information necessary to confirm the diagnosis.

Mac tried to focus more clearly on what Evelyn was saying, not just how she was saying it. From the thickness of Levi's medical records, Mac knew there was a lot of information to be shared; she didn't want to miss any of it. "You mentioned other cancers. Was Levi diagnosed with something else?"

"Leukemia was only the beginning."

Chapter 15

"Your Honor," Harold Neiman said in a very terse tone, "the conflict of interest is as obvious as the nose on your face." Mr. Neiman's flip remark referencing the judge's nose drew sharp looks from the other attorneys in the courtroom, and this apparently made him recognize his unfortunate choice of analogies.

"What I mean to say, Your Honor, is that Ms. MacIntosh cannot possibly serve as attorney, guardian ad litem, and foster parent for Levi Landers. How can the agency or the court or counsel expect open communication about the well-being of this boy if his foster parent is also his advocate?"

Apparently overlooking the comment about his nose, Judge Binnard responded, "I tend to agree with Mr. Neiman. It would be my position that alternative placement be found."

"Your Honor," Mac said as she stood up, "may I be heard?" As Mac prepared herself for her response to the judge regarding Levi's placement in her home, she found herself thinking about how well things had progressed between them. She felt that she had made significant headway in their relationship, as they had played baseball together all weekend long. In fact, Mac took him to school yesterday and this morning, and the two were beginning to develop a fairly healthy routine. The improvement in their schedule was drastic, and Levi had started to show signs of this improvement in his diet and sleeping patterns. "You may, Ms. MacIntosh," Judge Binnard said.

"Levi and I have established a healthy and well-balanced routine together. This factor alone may have little weight in your decision, were it not for the fact that the road leading up to this point was very difficult. Combine with that the fact that there do not appear to be any other foster families willing to accept him into their homes. Even if one could be found, it would not be in his best interest to force another move upon him. He is safe and comfortable and doing very well with me, and I would hate to see this significant improvement in Levi lost due to the overlap of my duties. I am doing my very best to see that his special needs are met while balancing all relevant interests in this case. I have spoken at length with Linda Sterling and Mrs. Landers about this very issue, and I am confident that I am adequately prepared to care for all of his needs in this case as both his attorney and placement."

"With all due respect to Ms. MacIntosh," Harold Neiman interrupted, "her response just now clearly illustrates one of the many problems presented by her possessing both placement and counsel positions in this case. For her to adequately meet Levi's placement needs, she's practically required to consult with my client. With her placement hat on, she can consult with my client without me being present. Do we really expect her to quickly forget or lose sight of the information she gains from these conversations when she switches hats and becomes Levi's counsel again? How am I supposed to defend my client when she's put in this type of unusual predicament?"

"There is a group home alternative," Karl Swensen interjected. "I spoke with Linda Sterling this morning and she acknowledged that there was a bed open at the group home."

"She also acknowledged to me that it would be detrimental to place a child like Levi in a group setting," Mac said. "Look what happened when he was in Mrs. Kelly's home. No offense to Mrs. Kelly, mind you, but Levi had a complete and utter melt down after he was teased by the other kids in her care. After running away from the placement, he physically harmed myself—which is exactly the reason that there are no alternative foster placements for him now. Placing Levi in a setting filled with other dependent children virtually guarantees not only a repeat situation, but something far worse. Regardless of our respective legal positions in this case, we are all obligated to pursue what is in Levi's best interests, and I don't see how any single one of us could honestly say that a group home placement would be in his best interests."

"What's best for Levi is for him to live with his mother!" Harold Neiman shouted at Mac.

"Okay, okay. Settle down." Judge Binnard had heard enough bickering, and it was time for him to regain some decorum in the court. "I do not allow tempers in this court. It is our job, especially in this setting, to show restraint and demonstrate that we can work things out. This isn't litigation, counselors: this is a family in crisis and it is our job to work together towards a solution. Are we clear?"

"Yes, Your Honor," Mac said. When no other attorney verbally acknowledged the judge's admonishment, Mac decided to sneak in another push for her position while apologizing for the brief exchange of words just had. "I want to assure you that all I want is for Levi to be safe, healthy and happy. He is a wonderful little boy. I have seen some of his issues–he's broken things in my house–but I am positive that with consistent love, support and guidance, that we will help him through this."

"Consistent love and support?" Harold Neiman snapped. "Exactly how long do you plan to be his pseudo-mother? Long enough for you to get a kid of your own?"

"Mr. Neiman, that type of comment is unnecessary," Judge Binnard said as he turned himself directly towards the offending attorney. "And I will not stand for that type of underhanded jab in my courtroom. If I hear you respond like that again, I will hold you in contempt. Do I make myself clear?"

Harold Neiman made sure to act the part of apologetic attorney, and uttered in response an emotionless, "Yes, Your Honor. I'm sorry Your Honor."

"I have to admit, Mrs. MacIntosh, that I am a bit curious as to why you would put yourself in such a dilemma. This is your first case in Juvi, and you've already placed your neck on the line by taking the minor in question into your home. I have been on the bench a long time, Ms. MacIntosh, and this is a first for me. What exactly are you doing and why?"

Mac found herself shuffling in her cute new espadrilles, which she'd chosen despite their lack of comfort because they went so well with her outfit. They'd been standing in court now for nearly fifteen minutes, and she'd begun to question herself for making that decision. "I don't have an easy answer to that question, Your Honor, because this case has progressed in a way that practically required it of me. I was there when Levi stabbed himself, which ended up putting me in a position where I felt more connected to him than I would have liked."

"You call taking Levi to a vet's office a required response as his attorney? How could that possibly be in his best interests, as compared to, oh, say, a people's hospital?" Harold Neiman interrupted.

Mac didn't wait for the judge to acknowledge Harold's insolence again, because she felt that he responding to the question could only help her cause. "Your Honor, I want the record to reflect that I took Levi to the closest medical facility available, given the emergency situation I was faced with. Levi was seen by a physician in that facility, as well as being removed from the cold, damp environment that I'd found him in. He received emergency treatment. I did what any parent would have done in an emergency."

"Ms. MacIntosh, you did just fine," Judge Binnard said soothingly, as if he were trying to personally reassure Mac that her immediate response to Levi's injuries were appropriate. He then turned his attention back to Harold, and the expression on his face showed his displeasure with counsel.

"Mr. Neiman, I'm going to do you the favor of not holding you in contempt right now. Don't take this the wrong way, I'm not intending to do you the favor, but my morning docket is delayed enough as it is - without having you taken into custody on charges. I'm going to warn you one last time to take a seat and keep your mouth shut for the rest of this hearing." Judge Binnard paused to glance at his watch, and then let out a brief sigh before he continued. "We haven't even started to argue the merits of the case and it's already practically lunch time. I have a trial that's resuming here this afternoon, so unless we get moving, this matter will have to be continued until later in the week. Counsel, have you been able to work out settlement, or do we need to go forward with jurisdiction and disposition?"

Karl Swensen spoke up. "Your Honor, I don't think we're going to be able to work this one out. Looks like this one is headed for trial. "

"What is the expected duration of trial?" Judge Binnard asked, obviously disappointed by the news.

Karl looked to the other attorneys around him as he responded, "There are quite a few medical experts involved, so I'd guess we'll need at least six to eight court days."

"I usually only hear trials in the afternoon, as you well know. You think you can try this case, with five lawyers taking a crack at all these experts, in six to eight afternoons?"

"Won't happen," John Trainor said. "It'll be two weeks. Trust me." It was the first time that Mr. Trainor had spoken. He'd represented Dr. Landers in a few medical malpractice cases in the past and was acting fairly low-key. His warm smile cleverly hid the bull-dog within him, and he'd established a reputation as a tiger when it came to cross-examination.

Luke Landers sat next to John Trainor, wearing his light blue scrubs and a sport coat over the shirt. He'd been in his scrubs an hour prior delivering his Tuesday morning C-section. Mac was intrigued by the fact that he was not sitting by Evelyn and contemplated why he would not sit with her when the case required the parents to present a unified front. It looked more like the dynamics of a child custody hearing in a family law court than it did a juvenile law dependency hearing.

"I think Mr. Trainor is right," Judge Binnard responded. "A trial in this case is going to take at minimum several weeks. I suggest you five go out into the hall and again discuss some sort of settlement before we proceed to scheduling a lengthy trial on the matter. Feel free to use my chambers if you think that might help with the process."

Evelyn whispered in Harold Neiman's ear, and he immediately rose to his feet. "Your Honor, Mrs. Landers has three other kids to take care of. She has time in the morning when the kids are in school, but the afternoons are very difficult for her. She has kids in a multitude of after school activities and she has just reminded me that Homecoming is next week and that she has pledged to help out. Her eldest son, Austen, is—"

"You are kidding, right?" Judge Binnard interrupted Mr. Neiman in a shocked and nearly mocking tone. "I've heard a lot of excuses for not being able to attend court, but Homecoming has never been one of them. I don't care if the Queen of England is visiting Mrs. Landers's home, she will be in this courtroom when she is ordered to be here. We're talking about her *other* son right now—the one who is sick and is not running for Homecoming King. I suggest she reconsider her priorities."

Mac had been thinking about scheduling to pick Levi up from school that afternoon when she was startled back to reality with the judge's admonition. Mac realized that she was in no better a position than Evelyn was when it came to her calendar, and grimaced at the thought of how a trial lasting for two weeks would impact her. Was she going to have to hire a babysitter? If so, who? No one in town wanted anything to do with Levi, as they appeared to be afraid for their own children's safety following the knife incident at Mr. Kelly's house. For that matter, the YMCA wouldn't even allow him in its after-school daycare. Mac knew better than to raise this issue with the judge, as she'd be scolded just as Evelyn was. Plus, it looked like she was going to get out of this hearing without having Levi removed from her home, so she knew better than to push her luck.

"You walk back into my chambers—all of you, right now—and see if you can work this thing out. Take a good, hard look at the petition and see if there isn't a compromise that can be reached. Report back to me when you've all decided to act reasonably."

With that, all the lawyers, along with Dr. and Mrs. Landers, marched through the courtroom and out the back door, into the hallway that led directly to Judge Binnard's chambers.

When Judge Binnard entered his chambers at twelve thirty, he'd hoped that enough time had passed to give some resolution to the matter. He'd expected at least for the parties to begin treating each other with a little bit more respect than he'd witnessed in the courtroom just an hour earlier. An hour was enough time for that, he'd thought. He had a trial starting in the courtroom at one-thirty, and he'd hoped to have an agreement to put on the record in this case before the trial went forward. Sadly, he realized that this was not the case as he entered his inner sanctum filled with a group of angry and bickering individuals.

"It doesn't look like we have reached a settlement," he said, as he took a deep breath. You are all ordered back here next Monday at one-thirty in the afternoon. Trial will begin. I will block out two weeks. Have your witnesses and evidence ready. There will be no continuances. Understood?"

In hangdog fashion, the lawyers and their clients nodded. Mac was the first to excuse herself and leave.

* * *

"You have a million messages to return," Megan said as Mac rushed back to her office after the failed settlement meeting in court. "Take a look at your chair. I've stacked the urgent stuff there. The rest of it looks like it can wait."

Mac thanked her receptionist and rounded the corner to her office. Sitting atop her chair in the middle of her office was a mound of pink message slips, which immediately drew to mind the image of her chair vomiting up a bottle of Pepto-Bismol.

Mac sighed as she began to rifle briefly through each message, none of which was from Jeffrey. All but one of these messages were marked urgent, and were from clients who requested an "immediate response." It was the single message not marked as urgent that piqued Mac's interest the most, as it was from her client in the Powder River toxic methane gas case. Mac realized that she hadn't talked with Beth Anderson in quite some time, and was intrigued as to what her call was regarding.

* * *

Beth owned a pristine and lovely ranch with her husband just outside Sheridan, and there the two ran a successful horse training class. Beth was the mother of Mac's former boyfriend, Greg Fisher, whom Mac had dated for years while living in Jackson Hole. Mac had not heard from Greg at all since their break-up, and rarely encountered Beth during her brief trips in town.

Mac decided this was the most urgent of them all, and called Beth first. She let the phone ring several times before anyone answered the phone, because she realized that Beth was often in the barn and had a considerable walk to catch the phone in the garage. Mac recalled that Beth had been unsuccessfully nagging Butch to install a phone in their barn for years, with Butch insisting that the sound of the ring would spook the horses.

"Hello Beth!" Mac was pleased to hear Beth's voice over the phone, remembering immediately how much she enjoyed the woman. "It's Mary MacIntosh, returning your call. How are things?"

Beth filled Mac in on how her life had changed after the Powder River case, including how the remediation project was going on the ranch, and how Butch's horse business was going. "We don't hear from Greg much. I guess he is back in Africa or South America. I never can keep those countries straight."

Mac thought to herself, "continents,"–but it wasn't polite to correct people, and it didn't much matter whether Beth knew the difference anyway. She'd lived all of her life in Wyoming and Montana and was perfectly happy living a somewhat isolated life on a horse ranch. Beth was an exquisitely beautiful woman with her striking dark hair and emerald-green eyes complemented by her slim figure, muscular from all the work she did on the ranch and from her horse training. She wore her long hair pulled back most of the time, and dressed fashionably - especially for a woman who spent a good deal of time taking care of horses.

"I haven't heard from Greg at all," Mac said. "Is that why you were calling?"

"Oh no, dear! The reason I'm calling is actually quite peculiar, but I guess that makes sense since I'm a peculiar lady sometimes. Ask Butch or Wyatt. They'd tell you as much." Beth laughed a bit and then paused. "The reason I called was to see if I could help you."

"Help me?" Mac asked in bewilderment. "Do you mean in finding Greg?" Mac asked, confused as to the sudden gesture of kindness. Mac had gotten a great result for them in the class action methane gas case, and she knew that Beth felt a wide range a gratitude for Mac's devotion to her ranchland. She couldn't see any other reason that Beth would be offering her help.

"No. This isn't about Greg. Well, not really. Although I'd like nothing better than to see you two back together again. I'm still sick over your break-up, but I've come to realize that Greg would make a terrible husband. I hate to say that about my own son—but it's true. You deserve a nice man."

"Thank you, Beth. I wanted things to work out with Greg too, but your son made some choices that I couldn't live with. I hope you understand."

"Shoot, that's not the point of my call at all, I'm just looking to see if I could return the favor you did for me when you fought so hard to save my ranch, livelihood, and marriage. Hell, I wouldn't be sane if it weren't for the fact that you stood by me when I really needed it."

"Thank you," Mac said, blushing from the praise. "You know I did it with pleasure."

"From what I've read in the papers and what I hear from townsfolk, you're the one who needs help now—and I'm telling you I'm willing to help if I can."

"Forgive me, Beth, but I have no idea what you're talking about. Help me with what?"

"The Landers boy!" Beth practically shouted, surprised at Mac's dense response.

"How can you help me with Levi?"

"Mac, when I met Butch, I had a two-year-old boy who'd never known his daddy. Greg was a rambunctious kid, and I was working full-time and trying to take care of him and make a life for myself. I will never forget the kindness I received from other women during that time. I lived in Bozeman, and there was this little old lady who lived in the next apartment over. Now, looking back on it, she really wasn't that old, but she seemed so at the time. She volunteered to help watch Greg after his nursery school ended so that I could work and have an occasional night out. I couldn't afford extra childcare. She did it out of the kindness of her heart."

"I didn't know that," Mac said.

"There are a lot of things you don't know. One thing I'm pretty sure that you don't know yet is how hard it is to be a single mom. If this kid stays with you for long, you are soon going to learn this for a fact. Trying to take care of a little boy while working to keep up with your house and chores and social life will absolutely take you to the mat. I promise you, there aren't enough hours in the day. From what I hear, this little guy is rambunctious–way more than my Greg ever was. You're going to have your hands full."

"I know, and I'm afraid to admit it for the fear of Social Services placing him in a group home. Truth be told, I have no idea how I'm going to be able to take care of him, run a law practice, prepare for trial, take care of my house, and, possibly, have a relationship."

"Are you dating?" Beth immediately asked.

Mac realized her slip of tongue. She didn't want Beth to know about her relationship with Jeffrey. Jeffrey lived in a far-away city and this offered Mac a certain amount of small-town privacy that didn't usually exist.

"My point is that I agree with you, and that I'm working very hard to try and balance my own life and career with caring for Levi. I'm curious as to how you could help with this. Whatever it is, I'm willing to accept any help you could give!"

"I'm offering to help you take care of him, if you want. I can pick him up from school on the days you need to work, and bring him out to the ranch. I am great with boys, as you know. I will teach him to ride a horse and take care of animals. I know that he has behavioral problems, but that's nothing that a good dose of my ranch can't cure. The only concern I have is his illnesses. I've heard that he has cancer and I am not good with giving medicine, but I'm willing to learn. My boys were wild, but they weren't sick much and I never quite got comfortable with playing nurse-maid. Now, don't get me wrong–when a horse or cow is sick, I've given injections and medicine, but that's not the same. I don't think I could give a little boy a shot."

"What makes you think that he needs shots?" Mac asked.

"His daily shots, Mac! Just 'cause I live on a ranch outside of town don't mean I don't hear the gossip!" Beth lightheartedly responded.

"What daily shots are you referring to?" Mac asked, unsure of what Beth exactly meant.

"The ones he needs to survive, after being poisoned by his mom so many times."

Chapter 16

"Seriously, Beth" Mac urged, "I need to know how you found out this information. If I'm going to represent Levi to the best of my ability, I need to understand exactly what I'm up against. If word is out on the street on this case as you're suggesting, then I need to be prepared to respond to that."

"I happen to know a bit about this case from a confidential source, so you don't need to worry. I don't want to share her name with you unless you can promise me that this conversation never took place."

Mac wasn't sure what the best response was, because promising anything to Beth depended entirely on what information Beth knew. Ultimately, Mac realized that both her friendship with Beth and her need for information were tantamount.

"I've been good friends with Linda Sterling for a long time, Mac. We're on the same ladies' bridge group and book club, so we see each other once a month at minimum. She's asked for my help on some other complicated cases of hers, and as a result she had me certified as a temporary placement for foster kids. Linda seems to think that the ranch environment here could be beneficial to kids, and I agree. Plus, I don't have to worry about any parents coming and demanding unscheduled visits with their kids, with Butch and Wyatt around."

"I see," Mac responded as she chewed on the top of her pen. "That still doesn't explain how Levi's case came up, though."

"Let's just say that Linda may have mentioned that she had an unusually difficult case, and that I might have mentioned to her how fondly I thought of my old attorney. Perhaps she put two and two together. I'm not in the position to take Levi in on a full time basis, but I'm more than willing to help out in any way I can."

Mac knew enough to accept the gift Beth was handing to her. She knew that she could trust Beth with taking good care of Levi in the afternoons and she knew that Beth could handle his outbursts.

"I feel like I'm dreaming, Beth. I can't even begin to tell you how much I appreciate this–you're an angel. I accept your offer!" Mac started to smile as she began to realize just how much of a help this would be to her in this case, and that she might actually be able to balance the rest of her work load now. "We just need to figure out a way to introduce Levi to your family and the ranch, because he gets easily disturbed when changes are being made in his life."

"I understand. Greg was the same way when he was little. He is still that way sometimes, but he compensates for it by taking jobs that allow him to be noncommittal to those he loves. I think that it's his coping mechanism. It breaks my heart."

"I-I-I'm not sure how to respond to that."

"You don't have to respond, I just want you to know that I don't blame you for the break-up. I know I used some harsh words with you on the courthouse steps in Casper, but I didn't mean it. I was overwhelmed with a lot of little things back then, and was able to keep an emotional balance mainly because I knew my son had finally met a solid and upstanding woman. When that started to fall apart, I crumbled."

"I'm so relieved to hear you say that, Beth." Mac replied, grateful to have that moment in time remedied so quickly by something as simple as Beth's kind words. "Not because I'm happy to hear that you crumbled, but because I appreciate you taking the time to explain that all to me. I was hurt by your comments, especially coming at a time when I was so devastated with what Greg was doing to me. I didn't want you to think that I did anything but my best in that trial and my relationship with your son."

"Well, I'm glad we had the moment for me to explain that to you, then, because I spoke without thinking. After the emotions had settled, I realized how inappropriate my comments had been, and really regretted saying them. You never know. Things can change. You two could cross paths one day, and under different circumstances find that you still love one another."

Suddenly Mac became suspicious over Beth's unexpected generosity. Was her gesture in offering assistance less an act of good will, and more a calculated set-up? Could it be that Greg was scheduled to be home within the next few weeks, and this was Beth's way of ensuring their paths would cross?

"Are you expecting Greg home anytime soon?" Mac asked with some trepidation.

"No, I don't think so. The last I heard, he won't be here until Christmas. Why? Would you like for me to pass on a message to him?"

"Oh no, not at all," Mac responded, a little too quickly. "I was just curious. I could always email him if necessary, but thanks." There was an awkward silence on the phone line. After the pause had gone on for almost too long, Mac asked, "Should I bring Levi out to the ranch one afternoon this week, or is that too soon? I think the sooner you meet him, the better. Maybe we can have a few visits prior to you picking him up from school next Monday."

"Linda already suggested that, and so she started the process of getting special funding approval for the additional transportation costs. Not that I'm not willing to pay for my own gas, mind you, but because she suggested that getting these extra costs approved on paper would make it all look better. I guess with the cost of gas so high these days, it won't hurt to have some help with that. We can work out the best way for you to pick him up here in the evenings after court. I think it would be good for him if we threw in an occasional trip to the park or library, which would mean that he stays in town after school, and it would be nice to keep him from spending all of his afternoons in a car."

"Good point. How does today look? I expected to be in court most of the day today, so I didn't calendar anything for other clients. Would you mind if I brought him out around four o'clock? Maybe he could feed Mocha."

"I don't know about feeding Mocha, 'cause she's acting a bit feisty today. You know how she gets sometimes. As for you guys heading over today, though, that's fine. We have a new colt that Wyatt is working, so maybe Levi could spend some time with her. I tell you, Mac, that pony is a princess and she trots around the stable like she owns the place. I think that's what is upsetting Mocha! Anyways, feel free to come on over with Levi today. I'm sure we'll become friends in no time."

As Mac hung up the phone from her conversation with Beth, she realized just how much of a weight had been lifted off of her shoulders. She wondered if this type of stress and conflict was common amongst single mothers, and if so, how women were able to successfully balance motherhood with their careers.

With only two hours remaining before she needed to pick Levi up from school, Mac began to put her multi-tasking skills to pace. She swiftly returned phone calls while checking her e-mail and reading the pleadings Pamela had placed on her desk. When the time to pick up Levi finally arrived, Mac had more than enough work to assign both Pamela and Megan to keep them busy for the rest of the week.

* * *

As had been the case for a few days in a row, Levi genuinely appeared to be happy to see her when she pulled up in the pick-up zone, and he got in the car without much ado. As they pulled away from the curb, Mac told Levi that they were going to drive out into the country to visit a friend of hers who had a colt that needed feeding. Levi got noticeably quiet.

"You like horses, right? You told me that they're your second favorite animal. Aren't you excited to feed a baby horse?"

Levi didn't answer at first. Mac allowed the silence to settle in. Finally, he responded. "I like horses. I just wanted to go to the park with you and throw the ball."

"I didn't know that, buddy! I went ahead and scheduled this outing thinking you'd love spending time with this horse. I tell you what, though, why don't we do both? I have your bag in the car with our gloves and balls,

162

so we can throw the ball at my friend's ranch, or we can come back into town later and throw it before dinner. How does that sound?"

"Really? You mean it? 'Cuz my mom used to always say that and we never did it."

"I mean it. In fact, let's go to the park first and throw the ball, and then we'll head out to the ranch. How does that sound?"

Levi's mood picked up again and they chatted nonstop about his school day on the way to the park. After throwing for fifteen minutes, Levi' arm was tired, so they decided that it was time to head out to the ranch.

It had been a long time since Mac had driven the winding road past Arvada, and she realized how much she missed the beauty of the rolling hills of Wyoming. Some of the most gorgeous plains country in Wyoming lies along U.S. 14, east of Sheridan, on the quiet scenic road that curves through mile-after-mile of ranchland and amber waves of winter wheat. The road meandered alongside the cottonwood-bordered Clear Creek which was lined with beautiful purple lupine flowers that clustered near the banks of the river.

Mac looked back at the sinuous flow of water as they climbed through rugged hills and down a long green valley filled with fine ranches and modern homes. She watched in wonder as Levi allowed his eyes to wander to the right, catching the rays of sun illuminating the peaks of the Big Horn Mountains. The purple mountains were majestic in their own right. To Mac, they looked like an old cowboy lying down on his back at the end of a hard day's work.

"The mountains are beautiful from out here in the country, aren't they?" Mac asked.

Levi nodded. He turned his attention back to the road, as he was busy counting the mile marker reflectors along the side of the road. The landscape was still marred in places where the methane gas development continued, but the Anderson ranch looked a thousand times better than it did when Mac had filed the Anderson's methane gas lawsuit. Mac was deeply pleased to see that the surface damage had been remediated to some extent.

Mac's mind began to race through the Anderson's lawsuit, and so she started to share the story with Levi as they approached the Crazy Woman ranch. Mac was surprised to see that Levi appeared interested in the lawsuit, and how they had to sue the methane gas company in order to get them to fix her friend's ranch.

"Why did your friend let the gas people on the ranch? Why didn't they just say no and make them go away?" Levi asked.

It was a good question, and Mac was happy to hear Levi ask it. Most people would think that property owners would have a right to refuse anyone to come onto their land and begin drilling wells. Mac didn't know how much Levi would understand about subsurface rights and easements and water rights, so she tried to explain it in the most simplistic way. She was surprised by his continued interest in the story, and his apparently sophisticated sense of problem solving.

"Why do they call it the 'Crazy Woman'?" Levi asked. It was another good question. They'd just driven under the ranch entrance which was framed by beautiful pine log posts and a rough-on-the-tires cattle guard.

"The ranch was named before my friends bought it. My friends know how important it's to not change things if they don't need changing, so they let the name stand. It probably wouldn't have been their choice of a name for their ranch, but they're pretty good sports. You'll like them a lot. Today, you're going to meet Beth. She's a very nice lady. She's a mom and has two sons—both of whom are grown-ups now. She takes care of horses out here."

"Is that her?" Levi asked, pointing to a woman riding a horse in the pasture.

"Yes, as a matter of fact, that is her. She's very nice and very pretty. I think you're going to like her."

"Can I ride the horse?" Levi asked as he pointed towards the horse visible in the distance. Levi was wearing blue jeans and a long-sleeved sweatshirt, and was certainly dressed for a ride, but Mocha was not the horse for any child. Mocha was Beth's horse and she didn't allow many others to ride her.

"Not that horse. Mocha is sweet, but she's particular about who rides her. We'll have to ask Beth if there's a horse you can ride. If not today, maybe another day. We have to save time to throw that baseball, remember?"

Levi nodded. He had been so well behaved over the past few days. Mac missed him when he was at school and couldn't wait to pick him up at the end of the school day. She wondered whether he'd had much one-on-one time before he came to stay with her, other than that spent in a doctor's office or a hospital. He seemed to thrive when they had that alone time together.

They parked the car and Levi hopped out of the back seat. He took off running in the direction of Beth and Mocha.

"Levi, be careful!" Mac shouted. "Don't run up to the horse–you'll scare her. You need to stop and let her come to you."

Levi stopped in the driveway, near the arena and waited for Beth. She waved to him. Levi started to wave back, but then suddenly appeared embarrassed. He hung is head as he stared down at his feet. Mac walked over to him and grabbed him by the hand.

"It'll be okay, Levi. Mrs. Anderson is a really nice lady. She might insist you call her Beth or Miss Beth or something like that–and that would be okay. She teaches people how to take care of their horses, so she's a teacher, like Ms. Kendrick. She loves children. She had two boys of her own. One of them still lives with her and helps her take care of the ranch and his name is Wyatt. You might even see him around here today."

Mac's mind turned to Wyatt for the first time in awhile. He was Greg's brother, but he and Greg were as opposite as day is to night, and they didn't agree on much. Wyatt was better looking than Greg–there was no getting around that. In fact, Wyatt was better looking than most men and he easily could have posed as the "Marlboro Man" with his rugged handsomeness.

Mac's train of thought was sidetracked when Beth trotted near. "Well, well, well, if it isn't Levi Landers, reporting for horse-keeping duty," Beth said as Levi looked up at her. "How are you with horses, young man?"

Levi looked down again. Mac squeezed his hand, encouraging him to answer.

"Fine," was all he could muster.

"Fine is good enough for me. Tell you what, let's waste no time and get started already!" Beth's warm face and enthusiastic smile were enough to warm any heart, and Mac appreciated her genuine interest in Levi. "I want you to slowly reach up and let Mocha smell your hand. Go ahead, now, but be gentle. She's very sensitive to smell and likes to get to know you that way first." Levi reached out tentatively. "It's okay, Levi, her ears are pointed forward which means that she wants to smell you. She'd let me know if she didn't want you to hold out your hand. Horses are good that way. They communicate all the time, usually with their whinnies or their foot stomping or their ears. Mocha is the queen communicator around here. If there's a problem, she'll let you know. Okay?"

Levi raised his hand a bit higher. Mocha, a caramel-colored quarter horse, lowered her head and smelled his hand. Levi giggled. "Her nose is wet," he said.

"That's good. That means she's healthy. She's been running around up in the fields. A wet nose is usually a good thing, when it comes to animals. It's actually good for people too, but moms usually think you have a cold and get all fussy about it. It's nature's way of defending against bacteria."

Beth was so matter-of-fact that Levi didn't dare question her. He had grown quick at questioning authority because he had been poked and prodded by doctors for so many years. At some point, he became wise to the notion that he could actually protest to having his blood drawn again. The power it gave him was rewarding.

Beth adjusted the reins to the front and made sure that the bridle was in place before saying, "You seem like a very responsible boy. Would you mind walking Mocha to the barn? I will walk on the other side to make sure she behaves like a lady, but you should know that she usually is on perfect behavior going to the barn because she knows that she's going to get a yummy snack if all goes well."

Levi looked up at Mac with wide eyes, hoping to get some reassurance. He'd never been offered such a responsibility before, and was excited at the thought of actually helping walk Mocha to the barn. Mac nodded. "Sounds like you're the boy for the job," Mac said.

Levi's eyes lit up as he reached for the reins and as they rounded the corner of the long, gravel driveway and into the massive red barn, Mac heard a familiar voice coming from behind them.

"Howdy there, partner. You must be one very special guy if Mocha is letting you lead her."

Wyatt was a little over six feet tall and he walked towards Levi with the confidence of a steed. His hair matched that of his mother, but his eyes were Alexandrite—a mixture of emerald and amber. He pulled the leather glove off his right hand and extended it to Levi. Afraid to let go of the reins, Levi just stared at his large, weathered hand.

"Don't worry about Mocha. She ain't going nowhere. The food is here. You can let go of the reins with one hand to shake mine, man to man." Levi cautiously let go of Mocha's reins momentarily and reached out to shake Wyatt's hand. Wyatt shook hard and smiled. "Nice, firm handshake you got there, son. That'll take you places in life. Gotta shake like you mean it. My dad taught that to me when I was your age." Levi nodded and grinned, enjoying doing something right for a change.

"I got me here a problem. Maybe you can help me fix it, Levi. See over here," Wyatt said, pointing to a stall in the back of the barn. "We have us here a new colt. Now, my mom likes to give them all these fancy names and I just like it plain and simple. She hasn't yet named this guy. Think you can help me give it a useful name before she takes dibs on him and calls him something like 'Windsor' or 'Frappucino' or something else ridiculous for a horse? Trust me, horses can get embarrassed. What more embarrassing than a bad name? They have feelings too and when they have to go through life being called 'Mocha,' for example, they develop certain personality disorders."

Mac let out a laugh as did Beth. Levi followed Wyatt to the stall and climbed up to the second rung on the closed gate. He broke into a large smile. "He's small."

"Today he is. In a week, he'll practically double in size. He's got a heck of an appetite, this guy. Whatdya think? What should we call him?"

Levi paused for a moment, and tilted his head with his hand resting gently upon his chin. The little boy was clearly taking the time to make sure he came up with a respectable name. After a few moments, Levi suggested "How about 'Mr. Pony'?" Levi seemed proud of his name. Though Mac could tell that Wyatt would have preferred something else, he didn't ruin the young boy's pride by letting him know that.

"Mr. Pony, it is. Good name. I think he'll be proud of it, don't you?" Levi shook his head in agreement and smiled so widely that Mac could see his molars. She'd never seen him so happy. "Mr. Pony, this here is Levi. He's gonna feed you and brush you. Would you like that?" Mr. Pony let out a little snort, which was more likely a sneeze, but Wyatt didn't let it go without notice. "See, he likes you already. Come on in here with me and I'll school you in horse etiquette."

With that, Levi and Wyatt unbolted Mr. Pony's gate and disappeared into a world of promise and hope.

Chapter 17

"I can't believe the judge let you keep him," Jeffrey said to Mac during the phone call she'd placed to him while driving back from the Anderson ranch. She'd described the court hearing to him in a cryptic way, hoping not to clue Levi on to the contents of their conversation. "They must be desperate for foster parents out West. Of all the times I've been in court, yours is the most egregious conflict of interest I've ever heard of. I can smell that one all the way over here."

"Things happen for a reason, Jeffrey, and sometimes appearances can be deceiving. You've said as much yourself about so many of the cold cases you're trying to solve. Please try to give me the benefit of the doubt here. I'm trying to do something good and make a positive difference, just like you do."

Mac could hear Jeffrey exhale on the other end of the phone. "There's absolutely no comparison to what I do solving crimes and what you're doing right now. If you ask me, you're aiding and abetting a crime. For that matter, I can't see any reason why that little kid should be taken from *both* of his parents. I can see if both of the parents are beating the crap out of a kid, but when one parent is accused of doing something wrong and the other parent isn't implicated, that kid shouldn't be placed in the house of his attorney. No wonder the system is so screwed up."

Mac bit her tongue, though she was clearly disappointed with Jeffrey's response. To change the subject, Mac asked, "How was your gala on Saturday?" She hadn't asked him about the gala before, because she knew he'd start grousing over the fact that she didn't attend with him. Following the comments he'd just made, though, Mac figured that a grumpy conversation about the gala would be better than the one they were currently having.

"It was actually very nice. I had a good time, even though I was one of the only people there without a significant other."

Without taking the bait, Mac responded, "Glad to hear that you had a good time. You deserved to be honored for your hard work."

With that, the conversation toned itself down somewhat and they were able to talk about more mundane issues. Mac was trying to nudge their discussion along, as Wyoming rangeland was notorious for bad cell phone service; she hated when her calls dropped because she often couldn't call the other party back for five or ten minutes. She mentioned a few times that she was close to town and needed to go, but Jeffrey was more conversational than usual.

"Any idea when you can come out next?" he asked. Mac told him that she wasn't sure of her schedule at the moment due to the circumstances. "I'm scheduled to be in the Denver office in three weeks on that wiretapping case I told you about. Maybe you could come down for the weekend and we could go back to that jazz bar in Larimer Square we liked so much. What do you think?"

Just as Mac was about to answer, she was saved by the poor cell service that she frequently complained about. She was grateful that she didn't have to answer the question.

* * *

After Mac and Levi got home, they finished his homework, ate dinner and got ready for bed. Levi was still beaming from his time with Mocha and Mr. Pony, and he'd talked non-stop about it since they returned. Mac was thrilled to see how much Levi had enjoyed their outing, and even more delighted to see that his excitement had translated into him helping her with the dishes and the garbage.

After completing all of their chores, Mac and Levi continued to read the book, *Hatchet*, aloud. When Mac's voice grew hoarse from reading, Levi took over and read a few pages to her. Some of the words were a little advanced for him, but Mac enjoyed watching him sound them out and read them within the context of the sentence, trying to figure out what the words meant. She applauded his efforts, and encouraged him to continue his attempts at figuring the words out on his own. Mac could tell that he liked the positive reinforcement.

When it was time for him to go to sleep, Mac tucked him into her bed and gave him a light kiss on the forehead. "Sweet dreams, Levi. I hope you dream about Mr. Pony tonight."

"That would be good. Or the Baseball Man. He hasn't come to one of my dreams for a few nights. I like it when he comes."

"Will you tell me the next time he comes? He seems to have interesting things to say," Mac said. She was still not quite sure how to feel about the "Baseball Man," and wanted to contemplate it further before mentioning it to Levi's psychologist.

"Can we go see Mr. Pony and Mr. Wyatt again? I like horses. I didn't think that I was going to like it there, but it was sorta cool."

Mac smiled. "That sounds like an excellent idea. Miss Beth and Mr. Wyatt told me how much they enjoyed you during the visit today. I'm sure they'd love you to come and visit them again. Maybe this weekend we can go again. Would you like that?"

"Yes!" Levi responded, grinning from ear to ear and shaking his head wildly up and down.

Mac got a kick out of Levi's physical response to that question, and even more of a kick out of watching him roll over to his side and fall asleep. After waiting a few moments to ensure that Levi really had fallen asleep, Mac went into her living room and dug through the box of Levi's medical documents that she'd brought home from the office. She started reading the charts and notes, which fairly accurately adhered to the information that Evelyn had told Mac on Saturday when they'd met at the school playground.

Mac reviewed the long entries that discussed whether the flu might have triggered childhood leukemia in Levi. According to the charts Evelyn was the one who insisted that Levi be tested for acute lymphoblastic leukemia (A.L.L.). Since nearly all children with A.L.L. achieve an initial remission if they're treated early, she insisted that he undergo bone marrow transplant surgery in conjunction with chemotherapy with cranial irradiation. Not all tests had confirmed the diagnosis, yet Evelyn was insistent that they treat Levi's symptoms according to the hypothetical diagnosis immediately. The charts clearly noted Evelyn's aggressive campaign for A.L.L. treatment despite the lack of a formal diagnosis, and even showed that she'd made threats to sue doctors and hospitals if the treatments were not commenced immediately. Mac found many forms documenting the hospitals issuance of informed consent to Evelyn, including detailed review of the histochemical, morphologic, immunophenotypic, cytogenetic, and biochemical characteristics of Levi's leukemia cells.

Mac found extensive notes in the files suggesting the doctors intended to cover their own hides with regards to their proceeding with a three-drug induction regimen using vincristine, prednisone, and asparaginase. Those CYA-type notes were probably smart, given that within three weeks of treatment, Levi tested neurotoxic. The treatments were suspended, and the doctors ultimately concluded that Levi did not, in fact, have acute lymphocytic leukemia.

Mac continued reading for several hours, and it wasn't until nearly midnight that she found herself barely able to keep her eyes open. She tucked Levi's records into the box and closed the lid tight.

By around two in the morning, Mac felt a nudge on her left arm. Blissfully asleep, Mac tried to ignore it, hoping that it was her cat. By the third nudge Mac could no longer pretend that it was Ted looking for a sleeping spot on the couch. Mac forced open her sleepy eyes, and found herself looking directly into Levi's eyes.

"He came back," Levi said, in a trance-like tone. This time, Mac knew exactly what was going on.

"Baseball Man?"

Levi shook his head yes.

"What did he say?" Mac asked as she began to sit herself up on the couch. She motioned for Levi to sit next to her, and put her arm around him as she awaited his answer.

"That I need to focus on teamwork. He said there are good players on my team and that if we all work together, we'll have a winning season."

"Sounds like good advice."

"He said I have to trust my coach. He said I have a good coach and I need to do what the coach tells me to do, even if I'm not sure whether it's right. He says the coach knows best."

Mac reflected on this last statement. "Well, I guess that's usually true."

"He told me to slide into second base, because there was something special waiting for me there."

"Did you slide into second base?"

Levi nodded.

"Well, what was there for you?" Mac prompted.

"Probably the best baseball card there is, and the one I've always wanted."

"Let me guess," Mac said. She thought she might know, as they'd been talking baseball cards for days and Levi had told her more than she ever thought she could know about the old-time players that he loved. "Yogi Bear."

Levi laughed out loud. "Yogi Berra! Not Yogi Bear. He's not a bear in a hat at Yellowstone."

Mac giggled along with Levi. "Close enough. You knew what I meant."

"You weren't right anyway." Levi responded, taking on the same serious tone he'd had before. "It was Honus Wagner, the Pirates' lead batter. He is the top second baseman of all time. I bet his baseball card is worth more than any other."

"In your dream, did you get his card?"

"Yep." Levi smiled, clearly enjoying the memory of the long desired card. "I picked it up and smiled and looked back at the Baseball Man, who was on home plate. He waved and told me to read the back."

"Did you?"

"Yeah, but all it said was 'JJ'–no baseball stats on Honus Wagner or anything. It was cheap."

"That's interesting. Do you have any idea what "JJ" means? Is that a baseball term or something?"

"No," Levi said as he shook his head. He immediately smiled and craned his neck up high as he changed the conversation. "When I woke up I looked under my pillow, hoping I'd really have a Honus Wagner card."

"Sorry, buddy. Maybe someday." As Mac said this, she looked at the clock before gently reminding Levi that it was the middle of the night. "It's pretty late. Maybe if you go back to bed right now, you'll be able to pick up the dream where you'd left off."

"Maybe. But that usually doesn't work."

"We can't control how our brains work while we're asleep, but sometimes if we concentrate really hard on something before we fall back asleep, we can kind of nudge our brain in the right direction," Mac said. Levi shrugged his shoulders in response, and left the room.

For the next hour, Mac lied awake on the couch wondering what "JJ" could possibly mean. After an hour of tossing and turning over the meaning of the dream, Mac finally got up from the couch and turned on the floor lamp next to her. If I'm going to lie here awake, I might as well do something useful, Mac thought as she reached into the thick stack of medical records.

Mac continued where she'd left off, and found that Levi's illnesses continued throughout his entire fifth and sixth year of life. Once the doctors were able to rule out leukemia, Evelyn apparently began a crusade to find out what was making Levi sick. Evelyn suggested nearly every possible diagnosis, regardless of how unlikely the case might have been. Mac read Evelyn's complaints of stomach cancer, and then pancreas cancer once it had been ruled out. Next came kidney cancer, then cancer of his adrenal cortex.

Evelyn pushed forward with each potential diagnosis, and when it was ruled out she immediately came up with another one. Evelyn's apparently final medical conclusion was that he suffered from multiple endocrine neoplasia syndrome, which is abnormal and uncontrolled cell growth in more than one endocrine organ.

Each time Evelyn suggested a new illness, an entirely new team of medical professionals was called in. Each of these new doctors apparently noted Evelyn's overbearing nature. One such note was found in regards to Evelyn's fixation over Levi having Werner's Syndrome. After the top physician on this disease in the country was summoned to Denver from Harvard University, he'd made the following note in Levi's charts:

> "Mother had two years of medical school and it appears she may be suffering from low self esteem as a result of her failure to complete her medical training. She is bossy and manipulative during the examination of the patient and will not allow the patient to answer questions himself. She arrived at our first appointment with medical books and copies of medical charts for me to review. When I explained that I would request whatever information I deemed relevant, she was imprudent.

> "I made inquiry regarding patient family history and determined that father/husband was an OB/GYN and that Dr. and Mrs. Landers met in med school, before she dropped out to support him. This information, coupled with Mrs. Landers's behavior in the exam room, led me to believe that she might be 'steering the ship' as it relates to child's condition.

> "Patient presents with a combination of odd and troubling lab tests, though none of these results support a Werner's syndrome diagnosis.

> "Patient did present with a slender body build, long and thin extremities, a high arch palate, a funnel chest, a high arch in foot, thick membranes surrounding the lips, and a reported tumor in the pituitary gland. Biopsy of tumor benign. Determined to be hyperplasia of the gland, cause unknown. Referred patient to specialist

dealing in elimination disorder issues. Urged mother to seek counseling for herself and her son.

"Mother agitated and apparently unsatisfied with diagnosis. Left exam room visibly angry and suggested that I return to academia (I quote, 'Those who can, do, and those who can't, teach.')

Sadly, Mac noted that this chart was not unique. There were a number of similar chart entries by other specialists that also noted Evelyn's zeal in pursuing certain diagnoses. Mac read about Levi's platelettes and fevers and vomiting episodes, documented by years of medical treatment. Just reading about his many past fevers and vomiting episodes began to worry her, and Mac stopped reading Levi's medical history several times to go check on him. *How could a ten year old kid who appeared so healthy have had such a tumultuous medical past?*

By four thirty in the morning, Mac had reviewed countless pages of Levi's medical history. Just as she was preparing to put all of the documents away and finally get some sleep, Mac saw something out of the corner of her eye that gave her pause. When she looked more closely at the document in question, Mac caught her breath.

Chapter 18

"Hello?" Mac answered the phone at five thirty in the morning. Though she normally woke up early to enjoy a morning jog, this morning was not one of them. She'd been up all night and hadn't been able to fall asleep until just about thirty minutes earlier.

"You sound sleepy." Mac heard Jeffrey comment quite observantly on the other end. "You're usually up with the crows." Mac noticed that Jeff's voice appeared friendlier than it had been during their last conversation.

"I was up most of the night . . . working." Mac forcefully lifted her body from off of the couch. As she began to wipe the sleep from her eyes, she realized Jeff didn't normally contact her this early. "Is everything okay?"

"Everything's fine. In fact, it's great. Remember that meeting I was supposed to have in Denver in a few weeks? Well, it was advanced, and I'm flying out this morning and I'll be in Colorado for the next five days." Mac could hear Jeff's excitement through the phone. "Can you come down and spend a few days? I'd really love to see you."

Mac let out a heavy sigh–loud enough for Jeffrey to hear. She got up from the couch and headed toward the kitchen to brew a strong pot of coffee.

"I take it that's a 'no'?"

"Jeffrey, I'm just making coffee. I'm not awake yet. Can I call you back?"

"I'm boarding the flight now. Don't bother."

"Jeffrey, don't be like that. I'm on thirty minutes sleep. I just need a cup of Joe to wake me up. I'll call you right back. It'll be another twenty minutes until they make you turn off your phone."

"Okay." Though the excitement had clearly disappeared from his voice, at least the icy tone he'd picked up during their brief conversation had also left.

As Mac hung up the phone, she proceeded to grind the coffee beans. Mac put her hand atop the grinder, in hopes to isolate the sound it made as much as possible and avoid waking up Levi. It was Friday and he had a spelling test, so she wanted him to sleep for at least another hour. Ideally, they'd review some of his spelling words after he got up but before they began the ride to school.

Mac stood atop the coffee machine as she watched her morning energy rush brew, anxiously awaiting some finished product. When she finally was able to pour herself a cup, she greedily began gulping it down before returning Jeffrey's call. She dialed but was immediately greeted by voicemail. His phone was obviously turned off. She hung up and set the phone next to her mug, but no sooner had she done that the phone immediately began to ring.

"Jeffrey?" Mac asked, the surprise evident in her voice.

"Uh, no." a male voice responded on the other end. "Mac? Did I call the right number?"

"Yes, this is Mac. Who is this?" Mac wondered who else would be calling her at this hour.

"This is Wyatt. Wyatt Anderson. Did I call too early? I'm sorry if I did. I figure that you're the type of gal that gets up early."

"Wyatt! No. I mean 'Yes.' Yes, I get up early. No, you didn't call too early." Mac stumbled out a quick response, clearly embarrassed for answering the phone as she did. "I'm sorry that came out so mixed up, I'm just really tired. I just finished chugging a pot of coffee, and now have to wait for my brain to catch up with my mouth."

"Well, consider yourself lucky. My mouth works faster than my mind."

Mac laughed. Wyatt's voice was ridiculously sexy. In fact, everything about Wyatt Anderson was sexy–especially his self-deprecating remarks.

"Shouldn't you be out riding a horse or feeding a cow or something?" Mac asked, as she held the phone with her shoulder and started packing Levi's lunch box.

"Shouldn't you be running a marathon before work?" Wyatt countered.

"Touché. No, I haven't been able to get out in the mornings with Levi here."

"Actually, that is why I'm calling," Wyatt sheepishly admitted. "I kind of told him that if he came out this weekend I'd show him how to saddle and ride a horse. Do you think that'd work out?"

"He's already mentioned how much he would like to ride a horse," Mac replied. "I'm sure he'll be very happy to hear that you called about this."

"Is tomorrow too soon?" Wyatt asked.

"No, tomorrow would be great. He'll be very excited. Perhaps it will give him incentive not to grouch at me so much when I make him practice his spelling words."

"Oh, man," Wyatt said, chuckling. "I remember Friday spelling tests. Worst day of the week for me, 'cause I'm just a terrible speller. Poor kid. Tell him not to worry about spelling–it's more important to know how to saddle a horse."

"I'm not sure I agree with that, but I'll let Levi know that you are looking forward to seeing him." Mac chuckled a little too hard in response before catching herself and sobering her tone up a bit. "You might not want to tell Levi that, either, otherwise I'll never be able to get him to study for tests again."

"Deal."

There was a pause in the conversation. Mac knew Wyatt wasn't much for talking on the phone, but since he was the one who initiated the call, she didn't want to cut him short. "What time should we come out?" she asked, keeping the conversation alive.

"How early can you get up on a Saturday? The earlier, the better when it comes to ranch life. There's a lot to do around here in the mornings."

"Can we tentatively plan between six and seven? I want to get there as early as possible, but I don't want to wake Levi up if he needs the sleep. Sound okay?"

"Sounds great. I'll let my mom know. She'll probably insist that you eat breakfast out here."

Mac groaned. "Your mom forced me to eat breakfast last time I was out there and I'm still trying to lose the five pounds I gained."

"You look perfect. Don't you worry about that, now. See you bright and early."

When Mac hung up the phone, she could feel her heart pounding. *Damn. Why does he have to be my ex-boyfriend's brother?* A pang of guilt swept through her as she realized just how strong her physical reaction was to Wyatt. She felt alive again, for the first time in awhile.

As Mac showered and dressed for work, she contemplated about how silly and giddy Wyatt's call had made her feel. When she woke Levi and told him about their plans to go to the ranch the following morning, the giddiness became contagious. He ate breakfast without prodding and even volunteered to practice his spelling words before they got into the car. He carried his own backpack without complaint and agreed to respell the two words that he'd missed. They went through the list three times on the way to school and by the third try, he'd gotten all twenty words correct.

"I'm gonna ace this thing," Levi said as he got out of the car in the drop-off zone.

"Of course you are." Mac smiled in response. "I can't wait to hear how you did when I pick you up after school. Have a great day!" Mac blew Levi a kiss, but he rolled his eyes. He'd already warned her that ten-year-old boys don't get kisses from their parents at school. Mac thought that it was cute that he included her in the role of "parent."

* * *

Evelyn had a terrible week. Things started going wrong for her on Sunday, and quickly progressed throughout the week. "I spent the better part of my afternoon explaining our son's medical history to his lawyer, and you spend your afternoon golfing and drinking. What's wrong with this picture?"

"First, our ten-year-old son *has* a lawyer. Second, we're not doing anything about him having a lawyer. Third, he's living with his lawyer. Need I say more?"

After hearing no immediate response from her, Luke turned towards Evelyn and continued. "What the fuck is wrong with this picture, Evelyn? What kind of legal system takes your kid away, appoints him a lawyer and then lets him live with her?"

"We have a chance to make that change at court on Tuesday, but you've got to come with me," Evelyn said. She could see that Luke had a few too many vodka tonics, and she didn't want to be too aggressive with her responses.

"Are you that tuned out that you don't know my schedule? I always have C-sections on Tuesday, and I have four this coming Tuesday. I've been scheduling them this way for about ten years now, because it gives the mother enough time to recover and return home by Friday." Luke was moving around the bedroom, putting some clothes away as he ranted. "The fact that you and both of our lawyers allowed another hearing to be scheduled on a Tuesday really pisses me off."

"Luke, I don't have any control over when the court schedules its juvenile hearings, and that apparently is only on Tuesdays. Our judge covers other kinds of cases other days–"

"Well, I do C-sections on Tuesdays. I guess no one gives a shit about my schedule." Evelyn could tell that Luke was getting himself worked up, and wished she'd gone to sleep instead of confront him. "The judge's schedule trumps *mine*? I save lives. I bring babies into this world. I actually do something good and worthwhile–he just fucks everything up for the kids I deliver."

"That is not fair. Our judge really is a nice man, Luke. I don't like what's happening here either, but he's just doing his job–"

"And I don't have a job to do? If I stopped working, Evelyn, I wouldn't be able to keep my four spoiled brats and their spoiled mother living the lifestyle to which they are accustomed."

"You're an ugly drunk, Luke." Evelyn muttered under her breath.

"What did you say? Do I hear you commenting on my drinking? That's funny, coming from you. You know, you really could use a drink yourself, Evelyn–lighten up a little. When was the last time you smiled? Laughed? Had fun? You haven't had a good time in what, sixteen years? No wonder I load up every now and then when I'm not on call. I need to escape the boring hell you call 'marriage'."

"Is that what you think? Our marriage is hell? Well, that certainly explains why you'd have a girlfriend on the side." Evelyn pulled the covers back and got out of bed. She took a few steps in Luke's direction. Her flannel pajamas hung on her like a frock. Black streaks of mascara followed the stream of tears from her eyes.

"Jesus Christ, Evelyn. You've been accusing me on having an affair since I was in medical school. Grow up, will you? I'm sick and tired of hearing you bitch at me about the same old crap. You need a new gig. A new shtick."

"What I need is a man who cares about his wife and four children at least as much as he cares about himself."

With that, Luke went into his side of the closet and began loudly pulling open some drawers. He stuffed clothes into a gym bag and grabbed his shaving case from the bathroom vanity. As he headed out of the master bedroom, he felt an object whiz by his head. He turned in time to see one of Evelyn's shoes smash against the bedroom wall. Luke Landers kept on walking.

* * *

Monday hadn't fared much better for Evelyn. Normally, she met with a few ladies downtown at the Sheridan Stationery for a book club meeting, but not this week. Apparently, Evelyn had "inadvertently" been left off the email reminder list. This, of course, seemed a bit contrived, since Evelyn knew that the e-mail was sent to a group list of which she was a member. Evelyn knew that she'd been deliberately "uninvited," and this gravely hurt her feelings.

In the past few weeks, Evelyn had been shunned by more people than she could count. Not only was she excluded from the book club meeting, but also the Homecoming Parade organizational committee and the girls' varsity volleyball state championship fundraiser.

Unfortunately, the community's exclusion of Evelyn didn't stop there. Evelyn was very aware that people had begun to avoid her when she was out shopping at the local market, and she was rarely given a wave by anyone when she drove down Main Street. Things had changed. Personal affiliations had cooled. Phone calls were not returned. People were no longer willing to be seen around her. It simply wasn't chic for people to associate with her.

Evelyn wasn't sure whether Tuesday's hearing had broken her streak of bad luck, or whether it was a day just like the rest. Luke, of course, hadn't bothered to show up for the hearing, which he'd made quite clear to Evelyn on Sunday. Judge Binnard didn't let the absence go unnoted and made quite a stink about the fact that Levi's father was in contempt of a court order.

Later in that hearing the judge had ruled that Levi could remain in his attorney's care, and Evelyn had mixed feelings about the ruling. Evelyn was not happy that Mac was taking care of Levi, but for some reason, she took solace in knowing that Levi was safe and seemed to be healthy. Evelyn wondered how Mac was keeping Levi from getting sick. She thought about the possibility that perhaps there was something in the Landers's home that was making Levi sick—mold, perhaps? Now that Levi was out of the contaminated environment, was he fairing better? Evelyn made a note to herself to call a mold inspector that morning.

* * *

While Evelyn was considering herself grateful for Mac's status in the case, Mac was actively researching Evelyn's life history. The day following the hearing, Mac's paralegal completed a full-scale profile search and was able to dig up salacious information. What Mac read was clearly not in Evelyn's best interests, and if any of this was admitted into evidence at trial, it would clearly demonstrate that Evelyn was not fit to be a parent.

Chapter 19

"This year Sheridan High School's Homecoming King . . . is Austen Landers!"

The gymnasium was filled with parents, teachers, students, and coaches, all dressed in the appropriate blue and gold to support their Broncs. The crowd had been buzzing with anticipation, curious to know who their next King would be. Austen wasn't nervous or excited, because he was fairly certain that he was the winner. When Austen's name was called over the mic, he simply smiled and bowed.

No one's excitement about Austen's win matched that of Evelyn. She stood tall and proud, clapping a bit too loudly for her handsome, blushing, son. It was as if Evelyn felt personally validated at that very moment–as if she could say to the world, "*See, I am a good mom. My son is Homecoming King. That doesn't just happen in a bubble. It requires good parenting.*"

As Evelyn looked around her, reveling in the moment, she noticed that Ben was clapping with the rest of them. Evelyn never knew what to expect from him, so she was very proud to see Ben happy for his brother. Next to Ben was Lauren, who was clapping and shouting loudly for her big brother. Evelyn had pulled Lauren out of junior high classes to attend the pep rally.

Luke was missing from the event, which was not surprising. Evelyn wanted to put on a united front and have the remaining Landers family present at the pep rally for Austen's win. Evelyn came alone, and Luke was supposedly at the hospital. Luke told her that there an unusually high number of women in the hospital requiring discharge orders before the weekend and that neither of his partners could make rounds for him.

Evelyn normally bowed her head as she played the role of understanding and supportive wife–but not this time. Why should she? Luke wasn't at all supportive of her needs, and she was tired of the relationship being a one-way street. Minutes before the pep rally started, Evelyn decided to call him at his office. Dr. Lander's receptionist told Evelyn that Luke was out for the afternoon. Evelyn then called the hospital and asked that he be paged. Evelyn told the operator that this was an emergency and figured that she could come up with some emergency by the time he answered his page. After several minutes, the hospital technician got back on the phone and told Evelyn that Dr. Landers wasn't answering his page and explained to Evelyn that this likely meant he was not at the hospital, especially since all of his patients had been discharged from the hospital that morning. Evelyn hung up after being told that the OB ward did not expect him to return to the hospital, unless there was an emergency labor situation.

When Evelyn realized that Luke was not at the hospital or his office, she figured that he would show up for the rally. Her spirits rose a bit, and she began to think to herself, *I'll show you small town people what winners the Landers are.* Evelyn's temporary boost of confidence was deflated when Luke did not show up. Outwardly, Evelyn appeared nothing more than a proud mother of the Homecoming King. Inwardly, she was a seething, angry lioness plotting her revenge.

* * *

"Good morning, Levi," Wyatt said as he pulled off his dirty leather gloves to shake Levi's hand. Wyatt was wearing Wrangler jeans, a light green t-shirt and a plaid jacket. His cowboy boots were covered in dirt and his cowboy hat had sweat on the brim. He'd already been working for an hour. "It's a bit chilly this morning. I didn't expect to see you before seven. You musta got Mac up before the roosters crowed."

It was true. Mac had taken him straight to her office after she'd picked him up from school Friday night, and he was so excited that Mac could barely get him to settle down. Mac's office was located on the second story of a historic building on Main Street, which was prime viewing for any town event, including the Homecoming Parade. Levi sat in her window with Ted, Mac's cat who came to work with Mac on a daily basis, and together they watched the homecoming floats pass, one by one. Each float had a theme, and Levi held Ted and explained what he thought of each float. Ted, a mellow tabby cat who was more like a dog, seemed to understand the conversation, and purred as he sat next his new-found friend.

Levi waved at Austen when his float went by, and when Austen spotted him in the window, he waved back. Austen then pounded his heart with his fist and then pointed at Levi–a gesture to show his love for his little brother. Levi mimicked the gesture back to Austen. Tears filled Levi's eyes as the float traveled out of sight. Mac noticed, but decided not to comment. Some things were better left unsaid–at least for a time.

After the parade, Mac took Levi home and they ate dinner together before watching a movie. She hoped that if they went to bed early, then they'd have a good chance of getting out of the house a little after six o'clock in the morning. To Mac's surprise, Levi got up at five, dressed himself, brushed his teeth, and begged Mac for doughnuts on the way out of town. With a very strong cup of coffee in hand, Mac acquiesced.

Mac considered calling Wyatt to warn him of their early arrival, but wasn't willing to risk the chance of waking up Beth to do so. Butch was out of town on a rodeo training circuit, and if Mac were in Beth's position she would take advantage of that absence and sleep in a bit. Had Wyatt simply owned a cell phone, Mac thought, this entire dilemma would disappear.

"Mornin' Mac. You look ready to go jogging, not riding," Wyatt said. Mac was wearing black running tights, a black running tank and a fire-engine red fleece pullover. Her long, curly, auburn hair was pulled back into a pony tail, which was concealed by a Nike baseball cap. She wore no makeup, so her freckles glistened in the early morning light.

"Actually, I thought I might go for a run when you and Levi take the horses out. I need the exercise."

"I don't get you city folk. If you work the land and exercise the horses, you get all the exercise you need, and then some. I work out from the minute I get up until nightfall just by doing chores around this place."

"If I could make a living playing outdoors all day, Wyatt, I would. Unfortunately, not many lawyers work the land."

"The world would be a better place if they did."

"I'll tell you what. I'll help you with any chores you want today if you let me get a half hour run in this morning. Deal?" Mac was desperate; she had become so used to her daily run that she felt absolutely sluggish and out of shape for the last week.

"Deal. I'll have Levi help me feed the cows and the chickens. I'm also going to take him across the way to help with the sage grouse and pheasant. By the time we're done with that, you should be back. Then we'll put you to work tamping fence posts while Levi and I learn how to saddle up Mr. Pony."

When Levi heard his horse's name, his face lit up. "Go ahead, Mac. I'll be good for Mr. Wyatt." Levi spoke up for the first time since their arrival without prodding. He looked happy and comfortable. Mac agreed and took off down the gravel country road, and immediately felt free as her feet hit the ground. Her breathing leveled as her pace settled, and soon she'd logged five miles. She didn't intend to run so far, but it felt so good to be free, and the stress of the past week melted away.

As she grew closer to the ranch, she saw Wyatt and Levi carrying buckets of feed towards the bird coop. She noticed that Levi was asking questions and happily following directions. As she observed the two interact, it dawned on her that Levi had probably not spent much time with a positive male role model. Luke was too busy with his medical practice, and all his free time seemed to be occupied by the older and more athletic kids.

"Look who's back," Wyatt said to Levi. Levi smiled and showed Mac his bucket of bird feed. He wanted her to feel how heavy the bucket was.

"You've been busy, haven't you?" Mac asked. She reached to pick up the bucket. "Wow, this weighs a ton. You must be strong to be able to carry this!" Levi beamed with the notion and showed Mac the muscles in his arms. He was still thin, but he had filled out some over the past few weeks, and there was a delineation of biceps showing.

"This kid ain't sick. He just needs to be out of doors workin' like a real man," Wyatt said. Mac shot him a look. She may have only had a child in her care for a short while, but she knew enough to recognize that kids repeated everything said in their presence.

"He certainly has been feeling well over the last few weeks, haven't you, Levi?" Mac asked. Levi shrugged his shoulders, as if he hadn't given his health much thought. Mac tried to immediately, yet subtly, change the subject. "What else have you two been doing in the last hour? Did you feed Mr. Pony?"

"Yes. And we filled his trouser with water."

"Trough," Wyatt corrected while smiling. "Trousers are what men wear. You didn't see any horses drinking out of my pants now, did you?" Wyatt good naturedly teased, while tousling Levi's hair.

"Oh yeah," Levi said, not taking any shame from Wyatt's light hearted comments. Wyatt handled the correction matter-of-factly and with a kind tone. "Mr. Wyatt let me brush Mr. Pony and Mocha, and we moved some of the cows from one pasture to another. Cows smell and they are stupid."

"Cows do smell," Wyatt agreed, "but some of 'em can be pretty darn smart. Remember the story I told you about the one who kept escaping?"

Levi smiled and tapped his index finger to his temple in unison with Wyatt. "He was a clever cow."

"Yes, she was. It was a girl cow and she was too clever for her own good. Kinda like Mac here," Wyatt teased as he winked in her direction. Levi seemed oblivious to the banter. "Did you know that my brother used to be Mac's boyfriend?"

Mac shot Wyatt an alarmed look, and then turned her gaze immediately to Levi to gauge his reaction. Levi looked up at Wyatt.

"She has another boyfriend now," Levi responded without missing a beat. "His name is Jeffrey. He is a doctor. He lives pretty far away. He gets mad because he never gets to see her. I think he's gonna break up with her. He doesn't like kids. Mac likes kids. Mac–"

"Levi!" Mac breathlessly interrupted, embarrassed to hear Levi sharing so many of her personal details with Wyatt. "You're telling Mr. Wyatt an awful lot of boring stuff now!" Mac tried desperately to switch gears without looking as embarrassed as she was. "Why don't you tell Wyatt something exciting about baseball. Did you tell Mr. Wyatt how much you like baseball?" It was a feeble attempt, but the best Mac could manage.

Wyatt winked at Mac to let her know that he was taking her bait. She didn't know whether to be relieved that Wyatt was helping her shift gears, or humiliated that Wyatt realized her desperate attempts to steer the conversation away from her love life.

"Oh, buddy, you didn't tell me about baseball!" Wyatt chided. "I love baseball! I don't get to go to games much because I have to work out here on the ranch all the time, but I sure do loving talking baseball. Who's your team?"

Wyatt listened intently, appearing to be genuinely interested in what Levi had to say. "My favorite team is the Cincinnati Reds," Wyatt responded, after Levi had told him all about his favorite players from each team in the National and American leagues. "When I was a kid, they were really good and my favorite player was Pete Rose." Levi's face lit up.

"Charlie Hustle?" Levi said.

"Yep. That's what they called him. How'd you know that?"

"Baseball cards. I collect them."

"That's cool. I used to do that, too. I don't know where my collection is. If I can find them, maybe you can have them. I don't have much use for them any more."

"Really? That would be awesome," Levi said.

With that, Levi and Wyatt wandered into the chicken coop to feed the birds.

* * *

Mac's cheeks were still a bit red from blushing as she left them to head towards Beth in the newly remodeled Anderson home. Beth was sitting in her newly-remodeled kitchen drinking her second cup of coffee and reading the paper. She welcomed Mac's company and offered to fix her breakfast. Mac declined, but accepted a cup of steaming hot coffee with a touch of skim milk.

"The house looks amazing," Mac offered. Beth agreed and took her on a tour. The Andersons used some of the money Mac had won for them in the methane gas toxic tort lawsuit to remodel their nineteen thirties ranch house. The kitchen now had modern appliances and granite countertops. The rest of the home had new hardwood floors and textured walls with accents of new color and fine wood finish work. After giving Mac a tour of the general areas in the home, Beth took Mac towards Greg's old room.

"I re-did the whole thing. He doesn't come home much, so I decided to turn it into a nice guest room. He hasn't even seen it." Mac didn't comment, because the last thing she wanted to talk about right now was Greg. The less she knew about him at this point in her life, the better. It took her a long time to get over the hurt and betrayal from her nearly three-year relationship with him, and she wasn't in the mood to dredge up any of those long suppressed feelings.

"Wyatt is great with kids. Levi is having a big time out there with him. Thank you for facilitating this—it is exactly what Levi needs."

"You can thank Linda Sterling. It was her idea. She is a truly gifted woman. She can see things that other people don't. She is great at her job and she really cares about the health and safety of the kids that she works with. I admire her very much." Beth said, as they continued their walk along the house. "She's brought a number of kids out here. They all love animals and most kids like to be useful, once they get over the idea that they might have to do some 'work.' I doubt Levi's ever done a stitch of work or chores in his life. He has an overbearing mom and a full-time housekeeper. In my opinion, that is a disservice to a kid. Kids need responsibilities and chores and they need to pull their weight in the family. That's what makes a family complete—when everyone is needed. Levi has been expendable in his family unit and that's why he is in the position that he's in. A crying shame if you ask me."

Beth took a long pull from her coffee mug. Her long dark hair was pulled back off her beautiful face, showing off her deeply set emerald eyes. Mac noticed that Beth had a few more grey hairs, but instead of looking out of place, they accentuated her face and made her look even more regal.

"Levi seems to be doing pretty well," Mac offered in his defense.

"It's a wonder, knowing what I know about his mother. For the cards that woman was dealt, she's done a pretty darn good job raising kids, but

I think this last one put her over the edge. I knew her growing up. Did you know that?"

Mac stopped dead in her tracks upon hearing this, and turned towards Beth while shaking her head. "In Montana?"

"We grew up in the same small town. Gardiner. Not far from Livingston. Her father was an alcoholic and very abusive. He beat her mother when he drank too much. But that's not the worst part. As Evelyn and her sister got older, he sexually molested them." Beth paused at this point, looking to Mac for her reaction.

"Was that just talk of the town, or did Evelyn ever tell you this?"

"Pretty darned near a fact," Beth responded. "Because after their mom figured it out, she shot him. And that was all over the news, too. After she got sentenced to life without parole, the girls were quickly put up for adoption. Evelyn and her sister were lucky because they were taken in by a family in California who had quite a good deal of money. They had Evelyn tutored and sent her to Stanford and then on to med school. According to Linda, most girls who are sexually molested have a hard time with adult relationships if they don't get the counseling they need. Linda doesn't think that Evelyn had any therapy to deal with the molestation and abandonment issues and that's why she's doing what she is doing to Levi."

Mac wasn't sure how to respond to Beth, or whether the conversation they were having was in itself appropriate. The research Pamela had done provided much the same information that Beth was telling her now, but she was not going to let the on to Beth. She'd yet to say anything about Evelyn's pregnancy resulting from this abuse, or the fact that Evelyn's first baby with Luke had died shortly after birth, and Mac desperate to hear her take on this—but she wouldn't be able to bring it up on her own. Mac didn't know whether Beth knew that Evelyn's twin sister, Elaine, mysteriously died of saffron poisoning.

"I can't even imagine the pain Evelyn has had to deal with," Mac finally responded.

"Sure you can. Your dad died when you were little. To kids, abandonment is abandonment, whether it is from accidental or purposeful acts. The horrible thing for Evelyn was that both of her parents left her. When that happens, I think that children harvest their anger in perpetuity."

"I spent some time last weekend talking with Evelyn. She doesn't seem angry. In fact, she seemed like a very concerned, caring mother. The parent that seems angry and distant is Luke."

"Dr. Landers is a first-rate ass. I wouldn't let that man deliver a calf, let alone a child. If I was in labor and he was the only person left on the planet, I'd give birth alone."

Mac laughed at Beth's insolence toward Luke. She'd forgotten how outspoken Beth could be, and how much she appreciated it.

"The older kids seem to have a pretty good relationship with him."

"That's 'cause they're teenagers, and teenagers are known to rebel from their mothers and turn towards their fathers. Especially in families where the dad is the sole breadwinner and mom stays home. Teens are extremely self-centered and tend to bond with the parent who can give them the most 'stuff.' Plus, mothers tend to keep a more watchful eye over teenagers and kids resent that at that point in their lives. They probably have a good relationship with him because he is never around and doesn't enforce the rules on them. He probably gives them cars and spending money and cheers them on in the sports that he likes. Believe me, most men are teenagers themselves–so they relate well to selfish adolescents."

"You seem to know a lot about kids."

"Raised two boys and I've had two husbands. That's an education in and of itself. And, remember, Linda is one of my best friends. We've talked about her cases for years. She performs psychoanalysis on each case and she often shares her insights with me."

Mac winced as she asked, but couldn't help herself. "What does Linda think is happening in Levi's case?"

Beth held her coffee mug with both hands and pulled it up to her mouth for a long sip. She hesitated before answering.

"She is confident that she can find him a good adoptive home."

"That means that she thinks both of his parents were involved in making him sick," Mac said.

Beth looked directly at Mac and gave her a slight, uncommitted grin and said, "Something like that."

Chapter 20

Following the events the preceding night, Evelyn awoke Saturday morning feeling isolated and alone. Luke had showed up to the Homecoming game, but it wasn't until the fourth quarter. He arrived in time for Austen's winning pass into the end zone, and gave Austen congratulations that made it appear as though he'd been present for the entire game. Luke disappeared as quickly as he had come, leaving Evelyn to physically coordinate the rest of the kids' evenings. All three kids ended up beating Luke home, and when Evelyn woke up Saturday, Luke was long gone.

As Evelyn reflected on how busy and hurried the previous night had been for her, she realized that Luke had been living the life of a playboy for quite some time now. She was tired of being his nanny and housekeeper, especially when the kids she was caring for were teenagers. Keeping track of teenagers was no small task, and probably compared to the energy required to parent a two-year-old. When Evelyn complained to Luke about it, his retort was often derogatory.

You worry too much. You are micromanaging them. Boys will be boys.

She could never believe that he would say that, especially given his line of work. He saw pregnant teenage girls in his office frequently, and should know the results of that type of lax parenting. The house would completely fall apart if she weren't constantly worrying, and nothing at all would get done. Ben would not get his homework done if she didn't ride him. Lauren would spend all of her time (and their money) on her cell phone talking with her friends. She worried about drugs and alcohol and fast driving and sex and peer pressure. She worried about college entrance exams and religious education and community service. Yes, she worried too much and she micromanaged the family, but that was her job as their parent. What she couldn't get was why Luke didn't share this attitude. Wasn't that a parent's job?

Apparently, it was not Luke's. His type of parenting was as lax as you could get, which was the same way he'd managed his life up until becoming a father. He'd skated through high school and college on his charm and wit and ability to persuade girls into doing his work. He was also blessed with the additional ability to toggle several girlfriends at a time. He casually juggled women, while simultaneously ensuring that each had an "assignment" to complete that would permit him the extra time to play sports and party and get good enough grades to make it into medical school. Once he got into the UCSD's School of Medicine, he met studious and responsible Evelyn who was a year ahead of him in her medical training.

His wit and charm had never failed him, and the biggest catch was the dependable girlfriend who became his dependable wife. Not only was she lacking a bit in self confidence, but she was outrageously loyal. Even though she was very smart, she'd dropped out of med school in her third year when she found out that she was pregnant with his child. To ensure that she'd continue doing his class work for him, he'd decided it best to marry her. She continued to support him through med school, despite having a full time job. Luke loved every minute of it, because it gave him the time to spend on Pacific Beach or La Jolla Cove playing beach volleyball.

Evelyn gritted her teeth as she thought how good and easy life had been for Luke. He didn't seem to mind that she micromanaged *his* life then, as he most certainly would not have finished medical school without her. It seemed that he didn't want her intrusion in his life only now, when he'd apparently used up everything she had to offer him. Times had changed. *Or had they?*

Evelyn lay on her side in her king-sized bed alone and lonely, thinking about the road she traversed to get to this point in her life and her marriage. She held her reading pillow to her chest and tightly hugged it. Why had she married a man who was so emotionally vacant? Luke was the opposite of what she needed in a man. Her own father was the extreme example of an emotionally vacant man and he had violated her in every way imaginable.

From that experience, Evelyn hoped and dreamed that she would meet and marry a man who deeply and unconditionally loved her. Why had she chosen to marry Luke, then? He was more like her father than unlike him, and the opposite of everything she'd hoped for in a man.

Evelyn shifted in her bed, getting more close to the root of her emotional dilemma than ever before. Perhaps it was no accident that she'd chosen to marry someone so cold and unforgiving, she thought. Maybe deep down inside, she was afraid of being loved. There was no doubt that Evelyn had little to no experience with love, and her marriage to Luke wasn't about to change that anytime soon. Was she really afraid of being loved? Did she choose Luke because he offered no threat in that department, and because she so desperately needed to be needed?

Well, Luke certainly was an emotional vacuum, Evelyn thought. She thought about his reaction to the loss of their first child, and realized that should have told her of things to come. When Luke reacted a bit relieved after their daughter died of SIDS after only six short months of life, she should have bolted. He clearly wasn't ready for a baby at that time in his life—as he was a fourth year med student with residencies and fellowships and board exams to think about.

Thinking about their first child brought up some old emotions in Evelyn, as she remembered her utter devastation at the loss of her beautiful, precious little girl, Ivy. She still had a hard time understanding the loss, given the circumstances. Ivy slept in a bassinet by their bed in their tiny apartment in La Jolla, and had been sleeping on her tummy ever since she could roll over on her own—which was a four month milestone.

SIDS was a relatively new hot topic at the time, and it had been suggested by most pediatricians that infants sleep on their backs without covers or other potentially suffocating objects in their cribs. Evelyn often tried to turn Ivy onto her back, but the little girl would immediately flip back to her tummy and suck her thumb until she was sound asleep. Evelyn shared this information with Ivy's pediatrician, but the doctor didn't think much of it. Some babies prefer to sleep on their tummies and once they can turn themselves, it is a hard habit to break. He cautioned about the dangers, but admitted that there wasn't much a parent could do.

Evelyn remembered the fateful night, which occurred during Luke's final exams in his senior year at med school. Luke had been up most of the night studying, which was not unusual considering his bad studying habits. Luke always procrastinated, and usually was forced into major cram sessions before tests. Evelyn had breast fed Ivy and put her down early because she had been particularly cranky that evening. Evelyn was exhausted from working a double shift, and slept soundly through the night.

Evelyn awoke with a start at five after having a vivid, yet terrible dream about her sister being raped by their father. Something told her to get to Ivy immediately, and so she darted to Ivy's bassinet. Ivy was still sleeping, but her coloring seemed wrong. Evelyn remembered vividly touching Ivy's cheek and how cold the baby's flesh was. Evelyn snatched the little girl into her arms and held her close to warm her up–but it was too late. Her lifeless body lay limp in her arms.

Evelyn screamed. Luke ran into their bedroom and found her there, on the floor with Ivy held tight to her chest. It was a horrible sight. He called the paramedics immediately, but there was nothing that could be done to save Ivy.

Despite the horrific death of his child, Luke didn't see the harm in leaving Evelyn to deal with the investigation and a trip to the morgue as he went to school to finish up his exams. Luke claimed that he'd had no choice; otherwise he'd have had to re-take Bio-Chem. At that point, Evelyn had been heavily sedated, but remembered thinking through her haze what medical school professor wouldn't offer some flexibility given the circumstances.

The harm was that Evelyn woke up in their tiny little La Jolla apartment alone, partially sedated, confused, hurt, and scared. She was a little girl again.

She would never trust her husband again.

That was the harm.

Death has a taste–a feel–a smell. Ivy's death smelled of salt air and it felt cold and it tasted sour–like day-old milk. For that reason, Evelyn could not wait to move from the cold and salty coast. She didn't care where they moved, it just had to be somewhere that didn't smell like Ivy's death. When Luke was stationed as an Army doctor at dumpy Fort Hood in Texas to pay off the remainder of his student loans, Evelyn was relieved. It was hot there and sandy and did not remind her of salt air and cold and sour. But something had soured with her relationship with Luke. He accepted his position with irreverent reserve. He hated the notion that he "owed" the government anything, and felt as though he had to "report in" to his superiors just like he had to his wife.

He felt trapped. Trapped animals escape. And that is what Luke did.

Evelyn didn't want to accept the notion that Luke intended to be unfaithful, but coming home day in and day out to a wounded doe was more than he could take. Luke resented being needed by Evelyn, and after Ivy's death, Evelyn needed to be held and consoled and loved.

Luke was busy on the army base patching up wounds from basic training exercises and attending to the sniffles of civilian children. He did not like general med and had no intention of being a general practitioner. It was boring to him. He had applied for several residencies and was hopeful that he would get accepted into either obstetrics or general surgery. He liked being under the gun and needed a profession where he was challenged in a time crunch. Waiting to hear from the various residency programs was making him restless and irritable.

Late one afternoon in the heat of mid-July in Texas, a beautiful young nurse from the OB ward dropped by to tell him that a group of doctors and nurses were meeting at the officer's club for drinks after their shift. This particular nurse had made her presence known to Luke on several previous occasions, which had flattered him greatly and caused a stir from deep within. Luke weighed the prospects: going home to a depressed wife, or enjoying a pleasant adult conversation over drinks during happy hour with colleagues. Luke didn't pause long to make his decision, which was clearly the latter.

To his credit, Luke had the foresight and courtesy during the early years of his marriage to call Evelyn and let her know that he'd be home a little late and to not wait for him to have dinner. As is too often the case, one drink turned into another and then another, and by nine o'clock, the good doctor was well on his way toward drunkenness. The lovely young nurse happened to live only a few miles off base, and congenially offered to drive him home. Luke didn't object when she pulled into her driveway, not his. In fact, Luke had little objections with the nurse that night.

When Luke was dropped off after their debauchery, it was at four in the morning and about a block from his driveway. Evelyn was sitting in their small living room waiting. Her evening sleeping aid had worn off and she was in the mood for answers, but Luke had few. Evelyn considered that a lesson learned, not a lesson to learn from. From that point on, Evelyn picked herself up by the bootstraps, got a job near the base, and made sure that she looked good when she met with Luke for the happy hours and the parties and the weekend trips. She did everything she could to become "fun" again–and reliable.

Evelyn wasn't able to do this entirely on her own, though, and grew to rely on the little pink pills that her psychiatrist called "mood stabilizers." When Evelyn swallowed each pill, she was also swallowing her pain about Ivy and about her unfaithful husband and her abusive father. The pills helped her squelch the uncontrollable feeling that she was drowning in a pool of pity. In therapy, she formed a friendship with a neighbor who was a hyper- religious Catholic, and she decided to join the same church. Through her new bond with this friend and with God, Evelyn took charge of her life again. She reaffirmed her belief that God borrowed her little angel Ivy to test her and that love required faith and forgiveness.

Her faith and ability to forgive were tested many, many times from that day in Texas. As Evelyn lay in bed reminiscing of the bad ol' days with Luke, she thought of how unnecessarily difficult her life seemed. She thought how it was the morning after the big Homecoming game, yet she had tears rolling over the bridge of her nose and onto her twelve hundred weave count Egyptian linen sheets. Life had really tested her, and in the process given her a strong faith and ability to forgive. She was running short on both.

* * *

Mac sat in Beth Anderson's kitchen, staring at the box of Levi's medical records that she'd brought with her. She thought about Beth's comments and how they might play out in a juvenile court hearing. Juvenile trials are markedly different than other trials. Though juvenile cases are technically civil in nature, the fact that a person's rights to their child are being infringed upon make it akin to a criminal trial. The case itself is confidential, and for that reason there are no jury trials and all of the case's hearings are closed to the public.

The informality of the proceedings comforted and frightened Mac. She felt relieved in that she would not be spending countless hours in attorney conference rooms attending depositions. On the other hand, she felt like she was in the dark about what had happened to Levi. His medical records, while voluminous, did not explain the causation of his symptoms and diagnoses. He'd had a number of bizarre and unexplained illnesses, including rare and potentially terminal cancers. What boggled Mac, however, was that upon further testing these cancer scares all turned out to be false or inconclusive. Mac was fairly certain that the prosecution would put forth the medical evidence and argue *res ipsa loquitor*, which means "the facts speak for themselves." Mac could only presume that Luke and Evelyn's attorneys would argue that they were not the only people coming in contact with Levi, and that if there were meddling hands involved, it weren't theirs. She could practically hear the attorneys argue how attentive they were as parents, and that they could not be at fault for the medical providers' repeated misdiagnosing of Levi.

Mac was well known for her zealous representation of clients. She was always well prepared for hearings and did more than her share of due diligence in formulating trial strategies. She was highly uncomfortable knowing that she was going to trial in a few weeks in an action that could irrevocably change the course of Levi's life. If the prosecution proved its case, Evelyn and Luke risked losing their parental rights and Levi would face being adopted, receiving a permanent guardian, or being put into a group home. Mac did not want any of those options for her client, but wasn't sure whether returning home was ideal, either–not until it could be determined what was making this poor little guy sick. He had no symptoms of any illness during the three weeks spent in her care, but there were many periods of time in his ten-year life that he had been healthy before getting diagnosed with a serious medical condition. That didn't seem normal to Mac. What if Evelyn really was sick, but the state wasn't able to prove up their case? If Levi were to return home and then ultimately get injured–Mac would never forgive herself.

As she flipped through Levi's medical charts, Mac was drawn to a single set of initials that were found on nearly every pediatric chart entry.

Chapter 21

The first Saturdays of each month, Dr. Kerr opened his pediatric clinic to all indigent children. To help compensate the free medical advice given, Dr. Kerr paid his staff only minimum wage for their hours worked that day. Janie Johansen didn't particularly enjoy working on Saturdays, and she was not alone in this sentiment. Nevertheless, Dr. Kerr believed strongly in working pro bono, and if his staff was truly interested in working for him, then they too would be contributing some of their time to the community for just one day a month.

It wasn't that Nurse Janie hated to help out underprivileged people, because she enjoyed volunteering. What she didn't like was being forced to volunteer, and to give up an entire weekend day to do it. Many shops were closed in Sheridan on Sundays, as was the case in many other small towns.

Today was such a day, and Janie was definitely grumpy. If it weren't for Dr. Kerr, she'd be engaged in her usual Saturday morning routine: a morning workout, followed by a trip to the nail salon and every so often, the hair salon. She had dry cleaning and marketing to do as well, as she liked to have all of these items finished by early afternoon so that she could spend time with her "guy" in the late afternoon and evening, if he was available. Adding insult to injury, today was one of the rare days when her guy was available most of the morning. Janie was in a sour mood, buzzing from exam room to exam room attending to snot-nosed kids and their demanding moms. She idly listened to the onslaught of complaints, making less than copious notes in the family medical charts and then scribbling her initials after each log.

* * *

When Beth returned to her kitchen, Mac was digging into the box of medical files. "Looks like you have a new office," she said, half joking.

"The prosecution is going to try to prove that Evelyn contrived all of these illnesses because she has a medical condition called Munchausen by Proxy, meaning that she is deliberately–"

"I know what it is," Beth said.

"Oh. Linda probably told you."

"Actually, I've read about it. It's not a new phenomenon."

"Right." Mac felt embarrassed for her presumptuousness. "I started thinking that maybe there was another common denominator. I've been going through these records looking for something consistent amongst them, and the one thing I've noticed is that each new medical issue began with Dr. Kerr's office. In each of those visits, the accompanying chart entries the initials 'JJ' after it.

"Nurse Janie."

"How did you know?" Mac asked with astonishment.

"Lucky guess."

"Really?"

"No."

Beth walked back over to her coffee pot and pressed the grinder making a loud noise. When she was finished, she pressed the start button and then turned toward Mac. The room filled with the aroma of fresh coffee as the brew started its slow and steady drip.

"Linda has done everything you are now doing in Levi's case. She has poured over his records trying to make sense of this for years. It is her job to conduct due diligence before charges like this are filed. It's not like a slam dunk case where a kid presents with a black eye or belt mark across his back. Levi doesn't have any outward signs of obvious abuse. Linda knew that this case would be terribly difficult to prove and terribly difficult to sell to the county attorney to press charges. She knows that there are three common denominators in Levi's case. One is his mother; one is his father; and one is Janie Johansen."

"Why isn't Dr. Kerr on the list?" Mac asked.

"He didn't see Levi each time he was brought in with symptoms. Sometimes Levi was seen by Nurse Janie and then a referral was signed off by her under his license for Levi to see a specialist."

"Isn't that illegal? She's not authorized to practice medicine."

"Linda thinks so, but feels that's another issue entirely."

"Hey! Hey!" a voiced boomed from the garage, followed by the noise of a door closing. Wyatt and Levi walked into the kitchen. Levi was smiling from ear to ear. "We got ourselves a couple o' hungry guys over here. What's for lunch?" Wyatt asked.

"Nothing, unless the two of you turn yourselves around and head straight for the mud room and wash those filthy hands of yours," Beth said.

Mac was dying to hear the rest of what Beth had to say, and what Linda's insight was on Nurse Janie. She'd hoped that Wyatt might take a few minutes washing his hands and she could squeeze out some extra information from Beth, outside of Levi's earshot.

Wyatt gave his mother a sheepish smile. At nearly forty, he was still her baby in ways, and he didn't seem to mind. Wyatt gently grabbed Levi by the shoulders and marched him back into the mud room and helped him with the soap and water.

"I have left-over beef stroganoff," Beth yelled from the kitchen. "And some chicken noodle soup."

Wyatt returned with Levi, shooting Mac's hopes at continuing the conversation with Beth. Both "boys" were holding up their hands, demonstrating how clean they'd made them.

"Stroganoff for me," Wyatt said. "What about you?" he asked Levi. Levi shrugged his slight shoulders, looking to Mac for guidance.

"Why don't you try a little? If you don't like it, maybe you can try some soup or we can make you a PB&J."

Levi looked relieved to know that he had another option. Beth pulled out a casserole pan from the refrigerator and placed it in the microwave. While it was warming, she poured two glasses of milk and set four places at the kitchen table. Mac offered to help, but Beth declined. She loaded four plates with the noodle casserole and handed them out to the hungry group. As they sat together for lunch, Wyatt told them about all the chores that Levi had so deftly helped him do. Levi was beaming with pride as Wyatt bragged about Levi's astute care of Mr. Pony.

"I get to ride him someday."

"You do?" Beth said. "Did Wyatt tell you that he has to be broken first?" Levi shot her a look of horror.

"Remember? I told you how we'd have to teach him to be nice and gentle when a human rides him. That's what my mom means by getting 'broken.' It doesn't hurt him. It just teaches the horse not to buck the human off and to mind the rider's commands."

"Oh," Levi said with relief. "I get to ride Wyatt's horse today!"

"Only if you eat a hearty lunch, young man," Wyatt said. "Horsemen eat. They need strong muscles. We're going to build some muscle on you before winter sets in."

Wyatt spoke in the long term, and made it clear that Levi was going to be involved in the Anderson Ranch for some time to come. Mac watched Wyatt eat, and noted that he was not self-conscious, nor overly polite. He spoke when he had food in his mouth and ate with large bites, however, he was conversational and comfortable. Mac noticed that Levi mimicked Wyatt at the table as well as the barn, and watched Levi shovel food into his mouth faster than she'd ever seen him eat. Normally, he was picky and it took a lot of coaxing to get a meal into him, but not this meal. He ate heartily like Wyatt and when Wyatt was finished, Levi ate even faster so that he could be excused with his new big buddy.

"Ask to be excused and clear your plate," Mac reminded Levi. He did and then voluntarily thanked Beth for lunch. Wyatt thanked Beth too, almost as if he was now mimicking the manners of a child, and then both boys dashed out of the kitchen. Wyatt stopped himself at the door jam at the kitchen and turned around. His chiseled face looked handsome and serious at the same time.

"Why don't you join us?" Wyatt said to Mac. "Levi is really quick and he asks a lot of questions. Some of 'em I can't answer. I need your smarts out there."

Mac felt herself flush. Wyatt was so pure in his analysis of life. He saw things the "country" way–old fashioned and wholesome. "Sure. I'll join you. Give me a minute with your mom to clean up the lunch dishes and I'll be right out." She picked up her plate of mostly uneaten food and took it over to the sink while Wyatt was exiting the kitchen. It was true that Mac wanted to help Beth clean up, but mainly she was on edge to finish their conversation. She didn't want to appear too nosy, so she continued to clean up a bit while waiting for Beth to make the first move. She brushed the food into the garbage disposal and helped rinse the remaining plates. She did not like casseroles of any kind–it reminded her of childhood when people brought over food to the house after her father had died.

"I got the rest," Beth said. "You go on out there and see to Wyatt and Levi. We can finish our conversation another time."

Mac was disappointed that they wouldn't be finishing up the loose ends with that topic now but was in no position to push the issue. She thanked Beth and then proceeded to walk out the back door, through the garage and across the shale driveway, which led to the giant red barn. The air smelled sweet, as though it had been sprinkled with golden warm honey.

When she found Wyatt and Levi, they were saddling horses in the barn. Mac was grateful that the barn smelled heavy with manure, as she'd not showered after her morning run and felt slightly self-conscious that she might smell of sweat. As she was smoothing back the whispies atop her head that were frizzy and flying about, she realized that she hadn't been so self- conscious about her appearance in some time.

"Hey boys, I'm here!" Mac said as she approached. Levi gave her a wide grin.

"We're going riding. And guess what? I get to ride Ginger. Wyatt said it was okay. He said that you can ride along. He saddled Mocha. He's riding Old Boy. Mr. Pony isn't ready yet."

Mac chuckled at the excitement she heard in Levi's voice. He looked like a kid on Christmas morning who had just noticed the presents under the tree, but was still waiting for mom and dad to wake up. "I don't know about Mocha, Wyatt. She gives me a hard time, don't you remember?" Mac asked Wyatt.

"That's why you're riding her. To show her who is boss. Mocha has control issues," Wyatt said. And then, under his breath, "She's perfect for you."

"I heard that."

Wyatt smirked. "I call 'em like I see 'em." Wyatt's dimples grew deep as his smile broadened. He stopped what he was doing with Mocha briefly to turn and wink at Mac. It was only a second or so, but for Mac, it felt as though time had stopped. After winking at her, Wyatt continued to school Levi on how to properly saddle a horse. Levi paid strict attention.

Mac looked at her watch and noted that it was already one o'clock in the afternoon. She needed to have Levi back to town by four o'clock for a supervised visit with Evelyn.

"We need to get riding. We have an appointment in town later this afternoon."

"Sure. No problem. We're ready," Wyatt said. "No control issues here." He winked again at Mac. This time, she winked back.

Chapter 22

"That was the best day ever!" Levi shouted as Mac drove them back towards Sheridan. The daylight was winding down and the bright rays from the sun shone over the Big Horn Mountains. Mac listened while Levi chattered about Ginger and the fact that he had perfect control over the old mare. "When I pulled on the reins to the right, she turned right and when I pulled to the left, she went left and when I pulled back she stopped," Levi proudly announced.

"Mocha was as good as Ginger," Mac replied, almost defensively. She'd actually had a difficult time controlling her horse during their outing, which was pretty evident to the boys. In fact, Wyatt teased her about it the entire ride.

"Uh-uh. Mocha kept putting her ears back, and didn't listen to you like Ginger listened to me. I heard Mr. Wyatt say so. He said I was a better rider than you."

Mac looked at Levi out of the corner of her eye, and realized he was dead on. "I think you are right," Mac offered in a conciliatory tone. It was good for Levi to feel like he was better than someone else at something. "You have a natural way with animals. Maybe you'll be a veterinarian some day."

"Lauren wants to be one of those. I don't think I want to be the same thing as my sister, because she'd be so much better at it. I want to do something that only I'm good at," Levi explained.

"I'm not so sure about that, Levi. First, I think you'd be very good at whatever you choose to do. You're a very smart kid. Second, I know for a fact that Lauren loves you very much and would be very happy to see you do anything well, even if she were doing the same thing as you. Anyways, Lauren might change her mind about her career, and if she does wouldn't it be a shame if you'd already given up becoming a vet for that very reason? You don't want to choose your career based only on what somebody else is doing."

"I don't want Lauren's dreams to change. I want her to be a vet, and I want to go back to my mom's house. I just want everything to be the same."

Mac realized that she'd framed her comment awkwardly, not having intended on upsetting Levi. "I know how much you miss your parents. It must be hard to have to hang around with me. I bet you miss your sister and brothers too."

"No, I don't!" Levi said in a stern voice, taking Mac by surprise. "I don't miss Ben at all. And I don't miss my dad that much. He doesn't like me because I can't play sports that good." Levi crossed his arms and pushed his chin down to his chest. In a much quieter tone he added, "Only my mom. I miss her. I want her back."

Tears formed in his eyes. His lower lip quivered as he spoke. He was trying so hard to fight back the tears. Mac wanted to tell him that he would be back with his mom soon, but she didn't know how to say this in a way that wouldn't risk her making a false promise to him.

Mac and Levi showed up ten minutes late for the visit with Evelyn. She sat on the park bench waiting, looking at her watch every two minutes. When they approached her, she went out of her way to ensure brief eye contact was made before dramatically looking at her watch.

"Sorry we were late," Mac offered. She was about to offer an explanation when Linda Sterling came to the rescue.

"Not a problem at all," Linda interjected. "You actually did a good thing in that you gave us a few minutes to finally be able to sit down and talk." Based on the look on Evelyn's face, Mac interpreted Linda's statement as meaning that Linda had been given an opportunity to calm Evelyn down. Evelyn looked awful, as though she hadn't slept in days.

"Mommy!" Levi said. He ran and hugged his mother. "Guess what?"

"What?" Evelyn asked, forcing a smile.

"We went horse back riding today. I got to ride a horse all by myself. It was so cool. I got to ride Ginger and when Mr. Pony is breaked I get to ride him. I cleaned up the barn and fed the chickens and–"

"Whoa, baby. Slow down," Evelyn said. "You are not really supposed to be riding horses. Remember? We haven't received your doctor's clearance regarding your platelettes yet." Evelyn looked at Mac while making this statement. "I told your attorney about your health history. The least she could do considering how fragile you are is to consult with me before allowing you to do something as risky as riding a horse, for goodness sakes."

"Evelyn, can I have a word with you in private?" Linda said.

"No, you may not. Anything you have to say should be heard by Mac too. She thinks she's his mother apparently. She gets to call all the shots."

"Mac, why don't you take Levi over to the play equipment? We'll be along in a minute," Linda suggested. Mac nodded and took Levi by the hand. After Mac and Levi were out of earshot, Linda turned her attention towards Evelyn. "Are you sure you're up for a visit today? I have to document everything that happens during a visit and your behavior isn't appropriate. Would you like to reschedule? You seem upset."

"I am not upset!" Evelyn shouted. "Why should I be upset? My baby is risking his life on a horse and I can't do anything about it. My other three kids carry on as if they don't have any parents at all and my husband believes that having a girlfriend on the side is completely acceptable. Why in the hell should I be upset?"

"Levi was not risking his life by riding on a tame horse. Mac can certainly make reasonable judgment calls with respect–"

"You're telling me that Mac can make reasonable judgment calls about Levi? Are you kidding me? That's a mother's job! My son rides a horse for the first time in his life and I am not even there to see it. And I am damn sure that she didn't take any pictures. I will never know what it was like for him because I wasn't there!"

"Is that what this is really about, Evelyn? That you're upset because Levi had fun with Mac, and not with you?" Linda turned towards Evelyn and looked her directly in the eyes. "If that is it, I completely understand," Linda said, patting Evelyn on the shoulder. "I would feel the same way."

"You have no clue how I feel," Evelyn said, as she jerked herself away from Linda's touch. "You don't have children, do you? In fact, I did a little research of my own this morning, and what did I discover? Besides Karl Swensen, not one of the lawyers in that courtroom last week has any children. How in the hell can you people make decisions about what is best about kids and families when none of you walk the walk or talk the talk? Not even the judge has kids. Rumor has it that he's been married four times but that none of these marriages resulted in any kids. And this is the judge who is deciding my case, the judge who presides over family and juvenile court matters."

"Look, Evelyn, everyone involved in your case chose juvi because they like working with families. It is true that some of the folks involved don't have kids of our own. Believe me, most of us wanted kids but for whatever reason, we weren't able to have them."

"You have an answer for everything, don't you?"

"No, Evelyn, I don't, but I can tell you that you are not helping Levi when you show up for a visit with him and you are visibly not yourself. You appear very angry–"

"I am angry. I have every right to be."

"Not in front of Levi. His time with you needs to be positive and happy. Since it doesn't look like you are inclined to change your mood, I am ending this visit."

"The hell you are," Evelyn said as she started to edge herself back in the direction of the playground. "The judge told me that I can visit with my son. Until you are wearing the black robe, you don't tell me otherwise." Evelyn turned towards the playground and began walking with a strong, quick, pace. Linda charged after Evelyn while gesticulating wildly towards Mac in the hopes of gaining her attention. When Linda's frantic gestures finally did catch Mac's eye, she pantomimed running her index finger across her neck.

Mac was quick to read Linda's clues and grabbed Levi by the hand. "We have to go now, Levi," Mac said. "We'll see your mom and Linda again soon." Levi nodded and took Mac's hand as she started to lead him away. As the two of them headed towards the car, Mac looked back to see how much space there remained between. Evelyn had a fierce expression, and began to run directly towards Mac.

Linda was still frantically running behind, and had closed the distance between them substantially. Linda jumped forward towards Evelyn with both of her arms outstretched, and was able to just barely grab the edge of Evelyn's shirt with one of her hands. While Linda was not able to completely stop Evelyn's movements, she did successfully stop her from making contact with Mac and Levi.

"Don't do anything that would harm your case, Evelyn. Please."

Evelyn jerked herself away from Linda, pulling the material of her shirt from the woman's grasp. She turned back in the direction of Mac and Levi, and realized that she'd lost the battle.

Several seconds passed before Linda had finally caught up to Mac and Levi, who were by Mac's car in the parking lot. Linda was out of breath and had red splotches all over her face. They stood in stunned silence for a moment before Mac finally leaned over and whispered in Linda's ear, "She looked like she was on something."

"I thought the same thing," Linda huffed. "I wouldn't be surprised if she called you in the next twenty-four hours. Be careful. If she sounds unstable, don't let her talk to Levi. He doesn't need any set-backs. He's been doing great this week."

Mac agreed. She reminded Linda that Levi had a starring role in a play at school on Monday and then said good-bye.

After securing Levi into his seat, Mac pulled out of the parking lot and drove back towards her apartment. Mac made a phone call to their local pizzeria and ordered a half vegetarian, half cheese pizza for pick-up on their way home. They'd agreed to have a pizza party and watch a rented kid baseball movie called "Sandlot" for their Saturday night entertainment. Since Mac usually spent her Saturday evenings at the office, it was a welcomed change.

* * *

Lauren Landers had been invited to spend the night at her best friend's house again, and she readily accepted. She'd spent most of her Saturday at the swim meet, and felt uncomfortable after neither of her parents had shown up. While she wouldn't normally have minded, that Saturday it had been embarrassing. Everyone in town knew her family's business, and everyone at the swim meet seemed to notice her parents' absence at the meet. Lauren was not particularly pleased, yet she focused her negative energy on her performance, and she ended up having a very successful meet, qualifying for the state competition in three events.

When Lauren told her mother about the swim meet later that evening, Evelyn blamed of her absence on issues involving Levi. *There we go again*, Lauren thought to herself. It's always about Levi.

Using Levi as an excuse for her inefficiencies of motherhood, Evelyn had not once thought about the impact this would have on the other children. After hearing countless times that their mother had not done something because of Levi, all of the children had grown to resent him. Lauren resented Levi in a big way that evening, but this was not the first time that she'd felt that way–and Lauren was pretty sure that it wouldn't be the last.

* * *

Ben Landers beat every opponent in his weight division at the wrestling meet. Ben was used to winning, but somehow, this win was bigger than most. Austen had actually shown up to cheer him on–and that was a first. At first, Ben figured that his older brother was there to steal his thunder–being that he'd just been crowned Homecoming King. But, Ben noticed that Austen did not showboat his way through the crowd.

Instead, he found a seat on the top row of the metal bleachers and gave Ben the thumbs up during warm-ups.

As the time grew near for his first match, Ben mouthed to Austen, "Where's Dad?" Austen shrugged his shoulders. He had no idea where Luke Landers was at the moment. Delivering a baby? Golfing? Saving their mom from yet another nervous breakdown? If he had to place bets, Austen would have put his money on the latter of the three scenarios, but he hated himself for being so cynical when it came to his mom. To her credit, she was almost always there for him and very involved in his life, even if she looked like she was going to crack at any minute. He felt sorry for her. He sensed her loneliness and her desire to be loved and accepted. Despite his age, he was mature for sixteen. Now that he had a girlfriend of his own, he was beginning to understand how important it was to treat a woman with kindness and respect. Austen knew that his mother was not treated kindly by Luke.

The whistle blew, jolting Austen's attention back to the blue and gold mat in front of him. Ben grew intensely focused and angry. Austen noticed how fierce his younger brother looked—as if he were waging war against a mortal enemy. Ben grabbed his opponent by the back of the head—a legal grab, but more forceful than most. He took his opponent down to one knee and then quickly reversed him onto his back. One. Two. Three. An easy pin.

Ben stood and threw his fists into the air. He was a warrior. An angry, vengeful, warrior. The crowd cheered, but no one cheered for Ben as loudly as Austen. Ben looked into the stands and gave his older brother the thumbs up sign. Austen returned the gesture. This time, Ben mouthed, "Where's Mom?" Austen shrugged his shoulders.

Ben shook his head in disgust.

* * *

"Bad dream?" Mac asked as she pulled Levi onto the couch. After eating pizza and watching a movie together, she had tucked Levi into bed. It was four in the morning on Sunday when she woke to a poke in the arm.

"Uh-huh. Baseball Man."

Mac put her arms around Levi who was now seated next to her on the couch. "Who was it this time?"

"Ty Cobb."

"Do you like Ty Cobb?"

Levi looked at her incredulously and said, "No one likes Ty Cobb. He had twelve batting titles, too. Still, even his teammates didn't like him. He was mean."

"What happened in your dream?"

Levi rubbed his eyes, as if he was too sleepy to tell Mac the story. "He got into a fight with the Baseball Man."

"Like a fist fight or were they using mean words?"

"Both. Ty Cobb started yelling at the Baseball Man and the Baseball Man yelled back and then Ty Cobb took a swing at the Baseball Man and socked him in the nose."

"Oh. That's terrible. Do you know why they were fighting?" Mac asked.

Levi was silent for a moment, apparently reflecting on his answer. "They were fighting because Ty Cobb called the Baseball Man's mom a bad name."

"That's not very nice. I'm sure that upset the Baseball Man. No one likes to hear mean things about their mom."

"I know."

Levi scooted away from Mac and then rested his head on the opposite end of the couch.

"Are you sleepy? Do you want me to tuck you back into bed? It's pretty early in the morning."

Levi sat quietly without moving, rubbing his eyes and apparently pondering whether he was brave enough to return to bed. Then, out of nowhere, Levi asked Mac, "Were you saying mean things about my mom to Mrs. Sterling today?"

Mac's eyes shot open. "Do you mean yesterday at the park?" Levi nodded.

"No, honey, not at all. I would never say anything bad about your mom." Mac silently added 'in front of you' to the end of that sentence.

"My mom was so sad and when she left and I heard you talk about her."

"Honey, I wasn't saying anything mean about your mom. I was just talking to Linda Sterling about how well you've been doing over the past few weeks and I reminded her to tell your mom about the third grade play that you are in on Monday. I think your mom had a tough day yesterday, that's all. I certainly wasn't saying anything mean about her. I'm sorry if you felt that way."

"No one in my family is nice to my mom. I think it makes her sad. That's why she cries all the time."

"Are you nice to her, Levi?"

"Uh huh."

"Good. The only person you have to worry about is yourself, because you can't control anyone else's thoughts, words or actions. You just keep being nice to your mom, okay? She loves you very much."

Levi appeared mollified by Mac's comments and willingly got up from the couch to return to sleep in Mac's bedroom. Just before he exited the living room, though, he turned his head towards Mac and said, "Do you think my dad loves my mom?"

Mac was caught off guard. "Of course," she responded without conviction.

"The Baseball Man doesn't think so."

Chapter 23

"Mars, Mars, we're going to Mars. Grab Gus and pack up the car. Come on, we're gonna see stars. Mars, Mars."

Levi was standing center stage, singing proudly as he practiced his role in the third grade play as the father in a family disgruntled over past summer vacations.

Mac arrived early for Levi's performance and sat in the front row, completely oblivious to the danger she was getting herself in by her seat choice; parents located in the front row were routinely ambushed into participating in the play. When the third grade approached the audience, asking if any of them were willing to fill in for the role of "moon" following an unexpected absence, Mac discovered by fire her poor seat choice. Mac looked towards Levi on stage to see if he'd noticed the request, and when he made eye contact with her she realized she had no choice but submit.

Levi smiled widely as he watched Mac approach the stage, and started to giggle out loud when the teacher tied a three-sided prop around her shoulders.

"You look so silly!" Levi couldn't resist shouting towards Mac, who was now on stage with him. Mac turned towards him and shrugged her shoulders while giggling herself, as there was no point in disagreeing with Levi.

"When you hear the words "banana cream pie," turn to the full moon. When you hear the part of the song where the dad has eaten his portion of the dessert, turn to the quarter moon. When you hear that Gus, the dog, has finished licking the plate, turn to the new moon. Got it?" the teacher asked. Mac nodded, though she feared she would miss a cue and mess up her role somehow.

As the children assembled into their spots on the auditorium stage, Mac peeked from behind the stage curtain scanning the crowd for Evelyn. Deep down inside, Mac was silently wishing Evelyn might not appear, but during her second perusal of the audience, Mac located Evelyn, who was dressed in a cream and navy sweater matched with a cream silk shirt. Mac hoped that the improvement in Evelyn's appearance from Saturday meant that her attitude had also improved. Mac noticed that Evelyn was not talking with any of the other parents, and her attitude suggested that she was being somewhat guarded. Evelyn kept looking over her shoulder towards the auditorium door. Was she expecting someone, perhaps Luke? Or worse, was she trying to locate Mac?

Mac heard the teacher whisper "curtain!" and darted back to her place amongst the children on stage. The curtains were lifted, and all of the children on stage started their performances on cue. When Mac shifted from full to quarter moon, the audience laughed. When the play finally ended, the children on stage were flush with excitement as they performed their bows. A group of parents rushed the stage as they sought out their respective child to congratulate. While Mac was lifting the heavy moon prop off of her shoulders, she noticed that Evelyn was amongst the crowd rushing the stage. Mac knew that Levi would be very happy to get kudos from his mom, and therefore she gave them a few minutes to themselves. In the thick crowd of parents and children, Mac lost sight of Levi and Evelyn for just a split second. When the crowd thinned, Levi was gone.

Mac gasped, unsure of where to direct her attention next. It had only been a moment, so they couldn't have gone far from where she'd last seen them. Mac ran towards the front of the stage and scanned the crowd below, but she couldn't see Levi or Evelyn. Mac quickly perused the crowd, but neither Evelyn nor Levi was amongst the group milling around the auditorium. Mac realized that some people had already begun to exit, and feared that Evelyn might have succeeded in doing the same.

Mac dashed to the front entrance of the auditorium, but still could not locate Levi. She started shouting his name. No answer. She shouted louder, and people around her grew quiet and stared.

"I'm looking for Levi Landers!" Mac shouted. "Has anyone seen him?"

Mrs. Kendrick, Levi's teacher, came running in Mac's direction. "What's wrong?" she asked. "Where's Levi?"

"I can't find him anywhere. He was by the back exit door with Evelyn when I was on the stage trying to get that moon off me. When I looked again, he was gone!"

By now, all of the parents were gawking at Mac. Some of the stares appeared to be genuinely out of concern. Other individuals seemed to be looking at Mac out of disdain, wondering who the crazy woman was getting all worked up over momentarily losing sight of her child in an otherwise safe crowd. Despite the attention she'd gotten, no one in the crowd spoke up.

"Has anyone seen Levi?" Mrs. Kendrick asked. "This is important, people. Speak up if you know something."

A woman standing near the stage raised her hand half-way into the air. Mrs. Kendrick swung her body around. "Yes, Mrs. Cassidy? Do you know where he is?"

"I-I-I think I saw him leave through the back door with Mrs. Landers."

"Wouldn't the alarm sound?" Mac asked.

"No. Due to accidental tripping, the alarm was dismantled at the end of last school year. She could have exited from that door and we wouldn't have heard anything."

Without waiting for another second to pass, Mac bolted through the crowd and out the emergency exit door. She looked right and left, but the playground of the elementary school was deserted. Dammit! If only she'd followed her instincts and rushed out the back emergency exit, and not just assumed that it would have made a noise if opened!

While still focusing her attention on the perimeter of the playground, Mac quickly reached into her purse to extract her cell phone. She punched in the numbers to Evelyn's cell phone, and let it ring six times before hanging up. Mac immediately pressed redial, and this time the call went directly into Evelyn's voice mail without so much as a ring. She left what can only be described as a garbled, panicky voicemail explaining that she was at the school and that she could not find Levi after the play.

As soon as Mac the call, she dialed Linda Sterling's cell phone. The call to Linda went directly to voice mail, leaving Mac no option but to leave Linda a message. She could feel her sense of panic and her heart was pounding wildly. What should she do next? Where should she race to? Where in the world did Evelyn take Levi? Mac ran towards the front of the school, but there were no signs of Evelyn or Levi there. She then cut through the front door entrance as she jogged towards Levi's classroom. It was dark and vacant, without any signs of them. Mac returned to the auditorium, hoping that perhaps Evelyn had returned with Levi and this was all just a crazy mistake. Maybe Evelyn had taken him to the bathroom and had returned him to the auditorium. As soon as Mrs. Kendrick saw Mac return, she began to shake her head, indicating that she had not found Levi either.

Mac realized that she was left with no other options, and that Levi had simply disappeared with his mother. Mac opened her cell phone and dialed 9- 1-1.

* * *

"Where are we going, Mommy?" Levi asked. He was very happy to see his mom, but he was not expecting her to grab his hand and rush them out the back door of the auditorium as she had. He was afraid that they were going to get in trouble for using the exit, as his teacher had told him that those doors were only to be used in the case of an emergency. When he told his mom about this, she immediately shushed him. Levi continued to whine to his mom that they were going to get in trouble for using that door, until Evelyn told him that they were allowed to use the doors because they were in an emergency.

"Is this an emergency, Mommy?" Levi asked, the fear evident in his voice. "Do I need to go to the doctor?"

Evelyn had described many of their urgent trips to Denver or Billings for medical treatment as "emergency trips," and thus, the word "emergency" tended to unnerve Levi. To him, "emergency" meant needles and tests and yucky medicine and x-rays and scans. It also meant long stays in hospitals, away from his house and his toys and his teachers.

221

"I am taking you home, honey," Evelyn stated as she quickly buckled them both into her car and turned the engine over. "You belong home with me. You don't belong living with some stranger in a one-bedroom apartment on the other side of town."

"Mommy, Mac isn't a stranger. She's my friend and she takes good care of me."

The words cut into Evelyn like a sharp blade. "Children belong with their mommies and daddies, not with friends. I'm your mommy, Levi, and I'm a good mommy. I love you. I have always loved you and taken great care of you. You belong with me."

Evelyn tried to remain calm and focused, and directed her attention towards the road in front of her. With each passing minute, Evelyn felt better. She was glad to have made it to the car, and ecstatic that they had successfully exited the parking lot without so much as a glimpse of Mac. She was supposed to be watching Levi, she thought, yet she'd allowed something like this to happen, anyways. It was a good thing Evelyn was back in the picture, because clearly no one else cared for Levi the way that she did.

Evelyn passed the stop sign that she normally would have turned at to head towards their home. The further away from the school, the calmer she felt.

"Mommy, you missed the turn."

"I know."

"Where are we going?"

"On a little adventure. Aren't you excited to be going on an adventure with Mommy?"

"Yes, but I have a book report on Jupiter due Friday. If I don't turn it in, I won't get a good grade in science."

"Don't worry about that, Levi, just think about how much fun we're going to have."

Levi looked out the passenger window, and then returned his gaze to his mother. "But Mom, this is my first year to get letter grades. Mrs.

Kendrick told us that the book report is a big part of our grade. Mac took me to the library last week so we could get started on my report, and we did a lot of research. We checked out some books and got a rough draft printed out. I need to finish it and turn it in. How am I going to get—"

"I said not to worry about your report, Levi. It is the *last* thing you should be worried about." Evelyn's tone of voice tightened with each word.

"But Mom, this is a big part of my grade. You said that if I don't get good grades, starting now, that I won't go to college. If I don't go to college, I won't get a good job. If I don't get a good job, you said that—"

"Forget it, Levi! Just forget what I said. You're only in the third grade, for Christ's sake. A stupid book report on Jupiter is not going to keep you out of college. Now hush, Mommy needs to think."

Levi fought back the tears. Her words were confusing him. He tried to be happy and enjoy his time with his mom, but his stomach felt queasy. After sitting quietly in his seat for a few more minutes, unable to calm his nerves, Levi finally asked his mom another question, "Can I get my Nintendo? It's in Mac's car."

"Not today. Maybe another day."

"Where are we going, Mom? I really want to know."

"We are . . . going for a drive. It will be like a little scavenger hunt."

"What are we looking for?" Levi asked, relieved to hear what was actually going on. This made more sense, and explained why his mom had rushed him out as she had. If they were playing in a scavenger hunt, they would need to hurry to beat the other players. They were already on the road out of town. Levi was happy to recognize a familiar sign along the road as he started searching for possible scavenger hunt items. They played this game sometimes on long car rides and he liked it very much.

However, Evelyn did not respond to his question.

Levi sat staring at his mom, clearly awaiting her answer. While looking to his mom, Levi noticed that she was acting a bit different than he remembered. Her last few answers had been slowish and her speech was slippery. Some of her words didn't sound right to him.

"Mom, are you okay?"

Again, Evelyn didn't respond.

"Are you okay, mom?" Levi repeated. "Mom, you're driving weird and I'm starting to feel car sick."

Evelyn kept driving at a high rate of speed, swerving across the double-yellow line. Her cell was ringing, as it had been since they got into her car. Evelyn ignored the phone, but it continued to ring.

"Mom, your phone is ringing."

No response.

"Mom, you should stop the car and answer your phone." Levi didn't know why his mom wouldn't just answer her phone, since it was sitting out in the open on top of the console between the driver and passenger seat of the Range Rover. After his mom continued to ignore him, Levi tried to reach over for the cell phone himself. From where Levi was buckled, however, he was unable to reach far enough forward to grab the phone. He thought about unstrapping his seatbelt to get the phone, but realized his mom was driving too fast for him to be able to do that. He was getting dizzy as it was.

Levi reached for the door to open his window, but the window was locked with the child-proof locking device. His mom never used that locking device, but for some reason his window was still not opening. Levi was getting desperate for some air.

"Mom, can you crack my window?"

No response.

Levi's heart started to race. What was going on? Why wasn't his mom answering him? This didn't feel like a game anymore, and the feeling of uneasiness had quickly returned.

"Mom, I want you to stop the car. I think I am going to throw up."

Though Evelyn maintained her silence, this time she did react. Levi felt the car jerking towards the right. He heard gravel from the edge of the road spin into the fender wells. The car began to fish tail. Evelyn responded by overcorrecting the skid, and their SUV began to spin and flip off of the road.

Levi held onto the door handle so hard that his knuckles were white. He felt an impact and his seatbelt cinched him backwards. His head banged against the passenger door window. When the car quit moving, Levi realized the car was on its side, and they were now stuck in some sort of ditch.

"Mom!" Levi cried.

Evelyn did not respond.

"Mom! You crashed the car!"

Nothing. Silence.

"Wait until Dad sees this. He's going to be really mad."

"Hush up!" Evelyn finally shouted. "Stop badgering me. Do you hear me? You need to shut your mouth! You're driving me crazy! Nuts! Bonkers! Just be quiet for once, Levi!"

"Levi could no longer hold back his tears. He burst out crying with a loud sob. "Mommy, my head hurts."

"I told you to hush up! Stop that crying. You are not a little baby anymore."

Levi wailed. He couldn't help himself. "I-I-I'm sorry, mom. I'm sorry for crying. I'm just–"

Evelyn jammed her shoulder into the driver's door, trying to pry it open. It was of no use. The smashed front end had buckled the front fender into the door. She climbed into the back seat and tried to open Levi's door. It would not open either. She shoved her cell phone into her purse and then climbed over the back seat and into the rear of the car and flipped open the back tailgate.

"Grab that bag. We are staying here tonight."

* * *

The sheriff responded to Mac's 9-1-1 call immediately. While standing in the elementary school parking lot, Mac rushed through the chain of events leading to that moment. The Sheriff's office promptly issued an APB for Evelyn. Contact was made with the family. Luke claimed complete and utter ignorance as to the most recent scandal. None of the children appeared to know what was going on, and the fact that each of them were left stranded supported their lack of knowledge. Lauren had been marooned at swim practice, as had Ben at wrestling.

After concluding the inquiry with Mac, the Sheriff told her to go to her office and wait to hear from him. The Sheriff went to the Landers residence to see whether Evelyn had absconded with Levi and taken him home. A search of the house revealed no signs of Evelyn or Levi.

The Sheriff told Mac to remain at her office and that he'd contact her if he heard anything. She obeyed, but time seemed to stand still. She stopped pacing for a moment and stared out her office window. The sun was setting. Birds were beginning to fly south for the winter. Fall was still in the air, with warm evening breezes yet cool morning freezes, encouraging the leaves to change color. But somehow, despite the fact that the season was early in its change, the birds were leaving early. Did they sense a premature winter? Was a storm brewing? Mac had an ominous feel about her—an inner storm.

Mac was helpless and alone. She racked her brain for whom to call to share her worry with. Mac was frozen in time yet in a flash second, decided that she could call Beth. Beth would understand.

She reached for her office phone and started to dial, when the intercom buzzed. Megan's voice boomed in, "Karl Swensen on the line." Mac took the call.

Chapter 24

"I can't believe that she took off with the kid," Karl Swensen said. "Recent evidence in the case exonerates Mrs. Landers. In fact, I just had a conversation discussing settlement terms with Harold Neiman and John Trainor. I don't know why Mrs. Landers would abscond with Levi at all, but especially so close in time to the trial."

"Were you thinking about dismissing the case?" Mac worriedly asked.

"No, no, we weren't going to do that, Mac. The evidence that has come forward since we filed the petition, however, suggested that Levi being returned to his parents' care might be an appropriate move. We had talked about releasing Levi to his parents on a CRISP Agreement."

"What is a CRISP Agreement?"

"It's a conditional return to the parents wherein they agree to abide by certain terms and conditions, and if they abide by the agreement and attend all the counseling, then within a certain period of time the case is terminated."

"Sounds a bit like probation to me."

"Exactly."

"I hope you don't mind me asking, but what evidence did you review that you considered as potentially exonerating the Landers?"

"I wish I could tell you, but I can't at the moment." Karl said.

"I understand that this case is confidential, Karl, but I'm a party to the action and Levi's attorney. I'm allowed to hear this type of thing, and I wish you'd share it with me."

"I know that, Mac, but we're still in the early stages of reaching a potential settlement, and if we aren't able to reach any sort of settlement than I'm going to be forced to put forth my case. I believe a portion of this case can be proven, Mac, but it's just not an easy win. There's a chance we could lose and Levi would return home without any protection whatsoever."

Mac understood Karl's point, but her concern at the moment wasn't burdens of proof or justice in the eyes of the law. Her concern was Levi, and she wanted to know whether he was safe, and if he wasn't, she wanted to do whatever she could to help him.

As if Karl could read Mac's mind, he offered, "Don't be so hard on yourself. I see this kind of thing more often than I'd like to admit. Most times, the parents bring the kids back because they have to. I've only had a few cases where the parent skipped town and were never heard from or seen again. Those situations are extremely rare, and very unlikely in this case. Think about it. Mrs. Landers has three other kids and a rich hubby in town. She'll be back."

"But will Levi?"

Mac let her own words hang in the air, like a dark cloud looming over the horizon. Karl didn't respond. He certainly cared about Levi, but Karl Swensen had seventy other cases to prosecute. None of the cases on his case load had any more personal significance to him than another, and the only reason that the Landers case was a forerunner for Karl was that it was drawing plenty of publicity. The publicity was not favorable to the prosecution since the Landers were upstanding citizens, so the pressure for settlement was coming from Karl's boss.

* * *

Mac heard a loud knock on the front door to her office lobby. It was pretty late, and she had just hung up the phone with Karl. She wasn't expecting anyone, and was a bit nervous about who was at the front of her office. She walked in the direction of the lobby and yelled, "Who is it?"

"My mom said that Levi is missing. What can I do to help?"

Mac suddenly felt a much needed sense of calm at hearing Wyatt's soft and reassuring voice, and immediately unlatched the front door to let him in. Mac immediately grabbed onto Wyatt, looking for something to steady herself from the waves of worry that she'd been bombarded with. Wyatt knew that Mac just needed a moment of calmness, and remained quiet until Mac finally extricated herself from his grasp.

"I don't know what to do," Mac tearfully said, as she pulled back from Wyatt and started to lead him back towards her office. Her voice was not calm, and it was obvious to Wyatt that she was very near the point of breaking out into full hysteria. "I don't know what to do. I am so worried about him. The sheriff said Evelyn took all of her antipsychotic medication with her, and now I'm completely afraid that she's going to overdose either herself or Levi. It's clear she's desperate right now, and you know what they say about desperate people."

"They do desperate things," Wyatt said. He shut Mac's office door, and leaned her towards the leather couch near her desk. "It is easy to jump to conclusions, and things might not be as bad as you're imagining." Wyatt sat himself down next to Mac on the couch, and put his hand on her knee. Mac looked up at him expectantly, waiting to hear what he was going to say next that would ease her mind.

"Think of it a different way. Say you were his mom and you'd been falsely accused of something. I'm not saying that this is the way that it is—but I'm just asking for you to run a hypothetical with me. So, you're accused of something against your son that you didn't do, and your child has been taken away from you. You decide to take the law into your own hands and you take him back. Would you hurt him?"

Mac stared quietly at Wyatt for a moment before finally answering a quiet, "No." Mac suddenly jumped up from the couch and started pacing her office. "No. But I'm not on antipsychotic medication."

"Maybe so or maybe not. But chances are—you would not hurt your own flesh and blood."

"People are more likely to harm their loved ones than they are strangers."

"I don't believe that. When crimes are committed, sometimes they are against relatives. But in the grand scheme of life, I'm bettin' that most victims of crime do not know their perpetrators."

"That's not true, Wyatt. Crimes amongst family members are a lot higher than I'd like to admit, and since I've started working as a lawyer I'm realizing just how prevalent domestic violence situations are."

"Since neither of us knows for absolute certainty the numbers involved with that sort of thing, let's just assume that I'm right. Okay? Let's assume that you're his mom and you are frustrated with the system and you want your son back. If you took him back, would you hurt him?"

"No."

"Well, I certainly doubt that Mrs. Landers is going to hurt Levi. I think she is frustrated and overwhelmed. I would be too."

Mac stopped pacing for a moment and thought about Wyatt's statement. He was probably right.

"Do you want kids someday?" Mac asked the question out of nowhere, and had no idea where the thought had come from. Mac turned towards Wyatt somewhat nervously, after having asked such a personal question.

There was a considerable pause in their conversation. Just when Mac was prepared to interject with an apology for the question, Wyatt stood up and responded.

"Of course I want kids. I can't imagine life without them. I just haven't met the right woman to be the mother of my children. My mom has told me at least a thousand times that the most important decision you make in life is the person you choose to have kids with. I've seen what happens when the father of your kid is a rotten egg." Mac knew that Wyatt was referring to his half-brother, Greg's, father. "Why?"

Mac stumbled for a response, because in truth, she didn't know why she'd just asked him that question. She walked over to her desk and sat down in her wing-backed chair and nervously shuffled through a stack of phone messages. "I'm sorry. I don't know why I asked. The words just came out of my mouth."

"No need to apologize." Wyatt then looked down at his watch, clearly noting that it was almost nine at night. "Anyway, why are you still here?"

Mac held her silence for a minute. "I have been taking care of Levi for the last three weeks. He comes home with me every day after school. We have dinner together. We read stories and get ready for bed and hang out together." Mac paused to take a deep breath, and her voice began to break when she continued. "I can't imagine going to my apartment alone tonight. I think I will crack up if I do. I know how silly this must sound, but I miss him and I just can't–"

"It's okay, Mac," Wyatt interrupted while placing his hands on her shoulders. He cleared away a stack of papers from the top of Mac's desk, and then sat on the corner of it. He took his one remaining hand from off of Mac's shoulder, and grabbed Mac's hands with it. He covered Mac's hand with his now other free hand, and cocooned her hand within his own two.

Mac was temporarily distracted, and noticed that Wyatt's hands were warm and soft in some places, yet calloused and hard in others. His knuckles were scabbed from working with barbed wire and his cuticles were torn in places. Yet, as she looked at his weathered hands, she saw responsibility and dedication and commitment. She knew that Wyatt was there for her, and she knew that he was also there because he was worried about Levi himself. Mac looked back up at Wyatt, clearly appreciating his presence.

"It is okay, Mac. It's all going to be okay. Levi is fine and you'll soon see that. His mom just made a mistake. She'll probably come to her senses by morning. They are probably safely tucked into bed at a nice hotel somewhere and they will come back tomorrow. You need a decent night sleep so that you are there for him when he comes back." He reached over with his left hand and raised her chin up so that their eyes met.

"*If* he comes back," Mac said, lowering her head. Tears dripped down onto her desk.

He gently pulled her chin back up. The tears flowed caressingly down her freckled cheeks. "Pessimism isn't going to help. He *will* come back. Don't you waste another minute thinking otherwise. Levi is stronger than you think. If he is in danger, I think he will figure it out pretty darn quick and he'll do something about it. Heck, I saw him save himself from bein' kicked by Mocha. He saw it comin' and he got out of the way."

"What?" Mac said. "When did this happen?"

"Saturday. Didn't tell you 'cuz I didn't think you needed to know. He was fine. A little spooked, but I congratulated him for paying attention to Mocha's mood and sensing her reaction. Mocha is mean sometimes. Levi is no stranger to meanness. He gets it. I can tell. People are just like animals when it comes to just about everything, including displaying moods. I watched Levi watch Mocha–and he noticed that she was getting anxious and he backed off. I bet you dollars to doughnuts that he has a brother who gets mean on him without provocation and Levi knows how to get himself away from the undeserving punishment that's coming his way."

"Did he tell you about Ben?" Mac asked with a softer tone.

"Yes."

"Ben's a bully. Takes his frustrations out on his little brother."

"I think you should be a psychologist."

"A head doctor? That's the last thing I would be. I like animals, not people. Remember?"

"You just said that you wanted to have children. If you don't like people, why would you want to have kids?"

Wyatt paused and shook his head. She knew that she was being a contrarian, but she couldn't help herself. She waited for him to answer the pointed question.

"I like people, I just don't like *some* people." Wyatt lowered his head a tiny bit, to make sure that he was able to make eye contact with Mac. "I'm square with animals. Some are born mean and that's just their disposition. I leave 'em alone. Some are gentle. Some are playful. You get it. But people don't usually fit squarely in a category. Some really mean-spirited people come off as real nice at first, and then, over time, you learn that they really aren't nice. That's what I don't like about some people. They play charades. Levi is not like that."

"You didn't find him on the banks of Goose Creek with a knife stabbed in his thigh."

"True. But if someone was dragging me to the doctor all the time, and I didn't have time to be a kid, I might poke myself with a knife too. If my folks were willing to let every doctor and nurse in the United States poke me with needles, then I might take it upon myself to jab my own flesh once."

Mac appreciated what Wyatt was saying, and his attempts at relaxing her.

"Heck, my mom has already told me what that kid's been through. He's spent most of his time at the doctor's and that all of his medical stuff was made up. He really wasn't sick at all, for Christ's sake. The kid hasn't had any 'kid fun' his whole life. I wonder when the last time someone took him fishin' or bike riding or let him throw rocks in a big mountain lake."

"What if–"

"You can 'what if' all night long but it ain't gonna help. What's gonna help is for you to go home, get some sleep, and let the sheriff do his job. Like I said, Levi's probably sleeping comfortably in a nice hotel somewhere and you'll hear from the sheriff in the morning. Let's get you home now. You hear?"

As much as Mac felt like arguing her point, she was exhausted and she knew Wyatt was right. Her nerves were shot. Wyatt helped her load Ted into his cat carrier and helped her shut off the lights to the office. He followed her home in his truck and walked her up the flight of stairs to her second story apartment.

Suddenly, Mac realized that Wyatt was at her apartment, and that he'd never been there before. Mac turned to Wyatt as he set Ted's cage down on the floor next to the food bowls and opened the gate. Ted bolted out and immediately started eating from his dry food dish.

Mac flopped herself down on the couch and put her arm up over her head. She was truly exhausted, and though she wanted to sit up and be more appropriate with Wyatt in her house, she just didn't have the strength. She didn't notice when Wyatt walked over to her and gently slipped each of her high heels off each foot. She did, however, notice when he scooped her up from the couch and carried her to her bedroom.

She protested and grabbed at the door jam. "This is where Levi sleeps."

"Not tonight. This is where you are sleeping. You probably haven't had a decent night sleep in a month. I am tucking you in and I am going to sit here and babysit until you go to sleep. You hear?" His tone was commanding, but not mean.

Mac wanted to fight Wyatt, but knew it was futile. She really wanted to get herself more comfortable, too, but just didn't have the energy to do anything. As Wyatt placed her gently on her bed, she appreciated the softness of the mattress beneath her. Mac took a deep breath, and slowly allowed her eyes to close. The last thing she was aware of before succumbing to her sheer and utter exhaustion was the feel of Wyatt's hand brushing along her cheek.

Mac drifted into a deep sleep and found herself in a dream. In the dream, she was at a party where loud voices boomed over the lower dull-drum of conversation, yet she could not distinctly comprehend any of the words being uttered. It was like she was in an underwater cave, where every noise echoed after it resonated. She wanted to go home, but was unable to find the door. She needed her peaceful and quiet house, but every direction she turned looking for an exit produced more faceless voices booming with sound.

Panic started to rise within her as her desperation to leave increased. She had to find a way out. She could hear pounding, as if someone were knocking on a door, trying to get in. She suddenly realized that if she went in the direction of the pounding noise that she might be able to find a way out. She followed the sound as it grew louder, and finally found herself in front of what must have been the tiniest door she'd ever seen. It was like the door from *Alice in Wonderland.* Mac knew that she couldn't fit through the teeny door unless she shrank or the door somehow grew, but was unable to think of any ways to make either happen.

Her panic became terror as the silent alarm went off inside her. She was trapped.

Suddenly, everything surrounding Mac became silent at once. All of the loud yet unintelligible voices stopped, all of the buzzing disappeared, and every person that surrounded her from out of nowhere was turned directly towards her. Every eye was focused on her. Everyone was angry. They knew she was trapped and wanted out. The crowd grew intensely hostile and began to slowly approach her. She was ensnared in the corner of the room, confined, ambushed and deeply afraid.

She heard the pounding again. It was growing louder. Then she heard a voice. "Mac, open the door. It's me."

Mac's eyes flew open and she suddenly realized that she was back in her apartment. Mac rubbed her eyes and tried to force herself awake, while noticing on the clock that it was three o'clock in the morning. She searched her memory for the events leading her to this point, and recalled that Wyatt had brought her home from work and forced her to go to sleep.

She quickly looked around her to see if Wyatt was still there, but found herself alone. There was someone at her front door, however, and they continued knocking.

"Mac, are you there?" a voice called from her door.

As she was getting out of bed, groggy from her deep sleep and her strange dream, she heard another sound: her front door was suddenly opening. Mac's eyes flew open wide.

"Who are you?" she heard a voice ask at the edge of her apartment.

"Who are *you*?" she heard Wyatt ask in response.

"*Oh God.*" Mac said out loud. Wyatt *was* still at her apartment, and the person at her front door was Jeffrey. Mac bolted out of her bedroom and into the living room.

"Jeffrey, what are you doing here?" Mac said.

"What am *I* doing here? How about, 'What is *he* doing here'?"

Mac wondered the same thing. She didn't know that Wyatt had stayed. Mac glanced at the couch and saw that her pillow and blanket were askew and his cowboy boots were on the floor next to the couch.

"Uh," Wyatt said, sensing that Jeffrey was less than pleased, "I think I'd better go. Call me if you hear about Levi." Wyatt quickly walked over to the couch and grabbed his cowboy boots.

Sock-footed, he gingerly passed Jeffrey on the way out. "G'day," he said, as he left.

Chapter 25

Levi woke up in the middle of the night, freezing. He was not happy that they were spending the night in a shack, and even less happy to be as cold as he was. There was a gaping hole in the wall of the shack they were staying in, and it was letting cold air blow onto him all night long.

Why are we here, anyways? Levi thought to himself. He was pretty sure that his mom didn't even know whose shack this was, so why were they inside of it? Levi was worried about whether this was a crime; he'd seen enough "no trespassing" signs stapled to trees in forested areas to know that going on someone else's property wasn't right. Why would his mom risk getting them in trouble?

Levi was worried for his mom, and knew that her well enough to recognize that something was wrong. When they were driving away from the school, she was acting very strange. When she crashed the car into the ditch, he was certain she was lost. Still, she demanded that he get out of the car and bring his sleeping bag with him. He did as she said.

Evelyn had packed an overnight bag for Levi, a pillow, sleeping bag, and a stuffed dolphin toy. She had packed a bag for herself also, too, but apparently hadn't thought to pack herself a sleeping bag. After gathering their bags together and exiting the car, Levi followed his mom out into the woods. He wasn't sure where she was taking them, and from the random path she was taking, Levi wasn't sure his mom knew, either. They ended up walking forever until they came upon a small abandoned shed.

When they entered the old, musty hovel, it was still daylight. Levi wasn't sure why his mom brought them here, because the shack was empty and he was bored. They ended up sitting down on the floor inside the gross one-room shanty, and played card games for a few hours. By the time the sunlight had gone away and they could no longer see the cards, Levi realized how hungry he was.

"I'm hungry, Mom."

Evelyn looked at him for a moment, then back at the cards that she had been holding in her hands.

"Mom, I'm hungry. Can we go get something to eat?" Levi was holding his stomach for effect.

Evelyn looked at him quizzically. "No," she answered.

"But I'm hungry, Mom."

"Well then, you should have eaten lunch at school."

"But I did."

"You should have eaten more."

"I ate everything on my plate. There wasn't–"

"Stop talking back, Levi. I already gave you my answer, which was 'no.'"

"But I'm so hungry. Why can't I eat just a little something?"

"Because I don't have any food, Levi, that's why. All I have are two bottles of water and that's it."

"Well, can I have some water, then? I'm thirsty too."

"Goddammit, Levi, you always need something. You are the neediest kid I've ever known."

Levi coiled back, and his eyes began to fill with tears.

"You're always demanding something, and you're the reason our family has been driven apart."

"I'm sorry, Mommy." Levi started to cry. "Why would you say that to me? That's mean."

"Don't talk back to me! I'm still your mother, and you'll treat me with respect."

Levi was miserable, and didn't know what to say or do. His tummy hurt so much, and he realized that he must never have been this hungry before.

He did not feel safe or loved right now, and his mommy always went out of her way to make him feel both in the past. Something had changed.

Levi looked down at the deck of cards his mom had put back on the ground between them. Instead of just sitting around, Levi decided to pick up the cards and try to start shuffling them. As he awkwardly maneuvered the cards in his hands, his mom suddenly reached over and quickly grabbed them from his hands.

"You can't even shuffle right."

Levi opened his mouth wanting to say something right for once, but was at a total loss for words. He decided not to say anything, because everything out of his mouth up until that point ended up causing a fight. Levi ended up just sitting there silently in response, with his arm pressed up against his tummy to try and massage his tummy pain. He watched his mom, and saw that she unscrewed the cap to some pill bottles. She dumped a number of pills into her left hand and then, while holding the pills tightly, she unscrewed the water bottle. She popped a handful of pills into her mouth and then chased them down with a swig of water. She offered him some water afterwards. Levi accepted and drank the remains of the clear liquid.

They sat in silence for what seemed like an eternity. He wanted to talk to her so badly and make her happy and love him again, but he couldn't think of anything that seemed right. Evelyn was lying on the floor with her right arm flung over her face. Levi was sure that she was going to fall asleep and leave him awake and alone in the middle of the woods, and that scared him. He began to sneak through his mom's purse looking for a pen and paper, so that he could at least doodle to himself. When Levi found some, he realized that perhaps he could impress his mom with a demonstration of his improved writing skills from all the practice he'd had at school.

"Mom, let me show you how well I write! We're learning cursive in school, and my cursive is way better than my printing! Remember when my second grade teacher told you that I was going to have bad handwriting because I didn't practice enough? Well, she was wrong. My cursive is almost as good as the girls." Levi proudly scripted his name and showed it to her.

Evelyn lowered her arm from her face and propped herself up on her elbows. She looked at Levi's script and offered an approving smile.

Levi lit up when he saw his mom smile.

Evelyn remained quiet for a few minutes, with an expression on her face that made Levi think that she was contemplating something. After a few minutes, she finally spoke up.

"Levi, honey, your cursive is good. Tell you what. Why don't you write what I am about to tell you in cursive?"

Levi happily obeyed. He wrote until his hand was tired. His mom had a lot to say.

After what felt like hours, his mom finally stopped talking. By this point the sun had entirely disappeared, and the shack was pitch black. Levi was proud of himself for getting out the pen and paper, and doing something right for once that night. Levi heard his mom unwrapping the sleeping bag, and heard her call for him to join her in it. Although her words sounded funny to him, he did as he was told.

He tried to join his mom inside the sleeping bag, but it wasn't quite big enough for the two of them. Levi was only able to get half of his body inside, and that was only if he turned to his side. This wasn't comfortable, because the floor was hard and cold. Levi tugged as much as he dared to on the bag, trying not to disturb his mother who'd climbed in first and taken the majority of the material to herself. Finally, Levi decided that he'd get out of the bag and sleep on the bare floor, using the extra material from the bag to cover himself with like a blanket. This worked well enough for him to drift off to sleep for awhile, but he was asleep for only a short while before he woke up again bare and cold. He saw his mother next to him, who'd rolled over to her side and taken all of the protection from the cold with her.

When he tried to tug some covers back, he accidentally woke his mom up. She wasn't very happy about being woken up, and groggily complained for a little bit. Eventually she got out of the bag to go get some more of her pills, and then went back to sleep. Levi could not see her because it was too dark, but the sounds were all too familiar. Within a few minutes, she was in a deep sleep and he again lay there for what seemed like hours.

He was tired, cold and hungry.

Weariness eventually won out, and Levi found himself drifting into a hazy state, neither asleep nor awake. When the Baseball Man came to check on him, he was sure he was awake. It seemed so real to him. The Baseball Man handed him a baseball card with Ernie Banks on it. Levi flipped it over and saw written on the back, "It's a beautiful day for baseball. Let's play two."

"I don't understand," Levi said to the Baseball Man.

The Baseball Man replied, "Ernie Banks loved baseball the way you love your mom."

"I still don't understand," Levi said as he began to rub at his eyes.

"You can't sleep right now because your mom needs your help tonight. You need to show her double the love you normally show her. That means that you're gonna have to be brave and cold and hungry and tired to save her."

Levi sat up and looked around. It was still too dark to see, but the sky was beginning to lighten. He called out for the Baseball Man, but there was no answer. Within a few minutes his eyes had adjusted to the minimal light enough for him to be able to find his shoes. He put them on quietly, and then tip-toed to the wobbly door held in place by a weak wooden bracket. After slowly unlatching the bracket from the door, Levi quietly exited the shack and walked out into the twilight.

The nearly full moon lit the woods up around him, offering enough light for him to be able to retrace his steps towards the dirt road which led to the paved road of a two-lane highway. Although it was cold and dark and he did not recognize anything around him, Levi felt a sense of peace—as if he had been there before. He felt less alone than he had felt when he was next to his mom in the shack.

As he wandered toward the highway, Levi thought about what he was doing. He was too young to be walking alone in the middle of the night in the middle of nowhere. If his mom woke up and didn't see him in the shack with her, she'd be scared, too. He didn't want her to worry about him, and he didn't want to get in trouble, either. He decided that he needed to go back.

Levi turned around and headed back in the direction of the shack. On his way back, he spotted his mom's car resting sideways in the ditch. He'd almost forgotten that she had crashed. He reached up and felt the bump on his forehead–a subtle reminder of the accident.

He kept walking past the wreck, and quickly returned to the dilapidated shack. Levi opened the flimsy door, but this time without trying to mask the sound; this time he *wanted* him mom to wake up.

He walked to where she was laying on the floor and nudged her, but she did not stir. He nudged her a little harder, but again, she did not move. He felt her head, like she always did to him when she was checking for a fever, but she didn't feel warm. In fact, she felt kind of cold to him. Maybe the cold draft was freezing her head?

"Mom, wake up. Wake up," he said as he shook her as hard as he could.

She did not respond.

Suddenly, Levi was struck with a terrifying thought. What if she was dead? Maybe she got hurt in the car crash and died in her sleep.

"Mom, wake up. Please. Please wake up."

Still, no movement.

Levi panicked. He ran out of the shack and back towards the dirt road that led to the highway. He crossed the cattle guard and ran up onto the highway, yelling loudly the whole time. He hoped someone would hear him and come offer him some help, but the highway was deserted. Levi could not see any headlights in either direction.

He looked to the right and could see a light in the window of a house, but it looked like it was a long way away.

He looked to the left, but there was only darkness.

Levi realized that his only option was to go to the right, and hope to make it to that house with enough time to save his mom. He hoped and prayed that a bad guy wouldn't get him.

* * *

"No wonder you haven't been returning my calls," Jeffrey said to Mac.

After Wyatt left her apartment, Mac tried to explain the situation, but Jeffrey did not believe her. He was certain that she was having a fling with another man and using Levi as an excuse not to come and see him while he was at the Denver conference. "It's not just some coincidence that Levi turns up missing and your new boyfriend is spending the night. I think the evidence is pretty clear."

"Jeffrey," Mac started. "You are totally misunderstanding what is happening. Levi is missing. I am worried sick about–"

"I can see that. So worried that you had to have your cowboy over to console you."

"That is not what happened. Wyatt knows Levi. He's been helping me with him."

"The evidence keeps stacking up."

"I am not on trial, Jeffrey. This is not about evidence. This is about a little boy who was kidnapped by his mom and is now missing."

"Do you know how absurd that sounds? I hunt down serial killers who do the most egregious, outrageous crimes known to mankind. I ferret through evidence every day–anonymous tips that sound ridiculous but end up being legitimate and good tips that end up being wild goose chases. I can read a situation faster than anyone out there."

"Oh, really?" Mac replied. "Exactly what are you reading from this situation now?"

"Let's see . . . the woman you've described as a loving mom who picks her son up from school, and has doted on him for the past ten years, suddenly feels the urge to kidnap him. Unbelievable. There are kids out there who are beaten and abused and kicked around in custody battles–but here, you have two upstanding citizens who've had their son yanked from their arms and you accuse the mother of kidnapping?" Jeffrey turned and headed toward the door. Mac ran after him. He turned around briefly.

"And then, to top it off, I come to your aid and find some man spending the night in your apartment? You've lost all credibility with me."

"You've got to trust me, Jeffrey. Wyatt brought me home from the office and basically forced me to go to bed–"

"You can omit the details, Mac. I don't need to know another thing."

"That's not what I meant! What I meant was that I was exhausted and stressed and he insisted that I get some sleep. He must have fallen asleep on the couch. That's all there is to it."

"You expect me to believe that?"

"Yes," Mac said. She reached out to hold Jeffrey's hand. He recoiled.

"I'm not naïve."

"Jeffrey, I know that your first wife cheated on you and that you are still hurt by it, but I am not your ex-wife. I am not cheating on you. Wyatt is Greg's brother. We are just friends. He was trying to help me with Levi."

"Greg? Oh, you mean the ex-boyfriend that you dated for three years before dating me? Ahhh, the plot thickens."

"There is no plot. I told you exactly what happened. I was asleep in my bed. Apparently, he fell asleep on the couch. Not that I owe you an explanation, because I don't. All you need to know is that I told you I wasn't doing anything wrong."

"Been there, done that. I am nobody's fool."

Mac shook her head in frustration as she watched Jeffrey walk down the two flights of stairs that led to her apartment. She continued to watch as he got into his Ford Escort rental car and zoomed away.

* * *

Wyatt was unnerved by the confrontation with Jeffrey, and concerned about having put Mac in such a precarious situation. He didn't intend for his good deed to lead to such an awkward confrontation, and hoped that Mac wasn't angry with him for the mess he'd caused. He wanted to call her and apologize, but he didn't have a cell phone.

Wyatt instead drove along the lonesome, two-laned highway back towards the ranch, thinking about the nights events. *Why did I spend the night there?* "Darn it, I should've gone home," he said out loud to himself. For some strange reason, though, he just couldn't leave her there all alone and vulnerable. He didn't think that crashing on her couch would've been so stupid. He definitely didn't think that he'd leave in that type of haste, and had no idea why he felt so embarrassed about it all.

He reminded himself to focus on the road. At this time of morning, there were critters on the road. Deer and antelope crossed the road and seemed to be attracted to headlights of vehicles. Wyatt kept his eye on the ditches to the side of the road, looking for the red dilated pupils of creatures about to cross.

As he rounded the corner, he noticed movement on the side of the road. Wyatt instinctively slowed down, not wanting to make a hood ornament out of a wayward antelope. While slowing, Wyatt realized that the critter before him was not of a four-legged nature.

It was a human. A child. A boy.

Chapter 26

"Daddy," Lauren said to Luke. "I need to talk with you."

Luke Landers was sitting in the kitchen drinking an apple martini while rifling through the stack of mail. It was late Monday night, and Evelyn and Levi had been missing for several hours now. The sheriff stopped by twice and called a number of other times, to ensure that Luke understood the importance of him calling the sheriff immediately if he heard from Evelyn.

"Honey, it is late. You need to get to sleep. Didn't you tell me that you have a Greek Mythology test tomorrow?"

"Daddy, it's all my fault," Lauren persisted. She approached a few steps closer to the kitchen counter island, her bare feet shuffling across the travertine floor.

Luke looked up and saw her red glassy eyes, and realized that she'd been crying. He set the papers down and motioned for her to approach him.

"What's wrong, LooLoo? What's your fault?"

"Levi's sicknesses," Lauren wailed.

"Honey, that wasn't your fault," Luke said as he reached towards his daughter and wrapped his arms around her.

"No, Dad," Lauren cried, removing herself from his embrace. "I made him sick. I gave him mom's medicine." Lauren burst into tears.

Shocked and confused by her statement, Luke pulled away from his twelve-year-old daughter. "What medicine?"

Lauren let out a sob followed by a snorting cough. "The medicine that makes mom happy. Levi was really sad one day and so I gave him mom's medicine. I mixed it in his red Gatorade and he drank it." Lauren continued to cry. "After he drank it, they took him away from us and now mom stole him back and ran away and it is all my fault."

"Why are you doing this?" Luke asked. "Why are you trying to take the blame for something you didn't do? I know you didn't make Levi sick, Lauren."

"But Daddy, I did. Really! I gave him one of mommy's happy pills, you know, the pink and round ones. Mom takes them whenever she's sad, and so I thought it would help Levi. But now he's gone!" Lauren began to wail even harder.

"Lauren," Luke said, pulling his daughter back toward him, "Levi may have gotten sick after you gave him that one pill, but Levi has been sick over a long period of time. He wasn't taken away from us because of one mistake." Luke pulled Lauren away from him so as to make eye contact with his emotionally distraught daughter. "You did not cause any of this, honey."

Lauren dropped her chin to her chest. Luke took his index finger and gently lifted her chin so that he could see her eyes. Moments passed in silence as he stared into his daughter's sincere, sad eyes. Luke was surprised to see that his daughter remained just as distraught, despite his calm explanation.

"But Dad . . ." Lauren hesitated.

"But dad, what? I told you, honey, Levi has a long history of ailments and you could not possibly have caused any problems by doing what you just described once."

"I did it more than once."

Luke took both hand and placed them squarely on Lauren's shoulders.

"How many times?"

"I don't know, Daddy. I don't know." Lauren broke down in hysteria.

"More than five?"

"I don't know. Probably."

"More than ten?"

"Daddy, I don't know! I can't remember. I thought I was helping, I swear!" Lauren gulped in air, and the look in her eyes was desperate. "Levi was just so sad, so often. Mom was so sad, too, and I just couldn't watch it anymore. I didn't mean for anyone to get hurt or in trouble. I did it to make everyone better so that we could be a family again."

Luke's grip on her shoulders tightened. She felt the pressure of his fingertips dig into her shoulder blades.

"I'm sorry, Daddy. I will tell the police. They can take me away and give you Mom and Levi back." With that, Lauren slumped forward and buried her head in her father's chest and cried as hard as her body would allow.

Luke sat in stunned silence, faced with an awkward and difficult scenario. Luke finally picked up the phone, and did what he normally did in a time of confusion and panic: he called Janie Johansen.

* * *

"Levi!" Wyatt shouted while slamming on the brakes to his pickup truck. Before his truck came to a full stop, he shoved the gearshift into reverse and jammed backwards around the corner. His truck snaked backwards, nearly out of control, until it came to rest next to the reflector pole along the side of Highway 336. Wyatt lodged his truck into park and as the chassis rocked back and forth, he jumped out. Wyatt raced towards Levi, who was just about to crest the road. "Levi! Are you okay?"

Levi looked at Wyatt as if he were a stranger. It took him a few seconds to focus. Everything was a bit blurry to him and he was beginning to not feel well.

"Levi. It's me, Wyatt. Are you okay? Where is your mom? Is she okay?"

Levi looked up at Wyatt and then pointed in the direction of the shack.

"Is she over there?" Wyatt asked, not able to see into the darkness well enough to discern that there was a small structure just east of the dirt road.

"She's really cold," is all the little boy could say, and he sputtered out the words in a slow and slurry tone.

Wyatt grabbed Levi by the hand and then swiftly lifted him into the passenger side of his Chevy truck. He quickly buckled Levi in and ran to the driver's side. Before his seatbelt was fastened or the driver's door closed, Wyatt lodged the truck into gear and cranked the wheel in Evelyn's direction.

Wyatt saw the crumpled Range Rover in the ditch as they approached the shack. "You were in a car accident?"

Levi nodded and pushed his blonde bangs up to reveal the goose egg on his forehead.

"So you stayed in the Hendrickson's homestead?"

Levi shrugged in response.

"And your mom is still there?"

Levi nodded. "She's cold. She took too much medicine, I think."

"Did you take any medicine, Levi?"

"No, but my mom did. Twice."

"Did you drink or eat anything with her?"

"Water. She didn't bring any food."

At that point, they were in front of the shack. "Stay here and scoot into the back seat of the crew cab. I'm getting your mom and we're going to the hospital."

Levi did as he was told. He watched in wide-eyed horror as Wyatt carried his mother out of the shack and placed her in the front of the truck. She was completely pliant and limp, and her lips looked blue.

Wyatt strapped Evelyn's slumped body into the passenger seat and then ran back into the shack to gather anything that might contain the pill and water bottles. He shoved everything, including Evelyn's purse, into the sleeping bag and tossed it in the back of the crew cab.

As he sped into town, Wyatt whispered under his breath, "Mac's right. I need a cell phone."

Levi heard him. Until now, he'd forgotten that his mom had her phone in her purse. Usually, she left it in the car, but he remembered watching her grab it after the accident. "You can use my mom's." Levi reached into the sleeping bag and pulled out Evelyn's purse. He flipped open her phone and handed it to Wyatt.

Wyatt had never used a cell phone before. He glanced at it for a moment and then handed it back to Levi.

"Can you work this thing?"

Levi nodded.

"Call 9-1-1 and then give it back to me when they answer."

Levi obeyed, and was soon returning the phone to Wyatt. When the operator answered, Wyatt told her what had happened. The operator took all of the needed information from him, and prepared to dispatch an ambulance to meet them. After the call terminated, Wyatt handed the phone back to Levi and asked him to call Mac. "I don't know her number by heart," Wyatt admitted.

"I know it. Plus, it is stored on my mom's phone." Levi dialed. Mac answered. Levi wanted desperately to talk with Mac, but he handed the phone to Wyatt as he was told.

"I found him on the side of the 336, wandering around. They had a car accident. I think—"

"Oh my God! Is Levi okay? Where are you?"

"On our way into town to meet an ambulance. I think Levi's okay, but he's talking a bit funny and I'm afraid his mom might've given him something. And she's not looking too good, either."

"Evelyn? She's with you? Is she hurt?"

Wyatt tried to whisper into the phone. "Don't see any marks on her or anything, but I don't know if she's breathing. She's cold and blue and she ain't responding at all."

"What? Wyatt? Are you there?" Mac shouted desperately into the phone.

"Wyatt, I can't hear you. You are breaking up."

"I can see the flashing ambulance lights in the distance."

"Wyatt–don't hang up yet! Listen, when you meet up with the ambulance–"

Wyatt heard a thump in the back of his crew cab. He glanced back. "Oh shit. Levi passed out!"

"Oh God. Hurry! Speed if you have to. Please save our little boy."

* * *

Luke had tucked Lauren back into bed and told her that he would be back shortly. He then ran to his study and called Janie.

"She said *what*?" Janie Johansen said to Luke.

"Lauren said she gave Levi antipsychotic meds. She said she did it many times because the medicine made Evelyn happy and she figured it would make Levi happy too."

"Holy shit, Luke. Please don't tell me you believe her!" Janie incredulously replied.

"Janie, she was distraught."

"For Christ's sake, Luke. She's a kid trying to save her mom. Don't you see through this? She is trying to bail Evelyn out because she knows that her mom is in deep trouble."

"I don't think so. I can read my daughter pretty well. She's not one to lie."

"All kids lie," Janie snapped.

"Lauren doesn't."

"Don't be naïve. She's lied to me before."

Luke was surprised at Janie's response, and he was growing outraged at her belittling comments. He had been pushed to his limit that day, and having Janie accuse Lauren of lying was the final straw.

"I am quite sure that you can smell the sweet scent of a lie better than anyone." The words were sharp and Luke knew that he had gone too far. He wanted to retract, but weapons had been drawn.

Before she could edit her retort, she blurted, "Coming from the King of Lies, I consider that a compliment."

The wall between them was being constructed in a solid and unforgiving fashion. Yet, they both knew that if they drew enemy lines, they would suffer the consequences. Luke relented and softly offered a token.

"What if she's telling the truth? What if she did give Levi the meds?"

"Then it screws up our plan."

"Our *plan*? Is that all you can think about? What about my kids? What about Lauren? She could be prosecuted as a juvenile offender–charged with a crime, I'm sure. My family is being ripped to shreds and all you can think about is your *plan*?"

"Our plan, Luke. It is our plan. Don't even think of saying otherwise or I'll have my own attorney before you can blink an eye."

"Is that a threat?"

"I don't make threats. I make promises. I learned from the best, Dr. Landers. The difference is that I intend to keep my promises."

* * *

When Luke received the call from the ER, he quickly flashed from his conversation with Janie and accepted the call.

Lauren, who'd been unable to sleep, slowly and silently crept into the study.

Luke felt the heavy burden of his daughter's stare as he tried to listen to the details offered by the sheriff. The weight of grief lay between them–yet, in the moment of details about pulse and blood pressure and dilation of pupils, all Luke heard was the beating of his own heart.

How could a man cause his own family so much pain? The question rattled around in his brain as he raced to his car for the short, yet excruciatingly and agonizingly drive to the hospital.

Chapter 27

Facial expressions in hospital emergency rooms are roadmaps into one's soul.

When Mac entered the ER and glanced around, she saw pain, worry, regret, fear, blame, and anger. She did not know *any* of these people, but their facial expressions shared deep feelings with the strangers surrounding them. There was a mother holding a feverish child, constantly touching her little angel's forehead to see if her fever had reduced. There was a father with a clenched jaw pacing back and forth in front of his teenager's gurney. There was an elderly woman holding the hand of her husband who was hooked up to a chest monitor. Mac could almost predict what was going on in each of their lives, based entirely on their reactions to personal tragedy. Mac couldn't help but wonder about the larger picture, and the details leading up to these people being in the ER at this time.

When Wyatt charged into the ER a few moments later, Mac immediately knew the abbreviated version of what happened just by registering the panicked look on his face.

When Wyatt spotted Mac he immediately ran to her, grabbed her by the arm and pulled her out into the parking lot. "They are on their way," Wyatt said. There was something fearful in his eyes. "The ambulance is a few minutes behind me. I tried to keep Levi with me 'cuz I knew I could get him here faster, but the EMT insisted that they bring him."

"How did you find him?" Mac asked. She stood in the warm ray of the early morning sun, her business clothes rumpled from the day before and her eyes red with worry.

"I can't even begin to tell you how weird it was. I was drivin' along the road, lost in thought about my embarrasin' you by sleeping on your couch. I was paying attention to the corners of the road, only because I was afraid a critter might run in front of my path. Suddenly I saw the reflection of eyes on the side of the road. By the time I realized it was a kid and not a deer, I'd already passed him." Wyatt stopped for a moment as he began to shake. "Hell, if he woulda stepped two more feet onto the highway, I woulda hit him. I stopped and picked him up and he told me about the car accident and his mom. She's in bad shape, Mac. Real bad shape. She might be dead."

"Oh my God. What about Levi?"

"I don't know. He seemed confused when I first found him, and after we picked up his mom, he passed out. I'm real worried that she gave him some of these." Wyatt opened the sleeping bag sack and showed Mac the array of prescription drug bottles that were lying at the bottom of the bag like dead soldiers.

"There they are," Mac said, spotting the ambulance. "And there's Dr. Landers."

* * *

Dr. Luke Landers paced the ER as he waited the arrival of his wife and son. The ER rarely produced happy results. Luke knew this all too well as he anxiously awaited the arrival of his family. As Luke anxiously awaited the arrival of the ambulance, he looked around him and listened to the ER's noises. The frenetic pace of everyone around him matched in sync with the noises coming from the hospital equipment; lights were blinking, beeps were sounding, and voices were chattering.

This place was nowhere for a kid, and Luke was glad he'd refused Lauren's request to accompany him. He had woken their housekeeper before he left for the hospital, and instructed her to prohibit Austen, Ben or Lauren from leaving the house until he contacted her later. Ginny was accustomed to watching the Landers children, but not enforcing the rules with them. She promised Luke that she'd do her best, and hoped that the kids would listen to her.

Luke heard the siren of the ambulance and quickly ran through the sliding double doors.

"She's overdosed on antipsychotics," the EMT shouted to Dr. Shannon Tully. "Take her in first."

Dr. Tully assessed Evelyn's condition, rattling off a dozen questions to the EMT while transferring Evelyn's limp body onto an ER gurney.

"How's Levi?" Luke shouted.

"Vitals are decent, but he's not conscious," said the shorter of the two EMTs. "He's on oxygen and a drip. He's dehydrated."

Mac and Wyatt inched forward, trying to get a glance at Levi. He had a mask on his face and an IV in his arm. His color was better than it had been when Wyatt handed him over to the EMT crew.

"Levi," Mac shouted. "Levi, can you hear me? It's Mac."

As if on cue, Luke elbowed his way in between Mac and Levi. "Levi, it's Daddy. Can you hear my voice?"

Mac took a step back, respecting Luke's role as father and physician.

Wyatt grabbed her hand. "He's going to be fine. I promise you," Wyatt whispered. "He's a cowboy. He'll be back on the ranch before you know it, telling me which horse he's ready to mount."

"M-m-mocha," a small voice whispered.

"He's responding," Luke said. "I heard him speak." Luke reached over and removed Levi's mask for a second. Levi spoke again, "Mocha."

"Coke? You want some coke?" Luke said. "We can get you some–"

"Mocha," Wyatt interrupted. "He thinks he's ready to ride Mocha, dontcha, little buddy?" Wyatt sauntered around the gurney and took Levi's hand. "You can ride Mocha. And Mr. Pony. You can ride any horse you want. We just need to get you healthy, okay? Promise you'll do exactly what the doctors and nurses tell you."

Levi fluttered his eyelids open and closed a few times before locking glances with Wyatt. He managed a small smile. "I will." He closed his eyes again.

Luke affixed the oxygen mask back onto Levi's face and helped wheel him into the hospital. "I've got it from here," Luke said to Mac and Wyatt.

They stood helplessly and watched the ER doors close. Mac felt a conflicting pang deep in her heart. She hesitated for only a moment before deciding to charge into the hospital. She was not going to leave Levi alone.

Wyatt promptly followed her. He knew it was wrong to search another person's belongings, but something told him that under the circumstances, it was warranted. He'd been holding Evelyn's purse in his hands, and decided to see if there were any other drugs in there. He opened the purse and found only a wallet, keys, and a handwritten note.

* * *

"BP's down to seventy," the nurse yelled to Dr. Tully. "She's not responding."

Evelyn Landers was surrounded by a flurry of hands–each with an assigned task–moving quickly and expeditiously in their roles. Dr. Tully issued orders to her staff like a sergeant would in battle.

Luke was standing in the background, trying to keep an eye on both Levi and Evelyn. He would frequently dart in between the two curtains that separated Evelyn from Levi, doing his best to be there for both his wife and son.

"What'd she take?" Dr. Tully yelled.

"Psych meds," the EMT responded.

"Which ones? I need to know stat."

The taller of the two EMTs looked in Wyatt's direction. "You brought the pill bottles, right?" he yelled across the ER.

Wyatt nodded and reached deep inside the sleeping bag and pulled out six prescription drug bottles.

The EMT grabbed them and began rattling off names to Dr. Tully. "Seroquel. Haldol. Navane. Trilafon. Geodon. Paxil. Wellbutrin."

"Shit. Did she take all of them?"

"Trilafon is empty. So are the Navane and Seroquel. The others have a few pills left in them."

"Dr. Landers, was your wife on all of these?"

Luke looked like he was watching a tennis match, trying to simultaneously respond to questions from two treating teams. "I can't keep up, Shannon. She's always on something."

"Who's her doc?" Dr. Tully asked.

Luke looked sideways, as if he was a wolf caught in a trap and searching for an escape route. "Dr. Larhan was the latest, I think."

"That's strange," the EMT said. "Your name is on most of the bottles."

Luke looked at the EMT and then bit his lower lip. He was about to respond when the nurse interrupted them.

"BP's down to fifty, people. We're losing her!"

"Give her charcoal to induce vomiting. Now! We don't have time to second guess the dose!" Dr. Tully yelled.

One nurse shoved the needle deep into the IV plug and pushed down on the pump. The other nurse introduced a dark liquid through the oral tube that was inserted to pump Evelyn's stomach.

"BP's at forty. The antidepressants are making her heart stop, doctor."

"Defib!" Dr. Tully screamed.

The nurse grabbed the two pads and handed them to Dr. Tully. On the count of three, they sent electrical voltage through Evelyn's body.

"Thirty. We're losing her."

"All personnel!" Dr. Tully shouted. "Code Blue!"

Immediately, all staff left their respective posts and ran to her aid. Commands were responded to and orders were issued.

Meanwhile, Mac and Wyatt went to Levi's side and handed Mac the handwritten note that he'd found in Evelyn's purse. Mac read the note to herself and then softly reached for Levi's hand and pulled it to her cheek. She heard him utter a sound. Mac looked at Wyatt. He gently pushed the oxygen mask aside for a second.

Levi took a deep gasp. Wyatt replaced Levi's mask. Levi uttered again. Cautiously, Mac slid the mask partly off so that she could hear Levi speak. She leaned in close so that her ear was near his lips.

"The Baseball Man said that I should tell my mom that I love her."

Mac eyes filled with tears as she put the mask back on Levi's face. "I will tell her for you right now, okay?"

Levi nodded his head slightly. Tears began to stream from the outer corners of his eyes, making little streams into his curly blond hair.

Wyatt nodded his head to the right, and handed Mac Evelyn's cell phone. "Levi used this to call you on our way into town. After I met up with the ambulance, I fooled around with it a bit. I accidentally punched the button that looks like a tiny tape recorder and this message played. Listen to it."

"I will in a minute," Mac said, as she darted to the next partition. There was a sea of medical staff swarming Evelyn. Mac could not see her face. Disregarding the impropriety of the moment, Mac yelled out, "Evelyn, Levi says that he loves you very much."

With that, Mac heard the unforgivable sounds of a constant, low buzzing from the heart rate monitor.

"Again!" Dr. Tully shouted. Mac heard a buzz and a pop and the thud of a body landing on a gurney. "More." The sounds repeated. Mac could not bear to watch. She ran back to Levi's side.

"Your mom says she loves you too, Levi," Wyatt said.

Levi faintly smiled and whispered, "She's here with me now." And with those words, the sounds from Evelyn's partition stopped.

* * *

Wretched is the only way to describe the time and space that followed Evelyn's death. As Wyatt comforted Levi, Mac played the saved voicemail from Evelyn's phone. The message was from Janie Johansen.

"Evelyn, this is Janie returning your call. If you don't stop calling me and threatening me to end my affair with Luke, I'm going to turn you in to the police and get a restraining order against you. That certainly isn't going to help your case in court. Luke is going to leave you after the case is over. He told me so himself last night when he showed up at my door in the middle of the night. Your days as 'Mrs. Luke Landers' are almost over."

Mac replayed the message another time to make sure that she'd heard it correctly. She then went to Wyatt's side and together they re-read Evelyn's suicide note. Wyatt nodded and whispered to Mac, "No wonder the woman overdosed." Mac shook her head in agreement and slipped the note and phone into Evelyn's purse. She made a mental note to herself to give both to Karl Swensen.

Chapter 28

"All rise," the bailiff announced to the crowded courtroom. "Juvenile court is now in session. The Judge Binnard, presiding."

It was a crisp November morning and on her way to court, Mac noticed the crimson and yellow leaves were falling from the trees with rapid urgency. She wore her pinstriped, navy pantsuit with her hair swept into a loose chignon. Her lightly frosted lips were sucking coffee through a straw as she held her coffee cup in one hand and her briefcase in another. She walked into the courtroom at the same time that Judge Binnard entered in his long black robe.

Karl Swensen stood at the podium and began to clear his throat. Normally, Karl wouldn't have approached the podium until after the judge did the morning's calendar call, but today was quite different than most. The day's docket was unusually light, as the clerk had intentionally scheduled around the Landers trial.

"Your Honor, may it please the court. Karl Swensen appearing on behalf of Sheridan County Social Services Agency. The Agency is ready to proceed."

"Macy Green on behalf of Austen, Ben and Lauren Landers. We're also ready, Your Honor."

"John Trainor on behalf of Luke Landers. Ready."

"Mary MacIntosh on behalf of Levi Landers. Ready."

Judge Binnard looked over his glasses and into the galley. "Looks like we have a full house. Are the Landers children going to be in the courtroom? As you know, we normally don't have children present throughout the trial."

Macy Green spoke first. "Your Honor, Austen, Ben and Lauren are old enough to understand the nature of the proceedings. They are certainly mature enough to handle what is said by all the parties throughout this case. I would ask that they be allowed to remain in the courtroom."

"Do you anticipate that they will be called as witnesses?" the judge asked.

"Lauren will. I don't anticipate that either Austen or Ben will be called, but it is possible."

"Counsel?" Judge Binnard said. "Do any of you intend on calling Austen or Ben?"

In unison, all counsel said, "No, Your Honor," except for Mac.

"I might," Mac said, "and I believe that Macy Green might wish to reserve her right to call them for rebuttal."

Macy Green, a young lawyer without much trial experience, was grateful that Mac was watching her back.

"Uh, yes, Your Honor, I might want to call them later."

"Any objections, counsel, to having the children in the courtroom during their parents' testimony?"

"No, Your Honor," all counsel said, with the exception of Mac.

"What about Levi?" the judge asked. "Do you intend to call him?

"Yes," all counsel said.

"Your Honor," Mac interrupted, "I would ask that Levi not be present for the testimony provided throughout this case. Much of the information that I expect to see presented by the state throughout this trial will pertain to things that happened when he was very young. He probably doesn't remember most of it and it could be hurtful for him to hear about it in this setting. I have already secured the necessary arrangements for his care throughout the trial, as Linda Sterling has agreed to provide for him throughout this case. He will remain on call, so that when it is his time to testify, he can escorted by the Agency to the courtroom."

Judge Binnard agreed. "Are there any pretrial matters that need to be addressed, counsel?"

"Your Honor," Mac said, "I'd like to speak to the presence of the remaining Landers siblings in court. I know you've already stated that you would permit them to remain in the courtroom, but I want the record to reflect that I do not think that is a good idea. Since I'm not frequently involved in this area of the law, perhaps this happens frequently, but I just can't see how this could do anything but hurt them. I would think that these children need a good deal of therapy and perhaps a therapeutic setting would be a better place for them to deal with the issues that have brought their family before this court."

Judge Binnard looked at Mac with a mystical expression. He paused for a moment, considering his response. "Ms. MacIntosh, I assure you that none of the court officers in the juvenile system are numb to the effects of abuse on families. We deal with it nearly every day, and are quite familiar with the deep and painful issues that are litigated here. I understand what you are trying to say, and that your concern is for the welfare of these children. I appreciate your willingness to speak up to this issue, because I share the very same concern."

Judge Binnard turned towards the center of the courtroom, and continued. "It is my custom and practice to make a very clear record as to who is present in court and why, as many of these cases get appealed. It is the court's opinion that it is not in the best interest of the Landers children to hear the horrid history of how their family ended up in court. They know enough, I'm sure. They will remain outside the courtroom unless and until they are called as witnesses."

Mac nodded, and was pleased that she spoke up regarding the issue. She almost hadn't, because Judge Binnard had already ruled on the issue and specifically allowed the kids to remain in the courtroom. Mac knew it was never a good idea to disagree with a judge, especially not at the beginning of a trial. Still, Mac felt obligated to say something, considering how much the Landers children had all already been through. After all, it wasn't very long ago that they'd had to watch their once lovely and vibrant mother get lowered into the earth in a casket covered in white lilies.

Mac briefly thought back to the night before Evelyn's very public funeral, when the four Landers children held a private rosary shared at the church. Each child wrote their mother a goodbye note and the four envelopes were placed inside her casket. Levi gave her his favorite teddy bear. Lauren made her a necklace and bracelet with her bead collection. Ben slipped in his state championship wrestling trophy and Austen put in his homecoming king crown. After all the mementos were tucked around their devoted and beloved mother, the perpetuity blanket was placed over her and her casket closed for eternity.

The children would have to re-live her funeral over and over in their minds. Mac hoped that they would not end up similarly re-living this trial.

"Any other pre-trial issues before we get started?" Judge Binnard asked. No one spoke up. "Mr. Swensen, the prosecution may call its first witness."

Karl Swensen stood and buttoned the top button to his sport coat. "Your Honor, the prosecution would like to present the court with a brief opening statement. This court knows that openings are typically waived in these cases, but given how significantly the facts have changed since this case was filed, I believe an opening statement would be very helpful."

"That's fine, counsel. Proceed."

Karl Swensen took a stack of small white index cards from the breast pocket of his suit and set them before him on the podium.

"Your Honor, this case was initially believed to include the elements of Munchausen by Proxy. The State sought Levi Landers' removal from the home because Social Services believed Mrs. Landers suffered from a mental condition. It was the state's belief that this mental problem drove Mrs. Landers to make irrational and unsafe medical choices for her youngest son. During the detention hearing, the State met its burden of proving that Dr. Landers was aware of this substantial risk of danger yet did nothing to protect Levi.

"The prosecution has a duty of candor with the court, as do all attorneys. We intend to be brutally honest today and suggest that the prosecution cannot meet its burden today with respect to Evelyn Landers. It is well known that Mrs. Landers passed away last Monday. As sad and unfortunate as her death is, it is not the reason that I stand here today saying that the state cannot meet its burden as to her. The State cannot meet its burden as to Evelyn Landers because it has information suggesting that she was not suffering from Munchausen by Proxy. In fact, the evidence that you will hear today will tell you that Mrs. Landers was an exceptional mother, and that she did everything she could have done to ensure the health and safety of Levi.

Judge Binnard looked quizzically at Mr. Swensen, unfamiliar with such brazen statements by the prosecutor in a trial. He leaned forward in his bench, clearly intrigued with where the opening was going.

"The evidence will show you, however, that there was another woman involved in Levi's life that did want Levi to get sick. This woman wanted Evelyn out of the picture, and was willing to do whatever she could to make that happen."

"The State anticipates that Dr. Landers's attorney will argue that the State had it right the first time, and that Evelyn was in fact the source of Levi's injuries. It's very easy to lay the blame on a silent witness, and it's obvious to all that Evelyn cannot defend herself. Anticipating this defense, the prosecution will tell you now that it is aware Evelyn was not the most stable woman in the world. She suffered from depression, anxiety, an eating disorder, and low self-esteem, and her recent suicide is a clear example of her mental condition. Evelyn's mental state, however, was based largely on the abuse she received at the hands of her father as a child and then from her husband as an adult. While the state is unable to produce any direct evidence to Dr. Landers having ever inappropriately touched Evelyn, it will show that he was emotionally abusive toward her. It was this emotional abuse that contributed to Levi's medical issues."

"The purpose of this trial is to ascertain the truth, and the truth is that Dr. Luke Landers was having an illicit affair with Janie Johansen, Levi's pediatric nurse." Karl paused for effect, and turned to make eye contact with Luke.

"You will hear that Evelyn not only knew about the affair, but repeatedly asked her husband to end it. Dr. Landers refused." Karl looked pointedly at Luke. "It was this refusal that set the stage for this entire case, and created a complex web of betrayal and conspiracy. The affair created an emotional *ménage a trios* among Luke, Evelyn and Janie.

"The evidence will show that Luke Landers and Janie Johansen conspired to frame Evelyn as an MBP mom. If they could get her locked away, she would be out of the picture and they could pursue their relationship openly and notoriously without a messy divorce and without any custody proceedings."

"Evelyn was a good mother and Luke knew it. She was also a supportive wife. She wasn't perfect, but no person is. Luke was happy having a mistress, but Janie wanted more. She wanted to be 'Mrs. Luke Landers.' The doctor's wife. When Luke wasn't willing to make that happen, Janie took matters into her own hands. Let me play a tape recorded voicemail that Janie left on Evelyn's cell phone the day that Evelyn overdosed on medication," Karl said, hitting a button on a recorder near the podium. The message played in open court and captured everyone's attention.

"For a long time, Dr. Landers suspected that Janie was involved in making his son sick, and he could have put a stop to it, but he chose not to. The State will show that Dr. Landers chose not to stand up for the health of his son, because he didn't want to sacrifice the sex with Levi's nurse. He put his ego and libido before the safety of his own son.

"Finally, Your Honor, there will be an issue presented in the case as it relates to Lauren Landers. The State fully anticipates Dr. Landers's attorney to present testimony suggesting that Levi's sister intentionally medicated the boy with his mother's anti-psychotic meds, which the state cannot and will not dispute. The fact remains, however, that the majority of the harm inflicted on Levi Landers came from Janie, and that his father was aware of what Janie was doing. The isolated incidents involving Lauren simply could not have substantially impaired Levi's health, and in no way eliminates the criminal actions undertaken by Janie and Dr. Landers."

Karl Swensen finally put down the note cards, and looked up to the judge for what appeared to be his final remarks.

"Your Honor, I know I've been long-winded, and I apologize for using up so much of the court's time delivering an opening. I believe it is important for me to explain how and why the State's theory has changed, and why we continue to pursue this case against Dr. Landers. The prosecution intends to prove, by clear and convincing evidence that

Luke Landers continues to pose a substantial risk of danger to the physical and emotional health of all of his children. The State will be asking for the three remaining Landers children to be removed from his care and placed in suitable alternative placements.

"Evelyn Landers has no extended family members. Her biological parents are dead as well as her adoptive parents. Her biological sister is also dead. Social Services is in the process of searching for non-related extended family members or other qualified caregivers who can serve as legal guardians, adoptive caregivers or de facto parents to these children. And with that, the prosecution is prepared to call its first witness."

"Thank you, Mr. Swensen," Judge Binnard said. "If any other counsel wishes to give a *brief* opening, I'd ask that you reserve it until it is your time to put on your defense. You may proceed, Mr. Swensen."

"The prosecution hereby marks for identification and moves into evidence the detention, jurisdiction and status reports prepared in conjunction with this case. The Agency shall make Senior Social Worker Linda Sterling available for cross-examination regarding those documents."

"Any objections?" Judge Binnard asked.

"No, Your Honor," all counsel answered in unison. It was standard procedure in a juvenile court proceeding that the social worker's reports were accepted into evidence.

"The documents will be hereby moved into evidence," Judge Binnard said. "The prosecution may call its first witness."

"Thank you, Your Honor," Karl Swensen said. "The prosecution calls Dr. Kerr."

Chapter 29

"Mocha's crabby today," Levi said to Wyatt as they were performing the morning chores on the Anderson Ranch. Levi spent the previous night in Beth's care so that Mac could prepare for trial.

"Mocha *is* crabby. She's often crabby. Girls are like that," Wyatt said, while grinning at Levi.

Wyatt was thinking of one girl in particular, and for some reason he couldn't seem to get the thought of Mac out of his head.

"You like girls, don't you?" Levi asked with the straightforwardness of a ten-year-old.

"Of course I like girls," Wyatt quickly said as he turned towards the little guy and smiled. "Just not the crabby ones," Wyatt added with a wink.

"You just said *all* girls are crabby, so that means that you don't like any of them." Levi had a smug look on his face, apparently pleased at himself for catching the inconsistencies.

"First of all, I said that girls are *often* crabby. Secondly, I said that I liked 'em." Wyatt's voice was jovial as he pointed out the distinction in his choice of semantics, because he wanted to make sure that Levi knew he was just having fun and not in any way being critical of him.

"Do you like Mac?" Levi asked after a short pause. When Levi asked this question he tried to mimic Wyatt by winking and grinning at the same time, but he ended up creating a facial expression of his own: both eyes tightly squinted shut, and a big smile dominating his little face.

"Sure I do. Don't you?" Wyatt responded while laughing out loud at Levi's cute facial expression. "She's a nice girl, don't you think?"

Levi nodded in agreement, as he truly did like Mac. He continued working on his assigned morning chores in silence, happy to be spending time with Wyatt.

"Mocha ate all of the oats you told me to give her, and now she's just knocking me in the shoulder," Levi said.

Wyatt walked across the barn to where Levi was standing and squatted down next to the horse. Wyatt took a moment to examine the feeding bucket and quickly examine Mocha before he stood back up.

"I think she's pregnant."

"Huh? Who?" Levi asked with a confused look on his face.

"Mocha," Wyatt responded, his voice turning a bit more serious. "She's been eating like a pig and she's been acting crabby."

"You mean Mocha's gonna have a colt like Mr. Pony?"

"I reckon she might."

"How do you know?"

"I've been doing this awhile, and I can recognize it, I guess."

"But how can you tell she's pregnant for sure?"

Wyatt stood with his hand cupped under his chin as he clearly pondered a good response to that question. "Well, I guess I can't tell you that for sure. I mean, I could take Mocha to the vet and pay him to tell me whether she's pregnant, but I think I'd rather let nature tell us and save the money for another day."

"I know the vet in town. He gave me stitches in my leg last month."

"The veterinarian gave you stitches?"

Levi was busy kicking the dirt with his feet, and focused his attention fully on the ground. "The vet was closest to the river," Levi finally said, without lifting his head up. "That's where Mac found me after I hurt myself."

"Well, you certainly have had an interesting life, Levi." Wyatt began to move towards the birds' roost, and nudged gently on Levi's shoulder so that he would follow him. After picking up a sack of feed, Levi began to move in pace with Wyatt towards the roost.

"You call spending most of your life in a doctor's office interesting? I'd much rather spend my time out here on the ranch, doing this sort of stuff."

Wyatt was happy to hear Levi say that, and he was happy that Levi was talking so openly with him. Mac hold told Wyatt about the Baseball Man, and it was clear through his recent counseling sessions that Levi needed to sort through his emotions.

"Doctors are okay when you're sick, but I'd much rather stay healthy so that I don't have to see them too often. Do you know what keeps folks healthy?" Wyatt asked while raising the wooden bar that latched the bird shed. When Wyatt heard no response, he answered his own question. "Exercise. Working outdoors. Fresh air. Good food." Wyatt took a moment to look directly in Levi's eye, wanting to drive home his point with the kid. "People who sit around all day and eat fast food junk end up fat and sick."

"Some people who work outdoors end up hurt and sick, too," Levi countered.

"Oh yeah? How so?" Wyatt asked.

"I met a guy with black lung when I was in the hospital in Montana, and he told me that he got it from working in a coal mine." Levi looked up at Wyatt as he thought a bit more. "I also met a guy there whose arm was cut off by a saw when he was outside working, and a lady who had cancer because she worked at the electricity plant."

"Hmm. I get your point," Wyatt said. He took the feed out of Levi's hand and filled the bin before quickly closing the door so the birds wouldn't escape. "But those cases seemed to happen indoors, buddy. The kind of work I'm talking about is the stuff we're doing now, outside and in the fresh air." Wyatt took a moment to emphasize his point by taking a deep breath of fresh air. "Speaking of the outdoors, we're having a big bird hunt next weekend here on the ranch. The pheasants oughta be big and fat for the hunt."

"Do the hunters just walk in and shoot them?" Levi asked, wide-eyed and aghast.

"Not quite," Wyatt said and winked, clearly pleased to have changed the conversation to one he was much more comfortable with. "We'll take each bird out of the shed by its feet, and then proceed to whirl them around a few times to get them dizzy. After a few spins, we'll set the pheasant free knowing that they'll be too dizzy to get very far." Wyatt started to shake his head a bit. "I guess it's worth the money knowing you're getting a healthy bird, and you're pretty much guaranteed to shoot a wild one.

"Can I watch?" Levi's eyes were opened wide, and he was clearly interested in the idea.

"We'll see, sport. It can get dangerous."

"Cool," Levi said.

"Speaking of cool, we'd better get you and your backpack loaded in the truck. According to Mac's outline, it's time to take you to school. School rhymes with cool, so school is cool, right?" Wyatt nervously chuckled, knowing exactly how un-cool it was for him to say that.

"Oh no, please let me stay? Please?" Levi had his hands grasped together, and he was looking up at Wyatt with the widest and most innocent eyes.

"No way am I going to get in trouble by ignoring Mac's outline!"

"Oh, come on, please? You said that kids learned more from working one day on a ranch than they learn in school all week."

"Did I say that?" Wyatt asked, grinning again. "If I did say that, then it's probably right. But it's not my call to make, buddy, because I already promised Mac and Mrs. Sterling that I'd have you to school on time. So, go in the house and get your backpack. My mom made you a lunch and she already put it in there. Then get in the truck and I'll drive you to school."

"Dang. I wish I could stay here with you." Levi hung his head low, like a dejected little puppy. He then added silently, almost under his breath, "Because I like spending time with you."

Wyatt had to muster up every square inch of resolve he had in him to avoid tears welling up in his eyes. He was normally not outwardly emotional, but something about Levi got him square in the heart. "I like it with you too, buddy. You're a good ranch hand."

Levi smiled before he ran off towards the ranch house. In the brief exchange he'd had with Wyatt, he'd been able to put aside his sad thoughts about his mom and just be happy for a moment being a kid.

* * *

During a break in Dr. Kerr's testimony, Mac took a brisk walk around the perimeter of the courthouse. She appreciated the fall sun beaming down upon her face, and gulped in several deep cleansing breaths of fresh air. She had decided to bring her cell phone along with her so that she could follow up on some of the voice mail messages awaiting her. Most of these messages were from clients wanting to know when she'd return their calls. Mac sighed, as she realized how many things had fallen to the wayside in the past month while she was consumed with Levi and his case.

Mac's clients weren't the only ones feeling deprived of her time and attention. Mac heard Jeffrey's voice on the next message, and tightened up with trepidation. She was a bit surprised at her physical response to hearing Jeffrey's voice, but she was honestly dreading another verbal onslaught from the guy she had thought was "the one." Her spirits lifted when she heard Jeffrey apologize for not waiting around long enough to hear her side of the story following his surprise visit to her apartment. Mac's relief was short- lived, however, as Jeffrey quickly turned defensive when he began to suggest that she would have done the same thing had the roles been reversed.

Mac deleted the message and closed the cell phone. She realized that she would have been upset to find Jeffrey in a similar situation, but all she really wanted from him was an apology without the minor digs thrown in. Nevertheless, she returned Jeffrey's call by punching in the digits to his cell phone. Considering that D.C. was only two time zones ahead of Wyoming, Mac naturally assumed that he would still be at his office.

"Sorry to call you in the middle of the day, but I just got my first break in my trial," Mac said when he answered.

"Oh. I see." Jeffrey's voice sounded distant, and a tad bit hesitant, almost as if he didn't know with whom he was speaking.

Mac picked up on his tone. "Is this a bad time? Would it be better if I called back later?"

"Well, it is pretty late here," Jeffrey said as he made what sounded like an overly dramatic sigh. "It probably would be better for me if we chatted tomorrow."

"Are you serious? It's only one o'clock in D.C."

'I'm not in D.C., Mac."

Mac was stunned into silence, and a moment of dead air passed before she was able to regain her composure.

"Where exactly are you, then?" Mac asked as pleasantly as she could muster.

"Well, I'm not quite sure myself where exactly I am at the moment. I'm currently on a cruise, and assume I'm somewhere within the boundaries of Greece right now. I've always wanted to see the Greek Islands, and decided that I'd waited long enough. I really needed a vacation, and I haven't taken a good one in a very long time."

Mac was not frequently at a loss for words, let alone twice in the same conversation, yet she again was momentarily silenced by what Jeffrey was telling her. She had tried to get Jeff to go with her to Turkey, Greece and Italy last summer, but he'd shrugged her off saying that he was too busy. Now when she was calling him to settle their recent miscommunication, she finds him on a luxury vacation without her?

"Well, that sounds wonderful, Jeff, I hope you have a great time on your cruise. I'm heading back into the courthouse. Good bye."

Mac clicked off her phone and closed her eyes. She dropped her head back a bit, and felt the honey glow of the morning sun as it beat upon her face. Mac realized the significance of her phone call with Jeffrey, and sighed with the heavy realization that her relationship with Jeffrey was now officially over.

Mac quickened her pace and focused more energetically on her power walk; she was trying her best to distract herself from the flood of memories that had suddenly besieged her. She turned around and began to walk back towards the courthouse, and intentionally took slow, rhythmic steps to help calm her down. She felt her confidence slowly returning to her, and was nearly back inside the courthouse when her phone buzzed.

"I just wanted to let you know that Levi fed all the horses, cows and birds, cleaned himself up, and ate a man's sized breakfast this morning before I dropped him off at school." Wyatt was clearly proud of himself, and his voice communicated the huge smile spread across his face. "When I dropped him off at school, I followed your directions to a 't'. Not one of them snooty moms you warned me about gave me a dirty look, so I'm pretty sure I musta done it right."

"Thank you so much, Wyatt. I really appreciate you taking the time to call me with the positive update, more than you could possibly expect."

"My pleasure, Mac."

Mac felt her cheeks get a bit red, which caught her entirely off guard. She composed herself before responding. "I'm so happy to hear that Levi got to be a little boy today, and a happy one at that. Thanks for treating him so well. He really needs it."

"How's that hearing of yours going? Must be a slight bit stressful."

"Thanks for caring. The trial is going okay, though we haven't made much headway, yet."

There was a short pause in conversation, and Mac thought perhaps she'd gone a bit too far by suggesting that Wyatt's comments to her about trial were because he 'cared.' Mac thought she heard a stammer across the other line, and interpreted it as meaning that Wyatt might have something else to say to her. After just another second passed, Wyatt finally broke the awkwardness.

"You know I'm here to help, anytime. In fact, I can help out any single day this week with Levi if you need."

"Thanks. I'll take you up on that."

"Heck, I can help out with other stuff you might need this week, too—like if you need any errands done in town. I could run to the market for you or that sort of thing. I'm sure you don't have time to do that stuff when you're workin' a sixteen-hour day."

"You really are a lifesaver, you know that? I really appreciate your help, Wyatt, but I think I'm pretty set. I'm really lucky to have Pam and Megan working for me, because they take care of most of my errands."

"You wanna take down my phone number in case you do find yourself needing a hand?"

"Wyatt, I represented your family on the Powder River case. Do you really think that I don't have your phone number?" Mac smiled at the thought.

"No, I mean my *cell* phone number. I went out and got myself one of those today, because I figured it'd be smart for me to have one while Levi was in my care."

"I never thought I'd see the day that you got a cell phone. Welcome to the 21st Century." Mac took down Wyatt's new cell number, and logged it into her BlackBerry.

"See, even stubborn ol' cowboys can change their minds."

"Miracles never cease to happen, do they?"

They both chuckled.

"Mac, what do I tell Levi if he asks me about the trial? Linda Sterling told me to try to avoid discussing anything about his case with him, and if the conversation somehow came up to try and redirect his attention if possible. I'm afraid that won't be enough, though, 'cause Levi's both smart and persistent. What if he pointedly asks me about the trial, and continues to ask me until I give him a good enough response?"

"I think you should tell him the truth, Wyatt, and the truth is that you simply don't know. 'I don't know' is an honest answer and seems to work well with him. Try that and see how it works."

"Fair enough."

Mac looked down at her watch, and realized that she had just five minutes to head to the restroom before returning to court. "Wyatt, I really appreciate . . . everything. I need to run back into court now, so I should get rolling."

Mac caught her breath when she heard Wyatt's husky 'good luck' in response, and quickly disconnected the call.

Chapter 30

"You contacted Social Services, correct?" John Trainor asked Dr. Kerr.

"Yes sir."

"You contacted them to report Evelyn Landers and her possible mistreatment of Levi? Right?" Luke Landers's attorney began the line of questioning with Dr. Kerr that he hoped would elicit testimony beneficial to his client.

"Yes, sir, I did."

"Isn't it true that you reported Mrs. Landers because you believed that she was suffering from a syndrome called Munchausen by Proxy?"

"Objection," Harold Neiman said, "this witness is not an expert and is therefore not qualified to offer an opinion to this subject."

"Overruled," Judge Binnard said. "On direct examination, Mr. Swensen laid the foundation regarding Dr. Kerr's medical training in the area of child abuse. The witness may answer the question."

"I called Social Services because I thought Mrs. Landers might be suffering from Munchausen's by Proxy. If this were true, I believe Levi would have been at risk if left alone in her care."

"Would it be fair to say, then, that your concerns dealt with Mrs. Landers only?" John Trainor pointed out.

"Yes."

"And you indicated to Social Services that they should focus their investigation on Mrs. Landers, not her husband?"

"It would be fair to say that, however, I was not telling Social Services to exclude Dr. Landers from their investigation. As you saw in the formal documentation I prepared supporting that call, I was less specific to that matter. It was my job to protect my patient from potential abuse, and it was the Agency's and the court's job to determine the source of that abuse."

"Did you include in the written document you just referred to that Janie Johansen *insisted* on being Levi's nurse each time Levi came in for treatment?"

"No," Dr. Kerr said slowly. "Janie didn't cross my mind at all when preparing that report, because I was focused solely on what was bringing Levi to our office–not the treatment that we provided."

"Really?" Mr. Trainor began leafing through a specific document in front of him, and this caused Dr. Kerr to begin shifting in his seat. With his hand firmly planted on a specific page, Mr. Trainor continued. "Weren't you able to review Levi's medical chart before writing the referral, Dr. Kerr?"

"Well, yes, but–"

"Did you read all of the items documented in Levi's chart, Dr. Kerr?"

"Of course I did!" Dr. Kerr announced in a defensive tone.

"After reading all of Levi's medical charts, and preparing your written statement, you decided to omit the fact that Janie was present for every single visit?"

"I told you already, I didn't think about that."

Karl Swensen stood up from his seat. "Objection. Asked and answered."

"Let's keep the testimony moving, counsel." Judge Binnard nodded his head when he was finished, indicating to counsel that he may continue with his questioning of the witness.

"Thank you, Your Honor." Mr. Trainor said.

"While you were reviewing Levi's medical records prior to making contact with Social Services, would it be fair to say that you were focused on the suggestions Mrs. Landers made regarding Levi's medical diagnoses and care?"

"Well, I suppose that–"

"Your Honor, please direct the witness to answer with a 'yes' or a 'no.'"

Judge Binnard turned towards Dr. Kerr as he stated, "If the question calls for a 'yes' or a 'no' answer, please answer accordingly."

Normally, Judge Binnard would have interrupted Dr. Kerr himself with this admonishment, but in juvenile court cases he did so only upon the request of counsel. Judge Binnard had been on the bench for a long time, and had no doubts about his ability to give each statement in front of him the weight and credibility it deserved.

"I apologize, Your Honor." Dr. Kerr was definitely uncomfortable now, and beads of sweat began to appear on his temples.

"You may answer the question, Dr. Kerr," Judge Binnard instructed.

"Yes. My focus at the time was on Mrs. Landers."

"Which is why you steered Social Services in the direction of Mrs. Landers's being the likely source of Levi's mysterious and constant illnesses?"

"I suppose so," Dr. Kerr said, and pulled a handkerchief out of his jacket and dabbed his forehead. "But I wasn't trying to mislead anyone or to protect Janie. I was just looking out for Levi."

Objection. Move to strike," John Trainor said.

"Overruled."

"Your Honor," John Trainor stated as he was beginning to stand up and continue arguing his point to the judge.

Judge Binnard removed his glasses, and began to rub between his eyes. "Mr. Trainor, this is juvenile court, which is not your typical forum for trials. I know you're an experienced business litigator, and if this case involved a business dispute that required a jury to hear the witness's testimony, I might make a different ruling. In juvenile court, our focus always remains on protecting kids, and the rules of evidence are modified accordingly to achieve this goal. That means that most evidence presented during trial will ultimately get admitted to the record, counsel."

Judge Binnard put his glasses back on, and turned all of his attention now to Dr. Landers's attorney. "Dr. Kerr is not the one on trial here. He is a medical professional doing his job, and I want him to tell me what he did and why he did it. The more you interrupt, the longer this trial will take, so let's move on to the next question, counsel."

"I apologize to the court," John Trainor half-heartedly responded. He paused for a moment, trying to collect himself before turning back to the witness. "Dr. Kerr, you never suspected that *my* client, Dr. Landers, had anything to do with Levi's illnesses, correct?"

"That's correct," Dr. Kerr said, who was beginning to calm down a bit following Judge Binnard's comments on his behalf.

"Putting aside all the gossip and innuendo that has surrounded this case, Dr. Kerr, and focusing only on Levi's actual medical charts and history, you don't have any reason to believe that Dr. Landers abused his son?"

"Objection," Karl Swensen said, jumping to his feet, "calls for a legal conclusion and assumes facts not in evidence!"

"Overruled, counsel."

Dr. Kerr looked up at the judge expectantly, waiting for the judge to tell him what to do in response to this most recent objection.

"You may answer the question in front of you, Dr. Kerr."

"Yes, thank you, Judge." Dr. Kerr's smile had returned, and he appeared much more comfortable. "No. I do not."

"I have no further questions of this witness," John Trainor said.

After getting a cursory head nod from the Judge, Mac stood and walked over to the podium with her black evidence binder, a yellow legal pad and a stack of index cards. She took a moment to organize herself, and then began immediately after slipping the index cards into her pocket.

"Dr. Kerr, you testified on direct regarding Levi's long health history and all the illnesses that you believed he suffered from. Do you remember that, sir?"

"Yes," Dr. Kerr said and smiled, apparently relieved that he was no longer at the mercy of John Trainor.

"I'm handing you what's been marked as State's Exhibit 4, which has already been admitted into evidence." Mac approached the podium and handed a very thick binder to the doctor. "Do you recognize this?"

"Of course I do."

"For the record, will you tell the court what this is?"

"Well, it's the binder I had my office put together including all of Levi's medical records after being subpoenaed by the State." Dr. Kerr had his hands crossed on top of the binder, and appeared pleased with himself for not getting admonished by anyone thus far into Mac's examination.

"Open that up, please, and take a look at what I've marked with a red 'number 1' tab, copies of which have already been shown to counsel just now, Your Honor. Please tell the court what date that entry was made?"

"It looks like an entry for Levi was made here on January fourteenth."

"Thank you sir. Will you please tell me whether that entry was handwritten or typed?"

"Handwritten."

"Direct your attention now to the red 'number 2' tab. What's that?"

"Another one of Levi's entries, but this time for a visit on February twelfth."

"And was that handwritten or typed?" Mac asked.

"This one was also handwritten."

"How about 'number 3', Dr. Kerr. When was that entered?"

Dr. Kerr looked up at Mac without flipping to the third tab. "If you're going to ask me whether the notes were handwritten or typed for each entry in the binder, I can save us all time by telling you all of these entries will be handwritten. My office policy is to keep handwritten notes. I don't particularly trust computers yet, and prefer to write chart entries while the patient is still in front of me."

"Would it be fair to say that you have a reputation in your office about how you handle your notes?"

Dr. Kerr laughed, and responded in the affirmative too quickly for any attorney to object. Dr. Kerr obviously knew where Mac was going with this question, and had no problem responding to it. "Yes, Ms. MacIntosh, I am an avid note-taker. I am known in the office to manage the files well, and I like to make sure a patient's file is thoroughly documented."

Mac smiled at the doctor. "So, you're telling me that you are normally in charge of entering the notes into a patients file, then?"

Dr. Kerr sat up a little straighter, answering, "I do my best to keep all the files up to date, yes."

"In fact, -- and don't take this as a slight to your profession, -- you have quite nice handwriting for a doctor, don't you?"

Dr. Kerr smiled again and his chin lifted slightly in pride. He clearly liked the type of questioning he was getting from Mac, and he appeared much more at ease than before. "Yes. In fact, my wife can still read the very first anniversary card I ever gave her. My children have inherited my nice penmanship."

"Going through all of the paperwork, doctor, it's clear that your handwriting is far better than anyone else's in your office." Mac smiled at Dr. Kerr. He smiled back. She was pleased that she had the doctor so comfortable on the stand, eating up all of her buttery questions.

"You ever get a chance to see Janie's handwriting?"

Dr. Kerr visibly reacted, huffing out immediately, "Her handwriting is terrible!"

"So I take it that you have seen Janie Johansen's handwriting, doctor?"

"Of course, she's my nurse. Her handwriting was extremely sloppy, and there were times that I was unable to read it."

"Let's return to the exhibit for a minute, Dr. Kerr." Mac continued smiling at the doctor, and saw him turn his attention to Levi's medical charts as requested. "If I told you that Levi's medical history reflected in

Exhibit 4 included six hundred thirty-four different entries in it, would you disagree?"

"Well, I haven't gone through and counted them, but that sounds about right."

"Take a moment to flip through those entries, doctor. Do you notice anything about the handwriting in front of you?"

"Objection. Relevance, foundation," John Trainor said.

"Overruled. If the witness notices anything about the handwriting, he may answer." Judge Binnard turned towards Dr. Kerr and nodded his head, signaling that his ruling was made and testimony was to resume.

Dr. Kerr began flipping through the exhibit, taking his time to check out each individual page. After flipping through approximately ten different entries, Dr. Kerr lifted his head. "Yes, I do."

"What do you notice about the handwriting, doctor?"

"That the handwriting in most of these entries is sloppy." Dr. Kerr continued flipping through the pages in the exhibit, and a frown suddenly began to appear on his face. Dr. Kerr looked back at Mac tentatively, suddenly curious about where she was going with this line of questioning.

"Do you recognize your own handwriting on any of the pages you just flipped through, doctor?"

Dr. Kerr had to return to the exhibit and flip through the pages for several moments before he was able to answer the question. "Yes."

"By my estimation, doctor, all but twenty of those entries were written by Janie. Would you disagree with that?"

"Objection," John Trainor said, jumping to his feet. "Relevance, assumes facts not in evidence, and since when did a lawyer get to opine regarding herself as an expert handwriting witness?"

"Your Honor," Mac said as she turned her attention directly to the bench, "the witness has already testified regarding his handwriting and Janie's. I'm not asking him to tell us whether the entries were in fact made by Janie, only whether it was possible that he had written only twenty himself. It's a perfectly valid question, especially in light of the fact that he's previously testified that he'd reviewed Levi's medical chart in its entirety on two separate occasions prior to today."

"She's right, counsel. It's a valid, relevant question. The witness may answer."

"It is possible," Dr. Kerr said. "I noticed it myself, actually. Most of the entries in Levi's chart are from Ms. Johansen."

"Why is that?"

"I don't know."

"Does Janie normally enter the notes on a patient for you in their medical charts?"

"No, I normally write the entries myself immediately after seeing a patient. If the diagnosis requires a referral to another doctor, I'll dictate the referral and the extraneous information to be transcribed by office staff later, but the immediate notation is done by me before I transfer the chart."

"Why were things done differently in Levi's case?" Mac asked.

Dr. Kerr paused, clearly thinking about the question. "I really don't know, because I never thought about Levi's medical notes as being done differently. Janie and Levi had a great relationship and I wanted to make sure that I didn't ruin the one happy connection he had with our office."

"What do you mean by that, doctor?"

"I think it's important that kids enjoy their visits to my office, but Levi had so many visits I knew he had to be getting unhappy with all the poking and prodding going on. He hated needles and could really work himself into a tizzy sometimes, but Janie had a remarkable way of calming him down. I felt that it was important that he like coming to the doctor since we had to poke and prod the poor little guy so much. I was grateful that she'd taken such a liking to him and was so helpful in calming him down. She was very good with him, so I guess I allowed more leeway in the situation."

"Levi got pretty upset at the office sometimes, didn't he?"

"Yes, he did."

"He threw big tantrums?"

"Yes, I would say so."

"Parents of other children in the office would complain about Levi's behavior, because it was frightening their own children? Right?"

"I imagine that is true."

"Do you imagine, or do you know?" Mac quickly responded, hoping to avoid any 'speculation' objections that would break up her flow. "I want you to answer me with information you know, Dr. Kerr. Are you aware of parents complaining to you or your office staff about Levi's behavior?"

Dr Kerr whipped up his head, surprised and not altogether pleased with the admonishment. "I did personally receive a few complaints, but I also know that my staff received more complaints than I did."

"Would it be fair to say that you didn't like getting complaints from other parents?"

"Well, no, I didn't like getting complaints. Like I said before, Ms. MacIntosh, I wanted children to enjoy the time they spent in my office."

"It would also be fair to say that you were relieved that those complaints were less frequent when Nurse Janie was tending to Levi during a visit?"

"Levi seemed to scream much less with Janie, so naturally the complaints were less frequent when she was involved. Yes, that's a fair statement."

"Fairly quickly after noticing this, you began to allow Janie more latitude when it came to her personally tending to Levi's care?"

"I guess you could say that."

"Was Levi a 'failure to thrive' baby, in your opinion?"

Dr. Kerr relaxed upon the sudden switch in questioning. "Yes, yes. Levi had a very hard time as an infant.

"What specifically did you base this on?"

"He was sick all the time. If there was a virus going around town, he got it. You name it, he had it. He was touch and go a few times."

"To be clear, some of the sicknesses Levi got as an infant were 'reflux' and 'elimination,' correct?"

"Yes, Levi suffered from those."

"Aren't those fairly common problems with infants?"

"Yes, in my experience, they are."

"And many of Levi's other illnesses during his early stages of life were also common amongst infants?"

Dr. Kerr paused, lost in thought for a moment as he recalled his repeated reviews of Levi's medical charts. Finally, he responded.

"Yes."

"You testified on direct that Levi's next diagnosis was 'Reactive Attachment Disorder.' Do you recall that?'

"Yes."

"The note in Levi's chart documenting this was prepared by Janie, correct?"

"Yes."

"How did you arrive at that diagnosis, Dr. Kerr?"

"Janie suggested the possibility of Reactive Attachment Disorder to me after having had long discussions with Mrs. Landers and looking it up in my medical books."

Mac was stunned.

"You let your nurse diagnose Levi?" Mac asked incredulously.

Dr. Kerr shook his head slightly from side to side for several moments, and lowered his head just enough to avoid Mac's penetrating gaze. He took a few deep breaths, and then he lifted his head back up to answer the question.

"Janie spent so much time with Levi and Evelyn that she had developed an insight that I thought was very helpful with diagnosis and care. I never allow nurses this kind of latitude, but Levi's case was such an anomaly."

"Dr. Kerr, did Janie diagnose Levi with any other of his medical conditions?"

"I was running a very busy practice and caring for many children. Levi was in my office several times a week. Basically, he would present with odd symptoms, and Janie and Evelyn would discuss the details of what brought Levi into the office. When I came in to perform the more detailed check up, Janie would have already offered a possible diagnosis to me, with an accompanying treatment plan. I reviewed the charted notes, talked with both of them, and spoke with Levi before ultimately agreeing with Janie's suggestions. I then referred Levi on to a specialist, and that's how it continued until the next visit."

Mac stood there, astonished at what she was hearing. As she was preparing a follow up question, Dr. Kerr appeared as though he still might have something to say on the topic.

"Is there more you were planning on saying, doctor?"

"Yes. I want you to know that I'm not proud about how I handled Levi's care in regards to Janie's involvement, and other than with Levi's case I have always done everything by the book. Saying this, I'm sure I'm setting myself up for a malpractice case and an ethical review, but I want to be clear about how Levi's treatment occurred. It was surreal at the time and his demand on my time was overwhelming. Quite honestly, I was happy that Janie and Evelyn would discuss the details. This went on for years, I'm embarrassed to say."

"Is it fair to say, then, that this is also how Levi was diagnosed with elimination disorders?"

"Yes, although they were more common than the 'reactive attachment' diagnosis and easier to identify and treat."

"It would also be fair to say that this is how Levi was diagnosed with 'pervasive development disorder'?"

Dr. Kerr hung his head in shame. "Yes."

"This disorder was less common that 'reactive attachment', though?"

"That's correct. Janie and Evelyn had both spoken about Levi's symptoms in great detail, and had informed that they did their own Internet research on the subject. This disorder was, as I recall, not included in the DSM III, so it was a new one that I was not well acquainted with. Their comments and suggestions made sense, and the diagnosis was listed in the DSM IV . . ."

"What about the final diagnosis–where Levi received chemotherapy? I think your chart notes refer to it as lymphoblastic leukemia, or flu-induced leukemia. Did you diagnose this independently, or did you have help from Janie?"

"That one, actually, came from a doctor in Denver at Children's Hospital."

"How did Levi come to arrive at that Children's Hospital?"

"Upon a referral from my office."

"Who suggested the referral?" Mac asked.

"Janie and Evelyn."

"When you met with Janie and Evelyn, who did most of the talking?"

"Objection," John Trainor said. "Hearsay."

"I'm not asking the contents of their statements, just who did more, Your Honor. It would still be a party admission, however, and it is not being used to prove the matter asserted," Mac said.

"Objection overruled."

Dr. Kerr's eyes had turned to the judge when the objection was made, but now looked back at Mac when he realized he was going to have to answer and continue this painful testimony.

"Janie, but she was my employee and more comfortable around me. Mrs. Landers was often emotional."

"Emotional how?"

"Nervous. Crying. Normal for a mom whose child is ill."

"Did you ever suspect that Evelyn was taking medicine?"

"Objection, calls for speculation," John Trainor challenged.

"Your Honor, Dr. Kerr is certainly in a position as a medical profession to make such an assessment. If he felt that a parent was under the influence, making it unsafe for a child to leave the office with that parent, his opinion would be given appropriate weight. I'm simply asking what he observed of Mrs. Landers."

"Okay, then I object as to vagueness." Mr. Trainor added. "The question is not specific as to time."

"Sustained. Rephrase," Judge Binnard said.

"In the last two years, did you ever suspect that Evelyn was taking prescription or non-prescription drugs?"

Dr. Kerr hesitated for a moment. "I knew she was on antipsychotics."

"How did you know?" Mac asked.

"Janie told me."

Chapter 31

"Dr. Kerr, were you aware that Janie Johansen was involved in an extra-marital affair with Dr. Luke Landers?" Mac asked.

Luke Landers jumped to his feet from behind the defense table and shouted, "How dare you?" Before his defense counsel could appropriately interject, Luke continued ranting at Mac. "You already forced my wife to kill herself, don't you think that's enough damage to my family? You have some–"

"Objection!" John Trainor said, jumping to his feet alongside his client as quickly as he could process the unexpected turn of events. He grabbed a hold of Dr. Landers and whispered into his ear.

"Sidebar, Your Honor." John requested of the Judge while subtly motioning for Dr. Landers to remain in his seat while he approached the bench. John kept focused on Mac intending to glare her down. Mac directly held John's gaze, not willing herself to back down to his bullying tactics. As the group of attorneys began to gather at the bench, Judge Binnard cupped his pudgy hand over the courtroom's microphone. He peered over his reading glasses at the bunch of them in a matter-of-fact way, obviously nonplussed by the pending heated sidebar.

"Your Honor!" John Trainor said without much attempt at keeping his voice down to a whisper, and his whining voice was audible throughout the courtroom.

"Keep it down, Mr. Trainor," Judge Binnard said sternly. "If you want the privacy of a sidebar, then you need to keep your voice hushed."

John gave Mac another dirty look, and drew in his breath before continuing. "You can't possibly allow Ms. MacIntosh to pursue this line of questioning. It is irrelevant, highly prejudicial, misleading, and will invite multiple layers of hearsay testimony."

Mac injected her response to John's objection before he could continue whining to the judge. "This is absolutely relevant, Your Honor, as it goes to both motive and opportunity. Levi's injuries occurred under Dr. Kerr's watch and in large part because he neglected his duties as a doctor by failing to supervise his staff. Dr. Kerr knew of the affair between his nurse and Levi's father, yet he did nothing to prevent Janie from having complete control over the young boy's medical treatment and care. Not only was it inappropriate for a nurse to independently document Levi's charts and practice medicine without a license, but it was borderline criminal given her relationship with Levi's father. I intend to lay proper foundations for every question I ask, Your Honor. In order to do so, I have to ask Dr. Kerr whether he knew about the relationship."

"Dr. Kerr is not on trial here, Your Honor," John Trainor said in an attempt to regain control of the sidebar. "This case does not involve the State Medical Board or whether his actions as a doctor were appropriate, and Ms. MacIntosh should be prohibited from questioning him on this. Ms. MacIntosh is clearly trying to divert this court's attention from the real matters at hand, which is whether this court should attempt at reunifying Levi with his biological father, as our law mandates. Nothing she's said is relevant to that matter, and whatever probative value there might be is outweighed by the prejudice this line of questioning presents for the record."

Judge Binnard raised his left index finger to his lips. "I agree with some of what Mr. Trainor has just said, however, what happened in Dr. Kerr's office is pertinent to the central issue in this case: whether one of Levi's parents caused or exposed him to harm."

Judge Binnard turned his attention towards Mac as he continued, "Ms. MacIntosh can pursue this line of questioning, so long as she limits her questioning to the extent of Janie Johansen's involvement in Levi's care and whether his parents were aware of the same. That includes whether she treated Levi as a physician would, or personally diagnosed him with any illnesses. Questioning whether Dr. or Mrs. Landers knew or reasonably should have known about Janie's inappropriate involvement with their son's case, and the potential harm it might have caused to Levi, is also appropriate."

Judge Binnard made direct eye-contact with each attorney in front of him. "This court is not a circus and this trial is not a soap opera. I don't care who sleeps with whom in this town, and I won't permit that type of gossip to enter the record in this case.

Turning his attention now back to Mac, Judge Binnard wrapped up the sidebar with a final admonishment: "Your offers of proof regarding the affair need be specific to causation, and must be done without any unnecessary details. You are to only question Dr. Kerr with regards to how the affair in question may have related to Levi and his medical care. Understood?"

"Yes, Your Honor," Mac replied as she considered the impact of his detailed ruling.

As the other attorneys returned to their seats, Mac stood quietly gazing at the witness box pondering her next question. Mac gave Dr. Kerr a slight smile, and Dr. Kerr hesitated only briefly before respectfully returning the smile. Mac finally determined how to proceed, and resumed her questioning of the doctor.

"I'd like to make an offer of proof at this time, Your Honor, regarding the question I previously asked Dr. Kerr regarding his nurse's affair with Dr. Landers. To lay the foundation that Janie Johansen was in love with Levi's father and having an extra-marital affair with him–"

"Objection," John Trainor said. "Ms. MacIntosh is testifying. Is there a question pending?"

"Sustained."

John looked at Mac triumphantly, pleased with himself for continuing to break her train of thought with the witness.

"I'm sorry, Your Honor. I was attempting to lay foundation in anticipation of Mr. Trainor's objections, but I'm more than willing to proceed with questioning the hard way." Mac smirked at John before returning her attention to Dr. Kerr.

"When did you first learn that Janie and Dr. Landers were having an extra- marital affair?"

Dr. Kerr looked at John Trainor apparently expecting another objection, but John continued taking notes without lifting his head.

"I've known for some time," Dr. Kerr said, his voice quieter.

"Let's try to narrow that down a bit, shall we? Levi's ten now. Did you know when he was nine?"

"Yes."

"Did you know when he was eight?"

"Yes."

"Seven?" Mac asked, not hiding the incredulity from her voice.

"I-I-I think so. I'm not sure." Dr. Kerr looked around, clearly uncomfortable with where Mac was going. "I found out two or three years ago."

"How did you find out?" Mac asked

"Objection. Calls for hearsay."

"Sustained."

"Okay, doctor, let me rephrase that. Did you learn about the affair when Levi was undergoing treatment for his misdiagnosis of flu-induced leukemia?"

"Objection! Argumentative! Assumes facts not in evidence! Move to strike," John Trainor shouted.

"Your Honor," Dr. Kerr said before the judge responded to the objection, "Do I have to answer that?" Dr. Kerr's face had grown ashen, and he withdrew a handkerchief from his pocket to dab at his brow. "And can this testimony be used at another trial? For example, at a malpractice trial or before the Medical Board?"

Judge Binnard nodded. "I'm not allowed to give you legal advice, doctor, but in short, the answer is 'yes.' Would you like to take a short recess and make a phone call?" Judge Binnard asked, implying that Dr. Kerr should consult an attorney before responding to Mac's questions.

"Yes, Your Honor. I think I'd better."

"We'll take a half-hour recess." Judge Binnard struck the bench with his gavel before immediately getting up and walking through the back door of the courtroom.

* * *

"Mac," Macy Green said from her position at the defense table, "as the attorney for the three other Landers children, I'm worried about where your questioning might take the case. If you prove that Dr. Landers poses a substantial risk of harm to Levi, the logical conclusion is that he also poses a risk to Levi's siblings. In that event all four of them end up losing not only their mom, but their dad, too. Do we really want to see them all end up in the foster system?" Macy sighed, clearly worried about these kids and their futures. She turned towards Mac and more softly said, "All I mean is that we need to sit and think about where this is all going. Perhaps we should talk settlement."

Karl Swensen leaned forward, injecting himself into the conversation. "I'm sorry, but there's no way I can settle this case, not now after the evidence that's just been presented. If Dr. Landers was involved in any way with this, it is my office's duty to pursue all charges in both juvenile and adult court to the fullest."

John Trainor turned towards Karl with an incredulous look on his face. "Are you kidding me? Do you mean to suggest that Luke faces criminal charges now, too?" John twisted his face in disgust for emphasis before speaking to Karl in a softer tone. "Karl, I've known you a long time, and I consider you a good lawyer and a smart man. Can't you see where all of this is going, though? If the trial continues in this direction, it's going to ruin Dr. Landers's reputation. Luke Landers is a great father and a remarkable doctor who brings babies into this world. Even if he was a crappy husband who had an affair, that doesn't mean that he conspired to cause his children any harm." John now turned towards Mac and spat out quite venomously, "I do not want to be responsible for making these kids orphans. I think that Macy is right, and we should start to discuss settling this case."

"We don't get to play judge and jury," Mac interjected. "If your client was involved in Janie's scheme, yet failed to protect Levi, then he shouldn't be allowed to be a father."

"Ever since you won that big methane gas verdict, you strut around this town like you own the place. Well, Mac, you don't own the town, you don't wear a robe, and you're definitely not thinking about what's in the best interest of these kids." John turned towards Macy, looking for support before getting more personal in his attack. "The problem with this case is that your womb is aching and you'll do whatever it takes to make Levi your own - even if it means lying about Dr. Landers."

Mac stood up from the defense table and walked out of the courtroom without another word. This case had gotten ugly and personal, and she knew it was only going to get worse. She was surprised that opposing counsel had ganged up on her like that, but she was not about to back down now.

Mac shook her head, trying to shake away her frustration. She became decidedly more cheerful when she considered what John said about her attitude changing following the methane gas lawsuit. He was right—she had changed, but not in the way he'd suggested. What it did teach her, however, was that if you gave these sorts of courtroom bullies enough rope while playing an honest game, they'd usually end up hanging themselves.

* * *

Wyatt took the rope in his hand and slipped it around Mr. Pony's neck. Mr. Pony immediately jerked back, unfamiliar with any sort of restraints on his freedom.

"Whoa," Wyatt said. "I need you to work with me here, buddy, because there's a little guy out there who really needs you."

Mr. Pony turned his head toward Wyatt, as if he understood. Wyatt slipped the rope fully around the horse's head and tightened the knot. Mr. Pony whinnied slightly in protest, but ultimately allowed Wyatt to restrain him and lead him out of the barn into the fenced arena.

"He's too young to break," Beth said. "Your father won't approve."

"Well, he's not here now, is he?" Wyatt responded with a mischievous grin on his face. He then turned and added more seriously, "I know what I'm doing, mom. Dad will be okay with it."

"What are you going tell Linda if Levi breaks something?"

"I'm not puttin' Levi on him yet, mom," Wyatt sighed in response. "I need to get the horse ready for that happening one day, though. Right now, Levi really just needs something to look forward to."

Beth shook her head.

"He's got a dad."

"His dad's an ass," Beth snorted. "A pompous ass who reminds me of Everett Fisher."

"Every guy you don't like reminds you of your ex-husband."

"For good reason, Wyatt. I call 'em like I see 'em, and my experiences with Everett taught me the hard way how to tell a good man from a bad one. I certainly don't need to be schooled on that topic more than once."

Wyatt continued to focus his attention on Mr. Pony, though he was considering his mom's comments and how they might apply to him. Finally, Wyatt asked his mom, "What do you think about Mac?"

Beth picked up a brush and began to gently stroke Mr. Pony, who began to calm down with her soft caresses. "I think Mac is a good woman. I wouldn't have had her as my attorney if I didn't."

Wyatt nudged Mr. Pony to begin a cantor. Mr. Pony was not in a cooperative mood and as he reared back, Wyatt tightened his grip, struggling for control. "He's got a mind of his own, don't he?"

"All creatures do."

"Some are tamable."

"And some aren't."

"Do you think I am, mom?" Wyatt looked to his mom with a dead-serious expression. "Do you think I should settle down and have a family?"

Beth felt the warmth of a grin embrace her. "Wyatt, you're a cowboy. This is who you are," she said, as she gestured around the open range that surrounded the ranch. "You are as wild and free as this horse."

When Beth saw that her comments had done little to ease the tension from her son's face, she continued more pointedly. "You'll make a fine husband and father, Wyatt, because that's what it takes–structure and guided freedom. When you find that woman who understands you and what being a cowboy means to you, you'll be a fine partner–just like your dad."

Wyatt remained quiet. When he still hadn't spoken up after several moments, Beth tried to lighten his mood. "Your dad's not perfect, though, I'll tell you that! After thirty plus years, though, I'll admit that he's pretty darn close." Beth chuckled, looking for Wyatt's reaction. When still there was none, Beth became more direct. "Look, Wyatt, I don't consider myself a nosey mom, so I'm not going to ask you what seems obvious to me. Please know that I'm here if you do want to talk about it or just vent to someone, okay?"

Wyatt nudged the horse again and the horse reared up. Wyatt cinched the rope tighter and repeated his prodding. Cowboy and horse danced around the arena, and with each loop Mr. Pony settled down a bit more. Wyatt whispered into the colt's ear soothing and consistent praise, and the horse appeared to respond to the kind soul guiding it. Together, they looped around and around until, an hour later, the colt allowed a saddle to be placed on his back.

"He's gonna be a good horse," Wyatt said.

"Yes, he is. He's a beauty, that's for sure." Beth smiled at her son, obviously proud. "You remind me so much of your father, Wyatt. You are both very encouraging and patient."

"Thanks, Mom."

Beth smiled and turned back toward the ranch house.

"Mom?" Wyatt asked as soon as she began to leave. "Would it be okay if I asked Mac out on a date?"

Beth turned back towards Wyatt, a look of confusion on her face.

"I just mean, she did use to be my brother's girlfriend. Do you think it'd be alright if I did, considering all that?"

A look of comprehension registered on Beth's face. "Your brother broke Mac's heart a few years ago, and I was real sorry to see that happen. I know how much she cared about him back then, but Greg made his choice. His loss is your gain." Beth smiled at her son. "You know, that's not my call to make, though. That's between you and Mac, and if the two of you make each other happy, then it doesn't matter what anyone else thinks. You've always lived your life according to your heart and soul—don't stop now."

"Thanks," Wyatt said as he gave the colt a pat on the flank.

Beth tilted her head to the side—a gesture she made when deep in thought. Suddenly their tranquil conversation was disrupted by a look of panic streaking across her face. "What time do you need to pick up Levi?"

"Oh, Lord," Wyatt said, looking at the position of the sun in the sky. "I'm late!" Wyatt handed the horse's reins to his mom, and took off running.

Chapter 32

"You forgot about me," Levi said as he snapped another Crayon in half. Mrs. Kennedy sat quietly at her desk observing Levi's reaction to Wyatt. Levi was considerably calmer than he'd been when she told him that Wyatt had called and was running a bit late. She could tell from her years of experience that Levi was testing the loyalty of Wyatt's care.

"I didn't forget about you, buddy. I was working on a surprise for you at the ranch and time got away from me. Sorry."

When Levi heard the reason for Wyatt's tardiness, he closed the Crayon box and grabbed his backpack off the floor. Without skipping a beat he said, "I played soccer with fifth graders today."

"You must be gettin' good for them to let you play with them. After your homework is done, we can kick the ball around if you want. I used to play when I was your age." They proceeded out of the classroom, hand in hand. Wyatt gave an appreciative nod to Mrs. Kennedy on the way out. She returned his smile.

When they got to Wyatt's truck, Levi said, "Maybe Mac could play with us, too! I can't wait to tell her, she's gonna be so proud of me!"

"Maybe she can join us later, but right now she's working."

"When's Mac gonna be done with work?"

"That's a good question, but I'm guessing she's gonna be there awhile."

Without prompting, Levi proceeded to dig around in his backpack. After a moment, he'd removed his math book and math notebook and began working on a homework assignment. "We learned multiplication today," Levi offered.

"Are you kidding me? I didn't learn that until the fifth grade. You must be in the smart kid class."

"Nah, classes are just more advanced these days. That's what my mom–" Levi stopped himself mid-sentence, and then his eyes began welling up with tears.

Wyatt noticed. "It's okay, buddy." Wyatt reached over the seat and gave a gentle pat on Levi's knee. "Sometimes crying helps."

"I'm not crying!" Levi shouted. Tears fell down his cheeks like raindrops, and he wiped them with the back of his hand.

"Is that Mac walking down the street?" Wyatt asked, grateful for the distraction.

Levi craned his neck up high and peered out the window before nodding in agreement.

Wyatt pulled his truck onto the wrong side of the street and rolled down his window. Wyatt smiled at the sight of Mac, who was standing amidst golden leaves falling from the cottonwoods lining the street. "They kick you out of the courtroom?" Wyatt hollered out the window.

Mac turned towards Wyatt's voice. "Hey, it's my two favorite guys! What are you guys doing down here?"

"Heading to the store to get this guy a soccer ball so that he can teach me some moves." His tears had ceased falling and his smile was finding its way back to his face. "After he's done turning me into that Beckham character, I'm gonna give him a big, big surprise."

Levi's face lit up as soon as he heard Wyatt mention the surprise again. Levi then filled Mac in on his day at school, and how well he'd played soccer.

"I wish I could stay longer, guys, but I really have to get back to the courtroom. I only stepped out for a minute to get some fresh air."

"Are you coming to the ranch tonight?" Levi asked.

"No, sweetie. I am working tonight. I might be able to tomorrow night, though."

"Is my dad in there?" Levi asked, peering past Mac towards the stately building.

Mac was surprised to hear Levi's question, because she'd gone out of her way to avoid discussing the case with Levi. She'd never told Levi that today was his trial, and so she'd assumed that he was unaware. Mac quickly regained her composure, and as innocently as possible responded to Levi's question.

"What makes you think that, Levi?"

"I saw his car in the parking lot."

"Wow, you're really observant, Levi," Mac responded.

"Is he in trouble?"

"No, what would make you think that?"

Levi looked at Mac with disbelief. "For the medicine, silly. And for making my mom so sad."

Mac glanced at Wyatt and then back at Levi. "What do you mean about the medicine?"

"You know, the medicine he gave my mom. Is he in trouble for not telling her how much to take before she died from it?"

"Oh, honey, is that what you think we are doing in there?"

Levi shrugged his shoulders, almost nonchalantly. "No one tells me anything. My teacher says she can't talk about it with me, you're too busy to tell me about it, and Wyatt doesn't know what's going on."

"I tell you what," Mac said while looking at her watch. "I can't get into it right now because I'm late, but if you want to talk about it later with me I'm up for tomorrow night. I'm not trying to keep secrets, it's just that sometimes life is better without hearing all the details."

"By keeping secrets?" Levi asked incredulously.

"Not secrets, honey. It's complicated."

"My dad kept secrets from my mom and now she's dead."

Mac opened the back door to Wyatt's truck and climbed inside. She grabbed Levi's hands and looked him in the eye.

"Levi, I am going to come out to the ranch tonight and we are going to have a long talk, okay? I will answer any question, because I'm not keeping any secrets from you. You are smart, you are safe, and nothing bad is going to happen to you. Do you understand?"

Levi looked down at the floor. Mac couldn't decide whether he was embarrassed about their discussion, or whether he doubted her sincerity. Finally, he lifted his head and responded, "Okay."

Mac leaned over and gave him a big hug and a smooch on the forehead before she jumped out of Wyatt's truck. "I'll see you at the ranch."

"We'll wait for you," Wyatt reached for Mac's hand, and slowly lifted it towards his face. "Good luck in there, Mac." Wyatt then lifted her hand to his mouth and gently kissed it. He let go of her hand, waved goodbye, and was off.

* * *

Luke saw Janie as soon as he exited the courtroom and walked towards the water fountain just directly past her. He knew she'd be there, because she'd been subpoenaed. Janie would have gone into the court, too, but the lawyers had invoked some rule preventing anyone subpoenaed as a witness from entering the courtroom before they took the stand.

"Check your Blackberry," Luke whispered as he breezed past her. He was worried about Janie's reaction to Dr. Kerr's testimony, and fortunately the gag order in place prevented anyone from sharing that information with her. The last thing Luke needed was for her to cave in out of fear and end up admitting to anything and everything while on the stand.

Janie didn't openly acknowledge Luke as he passed by, but immediately pulled her shiny, red phone from her purse.

"Kerr knows. Testifying to affair, meds to E, charting L's file. B careful."

Janie quickly deleted Luke's message and returned the phone to her purse. When Luke came out of the bathroom, she nodded in his general direction. She pushed the loose blonde hair back from her face, and leaned back on the bench she'd been sitting on. Her form-fitting black slacks showed off her slim legs, and the white silk button-down blouse she had on showed off her décolletage.

Luke began pacing the hall as he waited for his attorney to exit the courtroom. Luke suddenly caught sight of Linda Sterling at the other end of the hallway and promptly made his way over to her. He began peppering her with questions about Levi.

Linda stepped back from Luke, who'd moved a bit too close to her upon his approach. She tried to explain that all of his children were in school where they belonged, and that he would not be seeing them in the building unless they were called as witnesses.

Luke nodded in silent agreement with Linda, though he received little solace from her comments. As he looked around him in somewhat of a daze, he realized just how much he needed a simple hug from his daughter. *How could I have betrayed my own children like this?* He thought to himself. *If only I could turn back time.*

He turned away from Linda and slowly took a seat on one of the hallway benches. Up until this moment, his life had proceeded at breakneck speed—working at his busy medical practice, attending his kids' sporting events, squeezing in family vacations, and maintaining Janie on the side. Suddenly, life put on the brakes and time began to move slowly around him.

When will this all be over? When will I get my life back?

At that very moment, Luke realized that his life was never going to be the same. He could lose this trial and lose his kids. He'd never contemplated that before, because he'd never lost anything. He'd skated through life, charming his way over obstacles. That's how he got into med school, and that's how he got Evelyn to make sure he graduated from it.

Guilt began to slowly register with him, and how Evelyn had lost part of herself over the past twenty years working to make him happy. The more Evelyn had given of herself, the more Luke had taken. He'd grown accustomed to the situation, and expected the freedom she'd provided him. Then entered Janie: young, beautiful, exciting, and completely unattached. She was the perfect accessory for a man who had everything, and Luke wasn't about to deny himself that pleasure.

Now, sitting outside of a courtroom where he was going to be judged for his manipulation and deceit, he was scared. It was the first time in his adult life that he'd felt frightened and alone.

As if sensing his vulnerable state, Janie walked over and sat next to him. She smelled wonderful–like vanilla and lavender and jasmine. Yet her smell reminded Luke of his shame. She reached for his hand, but he pulled it away. When she tried a second time, Luke got up and walked away.

She sat there on the bench in the sterile hallway of the courtroom, staring at him with a perplexed look on her perfectly made up face. "Where are you going?" she asked.

Luke glanced over his shoulder in her direction, but said nothing and kept on walking.

Chapter 33

The sun was nearly setting by the time Wyatt and Levi returned to the ranch. Wyatt noticed a chill in the air when he got out of his truck and was glad for the warm clothing Mac had prepared for Levi that day. Winter was approaching quickly, and soon the days would be shorter and the temperatures even lower.

When Levi hopped out of the truck, he threw his new black and yellow soccer ball down to the ground and began kicking it around the yard. Wyatt joined in, but after a few minutes began to coax Levi towards the barn.

"I got you a surprise in here," Wyatt said.

Levi's face lit up. "I like surprises now."

"Whatdya mean 'now' buddy? Surprises are fun!"

"Well, I'd never really seen a good surprise before, but I've been getting good surprises lately so now I like them."

Wyatt cocked his head to the side and removed his cowboy hat. "You telling me you've never gotten a good surprise before? Well, you sure got a dilly of one in store for you now!" Wyatt paused for a second, debating on his next question, but ultimately chose to go forward with it.

"What was it about surprises before that you didn't like?"

Levi threw the ball in the air and it landed with a thud near Mr. Pony's stall. The horse startled with the noise and set his ears back. Without missing a beat, Wyatt calmed him.

"Whoa," Levi said, mimicking Wyatt's tone. Levi's eyes suddenly focused on Mr. Pony's midsection, and his eyes began to widen. "Hey, he has a saddle on!"

"Yeah, I figured it's about time that he start getting used to it. Today was the first day he's ever worn one, and is the reason I was late to pick you up today. I was working on breaking him for you." Wyatt thrived on the excitement that was registering on Levi's face.

Levi reached through the gate and began to gently pat the horse on his flank. As though there had been no break in their conversation, Levi commented somberly, "My mom used to give me a surprise every time I had to go to a new doctor."

Wyatt shook his head, as the implication of Levi's history with surprises began to settle in. "So, if you had to go to a specialist or somethin' like that, she'd give you a gift?"

Levi nodded.

Wyatt was silent for a moment, and he had his hand poised around his chin in obvious reflection. "Well, that was pretty thoughtful of her, when you think about it. I'm sure she had a lot on her mind because things were really hectic back then, but she still went out of her way to try and take your mind off all those doctors' appointments and stuff."

"Yeah," Levi agreed nodding in agreement, though he didn't lift his head from Mr. Pony and had yet to make eye contact with Wyatt since beginning the conversation. "Still, getting a surprise meant that something bad was right around the bend, ya know?"

"Sure, I get it. I'm sure you woulda felt even worse if she hadn't gotten you those little surprises, though. You gotta give her credit for going out of her way to try and make those doctors' visits less traumatic."

She was his mom, and he expected her to love him and be there for him. He'd never actually stopped to think about her going out of her way for him before, or giving her credit for trying to protect him. Memories of his mom began to race through his mind, and he processed them while continuing to pet Mr. Pony in silence.

"Do you think my mom made me sick?" Levi finally asked.

Wyatt unfastened the gate to the stall while motioning for Levi to step back out of the way. "Why would she do that?" He asked incredulously.

"Your mom loved you very much, so I don't believe for one minute that she ever tried to make you sick."

Levi backed away as Wyatt led Mr. Pony into the arena. The horse reared a few times in protest before it settled into a trot. Wearing blue jeans, boots and a sweat-stained t-shirt, Wyatt trotted along beside him.

"Wanna be the first one to ride him?" Wyatt asked.

Levi's face lit up. "You mean it?"

"I do, but you have to promise to do exactly as I say. He's a feisty horse–a little like Mocha. If you don't listen to me, then you might get bucked off a few times."

Levi furrowed his brow. "Will it hurt?"

"I ain't gonna lie to you - it might. If you trust him, he'll start to trust you right back, and sooner than you know it you'll have come to understanding one another. When that happens, you'll do just fine riding him."

"Have you been bucked off before?"

"Dozens of times. Dad used to tell me that it builds character."

"Okay," Levi slowly said, a smile creeping back onto his face. "Just don't tell Mac–she'd freak out."

Wyatt let out a soft laugh and proceeded to hoist Levi up into the saddle.

* * *

"The prosecution calls Janie Johansen," Karl Swensen said.

The bailiff nodded in the prosecutor's general direction before exiting the courtroom. He returned a moment later, and in close tow was an obviously nervous Nurse Janie.

As the elegant blonde walked through the middle of the courtroom in the direction of the witness stand, her eyes were darting from one direction to the next. Just before she reached her final destination, she was able to make eye contact with Luke at the defense table. Janie had hoped to get a sympathetic gesture in response and was desperate to establish some

306

sort of connection with him. As soon as she caught his gaze, however, he abruptly turned his head and began whispering to his attorney.

The clerk swore Janie in and she climbed up to the seat located just to the left of Judge Binnard. As she was still settling herself into the witness stand, Karl began asking her some of his preliminary questions. Her head lifted in surprise, but she tried to quickly focus on the questions being asked of her.

"Ms. Johansen, why did you chart all the entries in Levi's medical records?"

"I didn't chart *all* of the entries," Janie defensively responded. "I only made entries into Levi's charts when Dr. Kerr instructed me to."

"You're telling me that Dr. Kerr instructed you to make entries into Levi's chart?"

Janie acknowledged her previous answer.

"Did Dr. Kerr normally ask you to chart entries into his patients' notes?"

"No."

"In fact, Dr. Kerr never asked you to chart entries in any of his other patients' notes, right?"

"That's correct, sir," Janie responded while nodding her head yes.

"Why Levi then?"

"His case was unusual, I guess."

"Unusual?" Karl asked. "Was that because you were having an affair with Levi's father?"

"Objection!" John Trainor yelled.

"Withdrawn," Karl said. "Unusual in that Levi was frequently sick and documenting his charts was important?"

Janie agreed. "He was in our office a lot."

"Part of your job as a nurse is to meet with the child's parent before Dr. Kerr does, is that correct?"

"Yes, because I need to get as much information as possible to present to the doctor, explaining the purpose of the sick visit."

"Did you ever suggest any possible diagnoses with Mrs. Landers during Levi's sick visits?"

Janie tucked her long blond hair behind her ears and began to fidget in her chair. "I didn't *suggest* anything to Evelyn. We met rather frequently, as Levi was in our office frequently. We'd discuss Levi's symptoms in detail, and I'd try and pinpoint the chief complaints before Dr. Kerr came in. Evelyn was always prepared with her research on Levi's symptoms, and more often than not had a predetermined idea on what Levi's problems were. It was then my job to document what she told me in Levi's charts on behalf of Dr. Kerr"

"I see. Did you ever discuss these diagnoses with Luke Landers?"

Janie hesitated, and glanced towards the defense table.

"I'd ask that you answer the question, keeping your eyes focused on me."

Janie looked flustered, but looked back at Karl and slowly responded in the affirmative.

"To your knowledge, did Luke Landers ever accompany Evelyn to Levi's appointments with Dr. Kerr?"

"I don't specifically recall, but he may have."

"Did Luke ever appear for a visit when you were the attending doctor—strike that, I mean, attending nurse?"

"No."

"When was it, then, that would you discuss Levi's diagnoses with Dr. Landers?"

"When I saw him or spoke with him."

"Where did these conversations take place?"

"I'd see him in more than one place, but most of our conversations occurred at his house."

"You went to the Landers's house often?" Karl asked, with a hint of surprise.

"Yes, I did." Janie further responded, "I had to take care of the kids from time to time."

"What about your apartment? Did any of these conversations take place there?" When Karl saw Janie again look towards the defense table, he quickly added, "Ms. Johansen? I'm over here."

"Yes, I know." Janie looked frazzled. "I can't recall any in particular, but they may have."

Karl nodded, silently indicating to the witness that he knew darned well that Luke had been to her apartment. "During the time that Levi was getting diagnosed with flu-invoked Leukemia, you were having sexual relations with his father, correct?"

Janie's eyes opened wide, completely caught off guard by Karl's directness.

"Objection!" John Trainor stood to his feet, in an attempt to inject more weight into his request. "Relevance, Your Honor."

"Overruled. The witness may answer," Judge Binnard said flatly before returning his direction to the witness stand. "You may answer the question, Ms. Johansen".

"Yes," Janie firmly responded, while drawing her shoulders back in a manner suggesting that she was quite proud of that fact. She again looked towards Luke, but had yet to establish direct eye contact with him. Before she could get admonished by the prosecutor again, she turned herself directly in his direction.

"You were in love with him, weren't you?"

"Well, yes," Janie responded less confidently than before.

"As you sit here today, you're still in love with Dr. Landers?"

"Yes," she admitted, this time not hiding her glances towards Luke as she looked for reassurance.

Karl disregarded her gaze, and immediately pounced with another direct question. "You wanted to be with Dr. Landers more than anything, isn't that right?"

"Well, I-I-I–"

"It's true that he'd promised to marry you, though?"

"No," she lied.

"But you told other members of Dr. Kerr's staff that the two of you were planning on getting married?"

Janie was silent for a few seconds, pondering her response. Karl obviously knew that Luke had promised to marry her, so she couldn't continue to deny it. "I guess you could say that we discussed the topic."

"You're aware that the laws of our state prevented Dr. Landers from marrying you while he was already married to Evelyn, aren't you?"

Janie huffed at the suggestion. "I know that, sir. He was planning on divorcing her."

Karl began nodding his head in response again, an almost imperceptible smile playing at his lips. "Yes, that's right. He told you he was going to divorce Evelyn for years, didn't he?"

"No."

"No?" Karl asked incredulously, before whipping around to face Janie directly. "Are you telling me after all those years of proclaiming his love for you, that it wasn't until recently that he decided to divorce his wife?"

"Yes, that's what I'm saying." Janie's feeble expression had turned into one of indignation.

"You must have found that to be quite humiliating," Karl suggested in a mocking tone.

"No, I didn't because I understood the circumstances." Janie gave a pleading sort of look towards Karl, as she continued less assertively with her response. "You see, Evelyn could be quite irrational. Luke didn't want to leave while she was unstable, for fear of the impact it would have on the kids and his practice. I understood that, being that I'm also a professional within the medical field."

"How altruistic of you. So, it's your testimony that you were patient with Dr. Landers divorcing his wife because you were concerned for the kids?"

"Yes."

"That's why you two decided to try and stabilize Evelyn by putting her on antipsychotic medications, correct?"

Janie flipped her hair past her shoulders in defiance. "No."

"No? You're telling us that at no time did you ever suggest to Evelyn that she should take medication to calm her nerves?"

"I don't specifically recall, no."

Karl Swensen began dramatically flipping through the pages in Levi's medical chart, and Nurse Janie looked on with obvious trepidation. He took his time turning the pages, trying to make her sweat a bit.

It worked.

Karl finally chose a page in the book in front of him, and turned his attention back to the witness stand. "Nurse Janie, are you telling us that on July tenth of last year you didn't suggest to Evelyn that very thing?"

Janie shifted in her seat. "No, I told you that I didn't recall. And I don't."

"Well, let me refresh your memory, then. I'm pointing to page one hundred forty-two in Levi's medical records, which have already been introduced into evidence. Would you care to look at that?" Karl placed Levi's medical records in front of Janie, and stood pointedly looking at her as he awaited her response.

Janie looked back at him in defiance, and gave a noncommittal shrug.

Karl quickly walked to the defense table, and laid down a sheet of paper in front of each attorney. He promptly turned back towards the judge, "Your Honor, I'd ask your permission to have the witness read the page I've flagged on the exhibit in front of her, a copy of which has just been provided to counsel."

Judge Binnard turned towards Janie, and instructed her to review the document to see if it could refresh her recollection to the matter.

Janie read it and nodded.

"Now that you've looked at the entry, has your memory regarding the events of July the tenth been refreshed?"

Janie nodded.

"I see you're shaking your head. Are you telling us now that you do remember suggesting to Evelyn that she take medications to ease her nerves?"

"Yes," Janie said as she closed the offending charts positioned in front of her.

"Did you ever discuss the medical recommendation you made to Evelyn with Dr. Kerr?"

"I don't remember."

"How about with Evelyn's husband? Did you ever discuss mood stabilizers with Luke?"

"Again, I don't recall. It was a long time ago," Janie insisted out of frustration.

"What were you wearing at the July 4th parade last year?"

Janie looked confused at Karl's blatant topic change. Without much hesitation, though, Janie was able to answer the question. "My red and blue stripped tank with a white skort."

"You answered that quickly, Nurse." Karl again turned his focus quickly to the witness. "You're sitting here today telling us that you can remember the specific outfit you wore to a parade last year, but not whether you discussed Evelyn's medications with Luke around that same time?"

"You are comparing apples and oranges," Janie said with a huff.

"Who came up with the leukemia diagnosis?"

"A specialist in Denver." Janie appeared relieved at the change in topics. "I don't remember his name offhand, though."

"Is that the one you found online and suggested to Evelyn?"

Janie was about to answer an emphatic no, but noticed that Karl had begun flipping through Levi's charts again. She decided to answer more cautiously. "I may have looked for a specialist online. Evelyn was frequently conducting her own online research, so there were occasions that I thought I'd help her out by doing a little research for her. She knew a lot about medicine, so I didn't doubt it when she suggested that Levi had leukemia."

"Really?" Karl stood directly in front of Janie, with his arms crossed over his chest.

"Yes. When Evelyn suggested leukemia, I thought I'd help by looking for a specialist to refer her to. I was trying to help her."

"Help in what way? You mean help her believe that Levi really was sick?"

"Objection," John Trainor said.

"Withdrawn." Karl continued without hesitation, "Ms. Johansen, tell me when the first time was that you and Dr. Landers discussed Munchausen by Proxy?"

"I don't know."

"You admit to having discussed that with him, though, right?"

"I guess."

"Which one of you thought of Munchausen first?"

"I don't remember."

"Do you remember the e-mail you sent to Luke several years ago to that matter?"

Janie's mouth dropped open, and her eyes flashed at Luke. When Karl's reference to her old e-mail still failed to draw Luke's gaze her way, she returned her gaze to the prosecutor. This time, she was not as surprised to see him start flipping through his exhibit binder.

"I've sent Luke e-mails before, yes. I sent the e-mail you're referring to because I was just trying to figure out what was wrong with Levi."

"And your concern for Levi had you suggest to your lover that his wife was suffering from a mental disorder?"

"Objection," John Trainor said. "Argumentative."

"Overruled," Judge Binnard said. "She may answer."

"I didn't suggest anything. Like I already said, I was just trying to figure out what was wrong with Levi."

"So you *weren't* trying to get Luke to leave his wife and kids by suggesting that Evelyn was sick in the head?"

"Objection!"

"Withdrawn. Janie, who diagnosed Levi with 'Failure to Thrive'?"

"Dr. Kerr," Janie said, sitting up a little straighter.

"But that's your handwriting in Levi's chart, isn't it?" Karl asked, pointing to a page in Levi's medical notes.

"Yes, I documented Levi's chart after Dr. Kerr made that diagnosis."

"Based on your suggestion?"

"No, Dr. Kerr made the diagnosis on his own, and it was based on Levi's lack of appetite, inability to keep food down, and low weight."

"What about 'Reactive Attachment Disorder'? *That* diagnosis was made by you, right?"

"No. Dr. Kerr diagnosed that."

"Really? But that's your handwriting again, correct?" Karl again pointed to Levi's records, another page of which had been tabbed for her review.

"Yes, I documented his chart there, too, after Dr. Kerr made the diagnosis."

"This was based on your suggestion, right?"

"No, I told you already that Dr. Kerr diagnosed him with Reactive Attachment."

"So when Dr. Kerr testified that you showed him an article on the disorder that you'd found in the *Journal of American Medicine* and suggested that it applied to Levi, he was wrong?"

Janie shook her head, clearly shaken. "I guess I don't remember."

"Do you read *JAMA* regularly, Ms. Johansen?"

"Of course. I like to be up to date on all areas of medicine."

"Do you subscribe to the magazine?" Karl asked.

"No."

"Where do you read that journal? Certainly not in the office, since Dr. Kerr already told us that he gets his copies sent to his home address."

Janie shifted nervously in her chair. "Luke gets it at his office."

"Is that where you read about 'Reactive Attachment Disorder' before suggesting to Dr. Kerr that Levi suffered from it - at his father's office?"

"I don't remember," Janie said. "It was a long time ago."

"Did you ever bring articles from *JAMA* or any other medical-type journal to Dr. Kerr's attention for any of his other patients?"

"Not that I recall, but I might have. I care very much about our kids and I am always considering their well-being."

"What about Jared Odell? Do you recall him?"

"Yes."

"Why didn't you research medical journals for information on 'Stereotypic Movement Disorder' for that little boy's rare diagnosis?"

"I don't know that I didn't," Janie said, crossing her arms over her chest while giving her answer.

"But you didn't make any entries in Jared's chart indicating that you'd gone out of your way researching his condition?"

"I don't know."

"Jared was diagnosed only two months ago. Wouldn't you remember going out of your way by researching his disorder, since you can remember doing the same for Levi many years ago?"

"It's been unusually hectic at the office lately. The beginning of the school year is very busy, and I just don't remember, Mr. Swensen."

"Fair enough. What about Tyler Abraham? Did you do any research on that little boy's Hodgkin's disease?"

Janie's expression became cross, and she turned towards the judge to see if he would allow this line of questioning to continue. None of the attorneys were objecting to the questions, though it seemed to her like there ought to have been at least one objectionable question out of the bunch. "Your Honor," she stated, "I don't see how this relates to the case, and I feel like Mr. Swensen is badgering me. Do I have to answer?"

Judge Binnard appeared amused by her statement. "Yes, Ms. Johansen. You must answer all questions asked of you unless you hear me tell you otherwise."

Janie nodded in silent agreement, though she felt silly from the judge's scolding. Finally, she returned to Karl with her answer. "I don't remember researching Hodgkin's."

"You don't remember, or you didn't?"

"I studied Hodgkin's in detail while in nursing school, so I didn't have the need to familiarize myself with the disease, no." She perked up with her answer, like she'd settled a score with the prosecutor.

"Oh good," Karl promptly responded. "Then you can explain the Hoxsey method to me?"

"The *what*?" Janie asked.

"The Hoxsey method, Nurse. H-O-X-S-E-Y. You just testified that you were familiar with Hodgkin's after studying it in great deal in nursing school. You don't know about this treatment for the disease?"

"No."

"But isn't that what Tyler's parents wanted their son to receive, against Dr. Kerr's recommendations?"

"I don't know."

Judge Binnard interrupted. "Mr. Swensen, I think I get the picture here. In an effort to keep this case moving, you can proceed to the next matter."

"Your Honor, I'm discrediting the Nurse's prior statement with regards to the deep concern she alleged she had for all of Dr. Kerr's patients. I have dozens of other examples that I believe need to be placed on the record in the event that this case gets appealed. It is highly relevant and is the foundation for the next line of questioning."

"I can't imagine that you've failed to lay adequate foundation for your next question, counsel. The record is clear as to your motives here, and

I'm sure that in the event this gets appealed that all the appellate judges will get it, as do I."

Karl Swensen looked disappointed as he returned to the podium where he kept his evidence notebook and legal pad. He flipped forward in the notebook as he obviously contemplated his next move.

"Your Honor, it is getting late and I have many additional questions of this witness. I'd request that we break for the day."

Judge Binnard made some notes on his legal pad. "Court is in recess until tomorrow morning at ten o'clock. I have a law and motion calendar in the morning. We will resume testimony after I am finished." With that, he stood and left.

Janie had been watching Luke for a reaction, but he continued to avoid making eye contact with her. When it was clear that he was not going to acknowledge her, she began to exit the courtroom. Janie waited for Luke to exit, in the hopes that his curt attitude was limited to the courtroom setting. He made eye contact with her as soon as he exited, and Janie raced towards him. Before she could utter a single word, however, his back was to her and he forcefully exited the building–leaving Janie standing alone and confused.

Chapter 34

"You're destined to be a cowboy, Levi," Beth said as she stood outside the corral, her sturdy arms resting over the edge of the wooden fence, watching Wyatt and Levi. Mr. Pony was being led around the arena by Wyatt, and Levi was riding happily in the saddle. Levi's smile spoke volumes as he held tightly to the reigns and listened carefully to Wyatt's instructions.

"Did you get all your homework done on the ride up here?" Beth asked. Levi nodded and let go of the saddle only long enough to give Beth a quick thumbs up sign.

"Well, you boys need to get inside soon so you can wash up before supper. Mac just called, and is already on her way."

"But I want to ride some more," Levi whined in protest.

"She's right, buddy. Anyways, Mr. Pony has probably had enough. This is his first day ever with a rider, and he needs a break. If we don't quit soon, you'll be saddle sore, too."

"But Wyatt, you said I could ride as long as I want."

"I said you could ride for a while, and it's now time for you and Mr. Pony to take a break. I've got some other chores calling my name that I need to get done before dinner."

Levi's face grew red with rage. "I'm not done and I'm not letting you make me get off!"

Wyatt watched in horror as Levi began to kick his legs about in protest. One of the boy's unintended kicks landed on Mr. Pony's flanks, and the horse reacted instantly. The colt reared up on his hind legs, flailing its front legs high in the air.

Levi's eyes grew wide with shock. He leaned over to hold onto Mr. Pony's neck, but the horse stomped down onto all fours before quickly rearing itself back up.

Wyatt jumped closer to Mr. Pony and reached for the lead rope in an attempt to rein the horse in, but the agitated horse responded by kicking and bucking more wildly than before. Wyatt felt as though time had come to a stop as he watched Levi fly off of the horse's back and sail through the air before finally coming to a thud in the dirt.

"Oh my God, watch out!" Beth screamed in horror.

Before Wyatt was able to push Levi out of the way, Mr. Pony stomped down, landing one hoof squarely on Levi's back.

"Shit," Wyatt yelled as he began to reel in Mr. Pony's ropes, hoping to prevent the horse from rearing up again. "Levi!"

Wyatt exerted every ounce of energy he could muster to corral Mr. Pony out of the arena and force him back into an empty stall. Wyatt shut the gate containing the colt and immediately took off running in Levi's direction. Beth had already jumped the fence and was on her knees beside the boy.

Levi lay face down in the dirt, both silent and still. Beth gently lifted his shirt up to reveal the area on his back impacted by the hoof, and evaluated his injuries.

"Oh, Lord," she said as she eyed the large bruise that was beginning to form around the four-inch lesion on Levi's back. She rolled him over so that he could breathe.

"Levi, are you okay?" Wyatt said. "Hey, little buddy, wake up."

After what felt like an eternity, Levi managed to open an eye and look up towards Wyatt and Beth hovering above him. He tried to lift his head, but it felt very heavy. He dragged his hand through the dirt and felt the gash on his upper lip where his tooth had cut through.

"Good thing you're tough," Wyatt said. "You sure taught that horse a lesson about bucking, didn't you?"

Levi began gently rubbing his chin, and tried to make sense of Wyatt's comments. Was he being teased for having made such a big mistake? Was he in trouble? After a moment of confusion, he tied to sit up. He desperately wanted to hold back his tears and be tough, as Wyatt had suggested, but he was hurt and afraid, and the tears naturally flowed. He caught sight of Mac entering the barn.

As soon as Mac saw Levi, she began running quickly towards him.

"Oh my goodness, Levi! What happened? Are you okay?"

"I hate you!" Levi yelled at Wyatt. "You think it's funny that Mr. Pony just stomped on me."

"Hey," Mac said, hushing her voice a bit. "No one is laughing at you, Levi." Mac turned towards Beth and Wyatt, looking for some support. She still had no idea what had just happened.

Picking up on Mac's body language, Wyatt jumped in. "Buddy, there's no way we'd be laughing at you. This was just an accident."

"There's no such thing as an accident!" Levi shouted.

"That's not true, Levi," Mac injected. "I realize your dad might have said that to you before, but it was under entirely different circumstances. If he were here now, he'd agree with us that this was an accident and sometimes accidents happen."

"No, you're wrong!" Levi shouted. "There is no such thing as an accident–this was my fault. Everything's my fault! If it weren't for me, my mom would be here right now!"

"No, Levi, that was not your fault," Beth said softly.

"It is my fault, I know it." Levi had softened his voice a bit, and lowered his head in shame. "The Baseball Man thinks it's my fault, too."

Beth and Wyatt both shot sideways looks towards Mac, hoping for an explanation as to what that all meant.

"When did he tell you that it was your fault?" Mac asked, hoping that her concern broke through Levi's angry façade.

Levi glared at Mac silently. After a minute passed without comment, it was obvious that the boy was intentionally refusing to answer her.

"It was Ty Cobb, wasn't it?" Mac intentionally sighed in apparent frustration, hoping to signal to Levi her disappointment with the mean-spirited baseball player. "He's the one who told you this, isn't he?"

Levi continued to stare at her with a stoned face, and didn't flinch upon the mention of Ty's name.

"Levi, Ty Cobb was not a nice man. You know that he was mean, because you told me so yourself. I'm surprised to see that you're letting him make you feel guilty, when you know what a troublemaker he was. Don't let him make you think that you are in any way responsible for your mom's death, because you're not."

Mac reached towards Levi's shirt and gently lifted the hemline to examine his wound. She was dismayed to see the swollen and purple bruise, which meant immediate medical treatment and prompt reporting to Linda Sterling. His lip needed treatment as well. "C'mon, buddy. We need to go pay Dr. Kerr a visit."

* * *

"There you go, all fixed," Dr. Kerr said with a genuine smile. The doctor turned towards Mac, "You should give him some Ibuprofen tonight, to help the swelling and the discomfort."

Wyatt had remained in the lobby during Levi's visit, and was feeling extremely guilty about how Levi's injury occurred. Not only was he worried about Levi's health, but whether the little guy would ever trust him enough to ride a horse again.

Mac overheard Levi apologize for kicking the horse and was relieved to hear that Levi wasn't holding onto the anger he'd displayed earlier. With that out of the way, she walked back toward Dr. Kerr's office. He was making a note in Levi's chart.

"Dr. Kerr–"

"Ms. MacIntosh–"

They both spoke at the same time and then smiled at the mutual interruption. Dr. Kerr continued quickly, "I know that we're probably not supposed to talk, but I can't let your unexpected visit go without making mention of one thing. I want you to know I have *always* held Levi's treatment and care to the highest regard, as with all my other patients. I would never do anything to harm one of my patients."

"Dr. Kerr, you really don't need to–" Mac interjected.

"Please, let me continue." Dr. Kerr nervously said. "When my wife and I moved to this small, beautiful town thirty years ago, she quickly noted how important it would be to stay out of the chirp den. My wife is a very insightful woman, and she correctly recognized the destructive nature of small town gossip, and she was right. Anyways, my point is that we've always gone out of our way to avoid the gossip around town." Dr. Kerr briefly paused, taking a moment to dab at beads of sweat forming along his brow.

"When I first heard the rumblings around town that I had been intentionally ignoring Janie's affair with Dr. Landers, I responded the way I always had: I ignored it. I never spoke of it with my wife or anyone else for that matter. It never occurred to me that it could have any ramifications on anyone other than myself, and most certainly not the Landers children. I did notice that Janie was overly attentive to them, but I presumed it was because she was a good nurse. I never would have connected that behavior to her affair, not for one second.

"In hindsight, I can see several warning signs that I simply overlooked. It is my fault that I didn't pay more attention." Dr. Kerr began to shake his head back and forth, obviously having beaten himself up over this point many times before. "Janie did pay too much attention to those kids. I was swamped with all the other patients, and by the time I realized that her behavior might be inappropriate, it had already been going on for quite some time."

Dr. Kerr looked Mac directly in the eyes and continued, "I can't tell you how many times I've kicked myself for not having said anything about this to Janie sooner. Had I, things might be different for the Landers family. What happened under my nose was wrong, and I understand there might be ramifications for it. I had a long talk with my attorney today. He told me that I should expect a medical board inquiry. My main concern isn't that, though, but that the Landers children do not end up in foster care.

They don't deserve it. I really don't think I could live with myself if that happens. What do you think Luke's chances are of keeping the kids?"

Mac normally would never have responded to that sort of question from a witness in an on-going case, but the current circumstances gave her pause. "I really don't know, doctor. The trial isn't over yet, and until all the evidence comes out it's anyone's guess. A lot depends on what happens when Janie gets on the stand tomorrow, and then whether Luke takes the stand after her. He may not. Given the possibility of them being charged with Evelyn's death, Luke might not want to testify. I'm sure his attorney's advised him that if he testifies to anything even remotely suggesting he or Janie were inappropriately involved in prescribing Evelyn's meds, that they could be charged in the case. If Luke does choose to invoke his Fifth Amendment rights in this trial, I think it's fairly likely the judge will find the allegations in the petition true. That, of course, would leave all of the Landers kids in foster care for a period of time. While the law requires attempts at reunification be made in general, that might not be the case here if Luke was charged with Evelyn's murder. That means the kids could be put up for adoption or long- term foster care."

"That would be a crying shame," Dr. Kerr said. "Those kids deserve at least one parent, especially after the loss of their mom. Luke's not really a bad guy, he's just selfish. The best possible outcome I could see would be getting Luke counseling to address that, and then returning all the kids to him. Without him in their lives, those kids' futures will be dramatically changed—for the worse."

Chapter 35

Luke Landers had to perform a C-section before trial even began that morning, which was stressful enough in itself. To make his day even longer, he was paged to return to the hospital immediately following the trial; two of his patients went into labor, providing the perfectly busy conclusion to a perfectly busy day. By the time he finally returned home it was dark outside, and he hadn't even seen one of his kids all day.

When Dr. Landers was unloading his personal effects on the kitchen counter, he finally was able to make contact with one of his kids. As Austen began updating him on the family events, he started to wish that he had completed the day isolated from his children. Luke rubbed at his temple as Austen explained that Ben had been sent to the principal's office for cheating. Before Luke was able to fully digest the news of Ben's troublemaking, Austen began describing how Lauren missed swim practice due to a carpool miscommunication. He didn't have enough energy left in him to reprimand Austen for injecting his own explanation as to how that miscommunication occurred, which dealt with the family's jumbled up life and jumbled up personal calendar.

Despite the negative attitude Austen had while delivering the news, Luke was happy that Austen was home at all. Since Evelyn's death, Austen had been spending the majority of his free time at his girlfriend's house. No matter how desperately Luke pleaded Austen to spend more time at home, Austen couldn't seem to be bothered.

Thank Heavens for Ginny, Luke thought. Their housekeeper had always been both reliable and dependable, but as of late she's also been the glue that kept the Landers house running. As Luke finally settled down to sleep following his hectic day, he realized that he should share his appreciation with Ginny herself.

Unfortunately for Luke, just as he dozed off into a blissful sleep, his pager beeped.

* * *

Ginny hustled around the Landers house, cleaning every nook and cranny—as usual. She was lost in thought, daydreaming about life working for another family. Ginny would never have *really* considered leaving the Landers family, but dealing with Luke had caused her to contemplate it for the first time. Working for another family wasn't really so far fetched, considering that she had become somewhat of a hot commodity around town as of late. Now that Evelyn was gone, Ginny found herself approached by a surprising amount of women offering her a job in a more "stable" home. However, Ginny loved the Landers children as if they were her own and knew that she would never leave them out of loyalty to Evelyn.

The problem was that Ginny had never liked Luke. She had witnessed many fights between the spouses. She felt that Luke was rude and demeaning to Evelyn, and it was no secret to her that Luke had a woman on the side.

Ginny shuddered as the image of Janie Johansen came to her mind. She knew Janie all too well. Ever since Ginny first met Janie seven years earlier at a cocktail party hosted by the Landers's, Ginny knew she was no good. Ginny remembered watching Janie interact with Luke on that day long ago and the foreboding she felt while witnessing Luke flirt with the local nurse. From that moment on, Ginny refused to refer to Janie as anything but "Quisling." Ginny had little doubts that Janie was just what the name implied: a traitor.

Though she'd never needed confirmation of her suspicions, the caller I.D. on the Landers's phone backed up the true whereabouts of Dr. Landers. If Janie could not get Luke to answer on his cell phone or respond to his pager, she would call the house. If Evelyn answered, Janie would use Levi as her excuse to call. But if Luke answered Janie's call, he immediately found an excuse to leave the house.

As Ginny sat around stewing over the family dysfunction, she suddenly realized that she hadn't checked the caller I.D. in days. She set down the carrots that she'd been peeling, and walked over to the kitchen telephone. She scrolled through the list of calls received earlier that day, and immediately recognized the familiar telephone number. According to caller I.D., Quisling had called seven times within the past twenty-four hours.

"Traitor," Ginny whispered to herself before returning to the carrots.

* * *

As Ginny was scrolling through the phone call list, Dr. Landers was performing another emergency C-section. During the surgery, his pager had gone off twenty-something times. He considered returning Janie's calls, but he knew she would only interrogate him about his having ignored her at court. Right now he needed to escape. He normally didn't jog–especially at night–but a good, brisk run followed by a long, hot shower sounded good to him. He headed towards the physician's locker room to change into a pair of gray shorts, a t-shirt and his worn-out Nikes.

As he took his first few steps outside, he was overwhelmed by how good the crisp air felt in his lungs. Luke picked up his pace as he neared Fifth Street, and was virtually at a full sprint by the time he headed out of town on a small, dirt road. As he began to wander past the old sugar plant that was being torn down for a computer headquarters, he realized how big Sheridan was becoming. More companies were discovering the favorable tax incentives within the town and relocating in increasing numbers. Between the methane gas industry and the influx of wealthy retired people, the town was changing and growing every day. Luke liked the changes. It was good for his business. As he slowed the pace of his run, he realized that this was the first time in awhile that he'd had some quality time to think. His mind was drawn back to the first time he laid eyes on Janie.

He was doing rounds at the hospital when he saw her, and her beauty stopped him dead in his tracks. She was at the hospital applying for a job. Luke liked the fact that she was self-assured–a thing that his wife did not possess. When she reached out to shake his hand, electricity bolted through his body. He felt the attraction instantly and made excuses to continue their conversation for over an hour.

It seemed like an eternity ago, Luke thought to himself as he started to climb a hill. As Luke reached the apex of the little climb, he suddenly was amazed at the depths of involvement he'd had with Janie's life–beginning from day one. Luke had suggested Janie work for a private doctor instead of the hospital and even called Dr. Kerr on her behalf.

The fit seemed apparent immediately, as Janie had excellent credentials and references. The only catch in Dr. Kerr hiring Janie was the fact that she was a divorcee without children. Dr. Kerr's wife worried about that. But, there was a shortage of nurses at that time, so Dr. Kerr offered Janie the job.

In appreciation for him taking the time to get her hooked up in a private office, Janie sent a thank-you that included a jazz CD and a gift card to the new latte shop downtown. Luke invited Janie to join him for coffee and the rest is history.

As Luke rounded the last curve and began his return towards town, he began to beat himself up over his having extended Janie that initial coffee invitation. It had been wrong and he knew it, but Janie was undoubtedly a temptress, while he was too eager to be led astray.

As his run came to an end, he yearned for the comfort and safety of his home. As he reached out to put the key into his Suburban, he was caught off guard by an unexpected voice.

"You're avoiding me," Janie said as she walked out from the shadows behind him.

Luke whipped around and saw that Janie was barely two feet from him. Her hands were firmly planted on her narrow hips, and her legs stretched out long from beneath her a tight brown, leather miniskirt. As Luke casually looked her over, he was surprised to see that she was dressed to the nines and did not appear in any way distressed. Her blonde hair was loosely draped up off her neck, and pinned in place with a brilliant, green jeweled comb.

"I'm not avoiding you, I'm just busy. I've still got my medical practice to run, in addition to the court case that will determine the future of my family."

"You can drop the attitude," she responded, as she switched her weight from one hip to the other.

"Oh yeah?" Luke was caught off guard by her arrogance, because he'd expected her to be moping. He recovered from his surprise, and retorted, "Well, you can drop the *Fatal Attraction* thing. I don't like being stalked."

"Get over yourself, Luke - I'm not stalking you," Janie said with a shrug of her shoulders. "I just have to talk with you about the text message you sent to me in court today. I couldn't decipher it, and it's been bugging me all day given how today's testimony made us both look. Before court starts back up tomorrow, I want to make sure that we're both on the same page."

"Getting nervous?" Luke chided.

"No," Janie snorted in response. "Just proceeding with caution, Luke. This is serious stuff."

"Since when have you proceeded with caution for anything, Janie?"

"I've always been cautious, Luke, and you know it - you're the one who throws caution to the wind."

"Yeah, right," he said without disguising his sarcasm.

"Oh please, who's the one here who has lived the past seven years quietly and under the radar? You or me? I never go out anywhere, certainly not anywhere with my man. I've stayed at home the past seven years, while you run around playing the role of doting and loving husband. I've been nothing *but* cautious, because you've always promised me a ring if I did." Janie turned to the side, and lowered her chin to her shoulder as she physically looked him down. "Quite frankly, I'm sick and tired of waiting around for you to honor those promises, and sick and tired of living my life so damned cautiously."

Luke realized there was no way for him to win this argument, and he was too tired to pretend to care. He turned his back to her and began reaching for the car's handle in front of him. "Listen, Janie, tomorrow's a big day and I'm exhausted. I need to go home and get to bed."

"Is that so? Might as well rest up good, big boy—'cause you're gonna see a whole new me on the stand tomorrow."

Luke paused, his hand still in front of him. He turned around, staring silently at Janie and seething. "What?"

"You think about that, honey. Keep in mind that I've documented everything. Oh, did I ever mention that Judge Binnard is single again? I'd be more than happy to hand some of that paperwork over to my new friend, 'cause he looks so lonely."

"What did you just say to me?" Luke asked incredulously.

Janie stuck her chest out in a boastful fashion. "What, did I stutter?"

"You're telling me now that you're going to get up on the stand tomorrow and lie, unless I kiss your ass? Tell me how that's not blackmail, Janie."

"What I'm telling you is to prepare yourself for my side of the story to come out at trial tomorrow. You've made it clear that we're no longer in this together. So you'd better get used to the thought of losing your kids and your practice."

Luke's adrenalin was already flowing from his run, and the new scenario Janie had just presented made his blood pressure rise. His mind began racing with all the possibilities that she'd just created for him—strange and terrible possibilities that he simply had never considered. Luke had always taken Janie's love for him as a given, and assumed that her devotion to him was without question. If what she was telling him now was the truth, then his picture of her had been entirely wrong. If she did turn against him mid-trial, then she'd end up beating him at his own game. Only this time, he had much more to lose than she did.

He had no choice. She had to be stopped.

Chapter 36

"Stay here tonight," Mac said to Wyatt as she exited her bedroom. "You can drive back to the ranch in the morning."

Mac had just tucked Levi safely into her bed, and made the suggestion to Wyatt after recognizing the late hour. She put the top on the bottle of children's Ibuprofen, and looked in Wyatt's direction for his reaction to her offer.

"I don't really have much of a choice," Wyatt said. "We drove your car into town, so my truck's still back at the ranch."

With the recent flurry of activity, Mac had forgotten that they drove her car to Dr. Kerr's office. "I'd have no problem driving you back, but with Levi asleep now . . ."

"There's no need for that, I'll just take the couch and we'll be on our way in the morning." Wyatt started moving the pillows around on the couch, forgetting that Mac had been sleeping on the couch since Levi moved in with her.

"The couch is a little crowded for two."

"Two?"

"I've been sleeping on the couch since Levi moved in, yet I'd have no problem sleeping with Levi tonight, but I'm concerned that my being a single woman might appear inappropriate."

"Hmmm—I'd offer to fill that role, but I'm not sure having his attorney's cowboy friend sleep next to him would appear any better."

"The couch is a pull-out, but it's a really uncomfortable mattress," Mac said, and let her words hang in the air until she realized that there was really no other option. "I guess we could give it a try, being that there's no real alternative. I'm so tired, I might not even be aware that I'm sleeping on the most uncomfortable bed in the universe."

"Okay," Wyatt quickly responded.

"Really? You're okay with that? You're not at all concerned about how that would look to Levi if he got up in the middle of the night?"

"I sleep on the right side of the bed," Wyatt said as he began to remove the sofa cushions from the couch. "I snore only occasionally, and that's when I'm really exhausted, so when I start snoring tonight just nudge me and I will turn over on my side."

Mac smiled as she listened to Wyatt describe the sleeping arrangements.

"I don't like covers, so don't you start pulling them up tight to your neck. You'll cinch me in and make me feel like I'm riding a bucking bronco. I need a glass of water next to me, because I always wake up at three each night thirsty. I wake up like clockwork at four forty-five, so I won't be needing no alarm clock."

Mac continued smiling, certain that Wyatt's monologue was driven by a sense of nervousness. She finally got up off the edge of the couch, nodding in comprehension.

"Perfect–I sleep on the left, and I snore when I'm exhausted, too." Mac caught Wyatt's eye and squeezed out a smile. "If my snoring wakes you up, though, you do not have permission to nudge me. I need my sleep tonight, so just let me be–okay? I have a love-hate relationship with the covers, and repeatedly kick them off before pulling them back up again all while asleep. It happens without me being totally aware, so I'm sorry in advance for me cinching you in. I also need water by the bed, because I get up at two each night parched. And while I don't need an alarm clock, either, I get up every morning at four-thirty. Oh yeah, and I wet the bed."

Wyatt's eyes were opened wide, but he appeared stunned and was currently speechless.

"Just checking to see if you were listening."

* * *

"I'm sorry I didn't treat you with more respect in court today," Luke said while rubbing his hair back from his forehead. "I've had a really stressful day, and I've meant you no disrespect. You have to understand how difficult this is for me, Janie." Luke sucked in his breath, hoping that he'd conveyed enough sympathy in his response to somewhat appease Janie. When she didn't respond, Luke continued. "Why don't we go back to your place, and let me clean up some while you light a few candles and pop open a bottle of wine. When I'm finished showering, I'll be in a better mood to sit down and talk, and we can see how this whole complicated mess of a trial has impacted you. How does that sound?"

Janie uncrossed her arms and took a step closer to Luke, but just before she made contact with him she seemed to think better of it. "I'm not so sure, Luke. It sounds to me like you're trying to appease me before I finish my testimony tomorrow."

He took a step closer to her, and extended his arms out in search of a warm embrace. "Come on, Jane Jane. You know me better than that. How long have we been together?"

Janie nodded, softening her glare.

"Look, I didn't want to ruin the surprise, but you might as well know now that I called my jeweler friend in La Jolla last week—the guy you met when we were at the convention last year."

Janie smiled slightly.

"I called him up in search of the perfect anniversary present for you, and . . ." Luke paused for dramatic effect, making sure to look her directly in the eye in the process. "Let's just say that I think you're going to be very happy when you see it."

Janie let out a deep sigh and took a step closer to Luke, obviously buying what he had to sell.

"I am sorry for the things I said," she said, as she began nuzzling her head on his shoulder. "You know I'd never testify against you."

"I know that," Luke said, as he began to pat her softly on the head. "You were just angry."

"I was hurt and . . . angry."

"It's okay, love. We've both been under a considerable amount of stress, but you should never doubt how much I trust or love you." Luke put a finger on her chin, lifting her head up to him. "Now let's go back to your place so that I can show you just how much I love you."

Janie smiled and gave Luke a light peck on the cheek and then threw him the keys to her Audi. "You smell, honey. You need a shower first."

"Oh, I'll shower. Don't you worry about that."

* * *

"Mac, wake up," Levi said.

Mac opened her eyes in a flash, immediately on guard. Levi was standing only an inch away from her face, and his face was covered with distraught.

"What is it, honey? Does your back hurt?

"Uh-huh."

"Did you have a bad dream, too?"

"Uh-huh."

"Was it that sneaky Baseball Man, again, honey?"

"Yeah," Levi sniffed. "But this time my dad was the Baseball Man and he was making me run the bases and he was yelling at me and he had a scary look on his face."

"That sounds scary, alright. Do you want me to give you some Ibuprofen for your back, and then lay with you until you fall asleep?"

Levi nodded.

Mac sat up and pulled back the sheets. As she hopped off the pull-out, she noticed Levi's eyes had grown wide.

"Is Wyatt your husband now?" Levi asked incredulously.

"No, no, silly!" Mac reached for Levi's hand as they walked towards the bathroom together. "We're only friends. We shared the couch tonight because it was too late for him to head home, and there was no place else in my place for him to sleep."

"But my mom says that men and women aren't supposed to share a bed until they are married." Levi caught himself, and appeared a bit embarrassed to have referred to his mother in the present. He lowered his head and whispered, "Well, that's what they say in church. And that's what my mom *used* to say."

"Your mom was right, Levi. Many people share her opinion, myself included." Mac decided that now wasn't the time to put his mom's opinion into question.

"If you really do believe that, than why are you sleeping with him?"

Mac took in a large breath, unprepared for this type of examination so early in the morning. She quickly racked her brain for an appropriate response, but was coming up empty handed given that it was two in the morning.

"I believe men and women should always treat each other with respect and love and kindness. I don't think there's anything wrong with two people sharing a bed if they're friends, there's no other readily available option. I'd have done the exact same thing if Wyatt were one of my old college girlfriends visiting me." Mac leaned over and tousled Levi's hair.

Levi appeared mollified as he followed Mac to the bathroom, and lifted his shirt without disagreement when Mac asked to inspect his wound.

Mac was shocked to see how much of Levi's back was covered in the deep, purple bruise, but she refrained from commenting. After using the restroom and drinking some water to wash down the liquid medicine, Levi followed Mac back to her bedroom. She lay down with him, and rubbed his shoulders until he fell back to sleep. She was exhausted from trial and from the stress of seeing him injured, and ended up quickly falling into a peaceful sleep alongside him.

* * *

"Are you almost done in the shower?" Janie whined through the bathroom door. He normally took two-minute showers, but he'd been in her shower now for going on fifteen minutes. "I opened the wine, lit some candles and I'm going to put on something sexy."

She waited for an answer, but there was no response.

"Luke?" she said. "Are you okay?"

Again, there was no answer.

The bathroom door was not locked. She turned the handle and entered the steamy room. "Luke!" she screamed.

* * *

Mac awoke to the smell of coffee brewing and the sizzle of something cooking. She rubbed her eyes before glancing around her surroundings. She dashed into the bathroom to brush her teeth before greeting Wyatt in her kitchen.

"Mornin," Wyatt said with a grin. "I'm assuming I was snoring last night, given that I woke up alone and all."

"You snored like a grizzly bear."

"Did I?" Wyatt's face registered his panic.

"No. If you did, though, I was completely oblivious to it."

Wyatt snapped her lightly with a dishtowel. "You're a funny girl, aren't you?" he said with a wry smile. "Hey, look who's up!" He inserted, as his head lifted in the direction of Mac's bedroom.

Mac turned around and saw Levi leaning on the corner of the kitchen wall observing their banter. He looked confused, so Mac walked over to him and put her hand on his shoulder. "Wyatt made pancakes for breakfast. Don't they look good?"

Levi looked at the plate on the table but did not respond.

"Do you feel up to going to school today? That's a pretty big bruise on your back."

"I can go to school," Levi quickly responded. "I don't like getting behind." "Okay, but I'm afraid you won't be able to play any soccer over recess today. I don't want you to get hit on the back during the game."

Levi agreed and sat down with Wyatt for breakfast.

"I got things covered," Wyatt said to Mac. "Why don't you take the opportunity and go out for a run this morning? You haven't done that in awhile, and it'll make you feel better."

"Music to my ears," Mac said as she dashed into her bedroom to throw on her running clothes. She came out in two minutes with her shoes laced. "Thank you," she mouthed to Wyatt as she quickly ran out the front door.

It was still slightly dark out and the air felt cold, while ominous- looking clouds were hovering over the horizon. A storm is on the way, Mac thought to herself. I hope that this isn't a bad sign of the kind of day ahead.

Chapter 37

Janie gasped as a pair of hands appeared out of nowhere and pressed themselves firmly against her mouth. It took her a few seconds to process what was happening, because spontaneous sex with Luke was par for the course. She quickly realized, however, that Luke's latex-covered hands were not covering her mouth in a playful way.

She tried to escape his clutches, but Janie's valiant attempts against Luke's firm grasp were in vain. After only a brief struggle, she felt his knee plunge deep into her chest, and immediately fell to the bathroom floor. Janie began writhing in pain, and began to gasp in both shock and horror.

As soon as her mouth was open Luke began pushing a warm, liquid-filled bottle towards her lips. She instinctively turned her head and pressed her lips together, but she was no match for his brawn and determination. Janie felt Luke's fingers firmly clamp onto her cheeks, then his index finger squeeze its way through her lips and into her mouth. She tried biting down on the intruding finger, but to no avail; a warm, sticky substance soon found its way into her mouth.

With Luke's hands planted firmly against her mouth and nose, Janie found herself unable to expel the foreign substance. She squirmed beneath Luke's grasps, but he was hell bent on getting the liquid down her throat. Janie felt his knee push harder into her chest, and she was nearly certain that her ribcage was going to snap.

With little else to do, Janie glimpsed meekly at her captor before slipping into darkness. Her last conscious thought was confusion, because the face in front of her was one she'd never seen on Luke before: a vicious sneer that was twisted by rage and distorted by hatred.

* * *

"All rise," the bailiff announced.

Judge Binnard entered the courtroom in his usual fashion, prepared for a day of testimony in the Landers trial. After getting situated, he looked down towards the parties seated in front of him and noticed that someone was missing. He looked to the clock on the wall, and then back down to the parties in front of him, and then let out a long sigh.

"Where's Mr. Trainor?" he asked without making any attempts at hiding his disapproval. "I stated in no uncertain terms that we would reconvene at ten o'clock this morning."

"Your Honor, Mr. Trainor is in the hallway trying to get a hold of Dr. Landers," Karl Swensen said. "From what I understand, Dr. Landers was unexpectedly called into an emergency this morning, but is currently on his way to court."

"That's not my problem," Judge Binnard dryly responded. "I made my intentions clear when we concluded yesterday, and I intend on resuming trial at ten o'clock - with or without the doctor's presence." With a swift turn of his head, Judge Binnard then directed Karl Swensen to proceed. "Your witness," the Judge said while nodding his head in the direction of the prosecutor.

Karl Swensen slowly rose to his feet with his mouth slightly open and an apologetic look on his face. "I'm sorry, Your Honor, but my witness, Janie Johansen, has not yet reported to court this morning either. I'm honestly puzzled as to her absence, since I spoke with her about her testimony yesterday afternoon. Even more curious, though, is the fact that she's not at work and not responding to her cell phone. Ms. Johansen has been cooperative with the subpoena process so far, so I don't know why she is not here." Karl looked up meekly towards the judge, "I'm aware that you specifically stated trial would resume at ten o'clock, but I'd ask for a courtesy recess at this time, so I can locate Ms. Johansen."

Judge Binnard stared crossly at the prosecutor in front of him. "Are you telling me that you're unable to call another witness out of order, counsel?"

"That would normally be the course, Your Honor, but as we speak there is an officer en route to Ms. Johansen's apartment. At this point,

I'm just as concerned about her well-being as I am with the procurement of her testimony."

"Alright counsel, I'll give you a recess this time, but consider it your last." With an unemotional face, Judge Binnard rose from his seat and exited the courtroom without further ado.

* * *

Luke calmly lifted Janie's face to one side, and made a mental note of its overall pallid and pinched features. As he let her face resume its resting position on the floor, he diligently continued documenting the duration in Janie's breathing intervals. When her pupils finally dilated and her breathing dissolved into nothing more than gasps, he nodded his head in approval.

As Luke began to hum in satisfaction, he noticed a puddle of urine slowly snaking its way across the floor. He shrugged his shoulders, simply grateful that she hadn't caused a huge mess by vomiting. As he lifted himself from his perch over Janie, he replaced his gloves with a fresh pair before turning his attention towards a more pressing matter.

As Janie's laptop slowly booted, Luke began composing a masterful document on behalf of his former girlfriend. He cleverly documented Janie's "sole and independent" actions in regards to Levi's medical conditions, ensuring that her intent of framing Evelyn came through loud and clear. After inserting several details that only the true culprit would know, Luke printed the letter on Janie's personal stationery and folded it into one of her monogrammed envelopes.

Luke returned to the bathroom with Janie's confession and removed one of her toothbrushes to wet and seal the envelope with. After securing the envelope, Luke carefully placed it atop Janie's desk. With that done, he marveled at his own genius. All he had to do now was pack up some of Janie's belongings, including Janie herself, and call it a day.

Luke placed Janie and her belongings in the trunk of her Audi, and then backed out of her apartment complex. As he drove along Highway 330, he patted himself on the back for carrying the carbolic acid on him.

When Evelyn so conveniently overdosed, he'd almost returned the precious vial to its proper place in the hospital. Almost, but fortunately he had not.

Luke easily found the path along the highway he'd been looking for, the remote stretch covered by trees he'd passed earlier during his run. He rammed the Audi down a ravine and into one of the trees, and then removed Janie from the trunk to place her body in the driver's seat. After buckling Janie in securely to her seat, Luke carefully hiked his way out from the desolate accident scene. A gentle dusting of snow had begun falling, so Luke made sure that he covered all of his tracks in the snow as he jogged back towards the hospital.

He showered and dressed in his scrubs immediately after arriving at the hospital, and had enough time left to spare to make his usual early morning rounds. He chuckled with delight when he heard that one of his partner's patients went into labor, and graciously volunteered to perform the delivery. While providing a documented alibi for him, the delivery did cause him to be a half hour late for court. Luke shrugged his shoulders for the second time in one day, confident that Judge Binnard would understand that the Hippocratic Oath required his attendance for the emergency C-section.

When Luke finally entered the courthouse thirty minutes late, his appearance corroborated his explained lateness. As he approached the group of attorneys huddled in the hallway like linebackers, he mentally organized what was sure to be a heart-wrenching soliloquy explaining his tardiness. Before he could deliver his Oscar winning performance, however, John Trainor removed himself from the huddle.

"Luke, I think you should sit down," John started. "I'm afraid I have some bad news."

Chapter 38

Janie's disappearance immediately spread across the small town, and within days became a major news story. When Janie's confession letter was later leaked to the press, these ramblings amongst townsfolk grew to an outright roar. Gossip and innuendo softly whispered amongst neighbors slowly picked up steam, and grew louder and bolder in the days and weeks to come.

While nearly everyone was talking about the details involved in Janie's confession, no one seemed bothered by the puzzling questions its existence presented. Media outlets reveled in reporting the letters' glorious details, without bothering to explain exactly what a 'confidential and protected' source was. Any concerns there might have been about Janie's letter getting publicized disappeared the moment the letter was read; how could any criminal investigation be impacted by the ramblings of an obviously guilty and subsequently remorseful other woman?

One channel in town announced it had exclusively obtained Janie's detailed involvement with the over-medicating of Levi Landers and repeatedly filled its viewers in on the insidious descriptions from one week to the next. Viewers absorbed every detail involved with Levi's prolonged medical history, starting with failure to thrive and ending with flu-induced leukemia. Gasps could be heard over television sets as reporters described how Janie frequently altered Levi's lab reports and injected him with animal feces in order to make him sick. Janie convinced Evelyn of Levi's symptoms and often suggested diagnoses, which Evelyn quickly bought into based on the lab reports.

Another local channel advertised that it had intimate knowledge concerning Janie's motives, and provided excerpts from the letter supporting its contention. An entire day's news was dedicated to Janie's attempt to frame Evelyn Landers with the poisoning of her son. According to Janie's confession letter, she forged letters from medical experts confirming false cancer diagnoses.

Another channel raked in viewers by describing Janie's despair over Luke's broken promises, and her realization that he'd never divorce his wife. Regardless of their particular claim to the Janie-story, all channels shared in the conclusion that Janie's letter was an act of cleansing her soul. Every news outlet appeared privy to the parts of Janie's letter chronicling her culpability, and as a result so had everyone in town. Janie was simply racked with guilt over her role in the potential demise of Luke's personal and professional life, and she expressed full accountability for every single action even remotely involved. No one doubted the letter's authenticity for one minute, especially when it concluded by referencing Dr. Landers pure heart and gentle nature.

Nine months of gossip and innuendo had passed by the time a teenager stumbled across Janie's mangled Audi nestled deep within one of Highway 330's ravines. After the car was finally wrestled from its tangled web within the snowy cliffs, Janie's body was sent to the Crime Lab for a perfunctory autopsy. The medical examiner's report was brief and to the point, and was issued without much delay given the lack of anything unusual in the case. No one in Sheridan needed a medical examiner to tell them that the manner and cause of Janie's death was suicide, because it was practically a foregone conclusion. When the medical examiner did ultimately issue his report establishing the same, it was done merely as a formality.

Had the examiner considered running a toxicology report on Janie, then perhaps he would have discovered what little residue of carbolic acid remained. Fortunately for Mac, she had a very good relationship with a pathologist in Jackson who had testified as an expert witness in several of Harry's trials. At Mac's request, Harry made a few calls and the pathologist asked the medical examiner in Sheridan to forward tissue samples from Janie to the Jackson lab under the pretense that he was conducting a study regarding tissue that had been preserved by natural elements. Within days, Harry faxed the lab results to Mac.

Members of the small and still tightly knit community felt nothing but sympathy for Dr. Landers, because he'd lost not one but two women in less than a year. While no one approved of his affair with Janie, they couldn't deny the impact her loss would still have had on the emotionally vulnerable man. He seemed to be handling matters well given the circumstances, though the gossip around town was that he conducted his grieving in private; Dr. Landers' brave face was merely a front to protect his children from any additional grief from these traumatic events. Many people considered Dr. Landers' single status as another selfless gesture towards his children. Mac, of course, knew better.

Levi was one of the better soccer players on the team securing his local team's forward position. His physique had filled out nicely, and he was slowly developing into an athletic young man. In less than a year since he was removed from an otherwise toxic environment, his body had outwardly recovered entirely from the earlier abuse.

As Mac took a seat in the bleachers for his Saturday match, she marveled over Levi's physical transformation. She cheered for her little guy as loud as her voice would permit, and silently gave thanks to the brave Judge Binnard, who'd granted her visitation with Levi. Providing a child's attorney with guaranteed future visits was uncommon, and Mac considered herself lucky to be able to remain in Levi's life. If it weren't for that ruling, Mac might never have known that Levi's Baseball Man dreams had significantly diminished. Mac was still frustrated that she couldn't determine the source of these nightmares, but was relieved to see that they were somehow being resolved.

As Mac leaned over to shout further praises for Levi, she saw Luke several rows ahead of her. Luke's involvement in Levi's life had improved proportionately with Levi's increasing athletic abilities, and he had started frequently attending the Saturday soccer matches. Luke looked up at that moment, and when their eyes briefly locked Mac felt a cold chill run down her spine. Mac was quite sure that Luke had been involved with poisoning both Evelyn and Janie. Mac swallowed the thought and forced a smile at the man who freely granted her time with Levi. She nodded her head and gave him the universal "I'm Watching You" gesture by pointing her fingers from her own eyes towards his. She made the gesture with an assassin's smile and secretly hoped that Luke would pick up on her awareness of his dark heart.

She kept Janie's lab results to herself for the time-being, unsure whether she wanted to forward them to the county attorney for prosecution. Levi seemed happy, as did Lauren, Ben and Austen. Despite the egregiousness of Dr. Lander's malicious acts, Mac couldn't bear to think of putting the Landers children through another nightmare.

Mac found herself forcefully shaking her head to ban the negative thoughts, and returned her attention Levi running around happily on the soccer field and to the cowboy seated next to her. She gently patted Wyatt on the back, softly giving praise to the man who'd been there for her in more ways than one when the Landers case was dismissed. She'd been dating Wyatt for a few months now, and enjoyed his respect and kindness. Mac had little doubt that his honesty and warmth were genuine.

"I taught him that move," Wyatt said, directing Mac's attention to Levi's fancy footwork with the soccer ball.

"How?" Mac teased. "You said that you don't like to dance."

"*That* is not dancing. It's dribbling. And I never said I don't like to dance. I just have to be with the right partner."

"Is that so?"

"I'll show you later," Wyatt said with a playful smirk.

"You've got a date," Mac said with a smile.

Dedication

This book is dedicated to my friend and editor,
Margaret Lopez Erpenbeck.

Books by Maureen Anne Meehan

Dying to Ski, a Mary MacIntosh novel
Snake River Secret, a Mary MacIntosh novel
Powder River Poison, a Mary MacIntosh novel
Pandemic Predator, a Mary MacIntosh novel
Poisoned by Proxy, a Mary MacIntosh novel
The Five, a Mary MacIntosh novel
Rodeo, a Mary MacIntosh novel
60 Dates in Six Months (with a Broken Neck)
Push You Away
Let Me Be

ABOUT THE AUTHOR

Maureen Anne Meehan received her bachelor's and master's degrees in education before becoming a lawyer. She lives with her family in Southern California, where she is a mental health judge and crafts legal thrillers, as well as nonfiction dating satire.